The Enemy Unleashed

Verdon ran for the end of the barge and swung the battle light in an arc. His chance to escape had finally arrived.

In moments he reached the ground, pulled out the cloak, and draped it over his armor. In the confusion of the battle Adralk would assume the predators of Darkfall had killed him as well as Restrad. The contingent commander might regret the loss of Restrad, but he would not waste a thought on Verdon.

Verdon hurried across the smooth ground where the treads of the heavy train had crushed the rock. Then he heard the rumble of the big doors on the last barge and felt a familiar rush of fear.

Adralk had loosed the sentinels!

WORLD OF ADEN
THUNDERSCAPE™

—THE—
SENTINEL

Dixie Lee McKeone

HarperPrism
An Imprint of HarperPaperbacks

HarperPaperbacks   *A Division of* HarperCollins*Publishers*
10 East 53rd Street, New York, N.Y. 10022

Cover illustration by Danilo Gonzalez

First printing: January 1996

Printed in the United States of America

HarperPrism is an imprint of HarperPaperbacks.
HarperPaperbacks, HarperPrism, and colophon are trademarks of HarperCollins*Publishers*

❖ 10 9 8 7 6 5 4 3 2 1

To Shane Hensley
Without whose genius in developing
THUNDERSCAPE and
The World of Aden
this book could not exist.

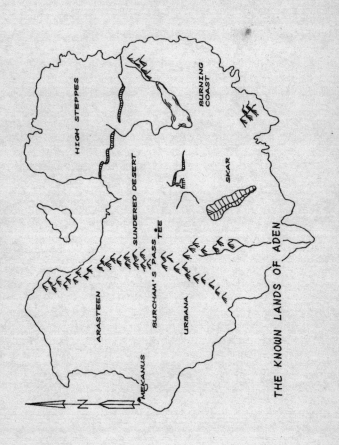

HIGH STEPPES

BURNING COAST

SKAR

SUNDERED DESERT

TEE

ARASTEEN

BURCHAM'S PASS

URBANA

MEKANUS

N

THE KNOWN LANDS OF ADEN

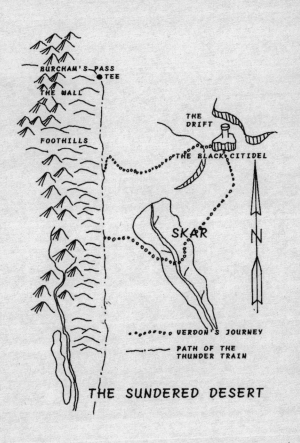

BURCHAM'S PASS
• TEE
THE WALL

THE DRIFT

FOOTHILLS

THE BLACK CITIDEL

N

SKAR

•••••• VERDON'S JOURNEY

——— PATH OF THE
THUNDER TRAIN

THE SUNDERED DESERT

1

Iliki hovered in the updraft of the heat rising from the Sundered Desert. The little ferran had the head, body, wings, and feet of an owl. A humanoid face with large round eyes looked out of an owl's feathered head. Unlike most ferrans he had six limbs. In flight he kept his arms and hands tucked under his breast feathers. The extra limbs gave him a humanoid flexibility, but he lacked the size and strength to fight against the dangers of Aden; he could stretch himself to fifteen inches, but relaxed he stood just over twelve.

His dual heritage gave him human intelligence while he maintained his animal wariness, and suddenly a sense of danger exploded in his head.

He dipped and swerved sideways, out into the bright sunlight. The pinions of an eagle's wing brushed his head as the bird swooped by, its grasping talons just inches away.

Iliki beat his wings against the disturbed air currents. A hundred feet below him the huge bird came out of its dive and soared again, searching the sunlit open space. It swept up the row of natural towers and started back again, seeking its prey. The eagle watched for another bird. It thought it hunted a small owl, but Iliki had the

advantage of human intelligence. A bird would have
panicked and streaked for the open air, trying to escape
the vicinity. The little owl-man swept back toward the
cliff, hovering close to the rock face. He stayed away
from the wind-worn horizontal fissures and shallow
caves. They hid a greater danger, the blind desert
worms that tucked themselves in crevices. They struck
out at any bird too intent on hunting to be wary.

A thousand feet away the long wind-worn rock column split, forming double towers. Iliki flew toward the
break and hovered just outside the break between
them, when the eagle spotted him. The giant bird
dived, and Iliki dipped between the two towers. He
stayed low, where the narrow space allowed his
smaller wing tips passage while the eagle's wider
wingspan kept it from following.

He hung in the bright afternoon sunlight on the
other side until the eagle flew over the tops of the double columns. When it dived, the ferran flew back
through the passage, into the shadows on the east of
the tower. They went back and forth a second time
and Iliki grew tired of the game.

"Go away idi-idio—bird-wit, or we'll keep this up
forever," he muttered. He would have to continue until
the eagle lost interest. He had no hope of outflying the
winged desert predator.

The third time Iliki flew through the break, the eagle
proved to be smarter than he expected. Instead of
soaring over the heights, it rose slowly. It judged to an
inch the space needed for its wingspan and flew
through the break just thirty feet above the ferran. It
drifted in the updraft off the sun-heated stone like a
malevolent shadow.

Concerned about the eagle, Iliki almost missed seeing the worm that lashed out of a shadowed fissure. In
a lightning reaction he whipped the air with his wings,
back-beating and rising out of the reach of the worm.
Above him the eagle saw its chance and dived. It
risked the strike of a worm to grab a meal.

Iliki felt the grip of one taloned foot as the bird caught him, squeezing the breath from his body. The sharp talons had not pierced him. He almost regretted not being killed outright. It would be better to die quickly than to wait to be torn to pieces by that ferocious beak.

In the eagle's determination to make his catch he had dropped too low to spread his wings. The bird fell. As it scrambled for a foothold, it slammed Iliki against the side of the cliff. Through a red haze of pain the animan saw the eagle's right foot scrabbling on the stone. The hope that the eagle might have to free him grew in the ferran's heart and suddenly died. The gaping red maw of a rock worm blotted out the sun as it closed on the bird-man. Again he expected to die, but the worm's wicked teeth fastened onto the bones and tough knobby skin of the bird's foot.

The eagle screamed in defiance and jerked. A coil of the worm's length whipped around one giant wing and across the breast of the bird. The worm jerked as the eagle clawed it. Orange ichor, the lifeblood of the annelidian splashed down the stone column. The worm's head and the eagle's foot both cushioned Iliki as they slammed into the face of the stone cliff again, but his head reeled with the blow. He struggled for breath, and what air did reach his lungs seemed devoid of oxygen. It stank of the rot within the worm's slow digestive tract. Another horror crossed his mind. What if he were swallowed whole?

The eagle still screamed its defiance. Its sharp beak tore into the worm's tough hide. More orange ichor dripped on the stone. The next cry of the eagle was weaker.

Then, as if answering the bird, an unworldly shriek caused the air to tremble. For a moment the world of the three, the worm, the bird, and Iliki froze. The strange, ultraviolent sound carried with it horrors beyond the shadows of the mind. A second, longer shriek threw the creatures into action. The worm released its grip on the foot of the eagle and whipped back into its cave. The sudden freedom threw the bird into the air.

The eagle, as panicked as the worm, spread its taloned feet. It fought for balance and a surface from which to leap into flight. Iliki tumbled away just before the strong claws found the side of the cliff and the eagle sprang into the air, fleeing the terrible sound.

Iliki tumbled onto a ledge of dubious but momentary safety before the sound died away. The small avian-ferran tested his wings. They were sore and bruised, but unbroken. He leapt for the open air, fled to a safe distance from the deadly stone caves, and hovered, searching the immediate vicinity. The eagle had disappeared and nothing else threatened him. While he drifted on an updraft he wiped the dirt and sweat from his face.

Years before, at the beginning of Darkfall, he had learned that mind-numbing terror had a short life span. By the time the second scream had started, the human part of Iliki's mind had recognized a mechanical quality about the sound. It carried shadows of horror as if the noise itself had passed something so terrible the imagination could not conceive of it. Still, it had not challenged or threatened him.

He hung on the light breeze and looked around, searching for danger, but the predators of the desert had fled.

As he listened he hovered in the cooling, threat-free air of the late afternoon. The unnatural scream had died. A new sound grew in his mind even before he became conscious of hearing it. Thunder, he first thought, but the sound continued too long to be the forewarning of a storm. An earth shake? He glanced up at the twisted shapes of the rock towers. They were still in the cooling air. Nonetheless, he wanted to make certain. His friend Kree, the lightning lizard, rested at the top of the gorge, in the shadow of a small mesa. Iliki had to warn him if any danger threatened his shelter.

He left the shadows and flew across the narrow gorge. A sunlit, solid stub of a shorter wind-scored stone tower provided him with a safe place to land. Through his feet he felt a slight tremble, an even vibration too rhythmic to be natural.

He flew toward it, knowing he had no more to fear from the eagle or any other flying predator. They had taken shelter or fled from the unknown.

Below him spread the desert, a tortured and angry land. The blistering sun beat down for years at a time without the relief of rainfall. Then the Pours, the rare but violent rains, beat the open lands to mud; the rushing runoff ate gullies into the barren soil. As one storm followed the other, though years might pass in the interval, they ravaged a land that lacked sufficient vegetation to heal itself of the scars.

The relentless sun, the one almost-constant feature of the desert, baked the mud that shrank as it dried. The level barren surface broke into hard, irregular tiles. The cracks between them could catch an unwary foot or hide a small predator.

And this was only the ongoing damage.

In a time before written history, legends told of the Great Freeze and the Vast Thaw. The slow movement of glaciers and, later, their melting waters had gnawed vast gorges and valleys in the flat land. They ate away the soil and softer rock, leaving towers, pillars and small mesas of harder stone. These geological anomalies, numerous where they occurred, were called desert forests. Further erosion by the digging of the desert worms and the constant winds cut and warped the stone columns into nightmarish shapes. Their striations of yellow, orange, and purple glowed angrily in the sunlight as if the bones of the land resented its destruction. Some valleys and their forests were small, others stretched for fifty miles or more and widened to more than half their length.

Occasionally springs found their way to the surface in these depressions. The underground water allowed the growth of sparse vegetation. Where there was

water and plant life, wildlife congregated, the herbi-
vores and the predators.

Iliki thought of himself as a predator's agent since
he watched better than he did anything else. His
saucer-shaped eyes appeared owlish. They had the
characteristic sharpness of a night hunter but without
an owl's sensitivity to the sun.

Like the rest of his kind, Iliki combined the traits of
humanoid and, in his case, avian genes. Other ferrans
considered him an oddity, even among the diversities
of his species.

Ferrans differed from each other as much as they did
from their double ancestry. They were half-human or
demi-human, half-bird, -beast, or -reptile. Most had
human or humanoid bodies with heads and extremities
that reflected their animal heritages. They usually combined the strength and senses of their bestial ancestry with
the flexibility of their human characteristics and intelligence. The individual double heritage of a ferran usually
accounted for its size. Ferrans often stood a head taller
than the human or the demi-human parts of their natures.

Born to an elf-lizard father and an owl-human
mother, Iliki had been carefully protected in his young
years or he would never have reached maturity in the
harsh world of Aden. He had been raised in a ferran village in northern Yzeem, south of the Sundered Desert.

Then had come the Darkfall. It began on that terrible
day when the blackness hid the sun. The nocturnals, in
every shape the horrors of the mind could conceive,
came out of the darkness. In an hour that left him in a
state of horror for weeks, his village was destroyed.
Iliki had seen his father devoured, his legs bitten away
even as he slashed at his attacker. He never discovered
what happened to his mother. Iliki had escaped only
because he could fly.

For weeks he struggled alone in a dangerous world.
Chance brought him across the trail of an elven caravan. The leader gave him food and shelter in return for
his scouting skills. No ability he possessed could have

warned the elves against camping near an ancient and forgotten burial ground. The nocturnals that rose up in the night and destroyed the elves had come too suddenly for his warning to help them.

He had traveled with other caravans, elf hunting parties, and even outlaws. At the moment his sole companion, a wounded lightning lizard, waited for him to spy out a likely meal. Game had grown scarcer in the broken rock and sparse vegetation of the high desert since the beginning of Darkfall. Most of the surviving animals were too fast for his purposes. He hoped to find a doran, a slow, heavily armored insect eater. Kree could make the kill and they would both enjoy the meat. Dorans were diurnal creatures; because of their heavy shells they feared little on the Sundered Desert.

But food was not as important as knowing if the shrieks could mean danger. First he had to discover what the strange sounds meant. As he rose higher in the hot air he saw a stream of black smoke, and the noise became louder.

A thunder train from Urbana!

He had not realized he was close to the Thunder Trail, the path carved and crushed by the huge, grotesque trains that periodically rumbled across the desert.

His fear gave way to excitement and curiosity. The mechamagical monster would not harm him unless he acted foolishly. If he came within bowshot, some shortsighted guard with an appetite for fresh meat might mistake him for a bird.

He chose another stone spire without holes to hide the desert worms. He hovered, lit, and paced back and forth, waiting impatiently for the giant machine to creep up out of the long valley and onto the flatter land.

And it did creep, he thought with disgust. Most creatures could walk faster than the train traveled. Living beings would doubtless be speedier for short spurts or even hours, but they could not continue the pace, day and night for weeks at a time.

The black column of smoke came closer. Two huge black smokestacks appeared over the rim of the valley, and for minutes they were all he could see. Still, they kept coming, getting taller and taller as they approached. Then he saw the pipes, a jungle of coiled and twisted tubes as if more than a score of giant snakes had been frozen while in a frenzy of motion.

They coiled around a huge vehicle of rust-streaked metal. The train moved on giant wheels that never touched the ground. Cogs on the perimeter of the wheels pulled wide bands of thick, flexible metal tracks that provided a constantly moving stable road-way for the monster train. He had heard tales of the trains and their tracks but had not believed them.

At first he lacked a reference to size the giant engine car. Then he saw independent movement on top of the monster and realized he watched a human on guard. His mouth dropped open. The wheels were at least twice human height. The roof of the engine car had to be at least thirty feet above the ground. In front of the engine car an angled protrusion like a double plow shaft added an additional threat to anything foolish enough to stand in the way of the train. While Iliki watched, the left track ran over a large stone. The rock crushed to powder, sending dust and dirt flying out from under the flexible metal.

Awed by the power, Iliki stared at the treads for several minutes. Then he raised his eyes again to the top of the train where a single human stood by a cannon. A ballista at the left corner of the engine car partially hid the man from the ferran's sight. Another mounted spear thrower flanked the cannon on the right. Two more ballistas stood at the back of the engine car. As the first of the barges came in sight, he noted they also bristled with the projectile weapons.

Iliki leapt into the air and flew closer for a better look. The man carried no bow, and the ferran had no fear of the cannon or the ballistas. The guard would not waste the ammunition for the heavy artillery on a bird.

Still he kept his distance as he rose in the air, impatient to see the rest of the train. The single guard riding on the roof of the engine car ignored him. The human watched for genuine threats to the train.

As Iliki drew closer, he saw ten barges linked together and to the giant engine car by coupling bars, thick as a man's body, attached to round couplers as big as the trunk of a lightning lizard. Armed ballistas had been mounted at all four corners of every barge. In the relative safety of the bright afternoon only one other guard rode on the roof of the train. He stood his duty on the rear car, leaning against a cannon. Occasionally the guard turned to make certain nothing threatened the center of the train. He focused most of his attention on their back trail.

When the first guard gazed ahead and the second surveyed their back trail, Iliki swooped in. He landed by the front left ballista on the fourth barge. He would be one of the few ferran on Aden who could boast of riding on a thunder train.

It was a rough ride, he decided, as the right tread of the barge slipped into a small gully. The barge tilted suddenly and the small ferran grabbed for the nearest available support. He caught a small handle on the ballista and it moved in his hand. The nut dropped and released the bowstring. A stout javelin shot out toward the nearest stone outcrop.

Startled by what he had done, Iliki flew up and away from the train, only looking back once. The guard at the end of the train stared up at him, laughing. The ferran laughed too. He could boast of a second experience. He had also shot off a ballista, one of the dreaded projectile missiles of Lord Urbane.

He sighed as he flew away. Those experiences would probably complicate his life. Who could hitch a ride on a thunder train, shoot off one of the weapons, and keep quiet about it? Certainly not a little owl-man. He'd never be able to keep the secret, and no one would ever believe him.

Before the coming of Darkfall, the children on the world of Aden begged for tales about great adventures. They listened, enthralled, to the ancient stories of the great wars and titanic battles. Sticks and strings became toy bows and lengths of wood served as swords as they played at war and fighting evils. Before the Darkfall, most people believed the old tales of major conflict were myth. The Golden Age, a thousand years of peace, had followed a treaty called the Peace of Rose. No wars spilled blood in the Known Lands. Aden still had its outlaws and the necessary authorities to subdue them, and its rulers squabbled from time to time, but they handled problems on the national scale by arbitration. Trade flourished between nations; the roads hosted hundreds of small caravans. Some crossed the continent; others only traveled from the agricultural areas to the nearby cities.

Then had come the terrible day when a great black cloud had turned midday to twilight. Horrors, many worse than the mind could imagine, rose up out of the earth or crept out of the shadows to destroy and devour the inhabitants of the Known Lands.

The children who had gleefully pretended to kill

each other no longer wanted to play at war. The children weren't the only ones to fear. Every city, every town was under siege. The traders suffered the most. Nocturnals destroyed the caravans before they had traveled more than a few days. Soon the traders decided no profit was worth the risk. Illness and death from starvation took many lives in the cities, while food rotted in the fields. The people in the outlying areas died at the hands of nocturnals because they lacked weapons to fight.

As time passed, the farmers decided to band together and hire mercenaries to protect their shipments of produce, so short trade routes were established again, but long-distance travel was still considered too risky.

When the king of Columbey died fighting nocturnals, Lord Urbane, the Iron Tyrant, took the crown of Columbey. He renamed the country Urbana after himself and ordered the building of the thunder trains. The huge, mechamagical engine cars could pull eight equally large and fully loaded barges without any decrease in speed. They traveled the length of the continent, picking up and depositing cargo on their regular stops.

The engine car, *Dominant*, powered the thunder train that Iliki had seen. The mechamagical monster lumbered across the desert, following the Thunder Trail, a path the *Dominant* and its fellow trains had cut through the desert. The sharp prow, like a twenty-foot-tall double plow shaft, could cut through forests and even small earthen hills when necessary. After eight years the prow blade was seldom needed. The passage of the trains had cleared and beaten out their roadway. Behind the sharp prow, the top of the engine car rose another ten feet. Small windows, heavily protected with bars and magic, allowed the mechamages who drove it to see their way. On the first journey, the blades and the engine car of the *Dominant* gleamed a newly painted black. The scoring of obstacles on the trail, the weather, and the acidic fumes of the train itself had eaten away most of the paint. In the late afternoon sun, rust glowed red in spots like the dried blood of vanquished foes. Not all the red *was* rust.

The fuming pipes partially obscured the top of the engine car. They cooled the escaping steam and turned it back into water, ready to be reused in the giant boilers. No wise man questioned the power that heated those giant steam pressure cauldrons. No one loaded any fuel aboard the *Dominant*. Periodically a shriek like an unworldly scream tore out of the bowels of the great engine car. The monster vehicle shuddered with the release. The surrounding air filled with a greenish yellow cloud. Those who heard the sound or breathed the fouled air suffered momentary visions of tortured faces and saw eyeless holes in skulls with rotting flesh. Their fears left them trembling in horror.

Compartments near the front of the 120-foot-long vehicle housed the mechamages that ran the train. Near the rear of the car two compartments inadequately served as quarters for the Iron Guard, who protected the train from attack. Despite the size of the engine car, the military contingent lived in miserably cramped quarters. When a train pulled its usual complement of cargo cars, eight, the guard numbered twenty. The ten bunks forced half the guard to remain awake and on duty.

Wooden paneling lined both compartments. The effort to damp the noise and heat proved as inadequate as the space. Both areas were windowless.

In the second compartment, a table and two flanking benches bolted to the middle of the floor seated ten. Above it hung a swinging lantern. The dim light reflected off the armor of eight members of the guard and the dirty plates that held the residue of their evening meal. It illuminated the scarred walls where guards, dressed in body armor, often leaned against the walls. Their armor scraped the wood when the huge engine swayed or bumped over rough ground. The odors of unwashed bodies, sweaty leather, and charred meat were so thick, Verdon felt he could see the stinking fog in the dimness. He could barely make out Contingent Commander Adralk Stunthfel at the other end of the table, the one advantage of the lack of light; Adralk was not a sight to bring pleasure to anyone. He had lost an eye two years ago; his lips were thick, wet, and the right corner of his mouth twisted in a scar. Short and stocky, he was a barrel of a man; contents—enough experience to give him his first command, a little shrewdness, but mostly bluster and resentment, the last directed at Verdon. The leader of the Iron Guard gave out the night duty assignments.

". . . And Worsten will take the rear cannon," announced Adralk as he leered at Verdon. He gave that order, like all the others, in a shout, the only way to be heard over the roar of the thunder train. The constant storm of noise invaded the minds of the guard until even their thoughts screamed over the din.

Seated near the opposite end of the table, Verdon frowned and nodded sullenly, accepting the most perilous night duty during the most dangerous part of the journey. At least he hoped he appeared resentful and successfully hid his satisfaction. For weeks he had hoped to be given the rear cannon watch, and at night, but he had hoped to get the assignment before the train crossed the mountains.

As the *Dominant* traveled south through Urbana, it had paralleled the border of Arasteen. He could have slipped off the train unseen, and with luck he could have been far away before his desertion was discovered.

The contingent commander could not have known about Verdon's decision, but had thwarted it for reasons of his own. He had kept the young guardsman on duty in the stifling galley or busy cleaning the guards' quarters. Adralk seldom sent him out on the roof of the train and then only to deliver messages or food to the guards on watch. Days had passed when he had no chores at all. His seemingly preferential treatment had turned the rest of the guards against him.

Adralk glared at Verdon with his left eye. The right,

a useless, milky white orb that constantly seeped between scarred lids, wandered aimlessly. Several of the other guards grinned at Verdon, taking malicious pleasure in the danger he would face. His position at the rear of the train put him far from help at the beginning of an attack.

". . . Unless Worsten has some other high-muckety relative that would object to his taking his share of duty," Adralk grinned, showing his stained and rotting teeth.

The younger guard had to steel himself against the reference to relatives. Adralk thrust with a verbal knife, knowing he twisted it in the wound of Verdon's recent grief. General Marchant Worsten had died a few weeks before, killed in a battle with nocturnals.

Adralk insinuated Verdon, the son of a high-ranking military officer, received special treatment. The commander lied, unaware he told a double lie. General Marchant Worsten was not the father of the youngest member of the guard, but since the general's death, only Verdon knew the truth. The lack of kinship had increased Verdon's grief for the man who raised him, protected him, and treated him like a son.

The insinuation that Verdon had received his position because of General Worsten's influence was also untrue. Verdon had won his place in the Iron Guard just like any one else—no, not quite like the others. Membership in the guard demanded each new applicant beat one of the current members in mock combat. Verdon had bested Adralk. The commander of the train's guard hated the youth who had beaten him.

Verdon had not known the depth of the man's resentment until Adralk had been given the contingent commander's position aboard the *Dominant* before it started its last long journey to the south. Within a week after the start of the trip he understood the motives behind his preferential treatment. By the time they were on the desert, the rest of the guard would hate him and he would not be able to depend on rescue when he found himself in trouble.

Verdon rose and pulled the wheel lock pistol from its holster. He made a point of letting the others see him check his ammunition. The train was three days south of Tee, beyond even the minimal protection of the rhanate, and could be attacked at any moment. The rules required every guard to have twenty rounds of ammunition for his projectile weapon at all times. Verdon made a show of checking his supply and frowned as if he had discovered he was short of ammunition, an excuse to enter the second compartment.

The windowless sleeping quarters ran the width of the train, fifteen feet where it tapered at the stern. Ten bunks, one five-cot tier on each side of the door, lined the wall dividing the sleeping and eating quarters. A deep set of shelves for ammunition, spare armor, and replacement parts for the weapons reduced the seven-by-fifteen-foot space to a two-foot-wide passage.

Sleeping guards filled each tier, partly hidden by their armor, which hung from hooks at the edge of the cots. Verdon wrinkled his nose at the stench of bad air. For nearly a year he had been trying to adjust to the odors, but he nearly gagged at the smell of sweat, urine, and bad breath from rotting teeth and an inadequate diet, all aggravated by the heat and lack of ventilation.

The designers of the train had not wasted valuable cargo space on the comfort of the guards. Between battles they lived in miserable conditions and stifling boredom, yet the duty was still the most desired in the military. The pay for a few trips allowed a penny-wise survivor to live comfortably for the rest of his life. He had the added reward of being feared and respected in the places where the train stopped and glory when he reached Mekanus after a long journey.

Verdon stepped beyond the bunks to the back wall. Shelves lined it from floor to ceiling. Most were filled with boxes. Thick leather straps kept them in place when the huge thunder train swayed over rough ground. He didn't worry about noise awakening the sleepers as he rummaged in the ammunition box for more projectiles for his wheel lock pistol. The roar of the moving train masked any sound but a shout in the ear or the blast of a weapon. His hands shook with excitement. He was finally able to put his plan into action. After a glance at the sleeping guards, Verdon removed the box of black powder pouches and tilted it, dropping several bags on the floor. When he knelt to pick them up, he slipped four extra pouches under the breastplate of his armor. He took four extra bags of ball shot from a box near the floor, tucking one bag inside his greaves and putting the other two down the neck of his back plate. He had just hidden the last of his stolen supplies when a whiff of fresher air warned him someone had opened the door behind him.

He concentrated on picking up the pouches of black powder. They provided him with an excuse to be kneeling and accounted for the time he spent in the sleeping quarters.

"Clumsy, Worsten, or just shaking from fright?" Adralk leaned close to speak in Verdon's ear. The commander's fetid breath hung around Verdon's head like a cloud. "Or looking for an excuse not to take up your station?"

Verdon stood, moving carefully to keep his stolen goods from being dislodged. He looked the one-eyed commander in the face.

"I'll go right now, and you can pick up the mess." He turned and walked out, hearing Adralk curse as he closed the door. He might pay for his insolence later, but if fortune smiled on him, he would never see the contingent commander again.

With three quick arrogant strides—foolish because the swaying of the engine could have thrown him off-balance—Verdon crossed the main compartment. He jerked open the door that led to the spiral stair and the roof of the car. He cursed himself for a fool when the fetid, unearthly fumes flooded into the compartment and caught him squarely in the face. He should have remembered the shriek of the releasing fumes. The last guardsman to enter the compartment should have closed the upper hatch to prevent the foul air from entering the stairwell, but Verdon would get the blame for it.

He held his breath as he raced up the spiral staircase, grinning as he heard the men below cursing because he had let in the stench. After their insults he had no sympathy for them. They believed Adralk's lie, and had used every opportunity to complicate his life. Breathing the noxious fumes was not an adequate revenge, but it was something. He had neither the time nor the inclination to do more.

Taking the steps two at a time, he raced up to the roof of the engine car before drawing another breath. The light breeze had blown away the fumes, and he sucked in the warm, dry air. The foul conditions below made standing duty more pleasant than waiting below. He stretched and looked around.

Thick black fuming pipes rose out of the rusted roof of the train and ran around the sides of the engine car like thick, twisted railings. They coiled and curled back on themselves and disappeared again into the car. Their placement left the corners of the car and both ends clear. At the front a large cannon thrust its blunt and deadly nose forward. At each of the tapering corners the heavy frame of a four-bolt repeating ballista sat loaded and cocked, and only the pulling of the anchor pin was needed to swivel and aim it.

At the rear of the car, two heavy braces, three feet apart and three feet high, formed the anchors for the springs of a cable extension bridge. The compression and extension of the springs allowed the bridge the flexibility needed for the changes in both horizontal and vertical direction as the train traveled through the mountains and winding valleys. The *Dominant* crossed thousands of miles of rough country on its journey from Mekanus in Urbana to Yzeem at the southern tip of the continent.

Sections of six-inch pipe ran along the side of the bridges and carried what the guards called the lifelines. The first, a thin wire cable, activated the alarm from the top of any barge on the train or the engine car. The other opened the door and freed the sentinels, the mechamagical constructs that helped to defend the train during a major attack.

Holding the handrail and walking carefully, Verdon crossed the first four extension bridges. As he stepped onto the roof of the fourth barge, he noticed the front left ballista had been fired and had not been reloaded. He paused, wondering if he should take the time to reload it, and decided not to. If some negligence caused more confusion in a night attack, it could only aid him.

Verdon's walk was longer than usual. Normally the *Dominant* pulled a full complement of eight barges. This trip, two others had been added. When he stepped onto the eighth barge, one of the additions, he felt an aura of magic shielding, but seeping through it came a horror that raised the hair on the back of his neck. He was crossing the top of the cars for the first time, but he had expected the feeling. The others who had stood watch on the rear of the train had been reluctant after their first watches, but they studiously avoided mentioning the two extra cars.

No one knew what they contained. No sensible person wanted to know.

The ninth, the other extra vehicle, gave him the same feeling, as did the tenth, but for a different reason. In the rear of the tenth, and always the last barge on the train, rode the sentinels.

When he reached the last barge, Sturwid, a hulking brute with a long jagged scar down his cheek, glared at him.

"You're late, and me not a drink since high sun," the big man snarled.

"Complain to Adralk, who should have sent someone," Verdon retorted. "I was on sleep period—I'm standing watch tonight, remember?"

"Yeah," Sturwid grinned. "Sticking it to you, ain't he?"

"It's cooler up here than in the compartment," Verdon said, beginning his check of the four pieces of equipment that would be his responsibility throughout the night.

First he checked the battle light. He pushed at the greasy handle and turned the lantern on its swivel. At the tug of a rope he sprayed the barely discernible twilight with a fifty-foot arc of unnatural red illumination. The pull of a second cord caused the red glow to disappear. All color washed out of the rocky ground and sparse bushes in the unnatural white glow. Inside the weatherproof covering, ten feet above his head, the light, a spell laid on by the mechamages, was enhanced by a reflector of brightly polished metal.

The red light helped the guards to locate potential attackers of the train while maintaining their night vision. The sudden switch to white blinded those same attackers for precious seconds and often halted them while the guards could clearly see their targets.

Next, he checked the cannon, mounted just to the side of the lantern. He used the ramrod to prod inside the barrel, noting the ten-inch discrepancy between the bore length and his exploration. He heard the clink of metal as he pulled it out. The weapon was "loose-loaded," filled with odd bits of chain and scraps of metal. When fired, it would spray a wide arc of devastation. He replaced the rod and checked the powder—dry.

The ballistas were loaded and cocked. He nodded to Sturwid and gave him the round metal disk that signified the change of watch.

When Sturwid had reached the fourth car, and was too far away to report on the young guardsman's activities, Verdon stepped to a hatch in the roof and opened it, exposing a compartment of long, narrow bags especially constructed to fit in the barrel of the cannon. The smell of resin-coated wood met his nostrils, and he sighed with satisfaction at the number still in the hold.

He moved to the far end and pulled out nearly a dozen before his fingers encountered a strap made of a different fabric. His supplies had remained hidden and secret. He expected them to be there. If one of the guards had found them, the furor would have been heard by everyone. No one could have traced them back to him, but Adralk would have known the provisions and the two wheel lock pistols had been placed there by an intended deserter. No one would have been above suspicion.

Verdon pulled out the sack and added the extra powder and shot to his stale food and water. He pushed the ammunition down below the folds of the cloak that must remain on top, ready for immediate use. He replaced his pack and the bags of resin-soaked wood and concentrated on his duty, watching their back trail. Occasionally he spared a glance down at the platform at the rear of the last barge.

The tenth barge of the train was the only other vehicle with space not used for cargo. At the end, directly below his feet, a compartment housed the sentinels. He shuddered at the thought of being so close to them, though he had never understood his dislike of their giant allies. His aversion was greater than usual because of the large number traveling on the train. The constructs were rare, and he had never heard of more than two or possibly three making a trip on the same train, but because of the extra cars and their mysterious cargo, this trip the *Dominant* was protected by half a score.

The sentinels were mechamagical constructs. The ten newly constructed sentinels aboard the thunder train were similar in build with human-shaped body armor. Like men, they had arms, legs, and heads, but they didn't move like men. They walked and fought with an inhuman precision. Slight hesitations punctuated their quick, jerky movements in an imitation of life that made his skin crawl.

The sentinels were constructed of manite. Lighter

and softer than iron and steel, manite was an inferior ore despised by the nonmagical, or those with only minimal powers. Dweomered, manite could withstand all the conventional armor and weaponry used against it. Unfortunately it was not as common as iron, but Urbana had several rich mines. With the growth of mechamagic, even small veins became the object of contention and even wars.

Wars over manite, wars with the nocturnals; all his clear memories were of times of strife, but there had been a time when everyone lived in peace. It only seemed a legend now. Verdon leaned against the cannon and thought about the Peace of Rose, which had begun the Golden Age that had been destroyed with the coming of Darkfall. His interest was not in the old lore, but the fact that he remembered it, and remembered when he had heard it.

He had heard it from his mother. . . .

A vague image grew in his mind. Why was the picture of the laughing woman so vague? He had been nine years old when his parents left him with Marchant Worsten. His memories of exploring the house, studying with his pedant, and learning about Mekanus were still clear, so why didn't he remember more about his parents?

Why had he been left with Marchant and why had he not missed his mother and father? They left him with Marchant because of some danger to themselves and, therefore, to him, he decided. They had been killed three years later. Why had he not mourned their deaths?

He automatically gave part of his attention to the surrounding terrain while he concentrated on the vagueness of his memories and found another misty image, though it should not have been vague, since its last occurrence was only a year before.

Periodically, normally about twice a year, Marchant was host to a stranger who arrived after dark and left before daylight. The tall, slender man had always been cloaked and hooded, his face partially hidden by a thick beard. His memory walked in a mist that prevented any precise description. Verdon had not seen him for more than a year. Without understanding what mental processes had led him to the knowledge, Verdon tied the stranger to the loss of his memories, and his absence with their return.

Was he a magician that came for the purpose of clouding a growing boy's memories? No, Marchant Worsten would not have deliberately robbed him of the memories of his parents—or would he? Yes, if he thought those memories were a danger to himself and a boy too young to understand that a childish indiscretion could bring about both their deaths. By taking Verdon's past, he had been protecting his future.

What future? Verdon thought sourly. To serve a ruler he hated, to serve as guard on the thunder trains and shiver because his mechamagical allies below were as fearsome as his enemies?

Speculating on the sentinels and their proximity in the late hours of the night could be worse than being under attack.

He concentrated on the terrain. The broken, wind-scoured high country of the Sundered Desert became nightmarish with the setting of the sun. During the day the purple, orange, and yellow striations of the rock seemed unnatural, angry in their brilliance. The long shadows and failing light turned the tortured shapes of the twisted rock into monstrous parodies of grotesque creatures.

Verdon spared a nervous glance toward the front end of the train. By full dark they would be traveling through a shallow valley the guard had named Peril Canyon. Tall, twisted towers of stone lined the narrow, relatively flat-bottomed depression. In the past seven years the nocturnals had attacked the trains twelve times in Peril Canyon. Twilight gave way to darkness as they passed the first of the stone towers.

Verdon hated Adralk, but he gave the man credit for

being a shrewd contingent commander. He had stationed a guard on every other barge. Every guard with the exception of Verdon stood near the front end of his car. Each kept close to the alarm cord that ran the length of the train. One tug on the cord would set off an alarm on every car and in the guards' quarters.

Seeing the other guards in place heartened Verdon. Then he realized the fallacy of his feelings. Their hatred of him, born of Adralk's lies, would prevent them from coming to his aid. He had heard of other guards who were generally disliked. He had never met any. They usually fell in their first major battle as doubtless Adralk hoped he would do.

A massive stone column moved. His mouth dropped open. The monster, it had to be a nocturnal, stood ten feet taller than the roof of the train, and was at least fifteen feet wide at the base. He had seen it as the train passed it. It had appeared to be just another column of rock, but two arms reached out as it approached the last barge.

Verdon activated the red light to get a clearer view. His first assessment was correct, it stood slightly more than forty feet in height, and looked to be stone. In the holes and crevices that resembled the wind scoring of natural rock, huge desert worms coiled and twisted, panicked by the movement of their lairs.

One of the other guards had seen the creature and the alarm shrilled over the noise of the train.

Verdon left the light and jumped for the cannon, jerking the cord that freed the hammer. The huge weapon fired with a roar and a billow of smoke that obscured his vision for a moment. When it cleared he saw the stump rock, less now than twenty feet tall, staggering, but continuing to follow the train.

Behind the stump, the top portion had fallen clear and it, too, kept coming. It pulled itself along on its arms while new legs slowly extended out of what looked like broken rock. He looked back toward the stump and saw arms rising from the sides. The monster could regenerate itself—themselves. His shot had created two creatures out of one.

The cannon shot had slowed it, or them, and the gap between the creatures and the train widened. Verdon grabbed a bag of powder, shoved it into the cannon barrel, and followed it with two scoops of loose metal. He rammed the load home, raced around to jab the powder bag with the prick and prime the powder.

Then he stood by, waiting for the creatures to advance again.

Verdon had fought nocturnals before, but he had never seen anything with the size and possible power of the forty-foot towers of moving stone that followed the train. As the space between the monsters and the train widened, he turned his attention and the beam of red light forward, sweeping the area around the last five cars.

Nearly a thousand feet ahead he could see the steady glow of the travel light that lit their trail. The mechamagic illuminator on the front of the engine car threw the rest of the barges into a shadowed silhouette like the yawning mouth of a black cave in the early morning light. On top of the engine car a battle light, a twin to the one Verdon used, swept the area around the front end of the train.

The engine had just passed a row of rock towers, called a desert forest by the people of the Sundered Desert. The forward guard had swept his light across the train and turned it forward again when Verdon saw the first movement. He grabbed for the alarm rope and tugged at it, setting off the Klaxon again as he focused his light on the row of columns.

Alerted, the guards swung the ballistas and fired at

the monsters that so closely resembled rock. The shafts entered the bodies for more than two feet. The nocturnals came on, ignoring the butts of the ballista shafts protruding from their bodies.

Verdon had no more time for the monsters attacking the forward end of the train. He swung his light back on the creature he had cut in half but had not killed. The stump end had grown two long arms and rapidly closed the gap. Verdon realigned the cannon and fired.

As usual, the roar of the cannon stunned his mind as the smoke hid the creature. When he could think beyond the roar, when the smoke had cleared away, he saw it staggering. Splashed against what looked to be blasted rock he saw the orange ichor and flesh of several large rock worms, but the creature of Darkfall continued to advance.

To qualify for a position in the Iron Guard, every member had to be proficient in personal arms as well as the use of the heavier artillery on the roof of the train, but they had been taught to work together during an attack. He glanced toward the front of the train. The guards were manning the ballistas on the forward barges, but no one else was defending the eighth and ninth cars. As he suspected, he was to be left on his own.

Fighting alone and with a huge enemy the cannon could not stop shook his confidence. A creeping horror, born of his lack of success, dulled his mind until he realized he was becoming lethargic. He shook his head in quick jerks. Who said he had to have support? He was trained to fight the evils of the night, and he could do it without aid if necessary.

He was in a try-or-die situation, so he'd better start trying.

So much for iron and steel, but perhaps fire would stop them. He jerked open a trapdoor in the roof of the train and pulled out a stiffened bag of wood bark chips. Holding it in one hand, he kicked the trapdoor closed and grabbed another premeasured bag of gunpowder. At the front of the cannon he rammed the powder home, pulled one chip from the sack, shoved in the bag, and gave it a settling blow with the ram.

He moved to the side of the roof-mounted weapon as he used his sparker to ignite the resin-soaked chip and tossed it into the barrel, stepping quickly away. From inside came a "whoosh" of fire as the chips in the bag ignited. The burning chips set off the black powder.

The fiery missiles arced through the air, struck both severed parts of the night creature Verdon had cut in half, and, to his surprise, hit another creature advancing out of the darkness. The highly flammable sap of the clermin tree burned fiercely and stuck whereever the chips hit. The stump of the first nocturnal, the nearest to the train, was freckled with burning spots. It stopped its advance and rubbed its thick stonelike arms against its body, trying to dislodge the fireballs, but they obstinately clung to its skin like burning leeches.

Close behind the first came a second monster. It stood more than fifty feet tall, but narrower at the base. The few chips that missed the first creature had hit it. The rock worms that hid in the crevices of its body writhed and waved like a multitude of fiery arms.

Movement next to Verdon caused him to start and pull his wheel lock pistol, but he whirled to face Adralk, who had arrived with Restrad, another of the senior guard. Verdon bit his lips to hide his smile as he saw the begrudging and quickly hidden respect in the contingent commander's eyes.

Restrad, an older guard who was slow, methodical in his ways, and bumptious about his exploits, raised the protective shield on the left side of his helmet and lowered the single-lens distance viewer over his right eye. He turned the light to get a closer look at the flaming nocturnals and considered them for a moment before he nodded.

"They can be destroyed with fire," he said, wasting precious seconds before stating the obvious; the man was a walking ego, living on past victories. Since Verdon had been on the train, Restrad had only taken an active part in two battles.

"I'll handle the cannon, you take over the ballistas at the front end of the car," the senior guard said to Verdon. Adralk grinned and nodded. He hurried back up the length of the car to pass the word to use fire. Doubtless he would take credit for the successful change in tactics.

Verdon nodded, understanding the motives behind the order. In addition to their pay, the guard won prize money for each attacker they destroyed. Every guard kept a tally through every fight and at the end of the battle they compared notes. By his constant insinuations that Verdon received privileged duty, the contingent commander had turned the rest of the guard against Verdon, but they would not cheat him of his kills. In the next battle they might need his verification of their own claims. Not even Adralk would be able to deny Verdon's three kills, but he could allow Restrad to take over the cannon and prevent Verdon from increasing his tally. They had all seen the ineffectiveness of the ballistas.

But had they?

While Restrad wasted more time surveying the dark landscape—he had not deigned to use the battle light—Verdon opened the trapdoor and pulled out another bag of resin-soaked bark chips. He carried it with him when he went forward to the front of the car.

He broke open the bag and pulled out a few pieces of bark, sticking one on the end of the barbed head of the loaded javelin. When he saw another of the towering nocturnals moving toward the rear car, he used his sparker to light the bark and took careful aim, not an easy thing when he had to sight past the flaming point and into the darkness beyond. His first shaft found its mark, plunging deep into the monster's body.

The result was better than he expected. He gave a whoop of victory as the creature resembling a rock column ignited from inside much faster than the three that had started to burn from the outside in. From the wound made by the spear its body fluid spurted out, flaming as it came.

Verdon's self-confidence returned, soaring like the

flames from the burning night creature, but he stifled his triumph, reminding himself he had no idea how many nocturnals were waiting in the darkness. He flipped the catches that held the rotating groove pan in place and turned it, bringing up another shaft.

Once he secured the groove pan in place, he attached a chip to the point, ready for his next target. Since nothing lurked close enough for accurate aiming, he rushed across the front end of the barge and placed bark on the javelin already loaded in the ballista on the left side of the car.

He stepped back, away from the second weapon, and looked around, looking for a target. Four cars up, three of the giant nocturnals were approaching the barges. The battle light at the front of the train illuminated them and the butt ends of the ineffective missiles fired from the ballistas.

He saw the flash and smoke from the cannon at the front of the train. Apparently no one else had thought of putting burning chips on the javelins or in the cannons.

He turned and saw Restrad coming up the length of the car, his stride adamant. The senior guardsman led with his shoulders, a sign of his irritation. Verdon could hear his shouting. He was incensed because the younger member of the guard had used the chips from the cannon on the ballistas, not a part of the practice drills. The man was a fool, Verdon decided.

Restrad's anger kept him from noticing his danger. A nocturnal loomed up from nowhere, right beside the last barge. With one sweep of its arm, which looked as rock-hard as any boulder, it plucked Restrad off the top of the train and thrust him into the giant maw that opened ten feet from the top of its pillarlike body.

After a moment of shock that stunned him into immobility, Verdon had three thoughts at once: the nocturnal had not had any teeth; he had to ignite the chips on the ballista and fire before the creature reached him; he now had the chance he had waited for since the beginning of the trip.

Before he finished the second of his thoughts he had ignited the chip on the javelin in the left rear ballista. The monster was moving toward him when he pulled the handle and slipped the trigger nut. The ballista's force at close range buried the javelin in the monster's body and it writhed as it flamed from within. It looked like a thick candle that had been burned until the flame was deep within the waxy shell.

Verdon ran for the end of the barge and swung the battle light in an arc. He saw movement off to the west, but at the moment nothing threatened the end of the train. His chance to escape had finally arrived, a latecomer but no less welcome for being tardy.

He jerked open the trapdoor that held the fire bark, shoved half a dozen bags aside, and grabbed his pack. He slipped his arms through the straps and, with it dangling down his back, climbed down the rear of the train.

In moments he reached the ground, pulled out the cloak, and draped it over his armor. In the confusion of the battle Adralk would assume the predators of Darkfall had killed him as well as Restrad. The contingent commander might regret the loss of Restrad, but he would not waste a thought on Verdon.

Verdon hurried across the smooth ground where the treads of the heavy train had crushed the rock. Then he heard the rumble of the big doors on the last barge and felt a familiar rush of fear.

Adralk had loosed the sentinels!

Verdon glanced back over his shoulder and ducked behind a scraggly bush. He watched the first of the huge man-made monsters as it descended from the train and paused to take stock of its surroundings. It emitted an aura of terror that had nothing to do with its size, as if something totally unearthly had been made a part of it. Even without the aura of terror it was awesome. Eighteen feet tall, a giant encased in ornate body armor. Manite trim swirled on the armor that ended in spikes curved like horns on the helmet, shoulders, and the joints of its limbs. Verdon knew the decoration acted as deflectors for magic that might be used against it.

In the metal fist, the sentinel held a war ax with a curved double blade. Four feet of honed edges gleamed in the reddish glow of the battle light at the top of the last barge. The eye slits glowed red and Verdon trembled as they swept across the bush that served him for cover. They seemed to linger for a split second.

Off to the right the movement of a giant nocturnal caught the sentinel's attention. It turned, raised the ax, and walked off. When the mechamagical machine moved, it proved its inhuman origins. Infinitesimal pauses punctuated the inhuman quickness of its steps, as if each movement had to be thought out and executed separately. Each action, once decided upon, was made with the speed of a striking serpent.

The first sentinel strode toward the approaching tower of the rocklike nocturnal, followed by a nearly identical construct. The others stepped off the slowly moving platform and strode up the length of the linked barges, two pairs ready to defend each side. They would soon be too far away to notice Verdon, so he watched the two who had reached the closest nocturnal.

The towering night creature was twice the height of the two sentinels who flanked it and attacked with their double-headed axes. The blades cut slashes in the tough hide, and dark fluid splashed onto the metal bodies, dimming the ornate trim of their armor. The nocturnal swung a thick arm and struck the sentinel on its left, flinging the big mechamagical fighter aside. The sentinel fell with a clatter of metal on stone, but scrambled to its feet again.

The rocklike right arm reached for the second defender of the train, but with a swing of the big ax the sentinel hacked off the limb. It fell wriggling to the ground. The second arm followed the first and then the first sentinel strode back to the battle, his red eyes gleaming with a terrible light. Working together, the mechanical men swung their axes in rhythm until they had cut through the broad base of the monster and the top half fell, leaving a stump fifteen feet high, still staggering on its broad, boulder-sized feet.

The sentinels paused, seemed to be listening, and then one shifted his ax to his left hand and raised his right. From the side of his arm a stream of fire shot out, burning into the hacked skin of the nocturnal. The stump blazed with the fury of the resin-coated bark Verdon had used to destroy the first of the attackers.

Both sentinels set to work destroying the rest of the body and the arms. In the light of the fire Verdon could see the rock worms that had nested in the crevices of the nocturnal fleeing the fire. Four came straight toward him, seeking the shelter of the sparse vegetation. The worms were predators natural to the desert, and as dangerous, for their size, as a nocturnal.

He waited as long as he could and then moved back, hoping to work his way into the surrounding darkness without attracting the notice of the sentinels. The mechamagical constructions were supposed to be allies of the Iron Guard, but in the heat of previous battles they had been known to kill their human allies.

He had backed fifty feet from the bush when a rock, buried under the sand, shifted beneath his left foot. He fell, his armor clattering. He scrambled to his feet, but the sentinels had heard the sound. He glanced behind him. Both crossed the crushed track of the train with long, inhumanly quick strides, their axes raised.

He could not outrun them; even attempting to fight those metallic monsters was ridiculous. He dropped his bag of supplies and whipped off the cloak. They would probably ignore the lifeless items. He turned to face them, hoping he could convince them he was an ally.

"I don't see any more nocturnals out here," he said as if he had been with them all the time. "Return to the train. I will go with you."

Did they even understand human speech, he wondered. They were controlled by the mechamages of the train. By voice command or by magic? By magic, he decided, as the leading sentinel raised his weapon. Verdon backed away. Behind the first, the second raised his own ax.

"I'm one of the guards from the train," he tried again, watching the first sentinel's blade, wondering if he would feel the pain, and how much.

The first sentinel's blade started down, but the second moved faster. He struck his companion. His ax crashed into the joint where his fellow mechanical's helmet joined his body armor, severing the head from the body.

Verdon stared, frozen in his disbelief. One sentinel had destroyed the other? He could not have been more surprised if the sun had suddenly risen. He watched as the giant helmet rolled away and the giant body toppled.

Slowly he raised his eyes to the second creature, who still stood with his ax in his hands.

"Vonny . . ." The voice seemed to come from some deep place beyond even the mind's imagination. The hair on the back of Verdon's neck rose as he realized the implication.

"Go safe, Vonny." The sentinel turned and lumbered off into the night, following the train.

Verdon stood in the darkness, shaking until his legs seemed ready to give out under him. When he felt he could no longer stand, he sat down on the thick leg of the decapitated metal body. His shaking had nothing to do with fear or a reaction from his brush with death.

Only one person had ever called him Vonny—his adopted father—Marchant Worsten.

Urbana rumbled with tales of how the sentinels operated. Some suggested the magicians of Lord Urbane raised the bodies of dead warriors to power the mecha-magical monsters, but Verdon had laughed at the story.

Now he had to believe. The sentinel that saved him held the body, or at least the spirit, of Marchant Worsten, a valiant warrior and a brave man. His adopted father, helpless in death, was being used by the dark forces of Lord Urbane.

4

Iliki tugged at the string that encircled his body just below his wings, tucking the "sword" inside it. While he wrapped the ends of the string around the "hilt," he reflected, and not for the first time, on the evils of Aden. It had a major failing, Darkfall and nocturnals notwithstanding. Aden was too large.

To accept the idea that he might be too small for his world would suggest some failing on his part. He discounted the possibility.

Swords, good swords, were made for dwarfs, elves, and humans, creatures that stood four, five, and six times his height with four, five, and six times his reach. He had taken great pleasure in the six-inch blade he had found on the dressing table of a wealthy house in Tee, but despite the jewels in the hilt, his enchantment had worn away with the edge on the blade. His weapon was an ornament for larger and wealthier people and never meant to be used.

His single skill, that of being able to fly silently in the night and slip into windows, stealing what he wished, did him little good. Most of what he found was too large for him to use or even carry.

Still, his "sword" had cut into the young sprout of a

barrel cactus, and he chopped away a chunk of the moist meat inside. He packed it in the scrap of cloth, knotted it, and flew up to the top of a rock spire, one that had only a single crevice, too shallow for any self-respecting rock worm.

He flew around the rock tower to be sure no rock worms endangered his perch and lit on the lip of the horizontal fissure. Just under the overhang he found a crack, a convenient grip for his clawed feet. He perched in the shade, protected from the hot sun and the eyes of any predatory flying birds. He had a clear view of the surrounding area.

To bad he couldn't remain there.

With nimble fingers he untied the knot in the scrap of cloth and took out one of the hunks of cactus, grimacing as he chewed it. The cactus tasted slightly bitter and he disliked the fibrous texture, but the juice quenched his thirst. More than just quenching, it refreshed. Still, given a choice, he would rather have had real water.

He did have a choice, he reminded himself. Only a few miles away, in one of the stone forests, a desert spring fed an oasis, but to be seen there might endanger his plans.

What plans?

What could he do?

He could wait, hang around, and hope for an idea or an opportunity.

He bent forward to spit out the fibrous leftovers after he had extracted all the moisture from the mouthful of cactus. He nearly swallowed it as he saw movement near the base of the rock spire.

A human! A human in a long cloak and hood. Iliki moved closer to the edge of the fissure as he spied on the new arrival.

A few yards away a second stone spire cast a shadow over a boulder. The man trudged over to the rock, searched all around it, and then sat down in the shade, removing the strings of a bag from his shoulders. Then he unfastened the cloak and let it fall.

Iliki nearly whistled in surprise as he saw the armor distinctive to the Iron Guard. The man had come from the thunder train! His helmet swung from a thong attached to his waist.

While Iliki watched, the human opened the sack and pulled out a waterskin, took a drink, and then brought out what looked to be bread. Iliki's mouth watered. He had not had bread for weeks.

He soon forgot the food as he considered the human. A member of the Iron Guard out in the desert alone? Had he fallen off the monster train that crept across the Sundered Desert? No, he carried a bag of supplies and wore a cloak to keep his armor from being heated by the midday sun. He traveled on the desert by choice.

Was he a spy?

Rumor said every country in the Known Lands worried about Lord Urbane's sudden rise to power and his steady increase of arms and trained soldiers. Iliki had heard every second person in Urbana over the age of ten took intense military training. He had heard that Lord Urbane, often called the Iron Tyrant, had more than a thousand military warships ready to sail and fifty thunder trains full of sentinels ready to attack any land that opposed him. He had also heard all the rumors were false, that people were making up stories out of their fear of Urbana. If those stories had reached back to the ruler of the land beyond the mountains, he might be sending spies into other lands to see if their fear drove them to prepare a defense.

But the human didn't appear to be a spy. Would a spy wear armor so distinctive it shouted his origins? The long cloak could not entirely hide it. No, not a spy, or he would have worn a disguise.

A deserter? Iliki had heard hordes of people fled Urbana. He had heard the new lord drove them to killing labor.

I heard a rumor . . . a man told me . . . you won't believe what a trader told me. . . . Iliki decided he would be a fool to act according to any of the stories that came out of the north lands beyond the mountains. If the man had deserted the thunder train, he might prove useful, but Iliki would watch him for a couple of days before approaching him.

And if he did, it would be from a position of strength, he decided. The world might be too big, but somehow he would find a way to be as strong as that mighty warrior.

5

The setting sun cast grotesque shadows across the Sundered Desert. Verdon eyed them with relief. Beneath his cloak, his armor felt like an encasing oven, but he dared not take it off and leave it behind.

His left shoulder ached from the unaccustomed weight of the bag of supplies. Earlier in the day he had redistributed the weight by cutting a strip from the bottom of his cloak to make a sash he had tied around his waist. On it he had strung the bags of ball and shot for his pistols and tucked the two extra gunnes into the makeshift belt.

He had not encountered a single danger in his all-night, all-day trek, but his luck might not hold, and he might need every advantage. And he would need every bit of luck he could muster.

Still, he was probably as safe on the desert as he would have been if he remained on the thunder train. He could die of thirst on the desert, but in that vast, unpopulated waste he might avoid the creatures of Darkfall. Aboard the *Dominant*, he had little to no chance of surviving the trip back to Mekanus. If the nocturnals who waited near the Thunder Trail to attack the train did not kill him, Adralk was not above shoving a knife in his back.

Other people survived on the desert, so he had left the *Dominant* confident he could manage. After a night and a day he was beginning to wonder.

When he left the train it had been traveling south toward Yzeem. Verdon turned west, at a right angle to the *Dominant*'s route as he headed for the mountains. Traveling would be slower, but water would be more plentiful on the slopes, and there might be game. Hopefully it would not be as wary as the desert hawk wheeling overhead.

Would travel be slower? he wondered as he worked his way cautiously down a rocky slope, careful to check for holes in the rock. He reached the bottom of a shallow wash and made better time. He rounded a turning and stopped short.

Directly in his path stood a ten-foot tiger lizard, a yellow-and-brown-striped carnivorous desert reptile. The breed had accounted for more solitary travelers in the Sundered Desert than the heat and lack of water. The creature sprawled in the dying sunlight, soaking up the last of the warmth, but it raised its head, its beady eyes fastening on the human. It surged to its feet, its short, stubby legs at right angles to its body. The flickering tongue snaked out from between pointed, three-inch teeth.

Knowing he could not outrun the lizard, Verdon ripped the bag of supplies from his shoulder and threw it to the side. With his right hand he popped his helmet on his head while with the other he drew his sword. Less than a second later, he held his wheel lock pistol. He didn't know if the lead projectiles would stop the creature, but perhaps the noise might scare it off.

Dream on, some disassociated part of his mind suggested as he slowly backed up, hoping the lizard would decide to go in search of smaller prey if it didn't feel threatened.

It either felt threatened or it had a large appetite. It moved toward Verdon, taking its time. It lumbered forward with slow, insulting arrogance, its eyes on the human until suddenly one foot sank into the sand. It hissed and jerked back, but it had disturbed a nest of giant sand fleas.

The area immediately in front of the lizard seemed to come alive as the sand moved and more than fifty foot-long sand fleas boiled to the surface. Many leapt in different directions, but more than a dozen jumped onto the back of the lizard. The reptile roared as the single claws of their feet dug into his tough hide. He thrashed his tail and crushed several, but his twisting and biting drew the attention of the others and in seconds the carnivorous insects covered the reptile.

Verdon swallowed and remained still, hoping the fleas would be too busy with the lizard to notice him. When they all seemed to be concentrating on the writhing, weakening lizard, he took a cautious step toward the bag of supplies he had thrown down.

Until then he had not seen the second group that crawled up out of the sand. The first leapt toward him; its mandibles snapped at his armor. He knocked it away with the barrel of his wheel lock pistol, and struck at a second with his sword. Then he felt a weight on his back and used his sword to cut the cloak's tie. It fell to the ground and he stepped away from it just as three fleas climbed its folds.

In the next five minutes the wisdom of keeping his armor proved itself. The repeated attacks of the fleas were frustrated by their inability to attach themselves to the metal.

Staggering backward, he retreated to the rock slope he had descended. He transferred his sword to his right hand, slashing legs and heads from the giant sand fleas until he had climbed halfway up the slope. The few that remained retreated to the sand and the easier prey, the dying and half-devoured lizard.

Exhausted, Verdon stood on the slope in the dying light and stared down at his bag of supplies and his cloak. To go back for them would be to invite a second attack. After walking a day and a night without rest he knew he could not handle another all-out fight. He circled the cleft and tried to reach his supplies from the other side of the gully, but the huge sand fleas sat grooming themselves on the sand as if waiting for him to descend from the rocks. He reluctantly turned away.

Twilight passed swiftly on the desert. His immediate problem would be to find shelter. If he could get a night's sleep, he might be able to rescue his supplies in the morning.

After a little searching he found the safest place in that part of the desert, the lair of the tiger lizard. The reptile lived in a shallow cave in one of the rock towers, hardly more than a ledge five feet off the ground with a little overhang for shelter. Bones littered the area, and the stench of a half-eaten carcass, almost masked by the stink of the reptile.

The vile odor would protect Verdon from any nocturnal that might pick up his trail. Tiger lizards hunted nocturnals as well as rock worms, so for that night, at least, he would have no cause to fear either. Still wearing his armor, he stretched out on the filthy ledge and fell asleep in minutes.

The next morning he woke with the sun. Every muscle felt bruised from sleeping in his armor, but his thirst had awakened him. His lips cracked and split when he yawned. His throat burned and felt filled with sand.

The rest had renewed his strength and he headed back for the sandy wash where he had left his pack and cloak. He circled the rocky slope at the upper end and walked along the rocky ridge that flanked it. He had thrown the bag to the side so it wouldn't be under his feet when the lizard attacked. With any luck at all he might be able to retrieve it without disturbing the sand fleas.

Then he saw it. He wouldn't be disturbing the fleas. He wouldn't have a reason. The sand fleas had shredded the bundle, as well as his cloak; the metal sockets and caps were all that remained of his waterskins. He bit on his dried lips with teeth that felt coated with sand and clutched the hilt of his sword. He shook with rage and frustration. It took effort to keep from charging down onto the sand to attack the fleas. He controlled the urge. The revenge would be foolish and even if he lived through it, he would have wasted his remaining energy to no purpose. After one long last look at the remains of his supplies, he gazed toward the mountains, just visible as a blue haze in the distance. Tee, the trading town to the east, might be closer.

He might have a better chance trying to reach Tee if he went back to the track of the thunder train. He might stumble across some remoras hurrying to catch up with the train and travel with them, or he might find a caravan traveling to Tee. The giant engine cars had smoothed out rudimentary road with their passage through the rough country and many natives used the Thunder Trail.

Within an hour he removed his helmet. On the desert a man could die of sunstroke in the main heat of the day, but long before the sun was high his brain would boil in the metal helmet. A few minutes later he removed his breastplate, tasse, cuisse, and greaves. He tried to continue wearing the kneepieces and gauntlets to protect himself if he stumbled and fell. An hour later they were so hot they nearly blistered his skin.

He trudged along with his eyes half-closed when he saw movement ahead, right in his path. A bird had flown up from a boulder. If he could shoot it, the raw meat might ease his thirst a little, but it had flown out of range. He continued on his way.

When he neared the boulder he saw a dark spot on it, and something greenish white. If he had needed to step out of his path to get a better look at it, he would have passed it by, but his direction took him right up to it. The dark spot looked like moisture. He touched the rock and felt the dampness. Then he picked up the greenish white pulpy mass and recognized it as plant fiber. The frightened bird had left it behind, he decided. Desert birds had to have liquid—why not from a plant when springs were scarce?

He squeezed the fist-sized fibrous mass, being careful not to waste the few drops that fell into his open palm.

He touched his finger to it and put it to his tongue. It had a slightly bitter taste. He had heard of desert plants that stored water and that their soft interiors could be chewed to draw the water out. Apparently the bird had found a plant, pulled away a portion, and Verdon had scared it off before it could get its drink.

"Sorry, friend, but you know where to find more and I don't," Verdon said through cracked lips. He chewed the fibrous mass, sucking out all the liquid. Instinct told him he should not swallow the fiber.

He continued walking, wondering how much further the two small swallows of water would take him. How long did a man live on the desert? People survived on it, but they knew its secrets, how to find water, what types of cactus could sustain them. He had never expected to cross the Sundered Desert on foot and had never made desert lore his study.

An hour later he saw the bird again. It landed a few hundred yards in front of him and flew off again. When he reached the spot, on a small rock he found another piece of damp, fibrous plant flesh.

"You stupid thing, if you keep putting it in front of me, I'm going to eat it," he muttered as he picked up the bird's leavings. The second hunk was half again as large as the first and he sucked three swallows from it. Half an hour later he found a third piece and knew the bird was deliberately leaving it for him.

Why? For what purpose?

The walking seemed to be easier as he continued. The small amount of liquid had not refreshed him all that much, but the hope of more kept him going. Two hours later the bird had not returned. He yearned for a rest and sat down in the shade of a tall column of rock. He nodded, nearly asleep, when a voice startled him. He jumped to his feet, his sword in his hand before he saw the bird. He blinked. The bird, the ferran, had a human face, but otherwise it looked like an owl.

"What . . . ?"

"I said sleep there and you won-won—you'll die,"

the little ferran stuttered until he found a way around whatever word he had originally intended to use.

"Glory ants," the bird-man said and a small hand and arm appeared from under his right wing as he pointed to two small mounds in the sand. "They're called glory ants because when they sting you get a sense of eu-eu-eupho—you feel great until you die. They stay underground until the sand cools off. My name is Iliki. I'll introduce you to my friends later."

"Thanks," Verdon said, and stepped away from the two small mounds. He picked up his armor and stepped out of the shadow when the ferran suddenly leapt into the air and flew almost in his face.

"Stop! Don't step on Milstithanog's tail!" Iliki cried, and then flew up ten feet over Verdon's head. "Don't hurt him, he didn't mean to step on you. Remember, he can't see you."

Verdon looked around. He had stepped off the sand onto a slab of rock, a bare slab of rock.

"Where?" he asked.

"It's safe now, he moved it," the ferran said. "It was right in front of you, but it's inv-inv—you couldn't see it. You can't see Milstithanog."

"Oh." Verdon eyed the little creature, sure it was lying about its unseen companion, but decided not to argue. He needed a desert-wise companion too badly to risk angering the little owl-man. If he could learn how to find food and water, he could make it to Tee, or even turn back toward the mountains.

"He's a creature from somewhere—not this world," the owl-man said. Both his hands appeared and he folded them in front of his chest and raised his eyes to the sky. I am truly blessed to have him for a friend."

"You can see him?" Verdon asked.

"Oh yes, he taught me the secret of seeing and hearing him. He's been trapped on our world for a long time and he was lonely, you see."

"The point is, I don't see," Verdon replied. "Were is this thing?"

"I wouldn't insult him if I were you," Iliki warned. "He can see you, and he can hear you too."

"I won't bother your friend," Verdon said, not believing a word of it. The little creature was trying to intimidate him, probably out of fear that Verdon might kill and eat him. "You're the one that left the cactus for me. I'm grateful, and if you show me where I can find more, you'd probably save my life."

Iliki flew down and perched on a rock, his head cocked to the side in bird fashion though he stared at Verdon with both his human eyes.

"What is your life worth to you?"

Verdon stared at the little creature, surprised because the ferran wanted payment for saving his life, and wondering at his own naïveté. The hard life of the Sundered Desert had been made even more difficult by Darkfall. People there took what they could get. "What are you asking?"

"Is your life worth another's?"

"You want someone killed?" Verdon had expected a demand for gold, and he was slightly shocked by the implication. But in a world where fighting had become a way of life, perhaps it was not so surprising.

"No, to save one . . ." Iliki moved his bird feet restlessly. "At least to rerescue one." His small hands came out from beneath his wings and he smoothed his feathers. "My fr-friend Cla-Cla—a sand elf. Clariel. The outlaws captured her four days ago."

"You want me to attack a group of desert outlaws alone?" He couldn't believe the ferran was serious. The Iron Guard considered itself the elite among the Aden military, an opinion not shared by the Iron Tyrant's shadow army or the Eye. The guard's reputation had risen considerably if anyone could believe a single member could take on an entire band of villains.

"You won't have to fight al-alo—by yourself," Iliki said. "I'll he-help, and so will Kr-Kr—her lightning lizard, and she'll be there too. I've tho-thou—worked it all out while I watched you."

"What about your big invisible friend?" Verdon asked. "If he's so dangerous, why hasn't he freed her?" He couldn't resist teasing Iliki about his imaginary companion.

Iliki looked up and to Verdon's right. "Don't be upset, he didn't mean anything by it," he said. Verdon told himself the creature couldn't exist, but he felt his skin crawl.

"He ca-can't," Iliki told Verdon. "You've seen the turquan stones these desert nomads wear? They're not mag-mag—they have no known power on this world, but they do on his. They drain his strength."

"Where did what's his name come from?" Verdon demanded, suddenly tired of this creature.

"He came into our world fr-fr—out of the mountains—from that way," Iliki pointed vaguely northeast, and Verdon felt the hair rise on his neck. He'd once heard an old legend about a gate in a range of mountains called the North Wall that led to other worlds and regions. Only master magicians understood and could reach those strange planes of existence. He glanced up at the empty air where the bird-man focused his attention when he spoke to Milstithanog. He decided not to tempt what might really be there. Since the Darkfall many things existed on Aden that had previously only lived in legend and nightmare.

"All I'll promise is to listen to your plan," Verdon said. He could not afford summarily to refuse. His life depended on his getting food and water.

Iliki suddenly flew up into the air and trilled a bird-like call. He landed and waited. Verdon snorted. He didn't say anything, but if the bird-man said he had a second invisible friend, Verdon considered striking out on his own again. He had heard the hot sun of the desert could drive people to madness. The little ferran might be insane. He was sure of it when he saw Iliki looking behind him, but a clatter of falling rock caused Verdon to spin around.

He stepped back a pace and reached for his pistol

before he thought better of pulling the weapon. Iliki had mentioned a lightning lizard, and Verdon was staring one directly in the mouth. In a mouth that could bite off his head at the neck with one snap of those powerful jaws.

Shoulder to shoulder it matched him in height, but fully erect it would stand nine feet tall or more, and was more than twelve feet in length. Its comparatively small front legs were as thick as his thighs, and its own thighs were thicker than his body. Standing out against the sky, the lizard was easy to see, but its pale brown hide with the irregular darker splotches across its back would camouflage it in the wild.

It balanced on three legs, holding its right hind foot off the ground. The outer toe and the claw from the middle toe had been lost in a recent fight. The lizard hissed softly at him and lowered its head, staring at the man with a glittering black eye showing out of a long slit of an eyelid.

"Beha-behav—be good, Kree," Iliki ordered, flying from his perch to land on the ground almost between the lizard's feet. "He is a friend—reolin—understand reolin?" When the little ferran used the elfin term for friend the lizard lowered his head until his blunt nose nearly touched his small feathered companion.

"He'll help us resc-resc—save Clariel. Save Clariel."

At the mention of the elfin name, the lizard hissed and gave a low whine. Verdon stared, surprised at the sound and the feeling it conveyed.

"Kree is a wonder among lightning lizards," Iliki said. "Most of them just tolerate their riders, but there's a clo-clo—special bond between Kree and Clariel."

"Ah, well met, Kree," Verdon said. Apparently the beast trusted Iliki enough to accept the stranger.

"Now this is my pla-pla—what I had in mind," Iliki said. He squatted on the rock and the fluff of his feathers hid his clawed bird feet. The big lightning lizard stretched out on the ground as if he, too, were listening.

6

Verdon had grudgingly given Iliki his due; the little ferran's plan *might* work. After Verdon had heard it, he admitted that trying to cross the desert alone could be as dangerous as the attempt to save the elf. The little owl-man had promised he and the elf would guide Verdon to the mountains when she was free.

Once Verdon had given his word to help free the elf, Iliki showed him how to recognize waterthorn cactus. The short, stubby desert plant hoarded water in its soft, fibrous flesh. He soon discovered why Iliki wanted to teach him about the plant. Verdon's sword could hack through the thick, sharp thorns easily. It took Iliki, with his diminutive arms and tiny, dull blade, nearly an hour to satisfy himself and half a day to quench the lizard's occasional thirst. Iliki had also shown Verdon the caroon, a thorny plant with edible flesh, but one the ferran could not manage alone. Fortunately, Iliki had found a wounded desert antelope and Kree had eaten well the day before. Like most reptiles, Kree's slow digestive system would not require food for another five to six days.

As they trekked after the outlaws that had captured

the elf, Iliki coached Kree on the plan. The ferran trained the lightning lizard to follow close on Verdon's heels, not a lesson Verdon appreciated a great deal. He ached from the tension in his muscles that came from knowing that the three-foot-long head hovered inches behind his own. That eighteen-inch mouth full of sharp teeth would not suffer a strain if the lizard developed an appetite and bit his head off.

The elf had trained Kree, and when he objected to Iliki's orders, the name of his mistress brought out a whine and instant obedience.

Twice a day Iliki had flown on ahead to watch the progress of the outlaws and discovered they had two other captives, a human male and a female dwarf. If the little ferran could cut the bonds of all three, they might decrease the odds against the rescuers. So at dawn, four days after meeting the ferran, Verdon crouched between two boulders and watched the camp of the outlaws.

The Sundered Desert was a place of deception. From a distance the flat, arid land appeared to stretch as far as the eye could see, but they came on sudden gorges, valleys, and depressions. Legend said great ice floes and wide rivers gouged the land in an ancient time called the Great Freeze.

In those depressions were the "forests" of the desert, the tall columns of water and wind-scoured rock. Often those depressions, with their stone forests, were also oases. The wildlife of the desert congregated in them; small herds of desert antelope, flocks of birds, and diggins of rock worms.

The canyons with desert springs also served as camps of desert-wise travelers. They used fires to keep away the worms rather than spend the nights on the plain, where their fires could be seen for miles and draw nocturnals.

Dawn had begun to lighten the sky. From his position between the boulders, Verdon could see three sail carts drawn up in a rough triangle around the outside edges of the camp. Within their area of dubious protection, a dozen desert outlaws slept, wrapped in blankets. Two were on watch. Fourteen in all.

"Either your ferran friend can't count, or he lied to us," Verdon muttered. The lightning lizard hissed a soft reply. Probably the latter, Verdon decided, since the guardsman would not have agreed if he had known the number they faced. But it was too late to back out; he had given his word, and Iliki had already flown ahead to cut the bonds of the prisoners.

Verdon could see a man sitting upright, tied to the inner wheel of a sail cart. A female dwarf sat by the wheel of another desert vehicle, her hands behind her back. From his place behind the rocks, a third cart hid the elf they had come to rescue.

While he waited, Verdon studied the desert vehicles, thinking they were slightly different from the type that usually used the Thunder Trail. They had sharp prows like sailboats; better to cut down wind drag, he decided. They were three-wheelers. An axle attached to two large wheels went through the bottom a third of the distance back from the prow of the cart. Each tiller was mated with a third wheel, which supported the rear of the vehicle.

Beside Verdon, Kree, the lightning lizard, raised his head, sniffed, and hissed softly. He scented or sensed the nearness of his rider. It had taken both Verdon and Iliki to keep him from invading the camp.

While Verdon watched, a gray shadow flitted from beneath the wagon where the man sat and took cover behind the dwarf. Iliki had taken Verdon's knife to cut the bonds of the prisoners while alerting them to be ready for the attack. According to the plan, the elf warrior would be the last to be freed and the bird-man would leave the knife with her, since she was a trained warrior. Moments later the flitting shadow appeared again to dip out of sight beneath the nearest cart.

Verdon counted to fifty and rose, taking care not to let his armor rattle as he worked his way carefully down the rocks. He could feel Kree's hot breath on his neck. Lightning lizards were not reputed to have a great deal of intelligence, but Kree obeyed the training he had been given. He limped along behind Verdon. They crept as close to the camp as they dared. As the ferran had said, the guards relaxed at dawn. The nocturnals could attack at any time—light did not deter them, but it did reduce their ability to remain unseen while sneaking up on their prey. The brigands would need a magician's prophecy to expect an attack from a lightning lizard, a member of the Urbanan Iron Guard, and an owl-man.

In the growing light Verdon saw Iliki as he left the third cart and rose in the air. The ferran fluttered to the ground not far from the nearest guard. His left wing drooped awkwardly as he scampered among the rocks, clattering small stones. He kept his back to the guard so he appeared to be just an injured bird, easy prey.

Verdon nodded, an acknowledgment of Iliki's courage and trust. His hand went to the holster that held the wheel lock pistol he usually used, but he left it in place. He had tucked the two extra weapons into a makeshift belt around his waist. They would be harder to free in an emergency. He pulled them both, cocked them, and held one in each hand as he stepped out of hiding. The outlaw's mouth would be watering at the thought of roasted bird for breakfast. Iliki trusted Verdon and Kree to kill the guard before the guard could kill him.

Verdon kept to the sparse sand to muffle his approach. He was still too far away for a sure hit with a pistol, but the guard drew his bow and aimed at Iliki.

Verdon stopped, raised the projectile weapon, and sighted down the barrel, but shooting even a criminal in the back without warning seemed treacherous.

"It wouldn't be fit to eat," he said quietly.

Verdon startled the guard and accomplished just what he did not want. The humanoid jumped and let go the arrow. It missed Iliki by an inch. The outlaw whirled around as Verdon sighted down the barrel and pulled the trigger. The nomad's chest exploded in a shower of blood, bone, and flesh. The nomad had been a ferran with a human body and the face of a large feline.

Inside the square of wagons, the blanket-wrapped sleepers leapt to their feet, their weapons already in their hands. Nearly half were human. The others were ferrans. Behind Verdon, the lightning lizard, startled by the sudden noise of the gunne, roared a challenge.

"Kree! To me! *Kalamba*!" a voice, almost like bird-song called from the nearest wagon. The lightning lizard roared a challenge and nearly knocked Verdon off his feet as it charged, limping and hopping toward its mistress. A human nocked an arrow to his bow, but he had not fully drawn it before he let fly to stick in Kree's hide. The nomad had the satisfaction of know-ing he hit his target just before the lightning lizard attacked. The muffled scream came to a sudden halt as Kree bit through the bandit's neck and spit out the severed head.

Verdon had tucked his empty pistol inside the scrap of cloth that served as a makeshift belt and pulled the third gunne from his holster. He planned to charge into the camp and fire both pistols as soon as he had certain targets, immediately decreasing the number of foes.

Seeing the huge beast-men changed his mind. Only two were human size, the others were larger. Two stood more than eight feet tall, with short, thick horns jutting out over tiny eyes in heads ridiculously small on such massive bodies. One of the giant rhino-men lum-bered toward Verdon, his thick lips drawn back in a snarl. In a massive hand with short fingers and blunt, thick claws, the monster held a blade that glowed with a dweomer.

Verdon took a step back, watching the creature as it approached. Luckily it wore no armor, only a wide leather belt that held a scabbard and a knife. Its legs, thick as Verdon's body, were protected with leather straps woven into openwork greaves. As the beast-man charged, Verdon raised his right arm and fired the wheel lock pistol directly into the bestial face. The upward angle of his shot sent the bullet into the monster's brain, killing it instantly. The momentum of the huge creature carried it forward and it knocked Verdon to the ground with a wild swing of its left arm.

When he fell Verdon lost the third pistol, the only one still holding a load. He glanced around, looking for it as he scrambled to his feet, but a thick-bodied, pig-snouted bandit charged toward him. Verdon backed up and dodged his attacker, giving himself time to pull his sword. This one, too, had a sword enhanced by magic. Verdon had paid a high price for the extra magic on his weapons and armor, so when the two blades clashed they flashed a blue glow. The leather thong wound around the hilt of the ex-guardsman's blade absorbed the shock, but the metal handle caused the boar-man's blade to vibrate in his hand until his tusked teeth chattered. Verdon's thrust caught the ferran in the side of the neck, and a twist of the blade severed his windpipe.

Verdon stepped back and looked around the camp. He had accounted for three of the enemy. Kree had scattered the startled, sleep-fogged kidnappers; some he had knocked off their feet with his lashing tail and others had been panicked into fleeing the immediate area. The lightning lizard had decapitated one and had just brought down a bandit with a swipe of a claw across the man's throat.

The elf rolled on the ground, leg-locked with a cat-human who struggled to get free to use the length of his sword, while a human attempted to stab her. He dodged the rolling pair as they struggled. Iliki, hovering over his head, swooped in and threw dirt in the outlaw's eyes. Across the camp the male prisoner, judging by his beard and dress, a desert trader, had just crushed a human's skull with a large rock. He jerked his victim's sword out of its scabbard.

The female dwarf had disappeared.

The six who had scattered at the first alarm had regrouped and come charging back into camp. They ignored the elf and her two adversaries. The two humans converged on the male prisoner, who had managed to gain possession of his victim's sword. Three, all ferrans, all crosses between human and types of desert antelope, moved cautiously toward the lightning lizard.

The second of the giant horned animen strode toward Verdon.

Where did these outlaws get magically enhanced weapons? Verdon wondered as he saw the glow on the blade the rhino-man brandished. Not that the big outlaw needed magic against the guardsman. Its sword and reach were half again as long as the young warrior's.

The animan's eyes blazed with bloodlust as it lumbered forward. It charged, head down, the short, stubby horn on its head pointed directly at Verdon. He backed up, stalling for time while he looked for a weakness. Weakness? His opponent moved with slow determination, but that could be deliberate intimidation. Bestial strength wedged itself into those huge muscles; bestial speed probably hid there too.

Out of the corner of his eye, Verdon saw the cart behind him and realized he had only a few feet in which to retreat. If he backed up to the side of the desert vehicle, he would be trapped.

He suddenly changed course, stepping forward, and swung his blade. A gap of two feet separated the adversaries when he began his swing. His blade met nothing but air.

The huge rhino-man gave a "whoomph," as the unseen force knocked the breath out of him. The outlaw rose six inches off the ground, lifted by an invisible impact that threw him flat on his back. Too surprised to make use of his advantage, Verdon stepped in again when the monster leapt to his feet, and the unseen force promptly knocked him sideways.

"Thank you, Milstithanog," Verdon looked up at the empty air in the only open space in the encampment. "I won't doubt you again. You keep him busy for a while."

Verdon hurried the few steps to where the three antlered ferrans slashed at the lightning lizard. The big reptile bled from a cut on his left shoulder and two shallow slashes on his neck. The first bandit, with two wicked horns nearly as long as his sword, noticed the movement. He looked over his shoulder as Verdon ran him through. The young warrior was still pulling the dripping sword from the outlaw's body when the second ferran swung his curved shashqa at the armored man. The blade clashed against Verdon's armor and bounced off. Before Verdon could raise his blade again, Kree reached forward and clamped his jaws on the outlaw's chest.

The lizard dropped the half-severed body to the ground with a roar as the third antlered humanoid charged. He slashed his blade against the lightning lizard's side and raked with the prongs of his antlers. When Kree drew back, Verdon dashed under him and caught the antlered animan in the throat. A red stream gushed from his neck to the ground, mingling with the lizard's blood.

Verdon looked around. The elf had dispatched her first opponent, and, as Verdon looked up, she ran the dead man's blade through the second. The male prisoner had accounted for one of his attackers and the other backed off, desperately parrying the weapon of the newly freed man. The bandit managed four steps before the ex-prisoner ran him through with an expert thrust.

The scrape of a clawed foot on stone warned Verdon he had not finished his fight with his last adversary. He turned and raised his blade just in time to parry a slash from the huge, short-horned rhino-man that Milstithanog had knocked to the ground for him. Apparently the demon from the other plane had decided he had done enough.

The clash of the two magically enhanced swords sent out auras of light in every color of the spectrum. Expecting it, Verdon had averted his eyes, but apparently the ferran had not. He blinked as if to clear his vision and Verdon took the opportunity to slash at the tree-thick arm, but the beast-man stepped back. The tip of Verdon's sword cut through the heavy leather gauntlet, but no blood stained the dark leather.

His vision clear again, the ferran lowered his head, his tiny, black eyes snapped in rage. His snarl, from low in his chest, seemed deep enough to be rising from the ground. Verdon backed up, parrying blows from the big sword that nearly knocked him off his feet. Then he felt the wheel of a cart behind him and knew he had nowhere else to go.

7

With each parry, Verdon felt his own strength and the magic in his sword weakening. The ferran used a steel sword, while Verdon's was manite. Manite held magic better than steel, but once the magic faded, his blade would be no match for the ferran's.

Behind the huge outlaw, Verdon saw the female elf and the human male as they both crept forward, hoping to take the ferran by surprise, but either acute hearing or a sense of danger alerted the rhino-man, and he whirled. One swing of his blade against the desert man's weapon knocked him off his feet and his second, delivered with lightning recoil, drove back the elf.

Verdon took one step away from the cart before the monster had turned to face him again, the giant steel sword upraised.

The young warrior knew neither his own strength nor the magic of his armor and sword could stand another blow, when suddenly a roar from beside him startled him into jumping sideways.

The ferran staggered back as a fist-sized hole appeared in his chest, heart high. He stumbled forward and fell.

Verdon just managed to step out of the way and nearly stumbled over the dwarf as she scrambled to her feet. Beside her the third pistol, the one Verdon had lost, lay smoking on the ground. She picked it up, smiled sheepishly as she handed it to Verdon, and dusted off her skirts.

"Thank you," he managed to gasp.

She nodded and slipped around the end of the cart, while Verdon looked around the campsite.

Thirteen bodies were sprawled on the blood-soaked ground, corpses in the grotesque positions of death. Neither the prisoners nor Verdon suffered any injury, but Kree, the lightning lizard lay on his side, his breathing labored.

The elf threw a wild look around the camp, realized they had killed their last enemy, and rushed to Kree. She knelt by him, singing under her voice as her hands moved along his side, trying to close the worst of his wounds.

Verdon recognized the song—more of a chant—a healing spell. It evoked deeply submerged memories of another type of magic, the power of the world's essence. His parents had been essencers, and he had been learning their arts when he was left with Marchant Worsten. His returning memories surprised him. He had once known how to heal!

Verdon wanted to use that forgotten skill to help save the lizard's life. The creature deserved to live. Kree was faithful to his mistress and a valiant fighter.

The elf's song faltered as Verdon approached. She watched him warily as he pulled off his helmet and gauntlets. Awkwardly kneeling—his armor prevented much bending—he touched the ground and began a litany of his own, calling upon the natural forces of the world to give him strength. He began slowly, working to dredge up the memory of each word, but as he spoke one, the next came more easily until they were rolling off his tongue as if they were physically connected.

His fatigue fell away. His body throbbed with a new-born strength, and the world seemed suddenly brighter and more beautiful. At the end of the call for strength he stood and put one hand against the lightning lizard's side. The words of healing came easier.

The elf had slowed the bleeding; Verdon stopped it. The deep gash in the lizard's side partially closed, but neither Verdon's magic nor the elf's had the strength to heal it completely. Still, barring another fierce battle, the creature's own body could manage the rest.

The elf seemed satisfied and turned a pair of appraising eyes on Verdon. He returned her gaze, as curious as she.

Like all elves she was all slenderness and points. The tips of her pointed ears reached almost to the top of her head and narrowed to join a tapering jaw and pointed chin. Even her winged brows and almond-shaped, tilted eyes added to the illusion of sharpness. Her skin was a deep bronze, her black hair still had a few glints of blue beneath its thick coating of desert dust. She continued to stare at Verdon for a moment and then, without speaking, turned back to soothe the lizard, who whined for her attention. Verdon left her and crossed the camp to pick up one of his discarded gunnes.

"My gratitude," said a voice behind Verdon, and he turned to see the newly freed male prisoner. The man's bronze skin and sharp features identified him as a desert dweller. His hair was also black but not as deep or as vibrant as the elf's. His thick beard still held the hint of artificial curling. His teeth, when he smiled, gleamed whitely.

"I thank you for our freedom and probably for our lives," he said as he held out his right hand, palm turned toward the young warrior. Verdon understood the customs of the Sundered Desert well enough to know he was being honored. In a land where water was scarce and washing was a luxury seldom to be enjoyed, to be given permission to touch another's hand was the highest compliment the desert people could offer.

Verdon stared at the hand; soft, without the calluses of labor, wielding a weapon, or handling a sail cart; an enigma. He was like a cosseted pet, one that has been accidentally abandoned, but when it finds itself alone, reverts to the instincts of its wild ancestors.

He briefly touched the fingers and palm of his own right hand to the one offered and quickly pulled it away, not knowing how long the touch was meant to last. If he gave any insult in accepting the honor, the desert man did not seem to take offense.

"I am Aktar, no one of importance, save to myself, and my life, though valueless, I owe to you," he said.

"I am Verdon Stramel," Verdon replied. The time had come for him to acknowledge his heritage and use his own name.

"You're a des—" Aktar's eyes widened and he broke off in mid-sentence, embarrassed. "Forgive my stupidity. Fear and lack of food has taken my wits."

Verdon understood what Aktar was too polite to say. "The Iron Guard will call me a deserter, but I was born a citizen of Columbey; I owe no loyalty to Lord Urbane or Urbana."

Urbana had once been called Columbey. Since the beginning of the Darkfall, nocturnals had killed far too many of its citizens, but most of the population remained. Yet with the change of name and the ruler, the country had changed. Shabby factory towns replaced the peaceful villages. The constant need for fuel to feed the factories had destroyed many forests and left others in shambles. Wide vistas of fertile farmland lay fallow. Pollution from the factories had ruined the rivers and killed the fish. The rain, falling through the pall of black smoke that hung over the land, killed vegetation.

Even worse was the dark magic that the ruler of Urbane had called upon to create his mechamagic, the thunder trains and the sentinels.

A clatter of metal drew Verdon's attention to the fire. A small blaze was beginning to eat its way along a couple of sticks of wood beneath a metal pan standing on a tripod. In the midst of bloody bodies, the female dwarf was stirring a batter and pouring it into the pan as complacently as if she were in her own kitchen. She seemed comfortable at the fire, a nurturer, he decided, not a fighter. That's why she had stayed out of the way during the battle. She had been so quiet and so many other things had been claiming his attention, he had not given her a thought.

The others were strange, exotic in their desert dress, with their full, loose clothing, caught up at the wrists and ankles with tight bands to keep the heat of the desert floor off their skin.

He had not noticed the clothing of the dwarf because it was familiar. She wore a traditional Urbanan style, a trilayered skirt, double tunic and short-sleeved overjacket worn in Mekanus and most of the regions north of Rose. The gray-brown color indicated she was a servant. Except for the very young and the very old, dwarfs did not show their age, so he had no idea how old she might be. Her broad, heavy-featured face had the ruddy, healthy glow of her race. The heat of the fire had heightened the color in her cheeks until they were as red as her bright hair, held back with a series of curved combs. Her dark blue eyes sparkled as if they were speaking. The only sound she made came from the clatter of pots.

"I believe our short friend has the right of it," Aktar grinned. "Our captors were not too free with the food, and if you came well supplied, I see no sign of it."

"I've lived off desert plants since I lost my provisions to the giant sand fleas," Verdon admitted. Hungry as he was, he looked around with worried eyes.

"But we can't stay here long. The smell of blood will draw the rock worms and nocturnals."

Aktar agreed with a nod. "The next question is, where do we go?"

"Tee is the closest large settlement," Verdon replied. The desert nomad had to know it.

Verdon gazed northeast. He had wanted to leave the train before it crossed the mountains, but it was as if the contingent commander had read his mind and kept him at duties inside the train until they reached the desert, where he had a slim chance of survival. But Verdon had survived, and he still wanted to reach Arasteen. He would have to get through Burcham's Pass before the *Dominant* returned and spread the word of his desertion. Since he had left the train during a battle with nocturnals, he hoped Adralk would believe he had been killed, but he could not be sure he had escaped unseen.

If he traveled through Burcham's Pass with a caravan, he would not be noticed. He might travel as a guard, or a trader, he thought, looking at the bundles in the carts. Since he needed clothing, he started a systematic search of the nearest desert vehicle. The outlaws had obviously raided a trader's caravan. He found several jars of spices that would bring high prices in Urbana or Arasteen, several crates of dried palm fruit and jars of oil from the southern reaches. In one cart he had discovered enough of value to allow him to pass as a trader.

He didn't waste a moment's thought on the rightful owner of the trade goods. The Worms never left anyone alive. Not alive and free, he amended, thinking of the three captives who had expected to be sold as slaves.

In a small chest he found two suits of richly textured clothing that were a reasonable fit. The chest held an elaborately embroidered cloak, combs, a small purse of gold, a scroll that listed half a year's trade records, and several other small possessions that had belonged to a minor trader. Verdon frowned at the flamboyant clothing, shrugged when he discovered it fitted him, and changed into it. No one would expect the wearer of such garments to be a deserter from the Iron Guard.

While he was searching the cart, the dwarf came over and handed him a large, inch-thick pan-bread cake. She smiled and bowed, her eyes bright as she offered it, but a nod that set her curls to bobbing was her only answer to his thanks.

Seeing the food, Iliki, who had been perched on the sail watching Verdon's industry, flew over to perch on the side of the cart. He eyed the dwarf hopefully, and backed off when she sneezed. She glared at the bird-man, sneezed again, and scuttled away, back toward the fire.

"She doesn't ca-car—like me, I guess," the owl-man said, staring after her. "But you could share wi-wi—give me some of that bread," He held out a small hand, and Verdon tore off a small chunk. They were both chewing happily when Verdon remembered he wanted Iliki to pass along a message.

"Tell your friend Milstithanog that I appreciate his help with that big nomad," he said.

Iliki nearly choked. His eyes, already large, stretched until the whites showed around the owl yellow.

"Milstithanog?"

"He kept knocking that big rhino-man down. If he hadn't, we might not have made it through that battle. I don't think I could have beaten that monster, not with that dweomered sword he carried. It was power-ful enough to slice through a thunder train—why are you looking so stunned?"

"I—uh—*the turquan*!" Iliki chirped suddenly. "I didn't think Milstithanog would have the strength to help us at all. I told you that at the start."

"Well apparently it didn't bother him as much as you thought it would."

"N-no, appar-appar—it didn't," Iliki said, looking stunned.

Verdon thought he understood the little ferran's emotions. In the last few days he had felt lost, too. Too much had happened too fast.

By the time Verdon and Iliki finished the first of the fried bread, Aktar and Clariel and the dwarf were eat-ing. Verdon walked over to the fire where they sat with their backs to the carnage of the battle.

The elf had finished her food and sat with her arms wrapped around her close-drawn knees. She stared at the small, leaping flames as if, by focusing her attention on the fire, she could shut away even the existence of the others. Verdon could sense the wall she placed around herself.

"Now that we're free, where do we go?" Aktar brought up the subject of their destination again. "We'll be safer if we stay together and protect each other, but you want to return to your people," he said to Clariel. The elf shook her head.

"It is a poor warrior who takes shame back to her people. I travel on the trail of the nocturnals until I avenge my lost companions."

"And how do you propose to do that?" Verdon asked. Her glare told him she had misinterpreted his meaning. "I just wondered if you had some plan."

"I will seek out nocturnals and kill them until I've killed a score of scores, or until they kill me."

"And add the waste of your own life to those already dead?" Verdon asked. He had the satisfaction of sensing the drop of her wall of isolation. Her face contorted in rage that immediately froze into haughtiness.

"I will forgive your insult, but only because you are human. You cannot understand the loss of lives that should have continued for centuries."

"I'm more concerned with the value of lives than with their length," Verdon retorted. "If you set out alone to attack bands of nocturnals, you'll be killed the first time you're outnumbered, selling your life for a thrust of a cheap sword. I propose to cost Darkfall many of its evil creatures before I'm done."

"It is true, a great warrior only sells his life at great cost," she admitted. "How will you do it?"

"Not by committing suicide, gloriously attacking against odds too great for success."

"So far all you've said is what you won't do."

Beside the elf, Kree was turning his head, eyeing first his mistress and then Verdon. Iliki, Aktar, and the dwarf were very still. Verdon was irritated with the elf, but not angry. He was struck by her insight.

"That's true," he admitted. "My only excuse is having all my plans upset. I'm trying to make new ones; deciding what I *won't* do is the first step, I suppose."

"You did choose a strange place to leave the thunder train," Iliki commented.

"Like Clariel, I made a vow. I swore to leave the train at the first opportunity," Verdon said. "Fate worked against me. Fate, or the contingent commander, I'm not sure which. By the time I was posted on a watch where I could escape unnoticed, I didn't think, I just left." He inclined his head toward Clariel, his gaze locked on hers.

"I let impatience drive me to risk my life on the desert alone. If I had died, I would have lost my life without striking a single blow against Lord Urbane or the monsters of Darkfall."

"You plan to cross the border into Arasteen?" Aktar asked. "We've heard rumors that war between Urbana and Arasteen isn't far away."

Verdon nodded; he glanced in the dwarf's direction and thought he saw her eyes flicker.

"I'd still like to reach Arasteen," Verdon said. "I've searched those bundles on the carts. They're trade goods. I might take some into Tee and use them as an excuse to buy passage on a freight caravan going through the pass." He looked at the silent dwarf.

"Do you want to go north with me?" he asked, believing the interest he had seen was an indication of her chosen direction. She answered with a vigorous nod.

"You can't speak?" he asked. She shook her head in reply.

"We don't know who she is, but she's obviously from Urbana," Aktar said, surveying the dwarf critically. "She's dressed like a servant, maybe a runaway."

The dwarf dropped her eyes.

"I cannot go to Tee," Clariel announced. "Kree

would not be tolerated there. To leave a loyal companion alone and wounded is to travel without honor. I will find shelter near here until he's healed."

"Many things have changed since the beginning of Darkfall," Aktar said. "Our people have seen sand elves and their mounts fight nocturnals. You'll find a welcome in Tee."

"We'll throw out enough cargo to make a place for him to ride," Verdon suggested, gesturing toward the largest of the sail carts. "The day wind is rising, so we should make ready to leave."

For the next half hour they checked the cargo on the vehicles, casting out the least valuable, but they kept all the weapons. Several bows and a good stock of arrows could save their lives. Clariel discovered her own weapons, taken from her by her captors. They rearranged what they kept to make room for the lightning lizard on the largest vehicle. Verdon decided to keep his armor, since they could well run into trouble on the way to Tee. He could always bury it in the desert before they reached the trading town. He considered wearing at least his breastplate and then discarded the idea. The plan was to take all three carts, and the armor would hamper his steering.

The discussion between Clariel and Aktar convinced Verdon they were both familiar with the operation of the wind-powered rigs. As a boy in Mekanus, he had learned to sail a small boat. The rigging on the wheeled vehicles was similar, so when they suggested taking all three vehicles he didn't object.

"If we lose a wheel or wreck one cart, we'll still have two," Aktar said.

They kept enough cargo to give Verdon the appearance of being a trader and, within an hour of the battle, they raised the sails. Verdon looked up at the coarse cloth woven from the dried fibers of the tall, reacher cacti. The fabric was coarse, stiff, and rough to the touch. Most of the nomads painted decorations on their sails, proclaiming their clans. The decorations on all three sails showed a small section of rock near the bottom, and a huge coiled desert worm reaching up nearly to the halyard.

"Worms?" Verdon demanded of the others. "Those outlaws were Worms?" He understood why the bandits had dweomered weapons, but he had a hard time believing two humans, an elf, and a lightning lizard had overcome a raiding party of the most dangerous and dreaded outlaws on the Sundered Desert.

The others nodded.

"How can we go to Tee or anywhere in these carts?" Verdon asked. "The soldiers of the rhanate will be after us as soon as we come within sight."

8

Clariel took the largest of the three carts with Kree sprawled in the bottom. Verdon had watched, torn between impatience and humor, as she tried to force the lizard to lie down in the cart. Kree hissed his objections, but obeyed her while she was looking at him. The moment she turned her back to raise the sail, he raised his head. When she turned, he dropped it again for the length of time she stood looking at him. They were like two puppets pulled by the same string.

The dwarf, mute and nameless, rode with Aktar, and Iliki went with Verdon. The ferran was too small to operate a cart but still insisted he knew all about them.

"Who would know more about the wind and its forc-for—behavior?" he demanded.

Their plan suffered a reverse from the beginning. Verdon's and Clariel's carts, originally the most heavily laden, had been sitting on a sloping shelf of rock. Aboard his cart, Verdon was securing the halyard to the mast cleat when Iliki landed on what seemed to him a slim length of wood that would make a comfortable perch. He had chosen the pivoting brake lock and his weight released the catch. The sail was already billowing from the rising wind and the cart shot forward, throwing Verdon off his feet.

He heard alarmed shouts from Aktar and Clariel as he scrambled for the stern of the craft, threw himself onto the seat, grabbed the sheet in one hand and the tiller in the other. The rock incline and the rising wind had acted together to shoot the cart forward. He spilled wind to slow it down. Iliki, who had flown up with a shriek of alarm, caught up with the speeding cart and landed on the aft sail leach, clinging to the reinforced outer edge of rough, heavy cloth.

"I thought you knew about these monsters," Verdon griped as he swerved to miss a boulder.

"I know about wind, not about whatever that was," Iliki glared down at the brake lock.

"Then from now on, stay on the gunwale," Verdon ordered. "I don't need any more surprises."

"What's a gunwale?" Iliki asked.

"The side of a boat. This looks and acts like a boat, so that's a gunwale."

"But it's a cart, so why not say side?" Suddenly Iliki's voice rose an octave. "*And why not say rock?*" he screeched and pointed ahead as Verdon jerked the tiller to miss the huge boulder in his path. He jerked too hard and the cart spun completely around. The sail jibbed, throwing Iliki from his perch. The ferran tumbled head over tail feathers and caught the wind under his wings just before hitting the ground.

Verdon pitched sideways but still grasped the tiller and the sheet to keep from falling from the cart. By accident, definitely no design of his, he was holding the sheet so the wind caught it and the cart was heading back in the direction he had come. The rusty metal fittings and dry wood of the mast groaned against the strain.

He passed Clariel's cart, missing it by inches, and then Aktar's. He saw the startled face of the nomad. The dwarf's red head bobbed up as she looked over the side.

"You forget something?" Aktar shouted.

"My place in line," Verdon shouted back, determined to keep his fiasco to himself. Then, using care and all the knowledge he could dredge up from his long-unused sailing lore, he turned the vehicle and took his place at the end of the column. A couple of minutes later, Iliki caught up with him and hovered just over his head.

"I think I-I—we'll *all* be safer if I fly ahead and spy out the trail," Iliki said.

"I didn't turn it over," Verdon snapped. What did they expect from him?

"Not thi-this time," Iliki retorted, and rose on the breeze spilled from the sail.

With Aktar leading and Verdon bringing up the rear, they left the rock towers behind. The carts slowed as they climbed the slope out of the small, deep canyon.

Once out of the depression the overall lay of the land appeared to be nearly flat and stretched away into the distance, but the view was deceptive. The Pours, the infrequent but violent rainstorms, had eaten small arroyos into the surface. Most of them ran east to west, where the rushing water that could not be absorbed by the parched land had fed into the canyons.

Not even Aktar could see them in the distance, and Iliki flew ahead to search out a safe course. On the flat plain of the desert the strong wind sent them forward at a good clip and without the ferran's warning a three-foot-deep gully could be the destruction of a cart and injury to the riders.

In the early morning the wind blew from the southwest, giving promise of a speedy trip to Tee. Before the sun was halfway up the sky the breeze died and the sails hung limp. They had traveled in a close convoy, so when they rolled to a halt, they stopped close together.

Verdon left his cart to join Aktar and the dwarf at Clariel's vehicle. The elf allowed the lizard to climb out onto the desert floor, where he sprawled on the hot earth, as contented on the ground as he had been uneasy in the cart. The elf walked a few paces away from the cart and stopped. She raised her face to the blazing sun and stood with her arms straight, held out slightly from her sides. Verdon recognized elf sensing and knew she could read the weather.

"It's a veering time," she said after a moment. "A breeze comes from the northeast, but not for hours yet."

The dwarf had brought a sack of food, a small water jar, and four cups. They ate the rest of that morning's pan-bread and a basket of sweet, sticky, dried palm fruit.

Aktar had carried a bundle cut from an outlaw's cloak. When he dropped it in the shade of the largest cart, it clinked. He had stripped the dead of their small possessions, their jewelry, purses, and knives. The bifid-blade katar seemed the most popular small weapon, but several outlaws had used kris knives. Mixed in among the knives were several ornate purses, small lacquered boxes studded with jewels, and more than two dozen necklaces and bracelets of pale desert silver set with turquan. Aktar saw Verdon eyeing the loot. The desert man's black eyes glittered.

"They could not be allowed to buy their way into Racharval with the property of those they killed," he said shortly.

Verdon nodded. Many people on Aden believed the spirits of the dead journeyed to a special perfect land. There were almost as many names and locations for this spiritual paradise as there were people. He had his own opinions, but he kept them to himself.

Aktar eyed the rest of the party, but as no one seemed to object, he began a careful evaluation, creating five separate piles of equal value. Verdon almost told Aktar to keep his share, but a sense of practicality overrode his pride. Around his waist he wore a wide, flat belt with jewels, gold, and platinum coins sewn inside. The government of Urbana paid their officers and the Iron Guard well. After Marchant's death Verdon had converted their property into easily portable assets. Still, he might not be able to recross the mountains and he had to consider the expense of living in strange countries. He had no idea when he could replenish his purse.

Aktar was watching him with shrewd, measuring eyes. The people of the Sundered Desert were reputed to be an avaricious lot, and put more trust in greed than in goodness. Verdon accepted his share, tucking a purse and two knives in his belt.

"Watching you fight, I'm surprised they were able to take you prisoner," Verdon said to Aktar. He wanted to know more about this smooth-talking nomad who was nothing like the small traders in Tee. Aktar might belittle his social position, but he spoke like a wellborn and educated man.

"Misfortune, the last of a string of mishaps," Aktar said "I'm from a tribe near the northern border. My people mine turquan and make jewelry." He held up one of the necklaces from the small pile of loot and eyed it with scorn. "I assure you, we do far better work. I was taking a year's labor to trade at Tee—"

"N-not alone?" Iliki interrupted, shocked at the very idea.

"Of course not. There were twenty of us, the rest warriors—I'm the clan's trader. We were attacked by nocturnals. I got away alive, but alone I was no match for the Worms." He waved a hand at the wagons and then turned a pointed gaze on Clariel. The elf sat with her arms wrapped around her drawn-up knees, staring out onto the desert.

"Our tales in that respect are much alike."

The elf had given no sign she even heard the conversation, but when the nomad spoke to her, she turned her head, giving him a sharp glare.

"Did *you* lead your people into the ambush that took every life but yours?" Clariel's tone was loaded with venom. Her eyes held such pain, Verdon almost choked on it.

"Yes, I did," Aktar met her glare with a steady gaze. "But even if I led, I was not to blame. I took what we all agreed was the safest path, I did all I could."

"I rejoice in *your* clear conscience," she snapped. "By your own admission you are a trader, not a warrior. A warrior, a leader of warriors, knows better than to lead a troop into an ambush."

"I kno-kno—am acquainted with one who didn't," Iliki spoke up. "Fa-fa—ill fortune worked against her, and she shouldn't blame herself for it."

"You speak from ignorance; you are untrained as a warrior or a leader." Clariel stared into the fire again, refusing to be placated.

"I know more than anyone else except you, since I was there," Iliki retorted, and then explained to Verdon, "I was flying scout for Clariel—I was watching for an ambush, and even *I* didn't see the nocturnals. I was not careless, they were too well hidden."

"How did the Worms capture you?" Verdon asked Clariel, wanting to direct the subject away from her guilt. Her self-recriminations, justified or not, were fruitless. "I've seen Kree in action, and he'd fight to the death in your defense."

"He was injured, and I had left him behind when I went hunting," Clariel said. "I ordered Iliki to stay with him, so not even he was along to warn me of trouble."

"Why did they take you captive?" Verdon continued with his questions, directing the last one to Aktar. The Worms were reputed to kill anyone they encountered.

Aktar shrugged, so Verdon turned a questioning gaze on the elf. She continued to stare out at the desert, but some sense not shared by humans seemed to tell her when she was being addressed.

"We were going to be sold—to be laborers in some secret mine, I think. One of the creatures taunted me with the threat of never seeing the sun again."

"A secret mine?" Verdon asked.

"I've hear-hear—they say the rhanate has found a vei-vei— some manite," Iliki volunteered.

"There are always stories," Aktar scoffed. The smile that seemed permanently fixed in place no longer reached his eyes. "There's no manite in the Sundered Desert, and for that I'm sorry indeed."

"If it's true we might be glad of it," Clariel said softly. "Having it could bring on war with Urbana." She looked directly at Verdon. "I recognize the risk you took to free us. My lack of gratitude is a failing in me. I know my duty to you, and I mean no personal insult, but I distrust the Iron Tyrant."

"You wouldn't insult me if you killed that monster who rules Urbana," Verdon retorted. "When Lord Urbane came into power and changed the name of our nation, he nearly destroyed the country. He enlarged the mines, destroyed many of the forests to build new foundries and the factories. The rivers are fouled and the air is full of fumes and smoke. Not everything made in those factories is fit to discuss under the clear sky."

"You mean the war trains and the armies of mechamagical men?" Iliki asked. The others looked up. Out of the corner of his eye, Verdon noticed the sudden stillness of the silent dwarf, but her blue eyes were staring at him intently.

"I'm not aware of any war trains," Verdon said, and saw their doubt. "Because I don't know about them doesn't mean they aren't being made." He wondered if they thought he was being condescending, but he was speaking the truth. "In Urbana not even the Iron Guard can ask about that sort of thing without being questioned by the Eye." Verdon had no need to explain the Eye. All the Known Lands knew about the band of fanatical priests led by High Inquisitor Gerrick Malanch. Officially, the organization was created to ferret out dopplegängers and the corrupted, people who were in service to the mysterious forces of

Darkfall. Unofficially, the Eye spied on the citizens of Urbana and destroyed Lord Urbane's political enemies. Tales of the tortures inflicted on their victims rivaled the horrors of the Darkfall.

Verdon gazed down at the little ferran. "If by mechamagical men, you mean the sentinels, there are still fewer than fifty of them. . . ." Verdon felt the horror and grief over his adopted father again. It had not lessened over the past few days. "Fifty are far too many, and they're what I meant. Their creation is as evil as the nocturnals they fight. It's far too dangerous to discuss them in the darkness and mention of them pollutes the daylight." He attempted to suppress his feelings about the sentinels, particularly Marchant Worsten. Dwelling on the fate of his stepfather might force him to foolhardy action.

"It must be as hard on an essencer to see the desecration of his forests as it would be for an elf," Clariel said. "Even sand elves of the desert revere trees, though many live their lives and die without ever seeing one."

"Are you an essencer?" Iliki asked.

"I'm not," Verdon replied, and saw the sudden narrowing of the elf's eyes. "My parents were. When Lord Urbane began destroying the forests, they placed me with General Marchant Worsten, my mother's cousin." He was surprised to find that knowledge on the tip of his tongue. "They died defending the forest north of Rose. They had taught me some world magic, but not a lot, I was too young. Mar—" Verdon found himself choking over his adopted father's name, turned his pause into a cough, and tried again. "Marchant raised me."

When they finished their second light meal of the morning, they took advantage of the relative safety and stretched out on the ground in the shade of the largest cart. The dwarf, who neither sailed a cart nor took an active part in the fighting, gestured that she would stay awake and keep watch.

Verdon had not slept well since he left the lair of the tiger lizard. He fell into a deep sleep and only awoke to hear his name being called. He felt the sun on his back; it had traveled across the sky and was halfway to the western horizon.

The bread was gone, but the dwarf passed out more dried palm fruit. Verdon's store of trade goods would be a little depleted. He was unconcerned.

The wind rose as Clariel had predicted. They raised the sails and continued their journey.

Tacking against the wind required more skill than running before it, and Verdon struggled to remember his seamanship, determined not to repeat his fiasco of the morning. The well-oiled wheels and the rear guiding mechanism gave the cart far greater maneuverability than a sailboat. After an hour of tacking toward Tee, Iliki, who had flown on ahead, came flashing back to land on the leach of Aktar's cart.

Verdon frowned as he saw the desert man's vehicle make an abrupt turn. In the larger wagon, Kree raised his head and hissed. Clariel was slower in changing direction, but she had nearly completed her turn when Aktar passed her.

Verdon, a little behind, was slower in his change of direction, but he was traveling back down his own trail when Aktar moved up to pace him. Iliki flew across to perch on Verdon's sail.

"Six carts, all headed this way, all with worms pai-pai— symbols on the sails," the little ferran panted, still out of breath.

"And when we don't join them, they'll know something's wrong," Verdon said, letting out the sail to increase his speed.

9

They fled before the outlaws were in sight, and Verdon hoped they would escape notice. That hope died when the six sails appeared over a rise behind them.

Iliki flew up to perch on the top of the mast and watched their pursuers. A few minutes later, when he had a moment to spare from watching the ground in front of the cart, Verdon looked up, but the little ferran had disappeared. Before he could build up a worry, Iliki came streaking back to land on the side of the cart.

"Fifteen," he said, his voice breathless and hardly more than a whisper. "Mostly human. They're more skilled at sailing, but their car-car—vehicles are more heavily loaded."

"Then we'll have the edge on speed?" Verdon asked.

"As long as we sail before the wind; as long as there is wind." Iliki launched himself into the air and flew on ahead to confer with Aktar.

"That's heartening," Verdon muttered. He knew the wind dropped with the sun. It rarely blew all night. Then what did they do? But there was no need to imagine trouble, it seemed to grow out of the sand.

A few yards ahead, the flat plain split apart into hundreds of arroyos, gullies, and gorges. The surface of the plain was torn asunder—Sundered. The name that had always seemed a colorful exaggeration took on meaning.

"How do we get through this?" Verdon shouted. Clariel spared him a brief glance before following Aktar into a deepening gorge.

And what if the wind doesn't dip this low? Verdon asked himself as he followed the others, but the breeze stayed with them and the slope helped to increase their speed. He gritted his teeth as he kept the sail flat out, scudding within inches of stone outcrops and careening around turns, half-expecting to pile into the rear of Clariel's rig at any moment.

As the canyon deepened, the walls rose around him, towering over the sail of the cart. From the depressions in the walls, rock worms, disturbed by the passing of the other two carts, lashed out, their blind heads waving about to catch unwary prey, their mouths open, waiting for an opportunity. From an outcrop, fifteen feet above the floor of a canyon, one worm reached out too far, and the top of Verdon's mast slammed its head as Verdon sped past. Orange ichor splattered on the ground behind the racing vehicle.

Like the carts, the wind seemed to be trapped in the canyons and kept them moving at a fast pace. Verdon, one hand holding the sheet and occasionally pulling it in when he was sure the passage was too narrow, had to keep the other on the tiller. He watched the striations as he sailed by until his mind was a blur of striped stone and jutting outcrops. Several times they seemed to be racing toward solid walls, but at the last minute Aktar angled off into the continuing gorge.

After a sharp turn the canyon widened out into a long, steep slope, but Verdon was staring down an empty passage. He was so intent on it he almost missed seeing Iliki, who flew out of an opening in the side and gestured him in. Verdon swerved at the last minute. His speed and the sudden turn combined to raise the left wheel completely off the ground. He found himself on a gentle incline that led up to the floor of a dim, shallow cave. Even with the sail luffing, he had to apply the brake to avoid hitting Clariel's cart. She was just climbing down, joining Aktar and Iliki, who hovered nearby.

"I hope you're right about this," Aktar called up to the bird-man.

"They'll think we kept on down the canyon if you're *quiet*," the ferran hissed. "And how much farther could we go with the sun setting?"

"He's right," Verdon said. "Instead of arguing, we had better clear out any rock worms we find."

"If it's not one-one kind of worm it's an-another," Iliki said as he perched on the side of the large cart and fluffed out his feathers as if he were settling down for the night.

"Before you go to sleep, check up near the ceiling," Verdon ordered. "We'll look around down here."

"Let Kree do it," Clariel suggested as the lizard climbed out of the cart. "He's quieter." She had found her own bow and her quiver of arrows when they searched through the cargo on the carts. While the lightning lizard explored the dim recesses of the shallow cave, she followed Verdon back toward the entrance of the gorge.

Verdon surveyed the area and wondered if they were close to the nest of the desert hawk that wheeled overhead. He hoped it would not alert the Worms to their presence.

He paused to check the charges of powder in his wheel lock pistols and loosen his sword. It had a tendency to work itself tight in the scabbard with his movement. Another shadow flitted above them as Iliki flew up to keep watch.

Above their heads, a ribbon of sunlight still brightened the upper canyon walls, but it had narrowed to only a few feet when they heard the clatter of wide metal wheels on stone. Verdon crouched behind a boulder, a pistol in each hand. Clariel had an arrow nocked to her bow, and Aktar stood ready with his sword.

The six carts careened down the canyon without noticing the sharp turn that led to the bowllike cave. Minutes passed, and the sound of the wheels receded in the distance. Aktar sheathed his blade and ran his fingers through his beard. Verdon had already seen enough of the desert man to know the gesture meant he was displeased.

"We've lost them for the night, but what about tomorrow?" I don't like having them ahead of us."

"Ahead of us?" Clariel's tilted eyes narrowed. "They have driven us south, but our destination is northeast, toward Tee."

"As long as we're in these canyons, we'll go where the wind takes us," Aktar said. "For that reason I would have avoided them if I could." He gave Verdon an apologetic look. "It seemed the best choice at the time."

"It probably was," Verdon replied. "We couldn't outrun them on the plain." He had given the answer Aktar expected, but he had the feeling something in Aktar's purpose had been revealed, and he wanted to clarify his position.

"My destination is Tee," he said quietly. He expected Aktar to agree and disclaim any desire for another destination, so he was surprised when the nomad smiled knowingly.

"I would not stop you from reaching Arasteen, but your journey could be futile."

"I don't think so," Verdon retorted, and turned away. Even if all his specialized knowledge about the Shadow Army and the thunder trains was already known to King Corben of Arasteen, he still had a good sword arm to offer.

"Who will speak for you in Arasteen? Who will introduce you to the authorities who can make use of your knowledge?" Aktar pursued. "Will they trust what you have to tell them?"

Verdon kept his face impassive, but the question of trust had never entered his mind. Why shouldn't they trust him? Then again, why should they? He was a fool to assume the suspicions that grew out of Darkfall would be limited to Urbana.

"Lord Urbane professes friendship with the rhanate," Aktar went on, his soothing voice too quiet for the others to hear. "But most of our people distrust the Iron Tyrant. The rhanate will pay well for any information you could give him. He could also give you an escort through Burcham's Pass and see that you reach the authorities of Arasteen."

"And you can introduce me to the rhanate?" Verdon asked doubtfully.

"Oh no, *I* am no one, but I have a cousin who enjoys the honor of being a magician to the court. My claim of kinship would get me a hearing with him. By our custom he is bound by obligation to you, since you saved the life of one who shares his blood."

The elf had stood quietly, saying nothing, her eyes shifting from one face to the other as the two humans talked. Verdon remembered that his parents had trusted the elves that lived in the forests of Columbey. He had a vague memory of his father saying they were not always as wise as many people thought, but they seldom told a lie. He gazed at Clariel, wondering what she thought about Aktar's suggestion.

Aktar seemed to sense Verdon's thoughts and widened his perpetual smile. "Our friend the dwarf is preparing to feed us again. I will assist her," he said, walking away. His excuse was a lame one, but it suited Verdon; he wanted the opinion of the elf. When the nomad was out of earshot, Verdon gazed again at Clariel.

"You heard his suggestion," Verdon said. "I'd like your opinion."

"Elves seldom concern themselves with the affairs of

humans," she said with a shrug. "The wise man looks inside himself for his answers. Do you have friends in Arasteen who would speak for you?"

"No," Verdon admitted. "I know no one there."

"This I know. It is true that by the custom of his people, those of Aktar's blood owe a debt to you. More than that I cannot say with certain knowledge." She turned away to watch the entrance to their shelter.

"You have an opinion?" Verdon asked.

"My people do not trust the rhanate. Still, he is no true friend of Lord Urbane. When you spoke of your worth, you meant knowledge."

"Yes."

"The sharing of bread, water, or wealth decreases the amount left to you, but not so the treasure of knowledge. The further it is spread, the greater is its power."

"Then you would suggest I go to the Black Citadel?"

"There are powerful mages in the court of the rhanate." She turned to look him in the eye. "You may even find a way to destroy the sentinel."

"Destroy . . . ?" Verdon choked over the word. "What sentinel?"

"The one that fills you with such horror."

Verdon felt as if he were choking. Unable to meet her steady gaze, he turned away. Out of the corner of his eye he saw the elf walking back toward the carts, leaving him alone with his thoughts. She had looked into his mind and read an intent he had not wanted to acknowledge.

Destroy Marchant Worsten? Kill the man who had taken him in, protected him when he was a child? But Marchant was already dead. His body was being used by those he hated, his spirit was trapped by necromancy in a foul non-life.

Yes, Verdon admitted; the elf had seen the desire he had not felt ready to face. To destroy the sentinel that was the undead Marchant would free his adopted father's spirit.

Aktar had said the rhanate would pay well for information on the Urbanan military and the thunder trains. Verdon would accept the nomad's offer, but the payment he asked would not be in gold.

He was halfway back to the sail carts, moving slowly in the growing darkness, when Iliki swooped out of the shadows.

"We won't have to worry about the Worms tomorrow," the little ferran said as he lit on the side of the cart.

Before Verdon could ask why, he heard screams in the distance. Aktar, who had stepped out of the shadows wearing an expectant expression as he approached Verdon, drew his sword. The dwarf stood, brushed the sand from her hands, and melded into the shadow of the largest cart. Clariel pulled the bow from her shoulders.

"The Worms ran into a group of nocturnals," Iliki explained with satisfaction. "They won't be chasing us anymore."

"Nocturnals," Clariel hissed, and spun around, trotting toward the entrance of the hidden gorge.

"Don't be a fool," Aktar called after her. "Leave it to the evils of Darkfall."

"Even the Worms are natural creatures," Verdon called back over his shoulder as he started after the elf. She was a shadow that was soon lost in the darkness, but he trotted down the long slope. Ahead he saw a flitting shadow that had to be Clariel.

He drew his pistol at the sudden movement just over his head, but he lowered the weapon when he saw Iliki's silhouette.

"How much farther?" the ex-guardsman asked, keeping his voice low.

"Not too far down the canyon," the ferran said. "Just beyond that next rock slide."

In the darkness the western side of the canyon was one long, featureless shadow, so Verdon trusted to the sharp-eyed owl-man to show him the way. The screams and shouts were louder; he could hear the clash of weapons and the deep, hair-raising howls of the nocturnals. As he followed Iliki, he saw a low ridge of rock silhouetted against a faint glow of a campfire.

He climbed the boulders to reach Clariel, who was fitting an arrow to her bow.

The small fire revealed six humans and two ferrans in a tight circle, holding off more than a dozen nocturnals. Ten dead night creatures and the partial remains of six of the outlaws were strewn around the campfire. Two of the still-living nocturnals vaguely resembled rotted human corpses, and one was falling as Verdon looked over the ridge of boulders. Several were only indistinct shapes, with arms that seemed to flow out of their bodies at will. One of Clariel's arrows left her bow and bit deep into the flesh of the nearest. The monster seemed undisturbed by the shot until the elf murmured a low chant and the arrow moved, tearing itself from the soft flesh. The long barbs that had been nearly invisible when she nocked the arrow to the bow expanded and tore a hole that both Verdon's hands could not span. Flesh, bone, and ichor spurted from the wound and the creature fell without a quiver.

The largest of the nocturnals was a cavern-mouthed worm with a dozen limbs, all ending in saber claws. It turned from the fight to suck up a porcine ferran. The dead bandit was gone in one gulp, his bulk stretching the worm as the creature swallowed. When the big nocturnal turned back to the fray and presented a vulnerable target, Verdon raised the first of his wheel lock pistols and fired. The ball hit the four-eyed nub of a head just behind the huge mouth. The worm fell, twitching in its death throes.

Four more nocturnals fell to the blades of the Worms, Clariel killed the second since Verdon had joined her, and he sent a bullet into the head of the second human corpse.

The remaining three creatures of the night backed away from the outlaws and approached the low ridge of rocks where Clariel and Verdon were hiding.

Verdon pulled his last loaded pistol and fired at the nearest, dropping it in the path of its companion. The second paused, as if trying to decide if it should eat the body in front of it or continue up the ridge for a better meal. Clariel put an arrow into it while it was making up its mind.

The eight remaining Worms left the fight to the elf and the human. The wind had died for the night, but the bandits shoved the vehicles out onto the slope of the canyon floor and rolled away into the darkness.

"They left you with the last one." Iliki, who perched on a boulder by Clariel, sounded disgusted.

"No matter, I have begun my count," Clariel said as she put an arrow between the bleary eyes of the last creature trying to climb the rocks.

Verdon had pulled his sword, but he sheathed it again.

"Your total?" he asked her.

"Nine," she said and trilled a low call. Verdon watched, his skin crawling as eight of the creatures twitched. Clariel's arrows jerked free of the bodies and came sailing back to her. She gathered them by the feathered ends of the shafts. When they climbed down the rocks she repeatedly thrust them into the sand until they were clean. The night was still as they walked back up the canyon to their own camp.

"Have you made a decision?" the elf asked.

"I'll go with Aktar to the Black Citadel," Verdon said. "And part of the price of my information will be a trade."

"You want knowledge in return," the elf said, and once again Verdon suffered the discomfort of exposure, as if his mind were naked and vulnerable to her elfin sight.

"Marchant Worsten was an honorable man," Verdon said, pushing away the uncomfortable feeling. "Unlike most commanders in Urbana, he never allowed his soldiers to loot the homes of the people they protected. They obeyed his restrictions because he

took care of them as well as the citizens. He hated
Lord Urbane and what he was doing to the country,
but as long as Marchant was allowed to protect the
people from the nocturnals, he stayed." Verdon kicked
a small rock out of his path. He had not spoken the
truth and felt the elf would know it.

"No, he stayed for another reason, he wanted to
help lead the people and give them heart when they
rose up against the Iron Tyrant. He loved Columbey,
and it broke his heart to see what Lord Urbane was
doing to the country. For his body and spirit to be
used by the mechamages—which he hated—must be a
living . . . an ongoing nightmare. If I can free him of
that shame, I must."

They walked on in silence until Iliki swooped down
and landed on Verdon's shoulder.

"The Worms are still fleeing down the canyon. If
they don't crash in the darkness, they'll be far away by
morning. There may be more nocturnals though."

"I hope you're careful when you spy on them,"
Verdon said. The courage of the little ferran worried
him. They needed Iliki's scouting abilities during the
day as well as his night sight, but apart from his value
to the troop, Verdon had developed a genuine regard
for the little character. "Can Milstithanog take a turn
on watch?"

"Uh-um—I don't thi-think so," Iliki said slowly.
"He's had to run all day to keep up. He's already
asleep."

10

The next morning Aktar led the procession of three carts down the length of the canyons. The breeze blew gently and Verdon enjoyed controlling the sail cart, but two hours after sunrise the wind picked up, roaring down the narrow passages as if enraged at being trapped. They spent the day whizzing by steep walls of colorful strata, traveling narrow passages at dizzying speeds. Late in the afternoon they came out on level ground again and Verdon felt the fatigue after the tension of the day.

They turned back to the broken country, a five-minute trip, to find a sheltered place for the night. The next morning they saw the carts of the outlaws who had survived the attack in the canyon. Before Aktar could order a change in course, the outlaws fled.

"So much for the cour-cour—bravery of the dreaded Worms," said Iliki, who had followed them far enough to make sure their escape had not been a ruse.

"They didn't have our advantage," Verdon said. "They knew we had only three carts, but the large one could carry twenty fighters."

"And they'd never thi—thin-suspect only two people

had attacked the nocturnals from behind the rocks in the canyon," Iliki replied. "They know you had half an army if you were willing to fight off nocturnals to get to them. No one would help them against the creatures of Darkfall." He cocked his head, birdlike, as he gazed at Verdon. "That would be ma-ma—insane."

"They could never understand the elf's need," Verdon said.

"Oh? And she was alo-alo—the only one there?" Iliki sighed, his feathered chest rising and falling as if he were resigning himself to the peculiarities of his friends.

Nothing else threatened them for the next four days, to the disgust of Clariel, who had not added a single nocturnal to her tally of nine. The wind held steady and strong, but they traveled at a less furious pace. On the flat plane of the desert, Verdon was able to relax and enjoy the ride.

On the afternoon of the fifth day Aktar brought the caravan to a halt just out of bowshot range of a small stone fortress. The defensive installation perched on the brink of a high cliff that formed the western barrier of the Great Drift. The travelers lowered the sails, and, with Aktar in the lead, they walked forward, moving slowly to show they meant no threat.

The soldiers of the fort, so often thwarted by the outlaw bands, saw their chance for revenge. They came boiling out of the fort, anxious to take the four prisoners. Twenty spearmen surrounded them. Their commanding officer, a small wiry man with a sharp face and a long scar across his forehead, ordered their arrest.

"We're not outlaws," Aktar said, relating the story they had all agreed upon. Since no one had ever escaped close contact with the infamous Worms, they decided the truth would never be accepted. They had agreed to say nocturnals had overrun their own caravan, and, while wandering in the desert, they found the three abandoned carts whose bandit owners had doubtless met the same fate as their own comrades.

"Aye, and tell another one." The captain of the guard

forced a loud laugh that echoed across the desert. His black eyes darted about, seeking hidden dangers.

"More like, they've got bold enough to spy out our defenses," suggested a large spearman standing beside his officer. His graying beard and the scars on his face and arms indicated he had been in the service of the rhanate for years.

"They'll be giving more information than they get," the captain said. "By nightfall we'll know the name of their leader."

"Would that I could tell you who leads the Worms," Aktar said with a smile. "You wouldn't need torture. I'd make you a gift of that foul name—"

"That you will," the captain interrupted him.

"But know if you lay a hand on me or my companions, you'll suffer for it." Aktar straightened and continued as if the captain had not interrupted. "My cousin, Akbaran Wiss, will take revenge for the spilled blood of his kindred."

"And Milstithanog won't care much for it either," Verdon said, hoping the name of the demon would cause the soldiers concern. He had never asked Iliki if the demon was a well-known creature.

Apparently it wasn't. His remark earned him a sharp blow from the butt of a spear that knocked him to the ground. He was uninjured, but he shook his head as if he was groggy. He spread both hands on the hard, sunbaked soil. With his head lowered, he mouthed a litany to gather world force and took a mental grip on the butt of the spear that still hovered over him.

As the weapon moved in the soldier's hand, the man shouted in alarm. With a strong mental jerk, Verdon pulled it from the spearman's grip and threw it out beyond the carts. The weapon spun in the air, tumbling end over end. The rest of the troop muttered and backed away.

"It wouldn't hurt *you* to do a trick like that," Verdon muttered under his breath, hoping Milstithanog heard him over the confusion. They could certainly use the invisible creature's help.

Aktar seemed to be the most surprised. "Then he really *does* exist," he said, staring wide-eyed at Iliki who hovered above them. "I didn't believe it."

"H-he doesn't like it if his frien-frien—companions hurt," said the little owl-man, whose voice held the hollow tone of awe. He looked around fearfully, as if even he had no idea where the next blow would come.

The captain of the guard glared at his troops.

"It was a trick," he scoffed at them. "Are you so stupid you're put off by elf magic?" He motioned a spearman forward. "Guard her. If she moves, opens her mouth, blinks an eye, or raises a finger—" The captain's order was lost in a gurgle. His eyes bulged and he dropped his sword. Both his hands went to his throat as he tried to pull something unseen away from his windpipe. He rose two feet above the ground; his legs kicked out desperately. Just as suddenly he fell, his knees buckled and he collapsed to sit gasping in the dust.

"It—it wasn't the elf," the soldier guarding Clariel told his captain as his companion helped their leader to his feet. Another picked up the dropped sword. "She didn't breathe."

"If it wasn't the elf, what was it?" The captain choked out the words. He could hardly speak, but he wasn't ready to give up control. Aktar repeated Iliki's description of Milstithanog, but the captain was still doubtful of an invisible creature. "Where is it?" he demanded. His sword was at Aktar's throat.

"He-he's th-there," Iliki pointed. "Bu-but you cannot har-har—injure him with your sword."

"We'll see," the captain growled, and ordered five spears cast in the general direction.

The spears flew, three continued on to strike the ground a full cast away. Two stopped in midair, paused and came sailing back, one striking the ground harmlessly in the center of the group. One grazed the captain's arm. Blood welled up and stained his clothing.

"Are you convinced?" Aktar demanded. "Perhaps now I can tell the truth that you would not have believed before. "We *took* these carts from the Worms with the help of Milstithanog, and because we did, we have information that the rhanate needs to hear."

The captain of the fort was convinced. His apologies and his efforts to make up for his doubt wore out his guests. They spent the night in the safety and dubious comfort of the outlying fortress. Iliki patrolled a spot within the walls. None of the rhanate's soldiers set foot within the area where the ferran said the invisible demon from the worlds beyond took his well-earned rest.

At dawn the three carts started their journey down the cliff face, on their way to the Black Citadel. A path, eight feet wide, had been cut in the cliff face. It zigzagged down the nearly perpendicular wall in four sections. At the top of each, a windlass, with stout ropes attached, lowered the carts. Verdon shuddered to think of the labor that went into cutting the trail down the cliff, but he was glad it was there. The alternative was to sail the carts thirty miles north or south and then make the return journey across the sands of the Drift.

He sat at the tiller with the sail lowered and steered his cart along the narrow path as the soldiers let out a long braking rope. Aktar had been lowered down the zigzagging path and was two levels below, traveling in the same direction as Verdon. Clariel's larger cart was between them, traveling in the opposite direction as she steered her way down the second level.

Aktar had reached the floor of the Great Drift when Iliki started down, riding on the back of the limping lightning lizard. Kree's weight could not be trusted to the windlass. Behind the lightning lizard the escorting soldiers were giving an empty area a wide berth.

On the sand of the drift, Verdon discovered the use of the wide, jointed rings that had been fastened to the sides of the carts. They fitted over the wheels, tripling their width, and kept them from sinking into the sand. The tiller was harder to handle, and the resistance of the sand reduced their speed, but they sailed along as smoothly as they had on the plain.

A junior officer from the fort traveled in the first cart with Aktar, so the dwarf rode with Verdon. He found the rolling dunes of the Drift fascinating when the sun was low in the morning, but with the loss of the shadows they soon lost their charm. Since the travel was easy, and he could afford to take his eyes off their course occasionally, he surveyed the silent dwarf.

"You can't speak?" he asked her, not really expecting an answer, but she nodded so hard her bright red curls bobbed. She waved her hands, as if casting a spell, and pointed to her mouth. She interrupted her hand talk to catch a comb the jerking of her head had dislodged. She readjusted it, pulling her hair back out of her face.

"Someone put a spell of silence on you?"

She replied with an energetic nod. Why a spell of silence, he wondered, since they usually wore off in time. If someone wanted to preserve a secret, cutting out the tongue, or cutting the throat was simpler and more permanent. Unless . . .

By careful questioning and her gestured answers he discovered the sturdy little woman was also a magician, and priests of the Eye had used a spell to limit her powers. By asking the obvious questions one citizen of Urbana would put to another, he learned she had been sought for questioning by the Eye, the dreaded investigative force of Lord Urbane. After every answer she pointedly looked around and raised a short stubby finger to her lips, signifying that she put her trust in him, but it was to go no further.

"You know I'm going to the Black Citadel to give information to the rhanate?"

She nodded, reluctantly, he thought.

"My information may be valuable. Shall I make it part of my price that the spell on you be removed?"

Her answer was to frown and prop her chin in the palm of her left hand. After a few minutes thought, she started counting on her fingers. After a few seconds of calculation she jerked upright, opened her mouth, and made a sound that was hardly more than a whoosh of air. She shook her head decisively, nearly dislodging another comb.

"It's wearing off?" Verdon asked, and received a confirming nod. He almost missed while trimming the sail.

"You don't want them to know anything about you?"

She shook her head as energetically as she had been nodding. Her blue eyes darkened and Verdon thought her sun and wind-chafed cheeks whitened a little as she considered. Perhaps the Black Citadel was not a safe place for wandering magicians. But how many places were, he wondered. With the coming of Darkfall, every ruler wanted every bit of magic power he could get. Some, like the Iron Tyrant of Urbana, wanted to secure and enhance their own positions; some just wanted to gather protection for themselves and their citizens. No matter the reason, they all wanted magicians and the dwarf would do well to keep her powers hidden if she wanted to remain free.

Their labored conversation over, the dwarf put a short stubby finger into the waistband of her skirt and pulled out a tiny object Verdon did not recognize. She laid it in her lap and waved her fingers over it. It slowly increased in size until a two-foot-long roll of parchment lay in her lap. When she unrolled it, he could see the fine lines of script and carefully drawn runes. Her red curls fell over her face as she bent her head to study her spells. The cart was just topping a tall dune. The others had already started their descent. Verdon raised his eyes from the dwarf to watch their path when he saw the cliffs ahead. He was looking at a mesa that rose out of the sand dunes of the Drift, and on the mesa a huge black tower rose above black walls.

In the bright sunlight and the sparkling sand, the Black Citadel rose like an evil presence that seemed unaffected by the bright sunlight.

And the dwarf wanted to keep her own secrets in that place. Perhaps she knew something he did not.

11

Aktar strode swiftly down the corridor, all semblance of humility absent from his stride. He approached two tall doors, ornately carved and trimmed in gold. The four guards who stood at rigid attention dropped their spears, barring his path. They had no intention of letting pass a ragged beggar, no matter how arrogant his attitude. In answer Aktar reached up slowly and pulled back the full hood of his robe, exposing his face. The nearest guard visibly paled.

"Ag-Aktar!" He bowed, not as low as he would to the rhanate, the ruler of the Black Citadel, but deeply enough to show respect to a member of the royal kindred.

The other guards bowed, raised their spears, and hastily stepped back, all but one, who hurried forward to open the door, his haste an apology for detaining a member of the royal kindred.

As the door closed behind him, Aktar strode across the richly decorated room. On a cushioned divan sat a man of average height and size, and from a distance a stranger would have thought him an old man whose last joys were his embroidered silk clothing and the wine he drank from a jewel-encrusted goblet. Closer inspection showed his face was leathery from the harsh desert, but the few lines on his face were battle scars. His glittering black eyes and sharp nose were reminiscent of a bird of prey and stood out in sharp contrast to his pale hair. The wide sleeve of his robe had fallen back and exposed a muscled right arm; on it two scars parted the dusting of dark, curling hair. He moved with the feline grace of a desert cat that had found a rich lair.

Though Ag-Aktar's hair was the traditional black of his people, they were alike enough in the face to be brothers. Their fathers had been twins.

The ruler of the Black Citadel rose as Aktar approached and waited while the arrival sketched a bow. Aktar's lack of humility would have earned any other a whipping for his insolence. The rhanate grasped the ragged, dusty man by the shoulders and shook him affectionately.

"Well met, distant cousin of Akbaran Wiss," the rhanate said with a mocking smile. He turned and poured wine from a slender ewer into a second goblet, a condescension that would have brought stares from the rest of his court.

"I spoke no more than the truth," Aktar said with a deprecating sweep of his hands. "You once said he held a claim of kinship on you, and that gives him a claim on me as well, does it not?"

"I suppose so, but what interests me is your decision to continue the masquerade." The rhanate picked up his goblet and sat back on the divan, motioning Aktar to do the same. "What is it about these travelers that holds your interest?"

"More instinct than knowledge," Aktar said as he made himself comfortable. "The human is a deserter from a thunder train. . . ."

"One of the Iron Guard? Do you think he knows enough to make torture worthwhile?" The rhanate's eyes narrowed as he considered the possibilities.

"He saved my life," Aktar cautioned, walking a narrow path between his own opinions and the power of his cousin. "That puts us both under the custom of obligation, but I suspect he's more valuable as an ally than as a practice subject for your irons." Aktar related Verdon's history and explained about the young man's adopted father. "He may have valuable information on the Shadow Army as well. Even the price he puts on his information might aid us."

"That is?"

"Some healing for a lightning lizard and dweomering of his own weapons. Also, he wants the magicians to tell him how to destroy a sentinel on the thunder train."

The rhanate had smiled at the simple requests, but he frowned at the last. "I don't want to disturb those trains—not now."

"Destroying one sentinel won't bring trade to a halt. If those mechamagical monsters can be overcome, the knowledge might benefit us in the future." Aktar had been giving the deserter's ideas careful thought.

"Can it be done?"

"Who knows, since to our knowledge, no one has succeeded. I suggested to Akbaran Wiss that he might tell the deserter he could do the job with a diamond cluster empowered by the mages of Aramyst."

"But the only ones we know of were on the Burning Coast—" the rhanate smiled as he realized the potential of a visit to the abandoned land.

Before the coming of Darkfall, the Burning Coast had been known as Aramyst. It had been a land of magicians, spotted with their towers. At the beginning of evil, rumor said the greatest destruction had taken place in Aramyst. Tales told of the destruction of most of the mage towers and of the earth itself catching fire.

His spies kept him informed on the activities of the Aramystans in Refuge, the last bastion of the once-proud nation, but no one ventured onto the coast.

"And we need to know what is happening in the land of the magicians." The ruler of the Black Citadel threw back his head and laughed. His white hair caught the light. "Aktar, I hope you remain loyal to your kindred. Your mind is too sharp for your loyalty to be doubted."

"But cousin, you know what wit I have is always at your service." The time had come for humility, a sop to keep the goodwill of his powerful relative.

"What about the elf and the dwarf that travel with the deserter?"

"The elf is no worry; a warrior consumed with guilt. Her mission in life is to destroy nocturnals until they destroy her. The dwarf is a mute, an Urbanan servant. Probably a runaway." He shrugged.

"And what about this creature, this demon from another world? Does it truly protect them?"

For the first time, Ag-Aktar's face lost its expression of confident hauteur. He shook his head in puzzlement, a slight frown creased his smooth forehead.

"I don't know what it is. I didn't believe it existed until I saw it in action. It does their bidding, I think." Aktar had worried about the power of Milstithanog, an unknown quantity.

"Just how powerful is it?"

Aktar spread his hands, signifying his ignorance. "Who can say when we don't know what it is? I'm not sure it's wise to enrage it by harming that group. I do know weapons won't harm it, not even spears dweomered by our best magicians, and Akbaran Wiss cannot even detect its presence."

The rhanate frowned. "Perhaps it's best we leave them unharmed. I don't want some demon from another plane running amok within the citadel. We'll see your deserter is paid all he asks for his information, and you can accompany him to the Burning Coast."

"My lord—" This was carrying loyalty too far. It would not serve Ag-Aktar to be away from the Black Citadel too long. The rhanate surrounded himself with ambitious companions who were not above creating doubts in the ruler's mind. Even a royal kinsman needed to be present to defend himself.

"I must send someone with them, someone I can

trust." The rhanate's words were clipped; the knowledgeable understood it was the firmness of decision. Ag-Aktar had lost the argument.

"If it is your will, my lord," he acquiesced, thinking he had been too smart for his own welfare.

12

Verdon forgot the two guards that escorted him through the narrow alley. The buildings of the citadel crowded close together, leaving narrow passages between. They radiated heat and most of the inhabitants took circuitous routes through the buildings. Verdon cared nothing for their secret ways; he was fascinated with his walk.

The black walls and pavement absorbed light as well as heat. Above his head he could see the azure sky but he walked in darkness. The ebony uniforms of the rhanate's personal guard blended with the walls. Their faces and hands stood out with an unworldly brightness in the black surroundings. His own clothing, a pale yellow tunic and green flowing pants covered by a pale gray robe, seemed to glow with their own light.

This was Verdon's first stroll through the Black Citadel. He had spent two grueling days answering the questions of the rhanate's generals. Kharhan Ostol, the oldest, and lowest in rank of the rhanate's commanders, kept insisting they torture Verdon to ensure he had told them everything he knew. Verdon had volunteered to undergo a truth spell if they doubted him. His added suggestion, that a spell might bring to mind details he had forgotten to mention and the generals had not thought to ask, convinced them to call in Akbaran Wiss, the rhanate's master magician. Even Kharhan Ostol had to be content when the mage judged Verdon's veracity to be complete.

Verdon was still absorbed by the anomaly of light and darkness when his escort led him through a guarded doorway. For the first two feet the walls radiated heat, but beyond them the stone, a porous dark gray, was so cool he shivered.

The guards led him through a maze of corridors, each wider and more ornate in its decoration. The last was wide as a hall. At intervals, low, ornately carved couches piled with silk cushions lined the walls. Low gilded tables separated the couches. Lit sconces glittered down on the eight well-dressed men who sat waiting. At the end of the hall they came to a black door trimmed lavishly in gold. Another pair of black-clad soldiers guarded the door, but they opened it as Verdon and his escort approached.

Verdon was surprised at the size of the rhanate's audience chamber. The marble floor, inlaid with obsidian, could not measure more than thirty feet in width or length. A huge chandelier of magic light sparkled above the center of the chamber fifteen feet above the floor. Above it distance and darkness hid the ceiling, but the height of the room made it the coolest Verdon had entered.

At the end of the room a dais rose six inches above the floor. A white-haired man clad in black with gold embroidery lounged on a pile of cushions, but as he rose, Verdon noted the pantherlike movement of suppressed strength. The man's nose, like the sharp black eyes that stared at him over an ornately curled beard, reminded Verdon of a hawk.

The ex-guardsman decided only a fool would underestimate the rhanate of the Black Citadel. Verdon's escort had given him instructions on the obeisance due the ruler of the Sundered Desert. He made his bow and waited. The rhanate nodded in recognition and signaled the guards to leave. With another sweep of his hand he motioned Verdon to take a seat on a couch near the center of the room. As Verdon turned to take his place he saw two other men in the chamber. Kalad Kamaad, the rhanate's ranking general, lounged on a divan to the left as if he were fully at home in the audience chamber. Akbaran Wiss sat on another seat against the right wall. Though the magician evidenced no fear, he was not nearly so comfortable with his surroundings as the general. The rhanate smiled at Verdon.

"Verdon Stramel, I give you a belated welcome to the Black Citadel. General Kamaad tells me the information you have brought us is indeed interesting. I would like to hear from your own lips why you chose to . . . leave the thunder train and Lord Urbane's service."

Verdon paused a moment before answering. He had answered that question so many times the words came out like a child's learned exercise. Still, it was the only answer he could truthfully give. Since Akbaran Wiss was an adept with truth spells, he dared nothing else. He was also considering the rhanate's use of the word, interesting. Verdon had closely watched the expressions of the rhanate's generals when they questioned him. Much of his information on the Shadow Army and the operation of the thunder trains was new to them.

"I was born a citizen of Columbey," Verdon said. "I see Lord Urbane as a usurper, Rhanate. Any information I can offer that will strengthen his enemies and weaken him is a blow for the freedom of my nation."

"But I am not an enemy of Lord Urbane," the rhanate said softly.

"Not at this time, and possibly never by your own choice, revered one," Verdon replied respectfully. "But the Iron Tyrant may not give you the freedom to choose. Forgive my speaking bluntly, but your magician can tell you I speak the truth as I see it. In his presence I would be foolish to lie."

The rhanate threw back his head and laughed. The movement exposed a scar on the side of his neck. Verdon suspected the man had won his position in battle.

"Very well, Verdon Stramel, we will value the information you have brought us, though we hope never to need it." The rhanate shifted on his divan. His smile disappeared. "We are in your debt, for your knowledge you bring us as well as the life of the kindred of Akbaran Wiss. You have asked only minor rewards, the healing of a lightning lizard, a sword to fit the hand of the ferran, the dweomering of your armor, and the knowledge of how to destroy a sentinel. The first three requests we can and will readily grant. The fourth is beyond even the power of Akbaran Wiss."

The rhanate turned his head, his eyes giving the magician permission to speak. Akbaran Wiss stood, his hands folded inside the full sleeves of his robes.

"When the sentinels first began traveling on the thunder trains, we sent a member of our order to Tee to investigate. Even through the walls of the train he felt the power protecting these mechamagical creatures. Only a magician of the ninth order or greater could destroy one if he were acting alone, and we have none that powerful."

"There has to be a way," Verdon insisted. Somehow he would free Marchant Worsten's spirit from that fell monster that imprisoned him.

"The magician did not say your situation was hopeless," the rhanate spoke up. "We've discussed it, and it might be possible . . . we think the destruction of a sentinel could be accomplished with a power cluster. Unfortunately the only ones we know of were left in Aramyst at the beginning of Darkfall."

Verdon listened without much hope. He had heard about the clusters of power, the misshapen diamonds that could act as repositories for stored magic. They were extremely rare, and all the known clusters were held by magicians of great power or were lost to the evil that had invaded the Known Lands. At the beginning of Darkfall, Aramyst had become a burning land. Ten years later the inferno still raged, according to the tales that had reached Urbana.

"The cluster held by the magicians in Theretorus might be accessible," Akbaran Wiss said softly. He spoke to the rhanate. "The tower of Theretorus, just inside the boundaries of Aramyst, is not all that far from the border of our own lands. If the Urbanan could get it, we could feed it the power he would need against the mechamonster."

The rhanate shook his head. "It would be a dangerous journey." He gazed at Verdon, as if weighing the odds of his success. "But if you choose to take the risk, Verdon Stramel, the magic of the Black Citadel is here waiting and will be at your disposal when you return."

For another thirty minutes the rhanate, General Kamaad, and Akbaran Wiss discussed the possibilities. When the audience was over, Verdon was convinced his only chance to destroy the sentinel depended upon retrieving the power cluster from Theretorus. Verdon considered the dangers, but they weighed lightly against what he saw as his duty to Marchant Worsten.

The rhanate promised to provision the journey. Since Verdon wanted to leave the following morning, he wasted no time in telling his companions of his decision.

"Rumor says there are hordes of nocturnals between here and the Burning Coast," Clariel said. "To vanquish one's foe, one must find them."

"You'll ne-ne—require a scout," Iliki said. "But I wo-won—refuse to fly over fire. Burned feathers won't hold me alo-up."

The dwarf pointed to herself and Verdon and made a gesture indicating they traveled the same path.

"And you'll need a guide through the desert," Aktar said. "Not that I'll be much help in putting out a fire."

"The journey will be miserable as well as dangerous. None of you owes me a debt," Verdon said, moved that the others were willing to go with him.

The dwarf tapped her chest and put her hands on her hips in an adamant gesture. He wondered how long it would be before she could speak, and if her attitude would be one of arms akimbo.

"You saved my life, so I owe you," Aktar said softly.

"I travel on the path of my enemies," Clariel said, looking out at the bright sunlight. To Verdon it sometimes seemed she was only half-alive in the full daylight. If he had not known about her grief and her mission, he might have wondered if she, too, were a nocturnal.

The stables of the Black Citadel were caves dug in the foot of the mesa. When the travelers arrived, they found the three carts loaded with supplies. Verdon's armor, originally black, was now the color of sand and barely gleamed in the torch light. When Aktar attempted to touch it with his sword, the protection the magician had put on it deflected the blade.

Kree, the lightning lizard, was walking around in a circle, his neck turned so he could look at his left hind foot. The magic of the wizard had regenerated his missing toe, though only the uninjured toe on that foot had a claw.

"Leave nature to replace the claws," Akbaran Wiss had said. "He won't be able to run as fast without them, but they'll grow back in a couple of months. Natural healing is always better than magic, and, in the meantime, he can travel without pain."

The cuts on the lightning lizard's body had disappeared under the magician's powers. Clariel smiled as she ran her hand over Kree's side where he had suffered a deep gash only a few days before.

Verdon laughed aloud when Iliki, given a true saber dweomered down to a six-inch length, flew around whacking at spiderwebs and attacking straws.

The rhanate's guards helped them pull the sail carts out onto the desert and raise the sails, and they discovered the rough fabric with the Worm emblem had been replaced. The new ones were trimmed with some runes for good luck and others to ward off misfortune. Verdon doubted the wishes expressed on the sails were the true reason for the replacements. The Worm sails might aid the desert fighters to set an ambush for the outlaws. Since the rhanate's forces had been more help to Verdon than the Worms, he wished success to the citizens of the citadel.

Aktar led the way and Clariel still sailed the largest cart, though Kree raced beside it, occasionally circling it in his healthy exuberance. Verdon brought up the rear again and the dwarf rode with him.

They had traveled steadily for an hour when the dwarf crept back to sit not far from Verdon.

"At last I can say it. Thank you for freeing me from the Worms," she said, straining to speak loud enough for him to hear, as if the volume of her voice had not returned. She told him her name was Rala. "And thank you for not revealing me to the rhanate."

"Were you in danger there?" Verdon asked.

"I don't know. It's rumored that a magician lured to the Black Citadel never gets away." She shrugged. "We live by rumor today, not by truth, but there's no truth in that place."

"They were good to us. They helped in every way they could," Verdon retorted. In his opinion the dwarf was carrying distrust too far. Her eyes snapped with scorn.

"To use a platitude that could come from the elf, 'A person who travels with a fool is a fool as well.' I never thought I would say that about myself."

"Explain that remark," Verdon demanded. He decided he liked the dwarf better when she was mute. "They did what they could to help us."

"Did they?" She gazed up at him. "Does it help for them to send you to face the dangers of the Burning Coast after a power cluster you could not possibly use?"

"Of course I'll be able to use it," Verdon snapped. "They wouldn't send me after it if I couldn't."

"Suppose I give you a spell," the dwarf said, sitting back and folding her arms as if she hugged a secret. "Suppose I could give you one that would destroy the sentinel. Would you use it?"

"In a minute if it were possible," Verdon answered. "But no essencer, not even one with my limited knowledge, can use a magician's spell. . . ." He stared at the dwarf's twinkling eyes and pursed lips. He nearly overturned the sail cart on the side of a dune while his attention was on her. Neither of them spoke until he had brought the vehicle back on a safe course.

"You're saying even if I found a magician's cluster and brought it back, it would be useless to me because of my training as an essencer."

"It's a magician's tool."

"And I can't use a magician's tool. I'll never be able to destroy the sentinel," Verdon said slowly. "What's the point in continuing?"

"You have every reason to continue down the Drift," Rala said. "They did tell you the truth when they said a power cluster would allow you to absorb and release enough magic to destroy the sentinels."

"But you just said—"

"I said you couldn't use a magician's tool," she finished his thought for him. "When you learned your first essencing spells, you set your course in your use of magic, one that cannot be changed. When you opened yourself to the acceptance of world power you destroyed your inborn ability to use rote magic. You can't change it now."

"Then what good would it do for me to have any power cluster?"

Her full lips thinned and a dimple appeared in her left cheek as her face tightened. Her eyes sparked.

"I had not thought you stupid! If you found your own cluster, it would be an essencer's tool, not a magician's," she snapped. "It would be just as powerful, but only subject to world magic. Power clusters are like people, their course is set when they accept their first magic."

"But how would I find it? They're not just strewn about on the ground or everyone would have one."

"If there is one to be had, I know where to look. If one is available, you will have it before the return of this thunder train." She tilted her head to the side, as if trying to make up her mind about him. "I offer no guarantees, just a possibility, and the price could be high. Just remember, for all his sweet words, the rhanate offers you nothing and you could pay with your life to bring back a cluster useless to your purpose."

Verdon's hands moved automatically, steering around a sand dune while he thought about her offer. She was right, he could not use a magician's tool. He should have realized it before.

Verdon's suspicions flared. He had overlooked the obvious flaw in the magician's advice because he had been unused to thinking in terms of world essence or any other magic. Akbaran Wiss should have known; he probably did. The ex-guardsman's rage welled up when he realized the rhanate and his magician had attempted to use his need to fulfill their own desires. Verdon decided he had been duped for the last time.

"I must know more," he said. "I've been manipulated since I left the thunder train. If I'm to make a decision, it must be based on knowledge, not upon faith in people who want to use me."

The dwarf frowned, bringing out the dimple again. He had decided it was sign of irritation.

"You chose a poor time to come to your senses."

Verdon could not repress his grin at her backhanded compliment. Thinking back, he wondered why he had been so trusting.

"I should have known the rhanate's benevolence had to have a purpose. He has a country to defend. If I were in his position, I'd probably use anyone and anything that came to hand. The protection of his people has to be his main purpose."

Rala nodded. "Successful rulers must, particularly

since the beginning of Darkfall. I don't fault him, I just warn you he is using you too."

"And If I go your way, you wouldn't attempt to use me?"

"Of course I will. If I help you to find a cluster, I'll have a claim on its use." She nodded emphatically. "The difference is, you and I are after the same thing, the downfall of the Iron Tyrant and any of his minions we can reach."

"You still haven't told me where this cluster is to come from."

"To do that would be to tell you a secret held by dwarfs for untold years. In three days we should turn from this southerly course and travel west. We will be on the way to intercept the thunder train and try our luck on its return trip from Yzeem." She shrugged. "Between us and the path of the train will be Skar. There are dwarf caverns in Skar, and if a power cluster is to be had, it will be in one of those deep caverns."

"That's all you'll tell me?" Verdon disliked knowing so little, but the set of Rala's mouth warned him he would learn no more. He considered his options: if he could not use a magician's power cluster, did he have any? If he could manage the power to destroy the sentinel that imprisoned Marchant Worsten's spirit, the only way he could be sure of finding the sentinel again was on the train's return trip.

Fear had convinced many nations that Lord Urbane had thousands of the monsters, but they were wrong. From the whispered rumors within Urbana he suspected the mechamages had made thousands of sentinels, at least hundreds, but nearly all of them had been failed attempts, and the useless creatures had been destroyed, their armor and body parts melted down and recast. Fewer than fifty operative sentinels existed, and the ten that traveled on the *Dominant*, guarding that mysterious and evil cargo, would be reassigned when the train reached Mekanus again. If the mechamagical monster that imprisoned Marchant

Worsten's body and spirit was transferred to other duties, Verdon might not find him again for years—or maybe never.

He dared not lose this one chance.

Could he trust the dwarf mage? Rala was dressed in the clothing of an Urbanan kitchen servant. In front of Aktar and at the Black Citadel she evidenced all the humility of a well-trained slave. When she was alone with Verdon, the guise fell away and she showed the self-confidence of a power user.

"I have three days to make my decision," Verdon said. "I'll think it over." He expected an objection, but the dwarf smiled complacently and readjusted the combs in her hair. Then she looked out over the landscape, leaving him to his own thoughts. High in the sky, a desert hawk drifted in a circle before flying off down their back trail. Verdon's mind seemed to drift in circles too.

13

"**Y**ou want to what?" Aktar stared at Verdon as if the warrior had lost his mind.

"I want to attack the *Dominant* on its return trip," Verdon explained. "If I go to the Burning Coast, the train will return to Urbana before I get back. Once it reaches Mekanus, it could be rerouted to travel to the High Steppes or into Arasteen. I might never catch up with it, never find Marchant."

"But you need a power cluster to destroy the sentinels," Aktar reminded him.

"If I don't have one, I'll do without," Verdon replied. "I won't lose that train." He turned away from the desert trader to find his cloak. He pulled it from the pack that lay beside him. The gesture served two purposes; he stopped the conversation and the objections. He covered himself to block the cool desert air.

The party had camped for the night in the last of the sand dunes that made up the Great Drift. In a valley between the dunes, Clariel had ordered Kree to dig a deep hole. At the bottom their small fire burned merrily, offering warmth and emotional comfort. The light was obscured from any distance by the sides of the hole.

Across the fire pit from Verdon, Clariel's eyes

gleamed in the dim light. A slight twinkle told him she glanced from him to Aktar and back.

"Have you any objection to changing course?" Verdon asked her.

"Nocturnals follow all paths," she said. Her tone spoke her indifference. The gleam of her eyes suggested interest. Little by little she was putting her grief aside, stripping it off, layer by layer. She sat with her arms clasped around her knees, as if physically holding herself together. Her feet in their close-fitting elfin boots seemed small and slender beneath the flare of her hem-bound trousers.

Rala rose and picked up the thin wooden dishes she had used for their evening meal. She moved a few feet from the fire and sat in the shadows, cleaning her bowl and cup with sand. Her attention to homely chores had become the lifeline of sanity on their journey through the angry desert.

Clariel had withdrawn into the meditation necessary to elf magic, so Verdon took her bowl and cup to clean with his own. Aktar followed with a sigh. The desert trader showed his resentment at every chore, but he no longer expected the dwarf to serve him.

In front of Aktar, she was as quiet as ever. Verdon also wondered about the trader, who had given up his occupation to travel with them. As the ex-guardsman wrapped himself in his cloak and lay down on the soft sand, he warned himself about being so suspicious of his friends. Rala had suggested the rhanate would use Verdon or anyone he could in his effort to protect his land. Any responsible ruler would do the same.

Aktar had wanted to help his rhanate receive the information Verdon could give him, but that did not make the desert trader an evil man, just a patriot. Verdon decided he fought too many shadows. He should conserve his strength for his real enemies, but as he drifted off to sleep, some distant part of his mind insisted he should not be too trusting.

■   ■   ■

The owl-boy Iliki perched on the crooked branch that his father had buried in the ground in front of the leaf-covered lean-to. He watched, giggling, as his owl-human mother flew around his elf-lizard father. Beneath her wings, her tiny arms waved in the air as she tried to reach around her larger mate. She was trying to grab a sack of solan roots he had dug while out hunting. They ignored the two fat pheasants lying on the stump. The ritual game was for her to try for the sack. They played it nearly every day, but the family never tired of the simple joke.

While Iliki watched his parents, Vorky, his father's trained hunting cat, nudged the little ferran, nearly pushing him from his perch.

"Sto-sto—quit that!" complained the little owl-boy. He moved further up the branch, but the cat nudged him again. The little owl-man nearly fell. He caught his balance and turned to glare at the cat.

The happy bubble of the family game burst, a dream lost to reality as he awoke to night on the desert. He struggled to keep his balance on the side of a sail cart and blinked his eyes at the darkness. Kree, the lightning lizard, had been nudging him. As Iliki glared at the lizard, Kree gave a low, rumbling whine; he was hungry.

"The magician h-healed you, you can hunt for yourself," Iliki grumbled. In answer he received another nudge from the lizard.

"You're sp-spoiled," the ferran grumbled. "You just like having someone hun-hun—find food for you." The lightning lizard hissed softly as if he understood and agreed.

Iliki stretched and spread his wings. He looked around the camp. Rala the dwarf, Verdon and Clariel were rolled in their blankets. Aktar, alert and on guard, sat in the shadows of a dune. Iliki drifted on a slight breeze to hang in the air in front of the desert trader. He explained the lightning lizard's restlessness.

"You should help him," Aktar agreed. "The sooner he eats, the sooner he'll be back to help if we're bothered by nocturnals."

Iliki reluctantly launched himself into the night.

They were near the edge of the Drift. Not many creatures traveled the dunes, but on firmer ground, small flocks of flightless murdos used their long, sharp beaks to extract liquid from the waterthorn's soft flesh.

After half an hour of flight he found a flock sleeping in a protected gorge and led Kree to the spot. He waited while the lizard killed three birds, two to eat and one to bring back to the camp. Iliki perched on the third carcass.

"No, th-this one is for us," Iliki admonished the lizard when it complained. "We have to eat, too."

The lizard hissed his objections, but the ferran ignored him. Clariel had taught the lizard to hunt and retrieve food. It would follow orders. Kree's objections came from his hunger, which would be sated with two of the large birds.

An hour later Kree trotted back to the camp with the third bird held carefully in his mouth. Iliki, flying overhead, thought he saw movement in the shadows by a dune. A hawk rose and flew off into the night. Strange, the ferran thought. Desert hawks were diurnal hunters.

He had nearly reached the camp when he saw Aktar. The desert trader was walking between the dunes, approaching the camp from the north. He was not far from where Iliki had seen the hawk. Why had the trader been so far from camp? To relieve himself? He was carrying modesty too far.

When Iliki arrived at the camp, Verdon, Clariel, and Rala were still sleeping. Iliki directed Kree to put the murdo in the largest cart. He perched on the side and closed his eyes. As he drifted off to sleep he forgot about Aktar's leaving his post.

When they left the dunes, Verdon led the way. With Rala's direction he sailed the cart southwest. Aktar brought up the rear. Clariel's cart carried most of their supplies, and if both the other rigs were damaged, the largest one could carry all of them and enough supplies to get them to their destination.

When they left the sand of the Drift behind, they removed the wide wheel rims and refastened them to the sides of the carts. The smaller, permanent rims made steering easier. The wind blew steadily from the east. For ten days they had been traveling across a plain of hardpan, occasionally dipping into valleys to search for springs and fresh water. Verdon's muscles ached from his constant grip on the sheet and the tiller, and he was bored.

On his trips aboard the thunder train, he had enjoyed his daylight duty. Knowing there was sufficient food and water, he was able to enjoy the view of an angry land, tortured to insanity. After staring at it so long, even the madness seemed to take on uniformity.

A well-beaten road ran from the Drift to Skar, but Rala had insisted they avoid it. Nocturnals watched the roads, and their mission was too important to risk. Clariel's disgust had kept her silent for three days but they stayed fifty miles south of the road. After ten days with nothing to do but steer a straight course, Verdon was ready to agree with the elf. Fighting was preferable to fatal boredom.

"What do you know about Skar?" he asked Rala. "How can anyone live in that hole in the ground?"

"How can anyone live on a ball, but that's what the world of Aden is," the dwarf retorted. "Skar isn't a fire pit dug by a lightning lizard."

"That doesn't mean much to someone who has never seen it," Verdon objected. "You're telling me it's large, which I knew. I've heard it's more than a hundred miles long." He had never believed the tale.

"Closer to twice that length and around forty miles across at its widest point," Rala added. "You don't think it strange that people should live on a mountain. Think of a mountain turned upside down, but Skar is deeper than the highest peak in the Wall."

"I didn't know it was that large," Verdon said. The Wall, the range of mountains that divided the continent they called the Known Lands, had peaks that disappeared into the clouds. "It's the home of dwarfs?"

"The slopes and caverns of Skar are probably home to a larger variety of races than any other area in the Known Lands," Rala replied. "It was originally settled by outcasts of different races, just a few of each. They were outlaws, thieves, political rebels. Through the centuries they multiplied and developed their own societies. It's a small world within a world. A few races trade with the desert nomads, but they do most of their trading among themselves."

"The dwarfs there, are they . . ." Verdon had been trimming the sail as he spoke. When he looked up Rala had turned away. She had raised one hand to shade her eyes as she looked southwest.

Verdon saw Iliki approaching. The ferran usually floated lazily on the breeze. This time he flashed toward them as if he were being chased.

"Trouble?" Verdon asked as the little owl-man landed on the side of the cart. He shifted his position, ready to turn the sailing of the vehicle over to Rala while he put on his armor.

"Where is Kree?" the dwarf demanded of the ferran.

"Not trouble," Iliki gasped, breathless from his flight. "We found a rapacian on the desert, wounded and nearly dead of thirst."

Rala stood and looked out over the desert, her face contorted with concern. "Where there's one there might be others," she said quietly.

Verdon considered the news. Obviously Rala shared his distrust of the reptilian races.

"A rapacian is still a natural," Verdon said after a moment of consideration, separating the people of the Known Lands from the nocturnals, the corrupted, and the creatures of the dark magic created by the Iron Tyrant of Urbana. "We can't leave a natural to be destroyed by the nocturnals. I wouldn't wish that on a Worm." He turned the cart, angling off on Iliki's back trail. Ten minutes later he saw Kree in the distance. Verdon slowed the cart and brought it to a halt by the lightning lizard. It crouched on the ground just out of range of the rapacian's long, wicked spearpoint.

Clariel's cart stopped just behind Verdon's. She jumped out, bringing a second waterskin, but she wasn't as friendly as the human.

"Harm my friend Kree and I'll finish what someone else started," she warned the rapacian.

"Kill him and be done with it," Aktar snapped. "You can't trust that reptile." His slur on the general species did more to slow the elf than to encourage Verdon. She threw the desert man a sharp glance and ordered Kree to back away from the wounded rapacian. The ex-guardsman bit his lips to hide his grin when he saw Aktar's mouth twist in chagrin.

The rapacian's eyes had flickered at the elf's threat. He understood the common patois that linked Aden's people. Verdon considered him. Standing, the creature would have been about his height. He understood why, wounded and alone, it had survived. The reptile was one of a desert variety and had adapted in color to its surroundings. Its earth brown scales were patterned with irregular black stripes. Lying flat, it could have been a part of the cracked hardpan of the desert. The scales were marred by a slash above the right shoulder and its thick right leg bent awkwardly at the knee, as if broken.

By their appearance, rapacians could have been close kindred to the lightning lizards, and were nearly as fast on flat ground. They were smaller, with shorter backs, but the shape of their heads was similar, though the smaller jaws of the rapacian were more angular. Above its eye ridges, pinions connected a four-inch ridge of pale skin that rose when the rapacian felt endangered. But despite the scales and the reptilian appearance, rapacians were humanoid, capable of great intelligence. They were limited in technology because of the physical clumsiness of their stubby, clawed front feet. For years they were considered ferrans, but in fact they were a closer kindred to Verdon than to Iliki or Kree.

The rapacian seemed to think its fate was Verdon's decision. It stared at him with orange, slitted eyes.

Verdon had brought a waterskin from the cart. He

kept his eyes on the humanoid as he slowly pulled the plug and let a few drops fall on the ground, showing the humanoid that the bag held water. Then he raised the skin to his mouth and drank, proving it was pure. Lastly, he reached out toward the point of the spear and hooked the thong over the shaft just below the point—a manite point, he noted.

"You've been fighting nocturnals," he said, knowing he could be wrong, but the assumption served his purpose. "If you fight the creatures of the Darkfall, we're allies." The rapacian ignored his overture.

"We're wasting time on that reptile," Aktar said, too disgusted for his usual diplomacy.

"Yes, we are," Rala agreed. She raised her hands and muttered an incantation. The rapacian raised his hands, trying to weave a warding spell against hers, but he was too late. The light in his eyes died to an entranced state and he relaxed in his half-crouching position.

"You will trust these people; they mean you no harm," she said softly. "You will trust. Speak your name and show your trust."

The reptilian humanoid struggled against her commands until she repeated them. She wove another spell, and he stretched out on the ground.

"Siskiel," he muttered, his word hardly more than a sigh.

"If he has friends nearby, we should leave," the dwarf said, and turned an accusing glare on Verdon. "If you want to save his life, use your healing powers on him."

Verdon knelt, putting his hands on the ground. With an incantation he called up the healing power. Before he was finished Clariel had joined him. While they prepared their healing spells, Rala ordered Siskiel to drink and then stretch out on the ground. Verdon pulled the scaly leg straight and used his spell on it while Clariel closed the wound on his shoulder.

"Help me get him in my cart," Verdon told Aktar when they had done all they could. The desert man hesitated and Verdon lost his temper. "Don't be a fool, he could be invaluable. He's another fighter if we run into the nocturnals. If we meet his people, we've saved and healed him. I've heard rapacians have a code of honor of sorts." Verdon understood the desert man's hesitation. The rapacian race was one of the most feared on Aden. They were a breed of nature's perfect killing machines; size for size, mechamagicians had never built anything to compare.

Rala kept the rapacian under her spell, ordering him to use his left leg to help in the progress to the cart. Neither Verdon nor Clariel could cast healing spells strong enough to totally mend his injuries. He would need a full day's rest before he could walk on his right leg. His right shoulder would gain its full strength in a few hours.

They continued their journey. Siskiel lay on the floor of the cart, aware, but still under Rala's spell. Verdon carefully explained the reason as Rala unwrapped a haunch of raw meat, a leg from a desert antelope Kree had killed that morning.

"We're heading for Skar," Verdon told the scaled humanoid. "Rala"—he gestured at the dwarf—"Rala says there are rapacians living there. You'll be safe with them until you have your strength back and can return to your people. The dwarf is keeping you under a weakening spell until you trust us." He didn't get a flicker of an eye for an answer.

Rala offered the reptile the haunch of antelope and at first he refused it. Verdon had heard of the rapacian way of eating their prey alive. Then the creature seemed to think better of his attitude and took the food.

While he was eating, Rala returned to the stern and sat by Verdon.

"You don't have any healing spells?" he asked.

"My healing skills are excellent," she said. "But why should I wear myself out when you and the elf can manage? I might be needed later on if we run into trouble."

Verdon knew she was right.

14

The rapacian slept in the bottom of the cart for the rest of the day and when they stopped for the night, Verdon and Aktar helped him to the ground. Iliki had found another flock of murdos and Kree had brought two back to the camp. While Clariel and Verdon roasted one in a fire pit, Siskiel ate the second with more relish for the fresh-killed meat.

By the next morning he could walk without assistance and Verdon had changed his mind about taking the rapacian with them against his will. He gave the reptile back his spear and explained he was free to go. The rapacian gave no hint he understood. He climbed into Verdon's cart when they broke camp.

"I guess he's decided we're not ene-enem—too bad after all," Iliki said, eyeing Siskiel with a proprietary air.

"He could be a member of the tribe of rapacians living in Skar," Rala said. "If he is, we're going his way." She had been standing by Clariel, handing her the cooking spit and their single pot to be stored in the large cart.

"Home is the desired place for those with free hearts," the elf said with a touch of wistfulness.

"As soon as I take care of my business we'll start to work on your tally," Verdon told the elf, but she shook her head, refusing his offer.

"None can free another's spirit of its debts." She climbed into the cart and called to Kree. He had over-taxed his newly healed foot the day before. His early morning hunt had left him limping.

As usual the breeze strengthened slowly, but less than an hour after dawn the sporadic gusts grew into a steady wind. Iliki flew scouting forays to search for a smooth path and keep watch for hidden dangers that might appear out of the valleys and gorges.

The sun hung halfway down the western sky when the little ferran drifted lazily on the wind currents as he returned from his fifth scouting flight. Verdon absently watched him as Iliki hovered for a moment. Then the little owl-man whipped up his speed, his wings a blur as he streaked for the caravan.

"Worm carts," he gasped as he landed on the side of the cart. He pointed east. "Six, and they're just ov-hidden by the rise. They're com—approaching fast."

Verdon gritted his teeth in frustration. He was less worried than frustrated. Sometimes it seemed the entire Sundered Desert conspired to keep him from his goal. He considered turning northwest, hoping to find some shelter where they might escape notice. Hiding might seem weak-spirited, but it might save time. As he turned his head, looking in the direction he wanted to go, Iliki shifted on his perch in agitation.

"No, there's a cli-clif—a drop off into a canyon. You can't take the car-carts down it."

"Our only choice is straight ahead?" Rala asked the ferran, who nodded, still too winded to talk more than necessary. He flew back and landed on the larger cart to give Clariel his news.

Verdon close-hauled the sail. He increased his speed until the force of the wind tilted the cart and brought its left wheel up off the ground. He spilled enough wind for stability and glanced behind him. Clariel had let out her sail and Kree crept to the left side of the cart, where his weight would give the larger vehicle more stability at higher speeds.

And they would need speed to outrun the Worms, Verdon decided. The tops of the outlaws' sails rose over the rise in the desert floor. In a few seconds he could see the carts themselves. The Worms smoothly changed course, putting themselves on a tack to intercept the companions.

"Move to the left," Verdon called to the rapacian, hoping the creature would understand the need. He was surprised and angry when the humanoid dived under the boom, continued across the narrow deck and over the side of the cart. Siskiel hit the ground in a run, limping on his weak leg, but he kept his feet. "He's a Worm!" Rala announced, full of outrage. Like Verdon she expected him to sprint for the approaching bandits, but he ran along their own track. He fell behind, allowed Clariel's cart to catch up with him and grabbed the side, heaving himself aboard.

"What's he doing?" Verdon asked, unable to turn and watch. He needed to keep a close eye on their trail. The cracks in the hardpan of the desert floor could be treacherous. Allowing the wheels to slide into the breaks parallel to their course could overturn a cart. The danger increased with their speed.

"He's just sitting in front of the mast, catching his breath," Rala answered. She had shifted and stood on her knees watching Siskiel. "Now he's moving back— he's picked up Clariel's bow and quiver—he's putting them down within her reach. I guess I was wrong."

Verdon watched the approach of the outlaws. They had spotted the travelers while they were slightly east of Verdon's group. Verdon reconsidered his options. To turn north would avail them nothing, turning east would only bring them closer to the Worms, and west was out of the question. Iliki had said the sides of the gorge were steep. Sailing out over a cliff was a surer death than fighting.

"I told you I shouldn't waste my strength on healing spells," Rala announced. She tugged a bundle of blankets closer to the left side of the cart, knelt on it, facing south. She began folding back the long sleeves of her tunic as if she were preparing to wash clothes or work the dough for bread. As Verdon watched her he could not prevent a grin at her mundane preparations.

In less than a minute he lost his desire to smile. The Worm carts were still too far away for him to consider using his pistols, even if he had a hand free, but the Worms had a longer range with their bows. A shower of arrows arced toward them. Two struck in the wood, four clanked against the curved metal wheel rims attached to the outside. Verdon glared at their pursuers, checked the ground in front of the cart to be sure he stayed on a safe course. The need to sit passively and steer the vehicle frustrated him, but he knew the dwarf's magic would be a better defense until the Worms were closer.

Another volley of arrows flew from the first Worm cart and he ducked, barely escaping a feathered shaft that arced over his seat. As he straightened, a bolt of fire struck the ground just behind him. He felt the heat, but passed it by.

Rala sent a fireball that burst against the right wheel of the leading Worm vehicle. The wood splintered as if the wheel had exploded. The cart tipped onto the burning shards, throwing five archers out onto the hardpan of the desert floor. One of the riders, a ferran with a boar's head, fell on a flaming splinter.

The second pursuer careened around the first and nearly capsized as it rolled over the fallen mast. The two front wheels crossed the heavy timbers, severely jolting the riders. The smaller wheel at the rear caught for a moment and spun the vehicle in a circle.

The other four Worm carts avoided the crash. A human from the lead vehicle stood and threw another fireball in Verdon's direction. He jerked at the tiller and tilted the cart until the left wheel rose off the ground, but the fireball sailed directly for him. Rala sent a missile to meet it and the two destructive forces met in midair.

Sparks flew in every direction. They barely missed Clariel's sail. Aktar, following, was not so fortunate. The tall canvas burst into flame.

"Milstithanog!" The desert trader's voice rang out, shrill with panic.

Suddenly Aktar's vehicle shot forward, as if it had taken on a life of its own, and drew abreast of Clariel. Aktar took advantage of the closeness and leapt across the narrow space, clutching the side. His cart spun away as the rapacian reached over the side and hauled the human aboard.

Verdon had been watching Aktar's progress in rapid glances as he shifted his attention between his path, the outlaws, and the desert man's plight, but the dwarf came back to relieve him.

"I'm out of missile spells," she said. "I'll take the tiller. You make loud noises with those abominations of yours." She pointed at the wheel lock pistols tucked in his belt.

Verdon crouched on the side of the cart. At every stop he had checked his gunnes to be sure the rough ride had not dislodged the priming, but he gave them another quick scrutiny. When he knew they were ready to fire he picked up his bow. Their attackers were not yet in pistol range. Wasting his limited supply of shot and powder would be foolish.

His first arrow cut through the neck of a Worm who had stood to take careful aim. Blood spurted from the human's throat and he tumbled over the side of the cart, clutching his wound.

Verdon's second arrow whizzed by the head of an antlered ferran. From Clariel's cart Kree gave a roar, recognizing the type of creature that had wounded him in the fight that had freed the prisoners.

With Rala sailing the cart, Verdon had time to see the activity aboard their larger vehicle. Aktar had taken the tiller. One of Clariel's shining arrows streaked toward the second Worm vehicle, which attempted to intercept her. By the flight of her arrow, she had been aiming for the human at the tiller, but he jerked back just in time to save himself. Her shaft neatly cut the sheet. The slender guide rope parted and the helmsman jumped forward, grabbing for the severed end as the sail whipped off to the left, well out of reach. The force of the wind whipped the boom around, knocking two of the passengers overboard. The crack of the splintering mast echoed across the desert as loud as a pistol shot.

The cart in the lead rapidly closed the distance. Verdon loosed four more arrows, but his targets were close enough to see his movements and ducked out of sight. Then the cart came close enough for him to use his gunnes. He crouched low, sighting down the barrel of the first pistol, keeping it less than an inch above the side of the cart. Obviously the ferran who rose to aim his bow was unaware their prey could be armed with gunnes.

As the echoes of the shot cracked over the desert, the left side of the ferran's head disappeared in a shower of blood, flesh, and bone. The second worm that rose to look over the side of the Worm cart and quickly disappear again was covered with his companion's gore.

Shouts, curses, and a shower of arrows from the third Worm cart caught Verdon's attention. The sail fell. Iliki streaked away from the top of the mast as a volley of arrows followed him. The sunlight reflected off his tiny sword.

The falling sail had also diverted the attention of the Worms on the last two carts. Verdon aimed his second pistol and caught an unwary human in the shoulder. On the second vehicle, a huge ferran fell over the side. Two of Clariel's magic arrows were flying back toward her. She lowered her bow to catch them in midair.

Suddenly the rapacian stood up and drew back his arm, ready to cast his spear. An arrow from the second

cart grazed his shoulder just before he let the weapon
fly. Verdon grimaced at the spoiled aim until he realized the reptilian had not chosen an individual as his
target. The thick, tough wooden shaft passed between
the spokes of the right wheel. Wood splintered, the
shaft broke, but not before it had brought the wheel to
an abrupt halt. The cart spun, tilted, and turned over
with a crash. Aktar neatly avoided the long mast.

Verdon attempted to aim his third pistol, but the
last Worm cart abruptly veered away, pulling out of
the fight.

The outlaws had given up the chase, but Rala and
Aktar kept the companions at their maximum speed.
Only two Worm vehicles had been destroyed. One had
suffered damage, but could be repaired. It would not
take long for the raiders to regroup and come after
them again.

At a shout from their second vehicle, Rala slowed
her speed until Aktar could bring the larger cart up to
flank her. Both knew enough not to allow the wind
spilled from one sail to block the other.

"Anyone hurt?" Aktar called out. Verdon concentrated on reloading his wheel locks and left it to Rala
to answer in the negative.

"Clariel says she can close the rapacian's wound
without help," Aktar said. "He's our only injury."

Iliki swooped down to land on the side of Verdon's
cart, his feathers fluffed out with pride and indignation.

"No one as-ask—inquired about me," he huffed.
"And I halted one cart all alone. I didn't nee-require
some great spear or a magic spell. I did it all by
myself."

"If you're not injured, stop complaining," Rala snorted.

"I did it, I cut the . . ." He turned to Verdon for
help.

"Halyard," the guardsman replied, grinning at the
boasting ferran. The little owl-man could seldom help
in a fight, and Verdon was glad to give him his due.
"And you did cut it," he said.

"And that ma-ma—caused the sail to fall," he said, sidling down the side of the cart until he came face-to-face with the dwarf.

Rala nearly lost control of the cart as she sneezed.

"That's it, you get away from me," she demanded. "I'm allergic to feathers! You stay away from me or I'll turn you into a sand fish!"

"Were you injured?" Verdon asked the little ferran, who backed away from the angry dwarf. He wanted to change the subject before the animosity between the dwarf and the animan drove Rala to carry out her threat.

"An arrow clipped the tip off one of my breast feathers," Iliki said, holding up the severed portion. It could have just as easily have be-be—I could have been hit in the head."

"Life might be simpler," the dwarf said as she sniffed and suppressed another sneeze.

The two carts ran side by side as they discussed their battle. Iliki remained silent. He inched his way along the rail and flew down into the bottom of the cart while the others talked. Verdon glanced at the little ferran and wondered why Iliki wanted the severed tip of the feather. He seemed to be hiding it. Verdon grinned and looked away as he recognized the ragged gray garment. Iliki was working the feather into the front fold of Rala's cloak.

15

"**W**e need to know if they plan to follow," Verdon said when they had rehashed their brief battle with the Worms. "Iliki, can you drift back and see what they're up to?"

"I don't think he should go," Aktar said hastily. The others stared at him in surprise. "They know about him now, they may be watching," Aktar explained.

"I have goo-goo—excellent eyesight," Iliki bragged, and fluffed out his feathers. "I can see them long before I get into the range of their bows."

"Our little friend is too valuable to risk," Aktar said with smooth persuasion.

Verdon and Rala exchanged glances. The desert trader had never evidenced any concern for the ferran. Verdon thought it over. Iliki could stay out of reach of the Worms' bows. The sun dipped toward the horizon, it would soon be night. Before they stopped they needed to know the intentions of the outlaws. Clariel took the decision out of his hands.

"Knowing the enemy's intent is the first solid step toward a defense," she said.

Iliki rose from the side of the cart and flew down their back trail. In a few minutes he returned, announcing the Worms had drawn all their usable carts into a circle.

"Most are busy working on their repairs, but two are digging a fire pit," the little ferran announced. "They won't follow us tonight."

"We should still keep going as long as we can," Verdon decided. The iron rims of the cart wheels traveled the cracked hardpan with ease, but every crack crumbled slightly from their weight. Behind them he could pick out their trail for three hundred yards, and the Worms were far better trackers.

In the larger cart, Kree lay on his side, his head propped on the cart railing as he listened. The rapacian looked over the lightning lizard's shoulder, his reptilian head turning as he followed the conversation. As far as Verdon knew, their newest companion still had not spoken.

Verdon continued to lead until in the dimming light they could barely find their bedrolls. He and Rala had decided it would not be wise to light a fire that night. Kree's hunting had provided them with a desert deer the night before, and they had roasted the carcass, so they would not go hungry. Iliki surveyed the area while Verdon stopped in a shallow depression. With Rala's assistance, Verdon was placing the chocks to keep the cart from rolling, when the little ferran streaked out of the night sky.

"Nocturnals," he warned. "Flyers!"

"I'm getting tired of this," Verdon snapped. "Every time I turn around it's another problem!"

"I'm sorry I bo-both—disturbed you." Iliki backed up. "Maybe if we ask them nicely, they'll go away."

"Can Milstithanog help us?" Verdon asked, ignoring the ferran's sarcasm. He had asked for it.

"He's uh—hun-hun—foraging, but I'll see," Iliki said, and flew up again.

"What's wrong?" Aktar called after the ferran.

Clariel, whose sharp ears had heard the conversation, shouted the news, including Iliki's announced intention to find Milstithanog.

Verdon remained crouched on the ground. Foraging? Foraging for what? Iliki had never said anything about what Milstithanog ate. How far away had the creature roamed on his hunt? Would he get back in time to help them? The ex-guardsman decided not to risk it. He put his hands on the ground and called up the world essencing power to strengthen the breeze. He pulled the chock away from the right wheel and the cart jumped forward though he had not yet raised the sail. He dashed across the hardpan and nearly tripped as he caught up with it. The second cart flanked him and Aktar spilled wind from the sail. Verdon hurriedly raised his own canvas while Rala managed the tiller. The rapacian had jumped aboard with Verdon and he added his strength to the human's as the wind threatened to pull the canvas out of their control.

Iliki returned to perch on the side of the cart and dug the small talons of his bird feet into the wood to keep from being blown away by the gale.

"Thank the Fates for Milstithanog," Aktar shouted over the wind, and took the lead, pushed by the wind.

Rala gladly turned the sailing of their vehicle over to Verdon. "Iliki, you shouldn't call such an obliging creature a demon." She perched on the pile of old clothing that had become her customary seat, folding her sleeves back as she prepared to use her magic.

"He, uh, he does help, does-doesn't he?" Iliki said quietly, his owl's head turning back and forth as he stared into the darkening evening. Without a word he launched himself and disappeared behind the larger cart's sail.

Verdon decided to let the others believe the demon had brought the wind. Keeping the company in good heart was far more important than receiving credit for his deed.

They were well under way before Verdon wondered about the wisdom of his actions. Their movement limited the number of fighters who could hold off the nocturnals. They also faced the danger of destroying their transport in the darkness. Still, the speeding carts, blown by the unnatural wind, would make it harder for the flying nocturnals to attack.

Aktar suddenly veered north. Rala shouted her disapproval, but her objections were blown away by the wind. Verdon followed Aktar. If they became separated, the nocturnals could overwhelm them individually. Then he saw the reason for the change in direction. Large boulders loomed up on his left, just a few feet off their course.

Iliki, with his excellent night vision, had guided Aktar and Clariel, Verdon decided. He felt better about traveling in the darkness. Now, if he could just free himself from the tiller . . .

As if his concern had been spoken aloud, the rapacian rose and crept back to the stern. He placed one clawed hand on the tiller and held out the other, indicating Verdon should give him the sheet. Verdon could tell by the way he slid into position that the humanoid knew how to handle a sail cart.

The ex-guardsman turned the steering over to the rapacian and waited a moment, checking to be sure the humanoid could manage. Then he went forward and picked up his bow.

He wondered what had happened to the nocturnals, and if Iliki had been mistaken, when a dark shadow swooped down, nearly hitting the sail. Rala raised her hand, loosing a fireball. The sudden light illuminated the creature, a rotting skeleton of a ferran with a human body, or what had once been a human shape. Clawed, skeletal hands stretched toward them as if mindlessly reaching for anything they could grasp. Tatters of rotting flesh still clung to the upper arms and torso and the thighs. Its forearms, shins, and feet were bare bones. The maggots that had eaten away the flesh still writhed on what remained of the body. The nocturnal opened its beaklike mouth, its target the rapacian manning the tiller. Rala's fireball struck it and it screamed, rising in the air like a wayward comet.

By the light of the burning nocturnal, Verdon saw four more laboring to catch up with the travelers. He spared a quick glance toward the larger cart and saw six flying above it. One of Clariel's magic arrows glinted as it rose in the air and pierced the head of a shadowy form with huge, tattered wings.

Rala sent a ball of green light flying toward an indistinct shape descending on Aktar. The light struck what appeared to be a small, roiling black cloud and it reeled away. Small bolts of lightning flashed within the cloud before it dissipated into nothing.

In the meantime, Verdon had been busy with his own bow. With his first arrow he split the decayed head of the nearest attacker. Rotted brains, maggots, and gore sprayed out over the desert floor as the body tumbled from the sky.

In the ten years since the beginning of Darkfall, he had seen hundreds of terrifying sights, but his stomach roiled with disgust as the decayed body crashed to the ground with a splat.

His second arrow caught the skeletal wing of a second flyer, and the brittle bone broke. The nocturnal fell, spinning down to the ground in the wake of its severed wing.

Rala unloosed two bolts of lighting, her first target a flyer directly overhead and her second a formless blob drifting down toward Clariel. Both exploded in flames as they fell, lighting the sky and the surrounding desert.

Just ahead, Verdon saw a small herd of racing desert antelope, panicked by the creatures of Darkfall.

Rala threw her last fireball at a creature hovering over the tip of the mast and rushed back to the stern.

"That's it for me, give me the tiller," she shouted to the rapacian over the howling of the wind and the nocturnals.

The reptile relinquished the tiller and scurried forward,

picking up one of the extra bows. He had just nocked an arrow to the string when they heard Clariel's scream. In the dying light of a flaming nocturnal they watched as the larger cart disappeared.

"Stop! Stop!" the rapacian shouted. His sibilants were drawn out, but his speech was understandable. He threw down his weapons and dashed for the tiller, but not in time.

Suddenly their vehicle tipped and fell. Verdon spun in the air, falling in the darkness. As he tumbled, he realized what had happened. They had reached the great gorge of Skar. In their attempt to flee the nocturnals they had sailed over the cliff of the giant fissure. He could fall for miles before he met his death.

16

Verdon tumbled, falling into the gigantic gorge. He fought to suppress the scream welling up in his throat. He had once heard all creatures screamed during fatal falls. From all around him echoed the hopeless cries of impending death. He recognized the hissing cry of the rapacian, Rala's softer, but terrified scream, and the roars of several nocturnals.

He knew the next sound came from his own mouth, a cry of shock and pain as the back of his legs stung from what could have been the lash of a whip. Almost instantaneously the pain hit his hips, his shoulders, and his left forearm. His head snapped back as the velocity of his fall suddenly decreased. The sting of the lashing was lost under the pain in his neck and a sudden loss of feeling in the rest of his body.

Surprise, hope, pain, and fear swirled around in his mind in a dizzying fog, as if some part of his mind tried to obscure and protect him from the reality of his suffering. Reflex, rather than solid thought, brought up his right arm as if he could physically hold his head on his shoulders. He barely realized his plunge decreased in speed.

The net onto which he had fallen—it had to be a

net—had reached the limits of its resiliency. For a fraction of a second he hung suspended, and then the wind rushed by his face as the taut strands beneath him sprang upward. He had a vague expectation of being thrown into the air and struggled to get a grip with his left hand. His mind told him he attempted to move his arm, but it seemed frozen in place. His right still held his head and refused his order to move. Some unconscious command to protect his head and neck took precedence.

When the net reached the apex of its bounce he felt himself rising. To his surprise he lifted only inches; his own clothing prevented him from flying into the air. The strands that held him bounced up and down in gradually gentling undulations. At first his fogged, dizzy mind was only barely aware of it. Then the pain in his neck eased and he could think with more clarity. He attempted to order his thoughts.

He had not fallen to his death. He still lived, but in what condition? The lashing pain of striking the net and then the numbness when his head snapped back half convinced him that he had broken his neck. He had been able to move his right arm, but not his left.

He tried again. He could feel his fist clinch, but he could only lift his arm the width of his sleeve which seemed caught on something. He wiggled his feet, but he could only bend his knees a little before the confines of his clothing held him fast. The numbness eased, the pain of lashing against the ropes returned. He welcomed it as proof that he still had feeling in his body.

It took another moment before the relief gave way to the reality of his situation. He had not fallen into a net. Nets weren't sticky.

He was caught in a web!

Arachnids wove webs.

Arachnids were carnivorous.

By the size and strength of the strands, these arachnids were gigantic.

To these creatures he was an insect, struggling fruit-lessly until, at his captor's convenience, he served the purpose for the trap, a meal at the arachnid's leisure. Total panic blocked his reason for several minutes. Then he reminded himself he was a thinking human, with a mentality superior to that of the creatures hold-ing him captive.

He forced himself to be still and stretch his senses, reaching into the darkness. He concentrated on the vibrations of the web and the sounds around him. Small tremors in the strands suggested movement, and it was not far away. From somewhere beyond his head a hollow, disembodied cry of a nocturnal, and a sudden shaking of the strands told him even their enemies had been caught, probably as they dived to snare their prey.

In the distance he heard Clariel and Aktar call softly to each other. He decided against shouting to them. Loud noises might bring unwelcome attention.

From all around him came the snaps, clicks, and barks of the night creatures that had followed them into the trap. He heard the bleating of the antelope.

"Verdon?" Rala could not be more than twenty feet away, he decided. Rala, Clariel, and Aktar had sur-vived to fall in the web. What had happened to Iliki, Kree, and the rapacian? He repressed the urge to call out to them. He might attract the arachnids to himself, and if they answered him, they could also be pin-pointed by the sound.

"Are you stuck too?" he asked Rala.

"Hand and foot," she said.

"Do you have a spell that might release us?"

"Release us to what? How far would we fall?"

Of course she was right. He wondered if the pain in his neck had addled his brains. When the ache receded he could draw his sword and cut away the strands—again, how far would he fall? Perhaps the net had caught his body and his mind had fallen into Skar's depths. He'd certainly lost it somewhere.

"We'll have to wait until daylight," Verdon said

reluctantly. He would have said more, but off to his right an eerie wail rose out of the darkness. The sound sent shivers up his spine and set his teeth on edge. He struggled to free himself, to get away from the creature that made the unearthly noise. He discovered his struggles only succeeded in fastening his clothing more securely to the strands. The sweat of dread, a fear of being devoured alive in the darkness, stung his eyes and soaked his clothing. The wail tore into his mind and continued, almost tearing away sane thought.

The sound stopped. The sudden silence had a breathless, waiting quality, like the eve of a storm. Time seemed to stop, too. The rope beneath his shoulders kept his body level, but the effort to hold up his unsupported head pulled on the muscles of his neck and his right arm. When he let it droop he felt as if his upper spine had been crushed into powder.

The silence had begun to get on his nerves when the wailing started again. He tensed, expecting an attack, and then realized the noise was no closer to him. The cry came from some nocturnal that was also caught, he decided. Perhaps with luck, it would draw the arachnid creatures that had strung the net.

Great. Wonderful thought. If the giant spiders, and by the size of the net they had to be giants, reached the nocturnal first, he would be treated to a preview of what he could expect.

The night seemed to deepen with his misery. Off and on the trapped creature continued the wail. After its sixth long call, a trill in the distance answered and Verdon changed his mind about the source. An arachnid guard, calling its fellows to an early breakfast?

After that the creatures trilled back and forth. He could make nothing of their sounds until a few minutes after the sky above the eastern rim of Skar grew light enough for him to make out the cliffs. The half-light had not brightened to the point of adding color to his surroundings when he saw the shape of the creature that had been wailing through the night.

His anger blunted his relief when he realized the terrifying noise had been made by the rapacian.

And the reptilian-humanoid had been answered!

Before hope could flash through his mind an arrow shot up through the web. It passed him less than five feet away. He had just time to notice the four prongs that extended back from the point and the slender rope attached to the rear of the shaft. Two other shafts rose and fell, one near Rala and another close to the rapacian. He tried to turn his head to see below, but had to be satisfied with the view nearly a quarter of a mile away.

In the growing light he could see a ledge hundreds of feet below the web, a shelf of normality below the nightmare of his entrapment. Sparse vegetation and a few stunted trees still kept their night shadows. As the daylight continued to increase, he could see another ledge further down. It appeared greener, but it was too far away from him to make out any details.

In the distance, indistinct shapes were creeping up toward the arachnid webs near Clariel and Aktar. Others ascended ropes near the trapped antelope. Two climbed close together toward a larger shape that could have been the lightning lizard.

He knew the shadowy forms had to be climbing ropes, but in the distance the creatures seemed to be crawling up the unsupported dawn light. He felt movement in the strands of the web. Someone climbed to help him, he decided, and then wondered if he was wrong. He could see a nocturnal twenty feet away struggling against its confinement. The creature raised its head to look beyond Verdon who saw an eight-legged arachnid crossing the web with a surefooted pace.

"Twist about," the rapacian hissed. "Move and shout; show it you are alive."

"So it will kill me quickly?" Verdon asked. Did the rapacian want him destroyed?

"Kreds eat dead, rotting meat when they can get it.

They will be drawn by the smell of the nocturnals. They will ignore us if they think we are still alive. With enough nocturnals to fill their stomachs, they will wait for us to die and start to rot."

The rapacian shouted his explanation while he shook the strands of the web. The kred stopped a few feet from him, turned its head as it inspected the reptilian-humanoid. Then it moved toward Verdon.

"Get lost!" Verdon shouted as he jerked, bouncing the web. He left his aching neck to support itself and used his right arm to pull his sword. His arm was stiff and sore, but the blade glittered in the growing light.

"Do not injure the kred," the rapacian called out. "Just waving your blade is enough to drive it off."

"It's not exactly my best friend," Verdon retorted, frustrated with the reptilian.

"But they *are* the best friends of the people in this part of Skar. The nocturnals caught in their webs never reach the depths."

Verdon shouted at the approaching arachnid and it stopped just short of his sword. It stared at him, and he felt his mouth go dry. In the growing light he could see the color of the creature, a deep gray-green that probably blended with the ground far below. Its five feet of swollen abdomen were fronted with a head eighteen inches in diameter, and two jagged saw blade mandibles extended from its strong lower jaw, all stomach and jaws with legs to move it about. At first Verdon thought the giant spider's body was covered with short horns, but they stirred in the breeze. Hair half the diameter of his wrist?

The arachnid absorbed all his attention, so he had been unaware of the approach of his rescuer until the flick of a rope around his waist startled him.

"Hu-man—" The soft reptilian voice close to his ear caused him to jerk his head around. He felt as if his head had been yanked from his shoulders.

"Keep shouting."

Verdon did as he was told. He swore at the arachnid, using every vile insult he knew. The noise and his movements convinced the giant spider he needed more time in the web and it moved on.

Freed to look around, Verdon found that the rapacian wore a harness with a lead rope he had attached to the ring in the arrow anchor. He secured the rope around Verdon's waist and tied it to the loop in the rope that supported him. Attached to the reptilian-humanoid's elbows and the inside of his knees were blocks of wood, held in place by thick leather straps. Verdon saw the marks of rope burns on them. This was not the first time the rapacians had climbed to the nets to rescue trapped victims.

"I will now cut away the web," the rapacian explained. "You will prepare for a short drop, and I will lower us."

Verdon watched as the rapacian dipped his right hand into a pouch at his waist. It emerged dripping a green slimy mixture. He swung from one hand as he dipped his right in the mess. Swinging from hand to hand, he worked around Verdon, cutting away the strands of the web. When the last one had been severed, Verdon's neck suffered from the short drop. The reptilian slowed their descent by gripping the rope with the wooden blocks between his knees and elbows.

Free at last to look below him, Verdon stared down from an impossible height. Above him the pronged anchor came down with them. The rapacian's grip on the rope dropped them in jerks as he rappelled them toward the sloping ground.

His rescuer suddenly stopped their descent and pulled his weapon at a fluttering of wings. Verdon looked to see Iliki hovering in the air just behind him. The little ferran stared at him and then at the rapacian without speaking. Then he streaked off toward the two rapacians that worked to rescue Kree.

Verdon's neck felt as if it were breaking, but at the end of every dizzying drop he was closer to solid ground. In the distance he saw Clariel and Aktar. They had reached the ledge. A rapacian carried the desert trader. Hurt in the fall, Verdon decided, hoping the nomad's injuries were not too severe. The elf and her rescuer waited for her lightning lizard to finish his descent. Verdon looked up and saw Rala just above him. To his right, two rapacians descended more slowly.

When Verdon's feet touched the ground he thought his legs would give way with relief. Not fifty feet away lay the shattered remains of his sail cart. The web had not held the heavy vehicle. If he and his friends had not been thrown clear, they would have been bloody pulp in the wreck.

"Thank you," he said to the rapacian, barely finding the breath to speak. "You saved my life, and I consider a life debt a matter of honor." He wasn't sure the words meant anything to the humanoid, but he felt a need to say something to express his gratitude.

"You will pay the debt." The rapacian grinned and, with a sudden flash of his arm, jerked Verdon's sword from his hand. His sharp teeth glinted with his smile. "The Mating Feast is in four days, and you will be my contribution."

Verdon stared at the rapacian. Before Darkfall, the rapacian Mating Feast was rumored to be the greatest horror on Aden. The rite took place before the traditional mating season, when both males and females ate live victims to increase their fertility. "We always use what we catch in the webs," the reptilian-humanoid grinned again and shrugged at Verdon's outrage. "You would have been dead by that time anyway."

17

Rala's rescuer had brought the dwarf over to join Verdon and the rapacian that held him captive. Her eyes flickered, the only sign she had heard the conversation, but after a moment she pointedly gazed at Verdon and then back at their captors. When he did not immediately understand her message she tried again.

Verdon understood. She was a spell caster. He should keep them busy while she attempted to free them. He had no idea what she had in mind, but he tried to draw their attention.

"You can't kill us, you owe us a debt of honor," he said, speaking loud enough to cover her incantation. "We saved the life of one of your people, at least he must be one of your people, he has the same markings on his head and back," Verdon continued, jabbering as fast as he could.

Both rapacians stared at him, but the one who had captured the dwarf glanced down at her and saw her lips moving. In a lightning fast movement he clapped his clawed hand over her mouth. Using a rag from one of the pouches at his waist, he gagged the dwarf. For good measure he whipped the dangling strands of the web around her, effectively tying her arms to her side.

Rala had made a good try, Verdon thought. Since she could not help them, any escape would be up to him. He gazed around the sloping ledge, hoping for inspiration, opportunity, anything that would help him. One of the extra bows from the Worm sail cart still hung from his shoulder, and he had a quiver of arrows. Both were firmly held in place by the strands of the kred web that still adhered to his clothing. He had all three of his pistols, but they were empty since he had used them in the battle with the flying nocturnals. If he attempted to load them, the rapacian who had been traveling with them would understand his intention and stop him.

He eyed the pile of wreckage that had been the sail cart, thinking if he could reach it, he might be able to use a broken wheel or a shattered piece of wood as a weapon. He waited until the reptilian-humanoid had looked away before he started his dash toward the wreck. His race for freedom lasted for half a step. The web strands that were still attached to the back of his pants tripped him and sent him sprawling on the thick, damp grass.

The rapacian turned and stared down at him. Then, with another of his sharp-toothed grins, he pulled Verdon to his feet.

"Do not injure yourself, human," he said pleasantly. "Bruised flesh loses its taste." He lifted Verdon to his feet and set the bound human down by a stunted tree, one of a few that grew on the ledge. The second rapacian brought Rala and plumped her down on the ground by Verdon. He noticed the dwarf had not been dropped with bruising force. Verdon swore at himself for not remembering the web strands that still held fast to his pant legs. He would not make that mistake again. He doubted he would have the chance.

When the rapacian turned away to greet an approaching group of his people, Verdon eased his boot knife out of its sheath. If he could free Rala, she might be able to finish her spell, but she sat two feet away from him on the left, and the strand of sticky web still bound his left arm to his side. He sawed at the web's strand just below his left elbow. He worked furiously, but he could see he would not free himself or Rala in time to get away from the new group of humanoids.

He kept watching them as he hacked at the tough strand of the web. Their actions were curious as they greeted Siskiel. Their language seemed to be all hoots and hisses, and he could make nothing of it. When the others spoke to Siskiel, their heads bobbed up and down in what appeared to be some sort of courtesy they omitted when speaking to each other. One stepped behind Siskiel and used the slimy mixture from his pouch to coat the strands of the web that still clung to the new-comer's hide. The ropy kred web fell away as soon as the mixture touched it. At first Siskiel's friends seemed to be overjoyed to see him, but their delight wilted when he snarled some objection and spoke rapidly.

Verdon could make nothing of what he said, but by the gestures the new arrival seemed to be telling his comrades about the wound on his shoulder and his broken leg. The others glared at Verdon and seemed to be in grudging agreement, but Siskiel had not finished his story. As he went on with his tale, his friends looked about warily. The only word Verdon understood was the name Milstithanog. Then Siskiel gave an order, nodded to Verdon and Rala, and trotted off down the ledge.

So much for any gratitude for saving his life, Verdon thought.

Verdon's rescuer and a second rapacian approached the tree, bags of the repellent slime in their clawed hands. Verdon tried to hide the knife, but the flat side of the blade had touched the sticky strand and he was still tugging at it free when the rapacians reached him.

"You will not need a weapon, human," his rescuer said pleasantly. "We, too, accept the debt of honor in the saving of a life."

"What does that mean?" Verdon asked. He kept a tight hold on his only weapon.

"Your large invisible friend will not need to destroy our people in saving you," he said as he spread the green slime on the web strand that held the knife captive. When the blade was free he waited for Verdon to restore the boot knife to its sheath. Both rapacians carried spears, and Verdon's small weapon would be useless against the long, manite-tipped shafts. He sheathed his weapon. Then both humanoids moved closer, grasped his arms, assisted him to rise, and turned him to face the tree. Verdon felt the wetness of the stinking slimy mixture as the reptilian spread it on the sticky strands of web. In moments they fell away and he could move freely again, but the odor of the substance that had removed them filled his nostrils. His stomach twisted a warning.

"And you will need no spells," one of the creatures said to the dwarf. "You will not be harmed by us.

"Thank you for the smallest of favors," Rala snapped when they removed the gag from her mouth.

"The life of our Siskiel is a debt recognized by all our people," the rapacian said, and pointed to his helper. "This is Woos. He will be your guide."

Woos bobbed his head, a greeting courtesy, Verdon decided. He nodded his own head in reply.

"I wonder which was worse, the web or this awful smell," Rala observed.

"You find it offensive?" the rapacian asked as if surprised. "It will soon disappear. Now we wait for your friends, and then I will lead you through the ledges of the Lakwar."

"Lakwar?" Verdon asked. He was surprised, never having known the reptilelike humanoids to call themselves by any term but their racial name. They were usually race-proud and tended to look down on any creature not a rapacian.

"It is the name we give ourselves," the rapacian replied. "In our tongue the word means The Driven.

Many centuries ago our ancestors were near an elf village in Yzeem when the time of Mating Feast approached. The elves who survived fled and carried the tale to the rest of their people." Woos looked surprised. "Who knew they would be so enraged? The elves outnumbered our ancestors by many thousands and our people were driven into Skar." Woos threw out his chest with pride. "We are a people of good appetite and our ancestors ate a lot of elves."

Verdon decided not to comment.

"Of course, we do not hunt or eat the people of Skar," Woos continued, sounding wistful and a little sad. Another rapacian approached, carrying a live antelope. He called to Woos, who left Verdon and trotted over to inspect the catch.

"The sooner we get away from these reptiles the better," Iliki said softly. Verdon looked up to see the little ferran perched on a limb just above his head. He had not been aware of Iliki's presence.

"They're not reptiles," Verdon said before he realized the ferran was being deliberately insulting. He let the remark go. He didn't feel capable of making peace between races.

"Luckily Siskiel saw the power of Milstithanog," Verdon continued. He suspected the ferran knew the truth, that Verdon and not the demon had created the wind that sent the sail carts racing across the desert and over the cliffs of Skar, but Clariel and Aktar were approaching with their rescuers and the elf had sharp ears.

"He wasn't much help when we fell into the web," Rala groused. "And you disappeared in a hurry."

Iliki shifted on his perch, his face twisted as if he were listening or thinking hard.

"He—ah—he fell into the web, too," Iliki said. "I could not help you, but I thou—suspected he could, so I was helping him to get loose. He was almost free when the rapacians rescued you."

Rala nearly bent backward trying to see the ferran.

"How could an invisible creature who can't be injured by a thrown spear get caught in a net?"

Iliki shifted again. "I—ah—don't kno-kno—understand it either, but who knows what laws apply to a being from another world?"

They forgot Milstithanog's vulnerabilities as Aktar approached without a rapacian escort. He walked unimpaired, his clothing streaked with green slime. He brushed at his trousers with wisps of grass. By his expression, the indignity of the stain and smell outweighed the importance of his safety. Clariel followed, trotting beside Kree, who still limped a bit.

"Luck favored us. We could have been with them," she said, looking up. The rest raised their heads to see what she meant. Thirty or more kred were devouring the nocturnals that had followed the company over the cliff and had been caught in the nets. Verdon shuddered as one of the arachnids bit into the leg of a still-living and struggling creature. The thigh and knee disappeared. The foot tumbled out of the sky. Rala bit her lips and turned away. Clariel, with elfin stoicism, watched impassively.

Neither Clariel nor Aktar mentioned their narrow escape at the hands of the Lakwar. Verdon and Rala exchanged glances in a silent agreement not to mention it.

"Well, we've reached the first ledge of Skar," Aktar said, as if he felt a need to change the subject. "What do we do now?"

"We go down," Rala said with decision, and turned to Woos, who had returned after admiring his friend's catch. "Do you know Overlook? How do we reach it and how long is the journey?"

The rapacian stared at her and wrinkled his scaly nose. "As the crandow flies, eight miles." He pointed almost due south. "Perhaps twice as far down."

"And how hard will it be to get there?" Verdon asked. The rapacian had said the Lakwar did not eat their neighbors, but he had not said they were on friendly terms.

"There are troubles," Woos answered slowly. "Before Darkfall the trading paths were always open. They were still usable a month ago. Now I cannot say."

Verdon glanced around at the others. He had planned to tell them they did not need to make the arduous descent, but Clariel spoke first.

"A journey is only shortened by taking the first step." Aktar seemed to agree. "If we're going, we should get started," he said. "We won't be able to climb in the dark."

"Eight miles south, sixteen down—that's not so far," Iliki said, stretching his wings.

Verdon held up the beginning of the journey to search through the wreckage of the sail cart until he found his spare shot and powder. His dweomered armor had not survived the crash. When he attempted to touch it with the knife from his boot, the blue glow proved it still held its protection, but he doubted any magic would have withstood that fall. The others collected the food that survived while he reloaded his three pistols.

When Verdon had tucked the third weapon into his belt, Woos led the way south, staying close to the cliff wall. They walked two miles over smooth ground before coming to a break in the ledge. They started down a rocky gorge. The uneven turns and twists made walking difficult as they used a path gouged out of the cliff by the runoff from the rare but violent desert storms.

The rapacians had taken advantage of the cut and carved stone stairs in the steepest places. The width of the steps and the height of the risers had been designed for the rapacians and did not fit the stride of humans, elves, or dwarfs. Woos descended quickly. The humans had more trouble, and Rala's short legs could not manage them at all. After the first hundred feet, Clariel suggested the dwarf ride on Kree's back.

"I don't think so," Rala said sotto voce to Verdon. She distrusted the lightning lizard almost as much as the rapacians. "We can't afford injuries," Verdon said. "And Clariel's making a concession." The elf had refused to ride the lizard, wanting him to heal completely before he carried any weight.

Rala gave in and rode the lizard. The first lap of their journey, probably no more than eighteen miles in a straight line, was doubled by the trail's twists and turns. The rough ground on the more gentle slopes, the wide, deep steps of the rapacians, and the companions' lack of sleep during the night made for slow travel. The gorge descended nearly two thousand feet, but they walked more than ten miles along its tortured course. The sun had dropped low in the western sky before they reached the next ledge.

They came out of the gorge into the shade of the kred ledge, but they could see the sunlight out on the wide, sloping plain. The two-mile-wide ledge was greener than the one above and slightly cooler. A few stunted trees shaded the large herds of desert antelope that grazed peacefully on the short range grass.

"Where we cannot hunt, herding must feed our people," Woos said sadly. "We do not dwell on what our illustrious ancestors would think of us."

"And cook your food?" Verdon asked. For the last half hour he had been getting occasional whiffs of roasting meat. He had tried to stifle the saliva his hunger induced, not knowing what might be roasting in the land of the Lakwar.

"Flesh ruined by the heat of a fire is not to our taste," Woos said, wrinkling his scaly nose in disgust. "So it must be for you the meat is being cooked."

"What sort of meat?" Aktar asked warily.

"Our daily diet is limited to antelope," Woos said, again with regret. Verdon didn't care for the hungry look the rapacian gave Clariel. Apparently his rapacian ancestors had enjoyed elf.

They rounded a jutting cliff spur and found two rapacians feeding a fire and roasting a small antelope. The humanoids had run a spear through the carcass and hung the weapon on two forked sticks over the flames. Unused to roasting meat, they had not turned it often, so part of the carcass was half-raw and the other parts charred.

The humanoids wrinkled their scaled noses as if they smelled rotten carrion and backed away from the fire the moment the travelers approached. Woos questioned them, and by their attitudes indicated that they accepted no responsibility for the mess they had made.

"The Siskiel ordered the meat cooked for you," Woos said, staring with disgust at the fire.

The travelers had no complaints. Between the charred and the raw portions there was more than enough for two meals. Rala and Verdon set to work carving away the usable portions and even Aktar helped, urged on by his hunger.

When the companions started to eat, the rapacians looked away, as if they had been viewing something too shameful to watch. They retreated to tear at several freshly killed carcasses, and Kree joined them. "We cannot travel the long gorge in the night," Woos told them after the remains of both meals had been cleaned away. "We will wait until morning." He pointed back into the shadows under the overhanging cliffs.

"The long gorge?" Rala murmured. "What did we just do, a skip and a jump?"

Verdon looked back into the shadows, where he could see the black mouths of several caves. He shivered, thinking nocturnals lurked in the darkness. Nocturnals were not afraid of the sunlight, but they preferred to use the shadows and darkness to sneak up on their quarry.

18

Verdon slept before the sun set and awoke after dawn only because Aktar roughly shook his shoulder. He sat up and looked around. The others had the alert looks of having been up for some time. He grinned, stretched, and stood up, grimacing at the stiffness in his muscles. Sleeping on the ground had not helped to ease the soreness caused by the long descent the day before.

Aktar, with unwanted instruction from Iliki, was putting out the fire and wrapping roasted meat in leaves pulled from a nearby bush. Rala was openly studying her spell scroll; it was the first time she had let the others see it and Aktar kept throwing surreptitious and dissatisfied glances in her direction, as if he resented not being told she was a mage. Clariel stood apart from the others as if in a trance.

"It's clear you had no fear of our hosts," Aktar said peevishly. The dark circles under his eyes testified to his lack of rest. Rala, too, seemed tired, but Clariel looked rested and more cheerful than she had been since her rescue from the Worms. Was she putting her grief and guilt behind her or looking forward to the possibility of being eaten alive? Verdon didn't discount the latter since she was determined to be punished for what she considered her failure in leadership.

The others had already finished their breakfasts, so Verdon cut away a chunk of the antelope cooked the night before and ate it as they began the day's trek. He expected to travel south, but Woos led the way north for just over a mile. They walked in the shadows, since the sun had not risen high enough for its rays to fall on Skar's eastern ledges. Out beyond the upper ledge of the Lakwar, a mist shrouded the view.

"The middle of the desert is a strange place to see fog," Verdon commented to no one in particular.

"It's not fog," said Woos, who walked just ahead of him. "Rain falls on the lower ledges."

"It couldn't be raining," Aktar objected. "Not here."

"Of course it could," Rala said. "The lower regions of Skar are much cooler than the desert. Where the hot and cold air mingle, condensation forms—along with thunderstorms," she added as a roll of thunder echoed down the giant fissure of Skar.

Woos spared a moment from watching their path to glance back at Verdon. The rapacian grinned at the human's fascination with the flashes of lightning in the dark clouds. The storm had upset a desert hawk, who streaked away to the other side of the gorge. Verdon decided there were more hawks on the desert than prey to feed them. Then he wondered why the idle thought bothered him.

"Is it the first time you have seen the top of a thunderstorm?" Woos asked with a grin. The others answered in the affirmative, and even Aktar grudgingly admitted he was seeing something new.

"The first time I've seen a lot of things," Verdon replied. What he had seen of Skar was fascinating, and he had no trouble admitting it. The vegetation, particularly the trees, was fascinating, and the rainstorm was a delight when he paused to remember that outside the great gorge, the desolation of the desert stretched for hundreds of miles in all directions.

Woos led the way to the mouth of a cave. Just inside, he distributed four unlit torches. He gave one to Verdon, one to Clariel, and one to Aktar.

"We will need light for a short distance," he said, struggling with his flint. Verdon pulled out the sparker that was a standard item in the Iron Guard survival kit. One end of a thin, U-shaped tension bar was permanently attached to the outside of a sparking cap. The other end was set to scrape against the cap's rough surface when Verdon tightened his grip on the two bars of the U. The friction sent out an immediate shower of sparks that lit the torch.

Clariel and Aktar had seen the mechanism before, so they had been waiting for Verdon to light his torch and theirs in turn. Woos stared at the sparker, his yellow, slitted eyes gleaming.

"Show that to the dwarfs," he said. "Soon we will have a brisker trade in Skar."

When the torches were lit, Woos led the way into the tunnel. In less than a hundred yards it connected with the dry bed of an underground stream. The passage narrowed and widened with the slope of the floor, but they walked on a smooth stone surface.

Iliki had declined to take the underground route. He preferred to fly down to the next ledge and wait. Woos had assured Clariel that Kree could get through the watercourse, but he would have to keep his head low. Verdon discovered he also had to stoop in a few places.

At the beginning of the descent they all complained of stiff muscles irritated by the constant descent, but in an hour the stiffness had worn away. They had been wary of a nocturnal attack, but Verdon had ceased to worry and had begun to enjoy the colorful striations of stone when they emerged into the daylight again. Looking up, they could tell they had descended further in two hours than they had in ten the day before. Looking down, they saw how far they had to go. Rala backed away from the edge of the three-foot path that angled down the side of a sheer cliff.

"It must be two miles straight down," she said, awed by the view.

They were still above the rain clouds, and the misty air partially obscured the ground far below. From the height of the ledge they could make out no features, only a greener plain than the one above.

"Your long gorge is taking some unexpected turns," Verdon told Woos.

"We come to the gorge soon," Woos said, and led the way along the cliff.

"Soon" proved to be two miles of tense walking on the narrow ledge, but again the rapacians used a watercourse that sloped in a southerly direction. The long gorge had fewer rocks and sudden drops. Only two short sets of steps had been carved in the steeper areas. The sun was setting as they reached the lower ledge of the Lakwar.

The range grass was greener and numerous trees dotted the wider plain. The more abundant grazing allowed for more and larger herds of antelope. Groups of twenty to thirty grazed in the afternoon sun or lay on the ground in the shade of the trees that spotted the plain. The rapacian herders provided their people with a large food supply.

Stone huts with massive walls had been built close to the wall of the gorge and marched down the hillside in oddly staggering rows. Their roofs were flimsy affairs, with tree branches laid over a framework of slender poles. The village, if village it was, seemed deserted.

"Stay here, in the sunlight," Woos ordered. He turned away, but Aktar was impatient.

"What is it? Where are you going?"

Woos turned with a snarl. "Do as I tell you, human! The Siskiel has said I must get you through our lands safely. I will do it if I have to kill you." The rapacian turned and trotted away.

"To ignore the advice of a good guide is to walk the path of the foolish," Clariel said. She whipped her bow off her shoulder and strung it, but made no move to follow

Woos. Verdon strung his own bow and moved each of his pistols, making sure they would be easy to draw.

The hair on the back of Verdon's neck rose as he heard an eerie call. Then he recognized it as the same sound Siskiel had made when they were caught in the web. In moments Woos came in sight, walking slowly, inspecting the ground. He paused, raised his head, and called again. A call answered from the south. The rapacian waved a hand indicating they should travel toward the call and broke into a trot. He moved with effortless ease, but faster than the humans could sprint.

Rala made no objection when Clariel helped her onto Kree's back. At a command from his mistress, the lightning lizard sped off after the rapacian with the elf running beside him. Verdon and Aktar brought up the rear, with no hope of catching up. Woos was half a mile ahead when he stopped and waited impatiently for the two humans.

"You still haven't told us what's wrong," Aktar gasped when he and Verdon caught up with the others. Verdon didn't comment. He wasted no breath on the obvious.

"What could it be but nocturnals?" Clariel answered scornfully.

"It is so, and we must reach my people before darkness," Woos said. He scratched his scaly leg as he mentally measured the distance they still had to travel. "Humans are too slow, we will not succeed. We must find shelter." He raised a blunt-fingered hand and extended a three-inch claw as he pointed to the south. "At least we will not be alone."

Verdon had also seen the movement in the distance. Six rapacians were racing their way. They approached with the speed that had made their people famous and feared throughout Aden.

"To the cliff," Verdon said. "Maybe we can find a cave for shelter." He led the way, wondering if he should have asked advice of Woos, but the rapacian didn't offer any objections. The approaching humanoids seemed to have the same idea. Woos passed Verdon, taking over the lead, and changed the direction to a more southerly course but still leading toward the cliffs.

The sun had disappeared behind the western rim of Skar when they reached a shallow cave, though the description was generous. It was only a shallow depression in the cliff. It would protect their backs and the roof would prevent attack from flying enemies. While Verdon stood in the entrance, breathing hard from his run as he inspected the shelter, the shadow from the setting sun moved up the wall and left them in semidarkness. He had seen enough to know the stone wall behind them was solid. Their shelter would be as safe as any.

The six rapacians had reached the cave only seconds before Verdon's party. One stood grinning at him.

"Travel is not so easy for you without the sail cart," he said.

It took a moment before Verdon realized the speaker was Siskiel. Many tribes or clans of rapacians lived in the Known Lands. They could be found any-where except in the colder regions. Some differed in color, skin markings, and crests, but those of the same family or clan resembled each other. The slight differ-ences in the patterns of color gave individuality to the scaly skin of the rapacians, but they were subtle. Unless a member of another race knew rapacians well, the slight differences within families or clans were not easily recognized. Verdon had never encountered the humanoid reptiles until he met Siskiel, and he had a hard time recognizing one rapacian from another.

"I'm glad we didn't take you out of your way when we brought you along," Rala said. "It might have been helpful if you had told us you belonged here."

"I thought it wise to learn more about you and your purpose," Siskiel said with no attempt at an apology. "Acts that appear merciful are often traps for the unwary."

"Since the beginning of Darkfall, trust has become a trap for the unwise," Clariel said softly.

"Do you ever join a conversation, or do you just make wise pronouncements?" Rala demanded of the elf.

"When useless talk fills the mouth, the ears hear nothing," Clariel snapped as she walked away. She led Kree to the back of the shallow cave and ordered him to rest out of the way of the others.

"And all her pronouncements are wise," Rala sighed. "Maybe that's what irritates me."

"Or maybe the ride on Kree's back left you sore in spirit as well as in body," Verdon said, dismissing the complaints of the dwarf. He turned back to the rapacian.

"In our ignorance we may have given offense to the Siskiel," he said. "We weren't aware of your importance. We still don't understand your position in your clan."

"Siskiel is the name always given to the future Sis-Rain, the leader of our people," the rapacian said. "To be the child of the leader is an honor—they say."

"You don't think so?" Verdon grinned at the irony in the humanoid's tone.

Siskiel didn't answer. He cocked his head, listening intently. Clariel had returned to the cave mouth. She, too, listened for a moment and whipped her bow from her shoulder.

"Nocturnals," she murmured. "They do not walk like ordinary creatures."

"Flying?" Aktar asked. He had been leaning against the cave wall, sipping from his water flask and resting. He walked over to join Verdon, Siskiel, and Clariel, sword in hand.

"No, they travel on the ground, but they don't walk," Siskiel said, his yellow, slitted eyes staring out into the darkness. He could hear almost as well as the elf, much better than a human.

"Four days ago they started coming up out of the rotting caverns. Some are bestial forms. Others . . ." He shrugged as if they defied description. Verdon assumed their shapes and sizes were too varied to waste time listing. It was not unknown for a group of nocturnals to be alike in shape and form, but more often they were a heterogeneous group of horrifying shapes.

The travelers and the rapacians stood in a line at the cave's entrance. Four of Siskiel's companions were to Verdon's left. Siskiel, Woos, and the seventh rapacian guarded the right. Verdon, Aktar, Clariel, and Rala watched from the center. Behind them, Kree surged to his feet in defiance of the elf's orders. He paced back and forth, hissing and barking short cries.

"The lizard senses the approach of the nocturnals," Siskiel said softly.

"He's calling for Iliki," Clariel replied, searching the dark sky. "It would be an unlucky arrow that brought down a friend."

"Here we go with the pronouncements again," Rala muttered as she rolled up her sleeves. "Anyone interested in knowing what's out there?"

"A spell thrown too early is one wasted," Verdon said with a grin. He could not resist baiting the dwarf. To himself he had to admit he needed the release of tension.

"Don't you start or I'll go out of my mind," Rala snapped. "The last thing we need is for —"

"Silence." Siskiel spit out the word too fast for his long drawn sibilants to be noticeable. Instead they caught the dying scream of an antelope. Rala threw a spell and a ball of light flashed out over the plain. More than fifty strange shapes dotted the plain. At first Verdon thought he saw boulders where no stones had marked the plain in the daylight. After the first moment of shock, the gray blobs directly beneath Rala's glowing ball retreated, but the others moved forward. Their outer surfaces appeared to be covered with moss, but they undulated as they moved.

A small herd of antelope dashed across the plain. One unlucky creature ventured too near one of the bloblike shapes. It glided forward and the panicked deer ran straight into it. The antelope's head fell off on the other side. As the gelatinous mass moved away, only the skeleton and head of the antelope remained.

Beside Verdon, Rala shuddered. "This is not my favorite type of beast," she muttered.

"Something tells me we have trouble," Verdon replied. He had been holding one of his pistols in his hand, but he tucked it back in his belt. The gunnes were not accurate at any distance and he wondered what a shot could do to harm the creatures. He pulled his bow from his shoulder, nocked an arrow to the string, and let fly. His first shot hit his target but with no visible effect.

"I was right, we do have trouble," he said, shouldering the bow again.

Clariel shot one of her dweomered arrows. The magically enhanced arrow caused the nocturnal to explode. It ripped apart into ten pieces. In moments each piece moved toward them.

"Do you have a platitude for that?" Rala asked the elf.

"Only the foolish warrior increases the number of the foe," the elf replied. She shouldered her bow and gave a musical whistle that called the arrow back.

"Where are the ferran and his invisible companion?" Siskiel asked. "It is time for Milstithanog to aid us."

"I don't know. Iliki should have met us at the bottom of the cliff," Verdon said. "We haven't seen him since we left the upper ledge." He was worried about their little companion. The kred nets could not catch all the flying nocturnals that plagued the area around Skar.

"If we can't kill them with arrows, and swords would probably just cut them into living pieces, what's left?" Aktar asked Siskiel. "What have your people been using against them?"

"These are new to us," Woos answered. "Four days ago nocturnals began coming up out of the rotting caverns. Most have been the rotting undead. We have not seen these creatures before. If they have passed the guards at the entrance to the caverns, I fear for our people."

The light ball Rala had created was only temporary and it died away, but not before it showed new arrivals closing in behind the others.

"Quick, before they get any closer," Verdon said.

"Pull up some of that dry grass, we'll try burning them." Fire had worked on the monsters that had attacked the thunder train. He wished he had some resin-soaked chips, but they were defensive luxuries left behind on the thunder train.

The overhang prevented direct light, so the grass was not as abundant as on the plain. Verdon dashed out, grabbed a handful of long, dry blades. He was trying to twist it around an arrow when Rala called to him.

"Don't waste ammunition until we know," she said and began an incantation. A fireball shot out from her fingers, passing over the first fifty creatures. It landed in a tight group of moving shapes.

An eerie scream hurt their ears as half a dozen creatures burst into flame. They jerked about, setting others on fire. In moments more than two dozen shapes were contorting in the flames.

"Good work, but next time you might take out that bunch," Aktar said, pointing to a close-packed group of twenty that were approaching the cave mouth. "They're getting close."

"And if they had each exploded into a dozen little creatures, did you want them landing in here?" Rala asked.

"A wise fighter keeps his danger at bay," Clariel remarked, defending the dwarf's actions. She had returned to the cave with an armful of grass and had tied a few strands to one of her magic arrows. Verdon whipped out his sparker and set the grass alight. Remembering what had happened with her first arrow, she angled her shot over the top of the closest, firing into another tight group near the rear of the approaching attackers. Again the magic of her arrow caused a nocturnal to break apart; the flying pieces were blazing when they fell among the rest of the tightly packed group and set them afire.

"Help me keep a count!" she shouted with glee and started making another torch. Aktar sheathed his sword and knelt, picked up a handful of grass, and wrapped a third arrow for her. She stripped the quiver

from her shoulder and dropped it by him as she
recalled her first arrow.

"It is a time of legend when the Lakwar are protected by an elf," Siskiel said, his slitted yellow eyes on
the female warrior.

"Honor requires payment of debts," Clariel replied.
"I trust your people will remember it if ever another elf
comes within reach of your claws."

In the light of the burning nocturnals a shadowy
shape flitted through the air, hovered, and then
swooped up as one of the rapacians raised his spear.
At a word from Siskiel the rapacian lowered his
weapon and Iliki dived for the cave. He landed by
Verdon, who knelt on the ground, trying to tie some of
the dry grass to one of his arrows.

"Wha—where did you go?" the ferran demanded. "I
couldn't fi-fi—locate you."

"You look as if you've had a good nap," Verdon
said, noticing Iliki's eyes. They were puffy with sleep.

"I just took a little res-rest," the ferran admitted.

"You can help with these arrows," Verdon said.
Siskiel and the other rapacians were trying, but their
large fingers, less flexible because of their retractable
claws, were awkward and ineffective.

Verdon shot four flaming arrows. His targets were
the nearest of the nocturnals, knowing Clariel would
not risk breaking them apart so close to the cave. He
hit every target, and had nocked his fifth arrow to the
bow when he realized their danger.

The flaming masses staggered about and set the dry
range grass aflame. The fire moved slowly toward the
cave. The defenders were in danger of being roasted by
their own defense.

19

Verdon looked out over the burning plain. The flames leaping from the nocturnals prevented him from seeing a path through the fire. Even if they found a way to escape the fire they were in danger of attack, but one risk seemed as great as another.

Siskiel knelt and stared into the face of the little ferran.

"Where is your friend Milstithanog?" he demanded.

Iliki tried to back away from the wide mouth only inches from his face. The rapacian prevented his escape by catching the ferran's wing in one clawed hand.

"I don-don—he's *coming!*" Iliki wailed. "He can't g-g—travel as fast as I can fly!"

Milstithanog was always somewhere else when they needed him, Verdon thought with a sigh. He knelt to pick up another arrow. He spared a moment to touch the ground and call up the earth force. The power surged through him, leaving him with a light-headed feeling.

"Let him go," he told Siskiel. "Iliki, fly up and see if you can find us a path through the nocturnals. If you can, Milstithanog might help us when he does arrive."

Verdon felt the power but he lacked an answer to their problem. If he created a wind to blow away the flames, he'd be spreading the conflagration across the Lakwar range, killing the antelope herds and any of the rapacians that happened to be in the way. Rain? No, the fire was their protection from the creatures of Darkfall as well as their danger.

Iliki seemed glad enough to get away from the rapacian. He stayed close to the face of the cliff as he rose on the air. Twenty feet above the entrance to the cave he hovered in the air and then dropped back again.

Behind the row of defenders, Kree paced in agitation, hissing and spitting at the fire. Clariel's reassurances fell on deaf lizard ears.

"Nor-nor—that way," he pointed to the northwest. "The gr-gr-grass is wet because a stream has floo-floo . . . "

"I know where he means," Siskiel said. "But how do we get through the burning nocturnals?"

The air in the cave seemed to be losing its oxygen. The heat singed Verdon's face; the discomfort made concentration difficult.

"We travel with fire," he said to Siskiel. "If we can find a way through, we'll need to hold off the cavern creatures. Tie the grass to your spears and we'll use them for torches. Iliki will have to find us a safe path between them."

Iliki, Verdon, Clariel, and Aktar helped the rapacians to wrap the remaining grass around their spears. Clariel and Verdon had been making good use of it, and not much remained. Siskiel frowned at the few blades of dry grass on his torch.

"I will not light it until it is necessary," he said. "It will not last long."

"Iliki, you'll have to find us a way through," Verdon said to the little ferran. He had turned his back to the plain as he spoke with the little owl-man. Iliki hovered just over his head and pointed northwest.

"Ho-how about that one?"

While the others shouted in surprise, Verdon turned

to see a path through the flames. The ground still smoked, but the parched grass no longer burned. Flaming nocturnals were still twisting and moving about to the right and the left, but an escape route had magically opened for the beleaguered fighters.

"Milstithanog arrived, I see." Aktar pulled his sword, shifted his belt, and picked up his sack of supplies, ready to travel. The others did the same; this time Rala climbed onto Kree's back before anyone suggested she ride. Verdon and Woos, who carried the best torch, led the way. The rapacian lifted his feet quickly, trying not to burn them on the hot ground. At first he jogged in place, not wanting to outrun the humans. Verdon knew he and Aktar were the slowest of the group, so he sprinted as fast as he could go; the desert man was hardy and could keep pace with him. Kree trotted along behind Aktar, still hissing at the fires that flanked them. One of the other rapacians passed Verdon and kept pace with Woos.

They covered just over a hundred yards when Verdon felt water splashing around his feet. They had reached the stream. They had also passed most of the flaming nocturnals. Another group of at least fifty mossy blobs had arrived to assist their comrades.

Rala threw a fireball that landed in their midst and then made a show of unrolling her sleeves. Verdon understood the meaning of her actions.

"That's it for the mage, the rest is up to us," he shouted at the rapacians. "Us" was incorrect. Their defense would depend upon the rapacians. There had not been enough grass for him and Clariel to make more torches, and Verdon had nearly emptied his quiver. Hers remained full since she could call back her magic shafts, but her arrows were worse than useless since they multiplied the danger. Using his sparker, Verdon lit the torches of the rapacians, and they waved the flaming brands at the nocturnals as they ran down the stream.

Rala had thrown all her fire spells, but she still had

another for a ball of light. It danced over Verdon's head as he led the way along the watercourse. Aktar still splashed behind him, followed by the others. Iliki swooped down close to the bright ball and drifted on the air currents just beyond Verdon's shoulder.

"You're outrun-run—distancing the rapacians," he said. "They stopped to fi-fi—ignite the last of the nocturnals."

Verdon slowed, but before he had stopped, Clariel passed Aktar and paced him. She ran easily, with no more effort than he put into walking. Her hair streamed behind her.

"A good runner does not slow until the race is won," she said, pointing off to the left, where the magic light ball showed another small group of nocturnals. They had surrounded a group of six antelope. As Verdon glanced their way, they caught one of the antelope, swarming over it, leaving nothing but bones in their path.

Verdon increased his speed and wondered how long he could continue the sprint. The water deepened for a short distance and shallowed again as the slope increased.

"Sis-sis—the rapacian is cal-call—I can't hear what he's saying," Iliki said, dipping and nearly flipping himself over as he tried to fly in one direction and look in the other.

"Clariel?" Verdon asked. He didn't have to say more. She shook her head.

"Our splashing is too loud for me to hear. . . ." The elf suddenly disappeared below the surface of the stream.

"Clariel!" Verdon shouted, and took a step toward where she had been. He lost his footing and sank into a strong, fast current. A flaying hand touched his, and, when he came to the surface, he looked into Aktar's staring eyes.

"What—what happened?" Aktar asked.

Verdon realized the shallow stream they had been

using for a path to safety had led them into a river. The shouts of the rapacians had probably been a warning, but they had not understood. Rala's magic light still bounced over his head, and by its illumination he saw a jutting boulder just within reach. He grabbed for it, but the sudden decrease in his speed broke his grip on Aktar's arm. The desert man swirled away with the current, his eyes wide with terror.

Verdon wondered if he should climb out of the water or follow Aktar and Clariel. He might be able to help them. He decided he was no braver than Aktar; letting go the safety of the boulder seemed to take more strength than holding on to it.

Making a decision became unnecessary. Kree, with Rala still on his back, went bobbing past. The lightning lizard's swinging tail struck Verdon and knocked him away from the boulder. He went spinning along the main flow of the river again.

The magic light still bobbed along over his head. He could see the rising banks on each side of the stream. The light made a sudden dip to avoid a stone cliff. The river went underground, taking Verdon and his friends with it. The cold fear that walked up his backbone had nothing to do with the chill of the water.

He struggled to keep his head above the surface and thought at least they had not been swept over a waterfall. He was glad that danger had not occurred to him before the river went underground.

But where would the stream take them? he wondered. Would they ever see daylight again? Going over a waterfall might be preferable to their destination. Up ahead he heard Rala complaining to the lightning lizard.

"Well, duck your head, you stupid thing!"

20

Verdon lost all sense of time as the water carried him along. Still, he wondered if he were not better off than the others; Rala's magic light still bobbed along over his head, dipping and rising with the height of the ceiling. The stream curved back and forth, sometimes roaring down steep inclines, sometimes slowing a little on gentler slopes.

The bobbing light showed him no shelves or side passages offering an escape, even if he could work his way out of the main current.

He shouted for Rala, offering and wanting contact. A swirling eddy in a bend of the underground passage pulled him under the water. He bobbed to the surface, shook the water out of his eyes and ears to hear:

". . . And if I ever give you the last of my lights again, I'll deserve to be plummeted into the dark with a lightning lizard for company!"

"I'm hurrying as fast as I can!" he shouted back, glad to know the dwarf and Kree were still somewhere up ahead. He didn't waste breath trying to keep up a conversation. He could just manage to keep his head above the surface. More time passed; he tired, and wondered how long he could continue to fight the current. His clothing seemed to weigh a ton. His arms and legs took on the weight of fatigue and his fear was lost under the effort to keep swimming.

The current slowed. He felt a breeze on his face and looked up to see stars. He bumped into a creature in the dark. A head and an open mouth full of sharp, gleaming teeth swung toward him. He desperately back-paddled until he recognized Kree's soft hiss and felt a nudge. Gratefully, Verdon looped an arm around the lightning lizard's neck and drifted in the water.

"Thanks for returning my light, but did you have to use it up?" Rala demanded. "There's barely enough light to see the shore. That way, Kree, and don't spare the splashes. No, a little to the left first, there's Aktar. We might as well give him a tow while we're at it."

The lightning lizard hissed his objections, but he obediently turned and, in minutes, Verdon gazed across Kree's neck into the tired face of Aktar.

"Where do you think we are?" Verdon asked Rala.

"Down a ledge or two," she replied. "I'm just glad we didn't end up in those rotting caverns."

Verdon silently agreed, glad he had not thought of them while they were still underground. If he had considered them as a final destination, he was not sure he could have continued his struggle for survival.

"Where is Clariel?" he asked, looking across Kree's neck at Aktar. "She was ahead of you."

The lightning lizard hissed at the mention of his mistress's name. Rala, who had somehow managed to stay on the lizard's back, stood, looked around and pointed ahead.

"She's just climbing the bank."

Two minutes later the others waded out of the water and collapsed thankfully on dry soil. Verdon looked around, and in the last of the light from Rala's magic ball, he checked his weapons and ammunition. His pistols were useless. The powder was wet. His bow still hung across his shoulder, but the finely braided leather of the string had stretched, and his arrows had disappeared in the river. His sword remained in its scabbard, and he reminded himself to move it occasionally while its sheath dried or the blade would be wedged tight. The stains of the green slime had disappeared from his clothing—small comfort.

They were not without weapons. Clariel's bowstring seemed in good condition, doubtless dweomered as were her arrows, which had not been lost. Aktar had trusted to his sword and had neither bow nor quiver. Luckily, Kree's claws and teeth were impervious to a soaking, Verdon decided. They might have to trust to his and Clariel's defenses. He'd often wondered if the elf had the power to read his mind, and he wondered again as she stood and looked around.

"Raise the light," she said to the dwarf. "It would be wise to see if there is danger about before it dies."

Rala sighed, as if asking why she had to manage everything. She flicked her fingers and the ball shot up into the sky. After a minute's survey, Clariel dropped to the ground again. The faintly glowing globe plopped down, to stop eighteen inches from the soil.

"The scent of the faerkin is in the air," Clariel told them, and pointed to an area of dense vegetation twenty yards away. The tall, leafy plants rose to a height of more than six feet. "That wall of growth is a field of eodwal. The fruit of the plant is a faerkin delicacy."

"Finally a straight sentence that isn't a platitude," Rala said. "I congratulate you."

"Wisdom dictates speech be understood," Clariel replied.

"I knew it wouldn't last," the dwarf groused as she gathered the folds of her skirt and tried to wring out the water. Verdon saw the elf duck her head and wondered if he had seen a smile, or if it had been a trick of the dying light.

"Hu-man-n!" The shout came from the water, the voice of a rapacian. Verdon stood up and looked out into the darkness.

"Siskiel? Woos?" Rapacian voices were too similar for human ears to distinguish one from the other.

"Kree!" Clariel rose and jerked up one hand.

"Vredenza!" The lightning lizard hissed its objections and plunged back into the water. In minutes it returned with two rapacians clinging to its tail.

Siskiel's yellow, slitted eyes gleamed in the starlight as he shook the water from his scaly hide. He dropped his spear to the ground and sat beside it.

"You do like fast travel, human." The rapacian's mouth opened and his teeth glittered in the darkness as he grinned.

"I thought we should escape the nocturnals," Verdon replied, as if the trip down the underground river had been the plan from the beginning. The glittering teeth disappeared.

"Is there an escape from the creatures?" Woos asked, his sibilants long-drawn with resignation.

"Not on Faerkin Fields," Siskiel replied. "The little people are in more danger than the Lakwar." He told them what he had learned since his return to Skar. Until that spring, Skar had been relatively free of nocturnals. The only creatures that had bothered them had been the flyers from the desert.

"It seemed as if the evil that is Darkfall had overlooked the existence of Skar," Woos added when Siskiel stopped to catch his breath and frame the rest of his story.

"At least this part of it," Siskiel agreed. "There may still be areas that are relatively safe, but many of the unused passages of the dwarf mines and the rotting caverns have spawned monsters in the past few months." He explained his abrupt departure after their rescue from the kred nets. He had been told of a pitched battle between his people and the nocturnals. His first duty had been to report his return to his father the Sis-Rain and to be certain the Lakwar ruler had survived the fight. He also wanted his leader's permission for their group to pass through the land of the Lakwar.

"Did you deliberately ride the river down, or did you

get caught in the current?" Rala asked when Siskiel finished his story.

"We chose it, knowing you had taken the water path. It can be a dangerous way to reach the lower slope. Luckily the run was not too swift," Woos said. "And we thought you might fear the worst if you were caught unaware."

"We did," Aktar grinned.

"I'm glad it wasn't too swift," Rala said, shaking her head in disbelief. Verdon understood her sarcasm, but it passed over the heads of the rapacians.

"Yes, it could have washed you down the lake to Faerkin Falls. If you had been swept under them, you would never reach the surface again."

"I understand your father gave us permission to cross Lakwar land," Verdon said. "But will he be angry because you followed us?" Then he sensed something he could not quite define. "Or did he tell you to learn why we are here?"

Siskiel's eyes gleamed again as if they were emitting a glow of their own. The muscles of the rapacian's face moved subtly, firming into determination though the smile remained. The barest shadow of learned authority and purpose warned Verdon that Siskiel took his responsibilities to his people more seriously than he had led them to believe.

"Since the coming of Darkfall, travelers do not often come to Skar," he said softly. "A few have been vergai, the corrupted ones—"

"If you think—" Rala had bristled at the suggestion, but Siskiel's clawed hand silenced her with an imperious wave.

"The vergai do not save wounded creatures on the desert, and I doubt they are attacked by the nocturnals. But you have a reason for being here, and we will learn what it is."

"And when you know, you might tell me," Aktar snapped. "I thought we were on our way to the Burning Coast to find a power cluster."

Verdon stared at the desert trader, wondering if the water had soaked his brain, or he had deliberately given away their purpose for being in Skar. But how would Aktar know what Rala and Verdon had discussed? They had not shared their plan with the others. They had not even told Clariel or Iliki. He stopped wondering about Aktar when he felt Siskiel's stillness. The rapacian seemed to be thinking with an intensity that sharpened his features.

"We've been run off our course," Rala said. "The Worms chased us a long way."

"Without the sail carts we need to cross Skar so we can reach the path of the thunder train when it returns from Yzeem," Verdon said. "My business is with the train."

Siskiel had stared at each in turn. Then he looked pointedly at Clariel.

"The price of my honor is four hundred nocturnals," she said quietly.

"What is the count?" Verdon asked.

"Fifty-two."

"It has to be more," Rala objected.

"I can only count fifty-two, since the first shot from my bow made twelve of one."

"How many more to go?" Verdon asked.

"Three hundred and forty-eight," she said so promptly the calculation had been made previously. "I cannot return to my people until I have cleansed my guilt in the blood of nocturnals," she told Siskiel. "Until then I go on the trail that offers the most danger, and that is with the guardsman."

"And I just try to keep up," said a voice from the darkness above the group. Iliki fluttered to the ground and glared at Verdon. "Why don't you warn me before you go dipping into caverns? I nearly flew into a stone wall!"

"The next time I know, I will," Verdon replied, but he still wondered about the presence of the rapacians. "How can you leave your people now? I thought you'd stay for your Mating Feast."

Woos stood abruptly and walked away from the group. Siskiel watched him a moment before turning back.

"I spoke out of turn," Verdon said by way of apology, though he had no idea what bounds he had overstepped.

"His mate was one of the first to be lost to the nocturnals. He will not take another this season, if at all. I have yet to complete my solitary journey. I suffer the shame of having failed and having lived only because strangers brought me back to my people."

"Forgive us, we beg of you," Rala snapped.

"All is forgiven. The shame will pass if I distinguish myself in other ways. Like the elf, I believe traveling on your trail is the shortest course to proving my worth to the clan."

Verdon wondered why these people seemed to think he would lead them into terrible dangers. Left to himself, he would like to find a safe place to hide, away from the dangers of Darkfall. With all his heart he wanted a quiet life away from the fighting. He had no idea what he would do with it, but decided he could find some useful work.

But if he could find a place free of nocturnals, he knew he would not be able to stay. As long as he could help to rid his world of even some of the evils of Darkfall, he would keep fighting. He would use his arm and every usable weapon.

He wanted to reach Arasteen with his knowledge—after he had freed Marchant. All his future plans had to wait upon his duty to his foster father. He refused to think beyond his desire to meet the thunder train on its return trip. He glanced down at Iliki who sat huddled on Kree's back, his feathers fluffed to keep out the chill.

"Did Milstithanog come down the river with us or fly down with you?"

"He's just coming out of the lake now," Iliki said. "The silly thing was afraid of getting his feet wet."

They heard a gurgle and a splash out on the lake and Verdon looked around, wondering why an invisible creature that nothing seemed to touch would make noise in the water. Or had something unseen made the splash? He turned back to see Iliki's mouth hanging open, his eyes huge and staring. Verdon gripped the hilt of his sword, the only weapon still usable.

"What is it?" he asked softly.

"I—ah—thought I saw something on the water," he said. "Out beyond Milstithanog."

"You did; I see a boat," Clariel replied.

21

Verdon stared into the darkness, but he was aware of Woos, who had picked up his spear and was holding it in a defensive position. Siskiel had also noticed and kept his weapon handy.

"Aren't the faerkin friendly?" the ex-guardsman asked.

"Usually, when they know we are coming," Woos replied. "We never invade their ledges without warning. In Skar, trust is not taken for granted, especially with nocturnals and vergai traveling our slopes."

Verdon thought about what he had heard and seen since he had arrived in Skar. They had been too busy traveling or fighting nocturnals to concentrate on the questions that had been in the back of his mind.

"Do any other races live on your ledges?" he asked. It had suddenly occurred to him that he might have injured his cause by having allies that were distrusted or hated by the other races.

"No." Woos shook his head as he stared out over the water. "In this part of Skar the races trade, but they do not mix, save when some special skills are needed." He spared a glance at Verdon and turned back to watch for the approaching boat. After a thoughtful moment he continued his explanation.

"Our ancestors did not choose this place; they were driven into Skar. At first they were too few and too busy fighting starvation to bother with the other races. We think the faerkin and the dwarfs who lived below them faced the same problems in the beginning."

"Like us, they were all few in number, and driven—people injured by the rest of Aden," Siskiel said. "Distrusting everything around them but too weak in numbers to war on each other. That was an advantage, I think. There is no bitter taste of hatred and death between us, but by the time the people of each ledge were secure and could afford to trust, we had each formed our way of life, separate from each other."

Verdon nodded. Skar, or at least this part of Skar, was certainly different from the rest of the Known Lands, where the races mixed indiscriminately. Some areas had a high concentration of a particular race, like the dwarfs in Top of the World in the North Wall, but even there, humans, elves, and even ferran were outnumbered but not rare.

"If the faerkin are not your enemies, why are you worried?" Clariel asked.

"It is a breach of custom to be in the middle of their lands without their permission," Woos said. "This is no time to build walls of suspicion."

Verdon heard the approach of the boat before he saw it. Renewed splashing followed a gruff voice giving orders and a high-pitched squeal, like an animal in pain, set his teeth on edge. Several moments passed before he identified it as the screech of metal against metal. Then he heard more splashing, and, at last, the dim outlines of a strange craft came into view.

He could see little of the boat itself; three large paddle wheels on the left side blocked his view, and, as the craft drifted and turned, he saw three on the right as well. Several light voices and the gruff one began giving orders, all overriding each other.

The boat backed up, the blunt stern angling toward

the shore. Fifty feet from the bank it came to a halt with more orders and more activity.

"You on the shore, be you friend of faerkin and dwarfs, or be you enemies?" a gruff voice called. "Declare yourselves or go to your long rest!"

Woos gave a sudden laugh and relaxed the hold on his spear. He drew a breath and opened his mouth to speak, but the elf was quicker.

"We are friends of all who walk the sunlit paths," Clariel called out the traditional answer of the elves.

"And to those who revere the bones of the world." Rala attempted to shout the dwarf greeting, but her voice was still so muted Verdon wondered if the dwarf aboard the watercraft could hear her.

"And we learn Aldag Strongarm still hides among the faerkin so he does not have to work for his keep," Woos shouted. "The river that travels your land is swift and tonight it brings more than water to feed the fields."

"Woos, you old dragon, is that you?" And, after a short silence that sparkled with surprise, "Don't just stand there staring! Get those critters moving and back up this barge, we've got friends to meet. Get ready to put out the boarding way. You there, move when I tell you! Get my friend Woos and his companions on board and find me my antelope fat! I can't hear myself think over that squeal." After several more shouted orders the boat backed toward the shore.

"That stern should be large enough even for Milstithanog," Aktar said as the boat moved closer.

Iliki had never mentioned the demon's size, but Verdon thought the desert trader might be right. The thirty-foot-wide stern of the craft extended back twenty feet from the paddle wheels. Ten feet from the low bank the boat stopped and a long plank extended out to drop neatly on the bank.

Woos strode up the foot-wide board. He stepped off onto the deck and stood grinning at the sturdy dwarf who glared up at him, arms akimbo. A desert dwarf, not as stocky as his kindred in the other lands, and darker in complexion. His face blended with his dark beard; his eyes and teeth gleamed in the starlight. "Hauling Lakwar is not my trade," the dwarf huffed. "And how will you be paying for your passage?"

"Don't be in such a hurry, short one. The fee will be paid, and more than you deserve, bush-face."

While the rapacian and the dwarf argued, the others boarded and Verdon looked around with interest. The lake craft measured a good eighty feet in length and ten paces across except for the bow. It narrowed to a blunt point, only a slight consideration to streamlining. It was hardly more than a raft surrounded by three-foot-high gunwales. In the center a platform rose four feet above the deck, and on it stood a young faerkin woman with her hand on the tiller. At the rear of the platform a short ladder allowed the small faerkin easy climbing access to the helm. Behind it and on both sides, square chests made of a light wooden frame-work and woven grass sides had been lashed in place with ropes. As a concession to a dangerous time, a three-foot-wide passage had been left between the cargo and the gunwales. More than a dozen faerkin stood guard duty, with short bows in their hands.

After his trip down the underground river, Kree objected to boarding the boat. Clariel coaxed him into the water, insisted he climb on board, and ordered him to lie down in the stern. Aktar insisted on explaining the presence of Milstithanog to the faerkin and warned them not to step into the empty area where he would travel.

Verdon wondered whether the demon had actually boarded the craft, and whether the desert man cared about the demon's comfort or just wanted the faerkin to know the travelers had a magic creature with them.

Woos and Aldag Strongarm traded tales about the nocturnals from the rotting caverns. Verdon had already heard much of the news, and he wanted to know what powered the huge, awkward craft. Inside the gunwales the eight-foot-tall paddle wheels were mated with treadmills. The inside mechanisms, made of slatted wood set in iron rings, held large mengari, heavy-bodied rodents. The creatures fretted, trying to climb the slats. While he watched the mengari, Aldag and Woos threaded their way up the side of the craft.

"Put the beasties to bed; we'll stay here for the night," Aldag ordered a faerkin. "The shallows will protect us."

Verdon blocked their passage so he walked on ahead of them until he came to a shelter built on the forward deck. The faint light from inside threw the framework's silhouette against the fabric of the walls. The temporary structure consisted of a series of panels, wooden frames covered with cloth, and lashed together with short pieces of rope. The ingenious structure could be re-formed in minutes to accommodate added passengers or to make room for more cargo.

Aldag led the way into the shelter, roofed with the same panels, supported by upright poles set in holes in the deck. Verdon ducked at the low entrance, intended only for dwarfs and faerkin. The pitch of the canvas roof allowed him to stand upright in the center.

Inside the shelter, faerkin lights bobbed close to the ceiling, bouncing over the heads of the individuals who entered. The light that had assigned itself to Verdon had considerable trouble as it attempted to stay above him. His hair brushed the ceiling and the glow bounced about his left shoulder.

"You'd better sit down, tall one, or you'll drive that little beastie into exploding," Aldag said with a grin.

Verdon looked around. Thick straw mats covered most of the floor, and he decided against using them because of his wet clothing. He sat on the floor and the light came to rest over his head. It settled in the air with a little bounce reminiscent of a sigh.

"It's food you'll be wanting, or I'm a lizard man," Aldag said. "And something warming to the stomach in your cup," the dwarf continued. He issued orders to the ten faerkin that had followed them into the shelter. Some obeyed with varying degrees of speed; four completely ignored him as they stared at the strangers.

Verdon watched as five knelt around a low table, preparing their food. He realized he was famished. He had not eaten since their short rest at noon the day before.

He was also interested in the faerkin of Skar. The little people, half-human, half-faerie, lived throughout the Known Lands. Like most people, he expected the inhabitants of Skar to be different, as if their life in the giant gorge had somehow changed them. They were the same as far as he could see, though possibly a little smaller than their kindred in Urbana. Only one stood four feet tall, topping his companions by at least six inches. Like the rest of his people, he had dark hair and his skin tone seemed to be darker than the Urbanan faerkin, but that could have been a trick of the dim lighting. Like their brethren in the rest of the Known Lands, they were slender, the biceps of their upper arms and thighs barely noticeable. They wore short, sleeveless tunics caught in at the waist with leather belts that bristled with knives, and each wore a short scabbard with the hilt of a blade rising above the waist.

They could have been mistaken for human children playing with toy weapons until one saw their faces. Their eyes, larger than humans', held the sadness of the ages. Like the elves, their faces seemed to be all points, but possibly because of their half-human origins, they lacked the delicate beauty of the elves.

The faerkin produced thick slabs of roasted meat in fresh, small, crusty bread loaves, and a bowl of yellow claws. Verdon tore off a piece of his loaf, a size that Iliki could manage, and gave it to the ferran. The travelers were given small cups of a highly spiced fiery ale. Verdon's first swallow burned his throat and warmed his stomach. He sat with Clariel and Aktar. Rala had stood in the doorway for a moment, looked around, and threaded her way between the mats to join an old faerkin who sat at the other end of the long shelter. Verdon could see little beneath the cloak that shrouded him like a tent.

While they ate, Verdon heard the drone of an incantation, one being spoken with the monotony of repetition. He paid no attention to it until Clariel gave a start and touched her clothing. Verdon rubbed a hand across his pants leg and his tunic. Even his sword belt was dry.

He laid aside his meat roll and checked the pouches of black powder still fastened to his belt. The grains were dry and free, running easily through his fingers.

"So you're traveling through Skar, wanting to reach the other side," Aldag said. When no one answered the dwarf, Verdon looked up and realized the dwarf had been addressing him.

"The desert outlaws chased us off our path," he said, sticking with the story they had told the rapacians. He had finished his meat roll and picked up the yellow claw, a tropical fruit that grew in bunches. He pulled back the skin and broke off a piece for Iliki, but the ferran was sharing Clariel's fruit.

"I need to reach the other side in time to intercept the thunder train coming up from Yzeem."

"Then you'll be wanting the water-vator." Aldag nodded as if the information confirmed his suspicions. "From there it be not far from the middle bridge of the Reaching Deep."

"If it's still passable," Woos said.

"Aye, if it be passable," Aldag agreed.

"Do you mean we'll have trouble crossing this bridge?" Verdon didn't care for what he heard. Perhaps the people who lived on the other side of the river were enemies.

"There's been trouble a century or more, but there's no saying but what the shadow dwarfs have put up the new span by now."

"It's possible to cross," Woos said when he saw Verdon's doubt. "Ten years ago we thought it was one of the most dangerous places in the Known Lands—"

"But the peril fades beside the evils of Darkfall," Aldag finished for the rapacian. "Still it be a long distance yet to walk, and rest is what you'll be needing."

The faerkin placed two mats together for the humans and the elf. Siskiel, who had been silent throughout the meal, and Woos settled on the floor, claiming that soft beds led to soft bodies.

Knowing the faerkin were keeping watch, Verdon took advantage of the security and slept well. He awoke to find himself alone in the shelter except for an elderly faerkin he had not noticed the night before. Verdon sat up and rubbed his face, knowing he would be hearing from Aktar and Rala about his late rising, but he didn't mind. As a warrior he knew the value of rest when he could get it, and he liked his sleep.

He found a pan of warm water and splashed some on his face, deciding he liked his luxuries, too. When he had dried his eyes the elderly faerkin had crossed the floor of the shelter. The wrinkles on the small humanoid's face moved with his smile as he handed Verdon a cup of steaming faerkin tea. "You slept well?" he asked.

"I did and thank you," Verdon answered. "I've learned to take my rest when I can get it and sleep as sound as I dare."

"And now you go to the shadow dwarfs to get a power cluster," the elderly faerkin said. He saw the surprise in the human's eyes and his smile softened. "In these times of trouble, magicians of like purpose assist each other. Don't blame the mage Rala for asking advice of those who know these lands. And it was necessary for her to tell us your need so we should advise her properly."

"I'm thankful for any help we receive," Verdon said. Since Aktar had blurted out the purpose of their journey, there was no reason to try for secrecy.

"What will you do when you have completed your quest?"

"I don't know," Verdon admitted after a few moments' thought. "I haven't thought beyond my present goal."

"You will possess a powerful weapon. Many will press you to use it in their behalf. Some will have genuine need, some will try to manipulate you out of greed."

Verdon stared down into his tea as he considered what he had been told. He knew the old faerkin was correct in his assessment, but he seemed to take it for granted that the guardsman would find a cluster. Verdon was less certain.

"Will you look at what the future can offer?"

Verdon wondered if he wanted to know. He kept staring into the cup. He was still working on his decision when the tea cleared, as if it had been changed to water, and an image appeared. He saw Lord Urbana. He heard no words, saw no movement, but felt the pull of desire. Riches unthought of were his for the taking. The rhanate of the Black Citadel next appeared in the cup, and other world leaders followed. They all offered wealth and power and Verdon was not too high-minded to feel greed for both. Beyond them, offering little but danger, were groups of people, some worn and tired with hard journeys, others, like the faerkin, were watching him with wistful eyes, offering nothing but gratitude. Everyone seemed to want something from him, and he felt the frustration of being only one person, of only being able to be in one place at a time. The images faded, the tea was just tea, but Verdon's mind was in a turmoil.

"Is this my future, to be pulled in all directions?" he demanded of the faerkin mage.

"It was not the future you saw unless you make it so," the elder said softly. "No magic can give you prophecy. What you saw was the truth hidden in the deepest recesses of your mind. Most of us know the result of our deeds before we act, yet for most of us our hopes or fears hide the truth. I have only stripped away your pretenses."

Verdon nodded. He knew the mage was right. Several times since leaving the Black Citadel he had banished wisps of random thoughts that were akin to what he thought he saw in the tea. Suddenly he wanted to flee Skar and forget about the cluster. The responsibility of ownership would be tremendous. He could do great good or great harm, and doubted he had the wisdom always to act in Aden's best interests.

"I-I could use it for my needs and pass it along to another, more powerful essencer, someone with more wisdom in its use," he said lamely. He still wanted the gem. He needed it to free Worsten.

"Once you take it you cannot pass it on," the faerkin said. "A power crystal controlled by a magician can pass from hand to hand, and in ancient times, wars were fought over them. One possessed by the user of the world force can only be wielded by the one who draws it from its bed in the world's surface. Wars could be fought over you, but not the crystal itself."

"You have a purpose in telling me this," Verdon said, knowing what the elder would say, but still needing to hear it. He felt as if he were flaying himself, because he would acquiesce without any intention of keeping his word.

"All people need help in these times," the elder said. "Many can protect themselves because they are large, strong, and knowledgeable in war. Our people, those of Faerkin Fields, are strong for our size, but we are small in comparison with most races and with the nocturnals. We have lived in peace for more than a millennium and are not warriors. Our protection has always been our value to our neighbors. We know little of battles. Few of our people can hit a target with a bow and arrow. You may think me selfish in asking for your help, but we are of value. Our crops feed many in Skar. They, too, would suffer because of our loss."

"I cannot promise anything," Verdon said slowly. He

had been intending to say he would return and assist
the faerkin against the nocturnals of the rotting caverns. A half promise would keep the old one from
pleading with him. But when he looked into those wise
eyes, he knew he couldn't lie.

"I may not live to return. I don't know what forces
will pull me once I have the crystal, or even if I can get
one."

"You could not speak fairer," the faerkin said softly.
"A promise I would distrust. I can see many paths in
your future. It is not magic that tells me this. The hope
and greed of others will pull at you."

"I think I fear those hopes and needs more than the
greed," Verdon said.

"You are wise to do so," the old one agreed.

They left the shelter and walked out on deck. Iliki
perched on the ridgepole of the shelter. Clariel was in
the stern of the boat with Kree, and Aktar stood in the
bow, staring out over the water. Rala sat in the sun-
shine, studying her scroll of spells.

On the port side of the boat, two faerkin were
attempting to remove one mengari from the treadmill
and put another in its place. The first playful animal
wanted to remain, the second wanted the wheel, and
the two creatures twisted their long bodies together as
they vied for the position. The paddle wheel raced,
throwing the boat off course. Aldag swore at the
faerkin and the mengari. Neither paid the slightest
attention.

The wide, low vessel moved with steady but stately
progress down the long lake between the cultivated
fields that gave the land its name. Occasionally he saw
small groups of dwellings and thought them tiny villages or farmsteads. A few were close enough to the
shore for him to see their sturdy wooden framework
and their woven grass sides. He spotted most of them
because of their high, conical grass roofs. One group
sat near the shore and tiny faerkin children played in
the shade of strange trees with single leaves six feet

long. Nearly as long were the clusters of green fruit that hung from the trees. Yellow claws, not yet ripe, he realized.

Verdon looked out on the placid lake and wished all of Aden could be as calm and trouble-free as the surface of that sparkling water. The depths of the lake probably held dangers—he remembered the gurgle before the arrival of the boat the night before. Darkfall had spread evil everywhere, and he considered the position he would make for himself if he found a power crystal.

Perhaps he could just turn around and follow his original plan. He could go to Arasteen, join King Corben's army, and let someone else do the thinking.

But what would happen to Marchant Worsten if he did? What other indignities would his foster father's spirit suffer at the hands of the Iron Tyrant's magicians?

No, he would continue, he'd try for the crystal, and pay the price willingly if he could free Marchant's spirit. But would he be able to release his foster father from his bondage?

22

The raft continued its stately way down the lake. Verdon could have walked faster, *Iliki* could have walked faster, but the travelers enjoyed the ride. The faerkin were intensely interested in everything around them. They watched the shore, exclaiming over and discussing every new field under cultivation, the height of the crops, the small animals that peered from beneath the bushes, and waved exuberantly at the faerkin they saw on the shore. They questioned the companions about the news of the outside world and were particularly interested in how their own race lived in the lands where they shared everyday life with humans, elves, dwarfs, and ferran. From the few questions Verdon asked, he learned that the few dwarfs who had designed their lake boats—they insisted they were boats, not rafts—and the dwarfs who maintained and ran the water-vator were their only constant contact with other races. Not all the land of Faerkin Fields was under cultivation. From the lake, Verdon could see numerous copses of woods. The villages they passed were set well back from the shore, and only the tall, conical thatched roofs were visible from the raft.

Faerkin Fields was Skar's breadbasket, and before Darkfall their produce had also added to the diets of many desert tribes. The dwarfs had handled the trading, and the little people never left the safety of their land. They were merry little tricksters and excellent thieves. They practiced their skills on each other and on the travelers. Verdon discovered he had lost a bag of pistol balls and two small black powder sacks when a laughing faerkin returned them.

As the morning progressed and they sailed further out on the ledge that made up Faerkin Fields, Verdon looked out onto the clouds that often filled the gorge. An hour later they had burned away and he could barely see the gray-green of the opposite slope.

"I feel as if I'm looking at a mountain," he told Clariel.

"It would be a large mountain indeed," she replied. "I wonder if the other side is plagued by nocturnals."

"Do you ever think of anything but your guilt?" Verdon asked.

"Is there anything else?" Her large slanted eyes coolly met his for a moment before she looked away. They were still filled with pain.

"I wonder whether you help or harm your dead comrades with your grief," he said slowly, trying to say what had been growing in his mind for days. "Does your pain help to free them or does it keep them bound to Aden?" For once he had her full attention, but after a moment she turned away and went back to scratch Kree's nose. She stood staring out over the water, but for the first time she looked south, toward her homeland.

At midday the raft stopped and backed up to a stone pier. The faerkin rushed to unload the cargo. The pier, the walk that led from it, and the structure half a mile away all looked to be the work of the rapacians. Verdon asked Siskiel about it as they left the raft.

"Yes, stone is easy for us. Nearly as easy as it is for the dwarfs. Wood is not. We lack the delicacy with tools."

Verdon remembered the well-constructed huts with the flimsy roofs on the lower ledge of the Lakwar.

"Our people trade in meat and hides," Siskiel continued. "The faerkin use little meat themselves, and our hides last a long time. Building the pier and the structures gave us credit for trade."

"Ready to hang in midair for five miles?" Aldag asked Verdon before the ex-guardsman could question the Lakwar about what they took in return for their labor. Verdon completely forgot about the trade balance of Skar. A drop of five miles?

"You're making a joke," Aktar said cautiously. He looked at Verdon, wanting confirmation.

"I've heard of the water-vator," Rala spoke up. "Is it as awesome as tales tell?"

"You'll soon see for yourselves," Aldag replied as they neared the first stone building. "You'll start your descent right away. We'll need the vator when we've unloaded the boat."

Verdon followed Aldag into the largest and tallest structure. It measured twenty by forty feet in width and its height matched its length. They followed Aldag into an eight-foot-wide passage between the walls that had to be at least six feet thick. Directly ahead a gate of iron rods prevented them from stepping off into a dark, square hole. Four paces beyond the first, a second hole went down into the ground. Thirty feet above their heads a shaft, thicker than Kree's body, extended from wall to wall and on it hung a gigantic cogged wheel, at least twenty feet in diameter. From where he stood, Verdon thought it was probably five or six feet thick.

The wheel rotated slowly. A chain, with iron links as thick as his arm, was slowly moving over it. The massive walls had dampened the sound from outside the structure, but inside the noise was deafening. The chain came up through the hole by the gate. In minutes a heavy coupling came into view. Attached to the coupling were four strong cables that widened into a square and, as the chain continued to rise, the travelers saw they were attached to the top of a wooden cage.

The frame of the eight-foot-square box was made of massive timbers. The floor and ceiling were solid, but the sides were wooden slats two inches thick and set eight or more inches apart. The boxy carrier came to a stop with the floor only inches above the stone pavement of the building.

Aldag stepped over to the wall, slid an iron bar forward, and turned it, using the hook at the far end to secure the cage so it would not sway. He then opened the building's iron door and, last, the door built into the cage.

"Enjoy your ride." He grinned at their visible doubts. "It's the easiest travel you'll have in Skar."

Verdon stepped cautiously aboard, followed by Rala, who made it plain she had no doubts about the invention of her people. Aktar hung back, so Clariel led Kree on board. The lightning lizard balked and hissed, but the elf's will prevailed. The large lizard was nearly twice as long as the cage, so his neck and tail curled around his body.

"Iliki, you ride with him," Clariel ordered. "He'll feel more comfortable."

"Trus-trus—put myself on that thing?" the ferran screeched back-winging as he hovered above their heads just out of reach.

"Never!"

"Get in here," Verdon ordered. If the little owl-man could keep the lightning lizard from panicking and trampling them, they needed the ferran.

Aktar and Siskiel stepped into the cage after the lizard boarded. Aldag had just closed the door when a faerkin came dashing up. He carried a bow and a quiver in one hand, an extra bundle of arrows in the other. "A gift for the desert man and arrows for the guardsman," he said, passing them to Siskiel.

Verdon shouted his thanks and just had time to place half the shafts in his own quiver when two faerkin lights danced into the cage and they started to move. He gripped the bars as they started down. The lengths of the chain, passing over the wheel, caused the water-vator cage to drop in small regular jerks. In the beginning their movement was barely perceptible. By the time the cage had lowered into the shaft in the ground, they were descending at a constant speed.

Kree shifted and hissed until Clariel rubbed his nose.

"How do they know they won't drop us?" Aktar asked, holding to a bar of the cage while he stretched to look over the body of the lightning lizard at the dwarf mage.

"On the other end of the cable is a second cage holding a tank of water," she replied. "They adjust the level of the water to maintain a balance."

"I just hope the tank doesn't develop a leak," Aktar muttered.

"How can that keep us traveling at a steady pace?" Verdon asked.

"I don't know," Rala admitted.

They continued down, moving slowly, but descending faster than they had when they took the switchback trails between the Lakwar ledges. Verdon guessed they had traveled a quarter of a mile when they heard the noise that had, until that time, been so subdued he had thought it was wind across a fissure in the stone of the ledge. It grew to thunder in the next quarter of a mile and then, by the faerkin light, they saw a giant water wheel and massive gears. The chain passed between a pair of cogs and Rala nodded.

"I guess the balance tank isn't the only reason it's called a water-vator," she shouted when they had passed the water wheel and the underground river.

They descended another half mile and light filtered in around the bottom of the cage. The two faerkin lights danced out between the bars and sailed back up the shaft as the passengers blinked at the daylight.

"What a beautiful view," Rala said, looking around with wide eyes.

To the east they could see the face of the cliff nearly a mile away. The same distance to the west a wide sheet of falling water hid much of Skar's western slope. They still hung in the shadow of an overhang that reached between the two. Far away to the west, the other side of the giant gorge seemed closer and greener.

"I'm glad it's not raining," Rala said. "Still the overhang might protect us."

Verdon put his head through the bars to look down and pulled it back quickly. Aldag had said the water-vator descended for five miles. That seemed an exaggeration, but they were more than a mile above the next ledge, high enough for his stomach to object to the view.

Iliki, who had been sitting on Kree's shoulder, walked along the lightning lizard's spine toward Verdon. He twitched his wings nervously. His round eyes sparkled, reflecting the sunlight.

"I don't like this," he said quietly. "Hanging in midair without the use of my wings is scary."

"Think of us, hanging in midair without wings," Verdon replied. "And where is Milstithanog?" He wondered why they always left the demon out of their travel plans.

"He's—ah—riding on top," Iliki said after a slight hesitation. "He doesn't mind the water-vator, he finds it interesting and thanks you for asking."

Verdon felt a stab of guilt. The invisible creature had helped them several times. Even if it sometimes went off on its own when they needed it most, it had saved their lives.

"Can Milstithanog help against those if they attack?" Clariel asked quietly. Verdon looked to the west, following her gaze. He thought he saw large birds, nothing to worry about until one disappeared on the other side of the waterfall, more than a mile away. Definitely large, he decided, when distance gave him a perspective.

"Crandow," Siskiel said. "Be still. If they don't see

movement, they may think the cage holds nothing but produce."

"Crandow are carnivores, but just natural creatures," Clariel said calmly. "To unnecessarily destroy what nature gave the world lessens all of Aden."

"Would you rather dine, or be dinner?" Verdon asked her as he checked his pistols, making sure the pans were full of dry powder and the balls were firmly wedged in place.

"They live by their natures while I live to fight evil," Clariel replied. "They exist by destroying other natural creatures. I destroy nocturnals. On the whole my life is worth more to Aden than theirs." While she spoke she strung her bow and fitted an arrow to the string. "Still, I will not kill them if they can be driven off."

"Iliki, can Milstithanog chase away the crandow?" Verdon asked the bird-man.

The ferran looked up at the solid top of the cage as if he could see through it. He shook his head.

"He's bu-bus—fully occupied just holding on."

"Perhaps the mage can drive them away," Clariel suggested.

Verdon frowned as he realized the elf and the dwarf seldom spoke directly to each other, but at that moment he lacked the time or inclination to consider their relationship. He glanced down at Rala, who shook her head.

"The crandow are not magical, but they have a resistance to spells," she said. "There are a few mages in the Known Lands who could drive them off, but I'm not one of them. The elf may have to choose between eating or being eaten."

They had been speaking softly, and as the crandow drifted closer, inspecting the cart, they froze according to the rapacian's instructions. Siskiel and Aktar gripped the vertical bars of the cage to steady themselves. Clariel braced herself with one hand on Kree's head, cautioning him to remain silent.

Verdon and Rala stood together with Iliki right in

front of them. The crandow hovered ten feet away, watching for movement. Satisfied the water-vator car held nothing of interest, it turned to soar away when Rala sneezed.

The sudden noise startled Kree into roaring. Siskiel jumped half a foot and dropped his spear. He slipped and nearly fell as he tried to catch it before it clattered against the wooden floor. He did not succeed. Rala sneezed again.

"That ferran is a menace," she announced as she tried to stop a third explosion. They had forgotten her allergy to the bird-man's feathers.

"I tol—warned you I shouldn't ride in this thing," Iliki said crossly.

"Now it's eat or be eaten," Clariel said calmly as she watched as the crandow turned back toward the water-vator cage."

23

Verdon held the first of his pistols in his hand as the giant bird swept toward the cage of the water-vator. When the faerkin had handed Aktar the bow and arrows, he had laid them aside as if he saw no purpose in them, but the threat of the crandow had changed his mind. He strung the bow and nocked an arrow in place. Clariel held her weapon with the shaft pointed toward the bottom of the cage, but she watched the large bird's approach.

As it came closer, Verdon saw it was no bird but a flying reptile, a winged predator with cunning, intelligent eyes glaring at him from a head that was more than half mouth and teeth. Fragile skin wings were powered by pectorals bulging beneath the dark, gray-blue skin. The flyer measured nearly fifteen feet from its head to rump and the long tail added another ten. Eight-inch claws poised, ready to grab its prey.

It flew within range of a good bowman, but Verdon held his pistol, at the distance as accurate and as useful as a tossed pebble. Aktar waited because he was no bowman. Clariel loosed a shaft, angling for the creature's wing. With the unerring accuracy that made her an excellent warrior, she pierced the hide, and the creature screamed, veering away, spun, as the velocity of the wind ripped the tear from the arrow, and slowed to regain control. It turned away and slowly glided west, across the gorge, a torn leaf, dependent upon the winds.

The arrow had barely passed through the wing when Clariel let out the musical whistle that called her shaft back again.

"That's done it, that's driven them away," Rala said with satisfaction as five other crandow turned to fly alongside their wounded companion. They flew so close together Verdon wondered how they could stay in the air.

"You've just made them reconsider their attack," Siskiel said. "They are not cowed so easily."

"What are they?" Verdon asked, watching as the five veered away from the one Clariel had hit. They were flying in a tight circle. They gave the appearance of being in council.

"Reptiles, we think," the rapacian replied. "I do not know if they have ever been classified. "Don't underestimate them. They are intelligent enough to use simple strategy."

The crandow continued to circle for several minutes and then split apart. One flew to the south, staying just out of range of Clariel's bow. She followed it with the point of her arrow and lowered the point.

"It seems to understand the limits of my bow," she said. "It's staying just out of range."

"So is that one." Siskiel pointed his spear at a second that hovered between them and the waterfall.

"They're flanking us," Verdon said, watching the first. It had swung north until the descending watervator cage was between it and its fellow attacker. He handed the cocked pistol to Rala and grabbed his bow. He could not compete with the elf's accuracy, but he would have a better chance with an arrow at a distance.

Both crandow rose in the air and dived on the cage at the same time. The angle of their approach presented the smallest target possible. Their speed brought them close to the cage before Verdon could even sight the bow.

Clariel sent an arrow flying toward the one attacking from the direction of the waterfall. She missed with a fatal shot, but she had creased the skin on the creature's head. It screamed and sailed away. The second broke off its attack just as Verdon sent an arrow in its direction.

Clariel called back her arrow, muttering at having missed her shot. They watched as the two flying reptiles sailed away to join the other three. The crandow circled again. Discussing tactics? "They're not leaving," Aktar said.

"They'll be back," Siskiel replied. He gripped his spear in his frustration. The beasts would have to reach the cage before he could assist with their defense. Verdon understood his feelings. The young future leader of the Lakwar hated leaving his safety in the hands of humans and an elf. He wanted a chance to prove himself.

Six of the seven in the cage watched anxiously as the crandow circled. Kree watched, but his attitude seemed to be idle interest. The reptiles were flying so close together that from the distance of nearly a mile they seemed to be touching wing tips.

"At first they sent in one, and the next time two," Aktar pointed out. "What if they all attack at once? We only have three bows."

"We won't have to worry about it until we're in the open again," Siskiel said.

The rest of the group had been looking up toward the crandow, so their entrance into another vertical shaft in the ground caught them by surprise.

"We haven't traveled five miles," Rala objected.

"Closer to three," Siskiel replied. His long-drawn sibilants seemed more noticeable in the darkness. "We are not yet at the bottom, only nearing the entrance to the dwarf mines."

"We can't shoot anything down here," Rala said. "I really wish you'd take your pistol back, Verdon. It's getting heavy."

"You two aren't playing with gunnes in the dark?" Iliki asked, his voice hoarse. "I don't trust those things in the daylight, and in the pitch-blackness, I object."

"If he doesn't take it, I may drop it and blow off one of Kree's feet—if I don't get one of my own," the dwarf replied.

Verdon fumbled to replace his arrow in the quiver, shouldered his bow, and reached out a hand in the direction of Rala's voice. His estimate was exact, too exact. He put his hand in her mouth and she nipped him.

"Ouch!"

"What were you doing? I'm not holding the pistol between my teeth!"

"I'll kill the one who shoots Kree," Clariel threatened.

"Be still, keep the pistol still," Verdon warned Rala. "Just let me find you—I've found your head. . . ."

"And that's my eye!"

"Sorry, I've got your shoulder, your arm—fate's fortune, you're pointing that thing straight at *me*."

"Will you two quit teasing?" Iliki pleaded.

"Just give it to me before it goes off," Verdon said, taking the weapon from Rala. As he fumbled in the dark his finger found the trigger before he knew what he held. The explosion in the confines of the shaft was deafening.

His head still rang when he heard the rapacian's sibilants. "Did you shoot anyone important?"

"Rala?" Verdon thought the gun had been pointed away from her but the pitch-black darkness confused him. Kree roared and surged up again. Siskiel and Aktar were shouting at the lizard, who pressed them against the side of the cage. Clariel threatened everyone, particularly Verdon and Rala.

"I think you blew out my eardrums," the dwarf answered Verdon. "Otherwise, I'm fine. Iliki?"

Kree hissed and fidgeted, but he settled down after a warning growl in Verdon's ear. Iliki complained, afraid he would be thrown off the lizard's back.

"I don't blame you, Kree," Aktar spoke up. "Being trapped in the dark with a group of madmen is not to my taste either."

"It won't be dark much longer," Clariel said. There's light below."

In another five minutes the cage of the water-vator came to a halt in a torchlit cavern. A dwarf stood waiting, holding an ax. As soon as the cage stopped he opened the door, stepped in, and closed it behind him. He gave a whistle and, before the others realized what had happened, the cage started down again.

"Obrin Quickfoot at your service," he said. Verdon just had time to see his courteous bow before the top of the cage shut out the light.

"We received word that you were traveling down to the bridge, and I have been assigned to be your guide. The trails are not difficult, but there are several blind paths."

"We thank you for your assistance," Verdon said.

"Quickfoot?" Rala repeated the name. "Are you related to the Quickfoots at Top of the World?"

"It is said we have relatives there, but I do not know any names beyond the time our people came to Skar."

"Your nearest ancestor in Arasteen?" Rala pursued.

"Stander, called the Digger, is the last that I know of," Obrin said.

"And he had two sons, Chamis and Regian," Rala said. "Chamis left to seek his fortune in the western area. . . ."

"And is my ancestor," Obrin volunteered.

"And Regian is mine," Rala supplied.

"And now we will be treated to a thousand years of dwarf lineage," Aktar snapped. "I'd rather listen to Verdon's pistols."

"Only 750," Rala retorted. "And don't give me an excuse to yank a gunne out of the guardsman's belt."

The rest listened as the dwarfs happily chatted about their lineage since the division of the two branches of their family. Aktar's complaint seemed to be for form's sake. Verdon had no avid interest in the history of a dwarf family, but the discussion filled the time as they descended through the darkness. They had caught up on four hundred years of lineage when the growing light filtering through from the bottom of the cage announced their imminent return to the open air.

The sun had moved far to the west, and they blinked as it blinded them after their trip down the dark shaft. Verdon dropped his gaze and turned to the east while his eyes adjusted to the change in light. They had emerged below a sloping overhang and, as Verdon judged the distance, they were a mile and a half above another ledge. The ground below them was even greener, and when he looked to the west again, he could see a few clouds. To the west and nearly on the level with the ground below them, he could see a huge ledge and a depth of the green that had to indicate trees. The clouds obscured his vision of the upper slopes.

Siskiel saw the direction of his gaze.

"Those ledges are elfin lands," he said. "The desert elves do not live in forests, but most of the others do, or so our tales tell."

"It would be a strange elf who did not revere the wooded lands," Clariel said, staring across the gorge. "Those trees are worthy of great reverence. They are larger than those in the tales of the Crystal Forest."

The ledge was at least ten miles away, so the others squinted, but their eyes could not compete with the long-sighted elf. Verdon looked over Kree's shoulder. Rala leaned sideways to peer around the lizard's rump. Only the lightning lizard, uninterested in the elfin wood, noticed their approaching danger. He hissed and barked short little roars. No one paid any attention to him until he shifted his position. Verdon glanced at him in irritation and noticed the direction of his gaze. The warrior looked up and jerked his bow off his shoulder.

"Crandow!" he shouted to the others as three flying reptiles swooped toward the water-vator cage. He pulled the second of the loaded pistols from his belt, handing it to Rala. He reached for an arrow as the first huge reptile slammed into the side of the cage and sent it spinning. The clawed feet caught the wooden bars and the screech of tearing wood blended with the scream of the reptile.

With his bow in one hand and an arrow in the other, Verdon had no time or hands to reach for another weapon. He jabbed the arrow into the tough hide of the monster's left foot, stabbing as if it were a knife. The crandow twisted, trying to get its jaws between the bars, but Verdon kept stabbing. The beast released the cage, dropped fifty feet as it caught the wind under its wings, and sailed up again.

The cage spun and swayed on its huge chain. The riders gripped the bars to keep from being thrown to the floor. Kree hissed and scrabbled, knocking Verdon and Rala against the bars that had splintered in the grip of the crandow. Verdon felt them give as he fell against them. He dropped his bow and his arrow as he grabbed for the lightning lizard's leg. Rala held on to his belt as she steadied herself.

"Don't drop the gunne," he warned her. He did manage to put a foot on his bow to keep it from sliding between the bars, but his first arrow was already falling more than a mile to the lower ledge.

"More coming," Aktar warned. "I can't shoot while we're spinning."

"Nor I," Clariel said. "The mage could help us."

"I'm busy just holding on," Rala snapped.

Verdon chose his time, released his hold with his right hand, and picked up his bow. He slid it over his shoulder and caught the side of the cage directly behind Kree. The bars seemed to be firm. He took a good grip with his left hand and pulled out his third pistol as another crandow swooped toward the cage. He waited until the flying reptile dipped out of sight and rose, its feet extended to get a grip on the bars. He fired into the muscular chest. Dark, nearly purple blood spouted from a hole the size of Verdon's fist.

The monster's scream lingered for a while as the wings collapsed and it fell out of sight. The noise of the gunne caused two others to soar away. They joined the remaining two and the four wheeled around the dropping vator car, staying just out of range of Clariel's bow.

Verdon watched them for a moment and then grabbed Kree's tail, wrapping it around himself. He kept his eyes on the wide flank of the lightning lizard to ease the dizziness caused by the spinning cage. With careful movements he loaded a charge of powder into the gunne he still held, and rammed a ball home. He found it more difficult to fill the pan, and spilled a full charge of powder on the lizard's back. The dizziness passed and he loaded his second wheel lock with less trouble. With weapon one in his holster and the second in his hand, he turned to search out the flying predators. He saw three.

"What happened to the fourth?" he asked Rala.

"I don't know, it just flew up and out of sight. It may have been the one you stabbed in the foot."

"Or it may not have been," Verdon said, staring uneasily at the ceiling of the cage. The scream from above him told him he was right. The carrier jerked and swayed.

"There's one on top!" Aktar shouted. He could have saved his breath, they all knew it.

"Give me a boost," Obrin shouted to Siskiel. "I know how to take care of that monster. Give me a boost."

"Don't put your arm outside the cage," Rala warned, but she was too late. With reptilian reflexes the rapacian had hoisted the dwarf, who thrust his right arm out of the cage, hacking with his ax. Verdon found a handhold, stepped onto Kree's left flank, and aimed his pistol to shoot over the top of the cage, roughly toward the center. The scream of a wounded crandow immediately followed the roar of Verdon's shot. The body of the bird, with one wing dangling, tumbled over the side of the cage and hung as if suspended, its jaws clamped to one of the four support cables attached to the roof.

The recoil of the one-handed shot nearly tore the gunne from Verdon's hand, and he lost his footing. He slid off Kree's back and fell against the already-splintered bars. They gave under his weight. He desperately grabbed for Kree's foot when the support cable, gripped by the wounded crandow, gave way. The cage tilted, and Kree slid down to trap Obrin and Siskiel and Aktar against the bars.

Clariel grabbed a handhold and swung her legs up over the shoulders of the lightning lizard. She landed halfway across Rala, who had been flung on top of Kree. Iliki fluttered at the top of the cage.

Verdon hung, half in, half out of the carrier, his weight balancing him against the tilted floor. Another crandow wheeled in, arrowing straight for him.

24

Verdon dangled half in, half out of the water-
vator car. On his back and nearly helpless, he
thought. He had been in that position before.
It was enough to engender a strong dislike of Skar.
Suddenly a weight fell on his feet and lower legs.

"I've got you," Clariel said.

"And just what is she going to do with you?" Rala
asked.

Verdon thought the dwarf had picked a bad time for
her sarcasm, until he raised his head and understood.
Clariel attempted to keep him from falling while she
nocked an arrow to her bow, hoping to drive off the
approaching crandow. Then Verdon realized a second
one was attacking. Not even the elf could manage two.

Verdon switched the empty pistol from his right
hand to his left and pulled the third weapon from his
holster. While the elf set her sights on one of the
attacking birds, he watched the other. He waited,
knowing the monster flyer had to be close enough for
the limited accuracy of the pistol before he fired, or
he'd never hit it.

Clariel sent her arrow straight into the wing joint of
the first attacker, and it tumbled out of sight. Verdon

waited until he could see nothing but a wide mouth full of teeth before he pulled the trigger. The foul breath of the flying reptile seemed to eat up the clean air when the crandow's head exploded, filling the area around him with blood, spittle, and brains.

The elf handed her bow to Rala and reached out a hand. With Clariel still sitting on his legs, he had the leverage to sit up, and she caught his arm, pulling him into the cage.

He spared a moment getting his breath and telling himself to stop shaking since he was as safe as any of the others. Safer, he decided, since their dwarf guide, the rapacian, and Aktar were pinned between the bars and the weight of the lightning lizard. They were complaining, and Kree hissed his agreement.

As if he had a need to torture himself, Verdon looked over the side of the cage. He realized they were only a hundred feet or so from the lower ledge. He would have been killed in the fall, but he would not have had to wait very long for his death.

"The last crandow is leaving," Clariel said, pointing to the diminishing silhouette. "We're too close to the ground for a successful attack."

"It is a wise bird that knows when it's beaten," Rala said, handing Verdon the third pistol.

"If you have time, we could use some help," Aktar complained. His voice was muffled; his face was pressed against Kree's side.

"I have new information for my people," Siskiel remarked. "Lightning lizards are heavy."

"Obrin?" Rala sounded anxious when the dwarf had not added his comments.

"I'm in the corner. I can't get out and I've lost my ax. Arms and hands in, everyone. It should be a rough ride from here on."

The cage bumped against the shaft walls as it sank into the ground. The sound of splintering wood and screeching cables accompanied them into the darkness. To Verdon, the possibility that the cage would disintegrate before they reached the end of the ride seemed worse than the attack of the crandow or falling in the open. At least in the light he could see his death coming.

No one spoke as the wood and cables continued to protest being scraped against the side of the shaft, but they had only been underground for five minutes when the cage righted itself as it came to a halt in a torchlit cavern.

"And look at this mess, will you now."

Verdon looked over his shoulder to see a disgusted dwarf staring at the carrier. The sturdy little humanoid shook his head until his beard waggled.

"That's what comes of doing favors for strangers."

"Sorry, but we didn't spawn the crandow," Verdon replied as he stepped out of Kree's way. The lightning lizard seemed glad enough to free the three he had trapped with his weight.

Obrin opened the cage door and stepped out onto the stone of the cavern floor. Kree pushed Siskiel and Aktar aside as he followed the dwarf out of the cage. The lightning lizard padded across the stone floor to the farthest corner of the chamber and stood with his back to the water-vator, his head turned to look back at it. Clariel called to him, but he hissed at her, making it plain he wanted nothing more to do with the water-vator.

"That lizard is smarter than I thought," Rala said as she and Verdon stepped onto the solidity of the cavern's stone floor.

Several more torches appeared from a passage that opened into the cavern from the south. Another dozen dwarfs exclaimed over the damage to the carrier, and one climbed up on top. He used a thick rod to loosen the coupling from the chain while four others wheeled another carrier out of the shadows.

"Ignore the complaints, we have troubles with the crandow from time to time," Obrin said as he led the way toward the passage, picking up a torch and lighting it from a wall sconce on the way.

Verdon followed, but as they left the cavern he paused for a quick look behind him. The dwarfs had pushed the damaged cage aside and had started fastening another in place.

The sun had been nearing the rim when they reached the bottom of the water-vator, so no one objected when Obrin suggested they stay in the lower maintenance caverns for the night. The dwarfs provided them with reasonable accommodations. Verdon, Aktar, Siskiel, and Clariel slept on the floor since the beds were designed for dwarfs and far too short for them. The next morning they learned that several flying nocturnals had bypassed the kred nets. The night monsters had flown down past the slopes of the Lakwar and Faerkin Fields to plague the dwarfs at the Sudden Door.

"We'll need to reach Overlook by nightfall," Obrin said as he roused them. "By the time we eat, shoulder our packs, and reach the lower door, it will be light enough to travel."

Very little light had filtered down into Skar when they began their journey. Rala refused to ride on Kree's back, saying after the ride on the water-vator she only trusted her own feet. Since they would not be able to travel faster than their dwarf guide, her shorter legs would not slow the party.

They walked in shadow most of the morning; the sun had almost reached its zenith before it fell on their path. Below them they could see the blue depths of the wide river that ran along the bottom of Skar. An hour before they felt the sun's rays they saw its reflection as if from a mirror. The reflected light did not come from the water but a point just above it.

"That's Overlook Castle." Obrin pointed at the reflection. Its towers are made of marble."

The trail down the cliff side proved easier than Verdon had expected. They were descending nearly five miles, and traveling south for eight. They lost very little time on switchbacks, and every time they passed

a turning in the path the castle's four marble towers
had grown with the decreasing distance.

Their destination was not always in sight. The trail
passed over small ledges and even behind low hillocks
that ended in steep precipices. The moister air and the
low clouds provided enough rainfall for trees, and
Obrin pointed out several clumps he had helped to
plant.

"Dwarfs do not live by stone alone," he said with a
grin. "There are times when we need wood, and it's
good for trading."

Verdon turned when he heard a shout from behind
them. Woos trotted down the trail, moving with
unhurried speed, but covering the ground faster than a
human could sprint. He had disturbed a desert hawk
that flew at his head before soaring into the sky.

"I decided I wanted to see this thunder train of
yours," he told Verdon. "And you might need an extra
spear." The rapacian carried a long quiver on his back
with the shafts of ten spears sticking out of it, similar to
the one Siskiel wore, though not as ornately decorated.

The two rapacians dropped back and chatted as they
walked down the trail. Until that time, Verdon had not
realized how quiet Siskiel had been.

Aktar kept throwing glances behind him at the two
reptilian-humanoids. It occurred to Verdon that some
of his companions had changed in attitude since they
began their journey from the Black Citadel.

The smooth-tongued desert man had lost his amused
tolerance and complained more. Clariel's grief seemed
to be easing with time and her growing count of nocturnals. Rala no longer pretended to be a servant, and,
while she could be impatient, most of her complaints
seemed to be for form's sake. Verdon wondered how
much he had changed.

He had noticed the dwarf had acquired another ax
while they were in the maintenance caverns and Obrin
kept glancing up at the sky. He seemed tense when
they were on open ground. Verdon also kept an eye

out, but he took care to make it appear he was interested in the scenery. He wondered if the crandow might attack again, or if Obrin expected danger from some other predator in Skar. He supposed the dwarf worried about the flying reptiles, but he refused to ask and worry the others unnecessarily. And it would have been to no useful purpose, he decided, since they reached Overlook Castle not long after the sun disappeared beyond the rim of Skar.

Obrin led the way up the wide stone path and opened the heavy door. It swung aside with no sound, and they walked into a huge, empty marble hall. Verdon was not sure what he expected from a mage's castle, but the spartan surroundings inside the entrance disappointed him. The wide expanse of empty floor, laid with square marble blocks, met empty walls.

Kree had entered with them, but the lightning lizard angled off to the side and curled up on the floor as if he had returned home. He showed no desire to continue further and Clariel seemed not to notice the absence of her mount.

The dwarf led the way across a chamber so vast that Verdon counted his paces. He had counted to a hundred before they reached a hallway that led past other empty rooms and up a stairway. Now and then a bench graced a passage or a large room, but most of the castle seemed unoccupied and unused. Still, it was definitely not deserted since it was scrupulously clean.

Obrin led them to a smaller chamber on the second floor, where a fire burned merrily in a fireplace, a worn, but thick, blue-gray rug covered the floor, and blue cushions covered several chairs and benches.

A small human with a high, domed forehead rose to meet them. His long white hair fell to his shoulders, nearly disappearing into his white robes. Verdon thought he had never seen such a serene and gentle face. The illusion disappeared as the magician looked at him. The eyes were as sharp as any rapier. The young ex-guardsman felt as if his mind had been pierced.

"Visitors from the world above," he said softly. "You are welcome, doubly welcome if you will entertain an old man with news." He offered them seats, and, before they had laid aside their packs, two younger mages entered with food and flagons. Verdon's held cluster fruit wine, but he could see foam on the goblets placed in front of Rala and Obrin, and the pale yellow of Aktar's drink, a strong sweet liquor made of fermented cactus flowers. Obviously the mages had known the number and the origins of their visitors long before they arrived. Iliki had been given a tiny cup that he could manage.

The travelers paid for their meal with all the news they had brought from the upper world, but Verdon had the feeling the mages marked time, listening for courtesy's sake. When Aktar asked questions about the castle, the answers he received were evasive, and the magicians countered with questions of their own. Verdon felt a power in the air, and the desert trader suddenly became too interested in explaining the goals of the rhanate's magicians to gather information of his own.

They were being manipulated, Verdon realized. Even Siskiel and Clariel spoke more volubly in Overlook than on the trail.

Verdon leaned back, resisted the force, and let the others talk. He had no objection to sharing what he knew, but it would be offered, not pulled from him.

Gilvaent, the master magician, suggested they might be tired after their journey and everyone began to yawn. Their eyelids seemed too heavy to stay open. The ex-guardsman felt the pull, but he resisted the magic.

He let the tendrils of his mind wander and felt the residue of an ancient malice in the stone of the chamber, long dispelled. When he tried to probe the present occupants and the goals of Overlook, he found Gilvaent looking into his mind, and a blank wall beyond those sharp, piercing eyes.

Verdon thought about the experience as one of the junior mages led him to a chamber with a soft bed, a single chair, and a chest of extra blankets. He sat on the edge of the bed, thinking about the master magician. If he had not been gazing up at the light, he would have missed seeing the image of Gilvaent emerge from it. The illusion grew in size and solidity from a pinprick until it seemed the mage stood in front of him. He could not make up his mind whether he saw an image or the solid form.

"Yes, there is power in you." Gilvaent nodded as if he were holding a discussion with himself. "But is there enough?"

"How much do I need?" Verdon asked, still resentful of the magician's intrusion into his mind. He hid no shameful secrets, but the invasion of his privacy rankled.

"This much," Gilvaent replied.

Suddenly Verdon's mind filled with black, roiling clouds. Creatures from the worst of his nightmares tore at his flesh. Searing pain and fear sent him swirling into a black void, where he knew and felt nothing.

25

Someone shook Verdon's shoulder. He opened his eyes and stared up at Gilvaent. He flinched, expecting another onslaught of the mental torture, but the magician smiled at him and stepped back away from the bed.

"How do you feel this morning?" the old man asked.

Verdon took a moment to mentally probe himself. He felt rested and energetic. His conscious mind relegated the memories of the horrors of Gilvaent's warning into the cubicle of experience. He would not forget it, but it would not affect his actions.

"Excellent," Gilvaent smiled. "You will manage better than we believed."

"Are you saying I have the strength to handle a power cluster?" Verdon asked. Everyone seemed to think he would succeed. For a few minutes at a time he was beginning to believe, and then his doubts would take over again.

"To use it yes, but how effective you will be I cannot say, or whether you will be able to withstand the powers that will try to twist you. Still, you might do some good with it, that is, if you can call one."

"Call it?" Verdon frowned. Rala had said nothing about calling it. "How do you call a cluster?"

"If you have the ability, you will have the knowledge when the time comes," Gilvaent replied. "You should leave now, before the others awake. There are those with you who cannot be trusted with the secrets you will learn."

Verdon wondered why magicians had to be so obtuse. Perhaps they thought speaking in riddles made them seem wiser than they were. As he left the chamber he saw an amused glint in Gilvaent's eye and knew the magician had heard his thoughts.

In the entrance hall of the castle he found Rala, Clariel, and Kree waiting with a young mage dressed in brown robes. An essencer, Verdon decided, since they usually identified with the richness of the soil. His newly acquired memories gave him an image of his parents wearing the same color and style of robe.

The essencer had the sharp features and coloring of the desert people, but when he spoke he used the universal accent of Gilvaent and the other mages. He introduced himself as Moncreed.

"It is not yet dawn, but we must hurry. The safest time to cross the bridge is at dawn." He opened the door, and they stepped out into the darkness, but a tiny glow lit the path as they followed the essencer. The light appeared in front of his feet and disappeared behind Clariel and Kree, who followed behind Moncreed, Rala, and Verdon. The path was smooth and hard. Verdon felt the essence of old magic in it.

They had traveled less than half a mile when they passed a strange structure that seemed to be solid stone. Verdon asked Moncreed about it.

"The abutment for a new bridge," the essencer replied. "The reachers have grown since the beginning of Darkfall. The new support chains are almost ready to be hung, but if we face an invasion of nocturnals, the work may be delayed."

"What is a reacher?" Clariel asked. Her sharp elfin

ears could easily pick up their conversation, and she had picked up a word full of unfamiliar meaning.

"Pray you do not learn," Moncreed said. "We do not speak of it this close to the Reaching Deep. Many believe to talk of it attracts its attention. I should not have mentioned it."

More magician's riddles, Verdon thought with disgust. He fingered his pistols in silence and thought about stringing his bow, but decided it could wait until they were nearer the bridge. A shadow drifted over his head and he looked up to see Iliki, who settled on his shoulder.

"You were leaving me behind," he snapped, glaring at Rala and Clariel, including them in his accusation.

"You were still asleep, and we wanted you to get your rest," Moncreed explained. "But now that you are here, you can accompany the elf on her mission."

"Your mission?" Verdon looked over his shoulder at Clariel. "You're not going with Rala and me?"

"Someone has to pay for the help we're receiving," Rala said. "The elf is going up a level." She didn't say any more, and Verdon refused to ask. He remembered being told that elves lived on two of the ledges on the west slope of Skar, and all elves were secretive people.

They had walked nearly four miles when Moncreed called a halt.

"We've made better time than I expected," the essencer said. "We'll stop for a meal and wait until dawn. The darkness under the bridge may be as dangerous as the light, but for different reasons."

Verdon could guess what he meant. Nocturnals roamed the seas and the rivers as well as the land. In Mekanus he had heard tales of ghost ships full of nightmare creatures attacking trading vessels. Since the beginning of Darkfall, safe nights belonged to history. Nocturnals could attack in the daylight, but all evil loved darkness where it could move in secret.

Moncreed led them to a flat grassy area, sat on the ground, and took food from his pack. When he had given each of them a crusty bread roll filled with meat and cheese, he handed around cups and filled them from a flask.

"Delicious," Rala said when she tasted hers. "Is it a concoction of magic?"

"Just the juice of the eodwal," Moncreed replied. "Like much of Skar, we trade with the faerkin." He sighed. "At least we did. The nocturnals may prevent travel, even in Skar."

The mention of nocturnals reminded Verdon of the danger of the reacher. Iliki perched on his knee, disdaining the damp ground. Verdon tapped the little owl-man on the head.

"Is Milstithanog with us? We may have a problem at the bridge, and if we do, we could use his help."

"I-ah—he's still back at the castle," Iliki said. "I can try to wake him."

"You don't need to pretend with the mages of Overlook," Moncreed smiled. "We see through your pretense."

Verdon laughed. "I didn't believe in Milstithanog at first, not until he proved he existed."

"But he doesn't exist," Moncreed objected. "I think I would know if we were accompanied by an invisible demon, or if there was one back in the castle. I know Master Gilvaent would be aware of him."

"He exists," Verdon snapped. "I'd be dead if he hadn't knocked that huge ferran off his feet when Kree, Iliki, Milstithanog, and I rescued the others from the Worms." Verdon listed the times the demon had assisted them.

"He didn't jerk the spear out of the hand of the rhanate's soldier, or bring the wind that blew us over the edge of Skar, because I did those, but he has undoubtedly saved our lives."

"I knocked down the ferran," Rala said softly. "It was one of the few spells I could manage before I could speak again. I also choked the captain. I did not turn those spears in midair or create the safe path through the fire on the lower ledge of the Lakwar."

"No, I turned the spears and laid a cloaking spell on the fire," Clariel admitted, and turned to glare at the little ferran. "So just what *has* Milstithanog done?"

"Nothing, because he doesn't exist," Moncreed laughed. "The four of you have created the creature, the ferran by telling you he existed, and the rest of you by using your own powers."

Verdon reached for Iliki, but the little owl-man leapt away. With his food in one hand and his tiny cup in the other, he soared up to hover over their heads.

"*You'd* need a big friend too if you were *my* size," he snapped.

Verdon reached up again as if to grab the little owl-man. "You little liar! You've let us believe he existed. Half the Sundered Desert and a good portion of Skar believes in him by now!"

"Like it or not, you have a well-known invisible friend," the essencer laughed. "And you may be stuck with him. No magic on Aden can rid you of what doesn't exist."

"You mean we'll need to keep up the ruse?" Rala demanded. "We'll have to keep throwing spells and give him the credit?"

"Not many people can walk in and out of the Black Citadel," Moncreed replied. "Few can demand and get the cooperation of the Lakwar or the dwarfs of the eastern slopes. You can give him credit for the way many strangers receive you."

"Wonderful," Verdon groused. "At least I can stop worrying about stepping on his tail—if he has a tail— or had one—or something!" He glared at Rala, who was laughing at his confusion.

"The eastern rim is visible," Moncreed said, and drained his cup. The others gulped down the rest of their breakfasts, and in minutes they were on the way down the trail.

In the growing light they could just make out the sil- very reflection of the river at the bottom of the gorge and the dark strip that spanned it. The morning darkness still drained the color out of the grass and the occasional tree when they approached the abutment and the building that stood beside it.

"The shadow dwarfs guard the crossing," Moncreed explained as a dozen stocky dwarfs came out of the building rubbing their eyes.

"Are they guarding it from us or for us?" Rala asked.

"They cross ahead of us, manning the weapons to protect us against an attack of the . . ." The essencer pointed at the dark water. "More we will not say until we are safely on the other side. I will stop here and gather what power I can." He stopped and knelt, putting his hands flat on the ground. His eyes took on the unfocused look of deep concentration.

Verdon did the same, calling up the power with no idea of how he would be able to use it. He felt the increasingly familiar exhilaration of increased strength and sharpness of mind. His vision had also sharpened or the growing light had made him more aware of the distance.

The suspension bridge had been built more than two thousand feet above the surface of the river. The abutment was three-quarters of a mile from the shore of the Reaching Deep. On the way down from Overlook Castle, Moncreed had told them the river at the bottom of the gorge was just over four miles wide. The world essence Verdon had called upon could not help him see into the fog that hung over the water. The bridge disappeared into the mist.

The dwarfs that had hurried ahead to man the defenses wore no boots, only soft leather slippers securely tied around their ankles. Moncreed, Verdon, and Rala removed their heavy footwear. Clariel's light elfin slippers made no noise at all.

As they stepped onto the ten-foot-wide bridge, they felt the movement as the light wind caused it to sway gently. Verdon felt as if he were walking into a nether world.

Two enormous chains, half again as thick as the ones on the water-vator, were the main support of the bridge. From their lengths hung three-foot cables connected to a series of metal strips ten feet in length. Bolted to those metal supports were wooden boards. The huge support chains provided a railing as well as the main suspension strength. Every few hundred yards a second link had been added to the chain, giving added support to weakened areas.

They had left the shore behind and were over the water when they came to the first ballista. The missile projector dwarfed the weapons on the thunder train, and had been constructed to fire down through a hole in the floor of the bridge. A cunning set of gears and levers allowed the dwarfs to aim it, and a framework extending ten feet in the air drew the two-inch-thick bowstring. A barbed point ten inches in diameter tipped the eight-foot-long shaft.

"They must have a lar-lar—huge target," Iliki whispered. He sat on Verdon's shoulder. He excused his desire to ride by saying the mist dampened his wings. Kree's skin was slick with moisture. Verdon hardly felt the weight of the ferran.

The fog that had seemed a light mist over the land thickened over the wide river. It muffled the sounds of the early morning birds and if it had not been for the scrape of Kree's claws, they would have heard no noise at all.

When they first stepped out on the bridge, Clariel whispered to the lightning lizard, trying to instruct him to walk more softly and not scrape his claws. With his limited intelligence, Kree only understood that he was being asked for something beyond his training and experience. He whined and whimpered his confusion until Clariel gave up.

Moncreed threw worried glances behind him at every scrape of the lizard's claws, but since they had to cross the bridge, Verdon stopped worrying. Kree would attract the attention of the reacher or he would not.

Half a mile beyond the first ballista they came to the first cannon. It had a longer barrel than those used on the thunder trains, but Verdon could not see the bore since it, too, pointed down toward the surface of the river. He had not seen a great deal of mechamagic used in Skar, but decided only magic could keep the shot in the cannon until it was fired.

The essencer had told them the dwarfs had installed four ballistas and three cannons on the bridge. They passed the third of the ballistas and two cannons, and Verdon believed they would make it across the bridge without trouble. The mist grew brighter with the sun on it, but it still obscured their view for more than a hundred yards. Then from far below they heard a giant splash and a gurgle.

Moncreed had been walking in the center of the ten-foot-wide span, but he dashed to the side and grasped the support chain, calling for the others to do the same. He gave up all pretense of silence.

"Go to the edge where we're easier to reach?" Clariel asked, staring at the essencer. "It is not wise to step toward your enemy—"

"Do as he says!" Verdon shouted at her. "If they fire the—" The roar of the cannon three hundred yards ahead of them was followed almost immediately by an explosion from the center of the bridge.

The weapon directly in front of them had been installed on the right and recoil bucked that side of the bridge up into the air. The tilt rolled along the flexible surface like a ripple on the water. Moncreed, Verdon, and Rala clung to the chain and rode out the wave, but Clariel and Kree lost their balance and slid on the smooth floor of the bridge.

They were still off-balance when the wave from behind them caused Kree to slide between the support chain and the flooring. Clariel reached for him, lost her balance, and went over the side.

26

The bridge still bounced when Verdon raced across to look over the side. Kree had not fallen. He clung with his teeth to the short cable that connected the bridge flooring to the support chain. Verdon ignored the lightning lizard and looked below. At first he didn't see the elf at all. Then, as the lizard swung, he saw her clinging to Kree's left foot.

As he watched, her grip slackened and she slipped, but the lizard had curled his tail and she caught it. He held her up, but his eyes, gleaming red in his panic, were staring at Verdon as if he expected the ex-guardsman to save him. The lizard's trust shook Verdon. His mind felt crushed under the weight of the responsibility, and the urgency undermined his ability to think.

"Kree can't ho-ho—he doesn't have much strength in his tail," Iliki warned, his round eyes wide, adding his own fear to Verdon's load.

"Your cloak!" Verdon demanded with a glance at Moncreed. "Cut it in wide strips and tie them together." Rescuing Clariel had to be their first priority, the importance of a thinking being over an animal. "We need fifteen feet or more," he called as he stared over the side. Far below the water gurgled and

splashed, waves of impending danger seeming to rise
out of the fog.

He stared down into the mist, not knowing what to
look for. When he saw the first tentacle rising out of
the mist he first thought it was a snake. Then he realized it lacked a head. It groped blindly, moving back
and forth in the general area beneath the bridge.

"Shoot it, shoo-shoo—do something, before it finds
Clariel," Iliki insisted as he hovered in the air over his
dangling companions.

Verdon attempted to swallow the knot in his throat.
His concern was not for himself, but for the elf, dangling helplessly below the lightning lizard. He took one
of the pistols from his makeshift belt, sighted down
the barrel, and replaced it. His bow would be a better
choice, he decided. He wanted to shoot at the tentacle
before it swung close enough to the elf to grab her.

He sighted along the shaft of the arrow, but the slim
tip kept undulating in the misty air. He shot but
missed completely. The tentacle rose within inches of
the bottom of the bridge. It swept around the lightning
lizard and the elf without touching them.

"Rala, we could use a fireball," he shouted to the dwarf.

"Quiet, it can locate us by sound," Moncreed said,
his voice just loud enough for Verdon to hear him.

"If it's interested in noise, it won't bother us," Iliki
said, turning his head to look west along the bridge in
the direction they had been traveling. Verdon tensed
as he realized the meaning of the clanks and bangs. He
had heard them, but in his concern for the elf he had
not considered their implications. They were louder
toward the west, but behind them in the mist, he heard
the same sounds, muted by a greater distance.

*The dwarfs were reloading the cannons! Another
recoil and ripple along the bridge would dislodge both
the lizard and Clariel.*

Rala appeared at his side, rolling up her sleeves.
The mundane action helped to bring the situation into
perspective.

"Keep those tentacles at bay," Verdon ordered, and rushed over to help Moncreed knot the wide strips of torn cloth. As the essencer knotted the last piece, Verdon measured it. Twenty feet, better than he had hoped, but still not long enough for what he wanted. He tied one end to his bow and knotted a loop in the other as he hurried back to the edge.

He had heard Rala's first incantation and her disgust as her first fireball missed. She cast another. As Verdon looked over the side he saw her hit a second tentacle that writhed and disappeared into the fog. The first wavered, dipped, and rose again, continuing the hunt.

Verdon played out the improvised rope. By crouching on the floor of the bridge and lowering his bow, the loop he had tied in the other end reached just below Clariel's boots.

"Fly down and slip the loop under her foot," he instructed Iliki. He knew the elf would not be able to support herself with one hand while she held to the lizard's slippery tail.

Iliki swooped off the bridge, caught the loop, and attempted to slip the elf's foot into it. His first try failed—the rope swung too low for her to get a purchase and hold it. Verdon raised his bow, drawing up the knotted cloth, and Iliki tried again, just as Rala threw another fireball over Verdon's shoulder. He had been concentrating on Iliki and the loop. He jerked the bow, yanked the loop out of the little ferran's hands, and sent the owl-man spinning.

While he waited for the ferran to fly back and try a third time, another tentacle rose out of the mist and neared the elf. Verdon reached in his belt and pulled out the pistol he had checked. He knew he ran a risk, laying it on the bridge floor, but he wanted it handy.

Iliki succeeded on his third try. Clariel's foot found and held the loop. She looked up, watching and raising her leg by bending her knee while Verdon pulled up the bow. When he and Moncreed hauled in the rope, working the knots over the side of the bridge, she used one hand to pat Kree. She spoke to the lizard in the elfin dialect. They all jumped at a clap of thunder when Rala sent a lightning bolt toward an approaching tentacle.

"Sorry, I was a little overenthusiastic," the mage apologized. "I'll be quieter next time."

Another strong tug on the rope brought Clariel up to where she could catch Verdon's hands, and he pulled her onto the bridge.

She didn't waste a moment getting her breath. She pulled the knotted cloth from her foot, jerked the other end from Verdon, and pulled it through the small loop, making a larger one.

"Iliki, put this around Kree's right leg," she ordered.

"We can't pull him up." Moncreed said what Verdon had refused to admit. "The cloth won't stand the strain."

"We can try," the elf glared at him. "I'll go over the side again before I'll let him become a meal for that monster below."

"We can try," Verdon echoed her sentiments. Kree had earned his right to their efforts.

Rala sent her last lightning bolt, this time soundlessly, but other tentacles had been drawn to the sound of the thunder. Clariel had dropped the loop over the side of the bridge and Iliki dived to slip it in place when one of the snakelike appendages rose, moving up past the lizard's tail as it groped for its prey. Verdon picked up the pistol and fired straight down over the side of the bridge.

He hit the tentacle. It jerked and struck Iliki, who was just flying away from Kree's leg. Both the ferran and the long limb of the reacher disappeared into the mist. Verdon fought back his impulse to shout for the little owl-man. Beside him Rala had clapped her hand over her mouth to stifle a cry. She swallowed hard.

"I never liked him, and I'm allergic to his feathers, but what has that to say to anything?"

Verdon didn't reply. He stretched out his hands, using the earth power to draw the air currents up from the water. The mist thickened as the wind grew stronger, strong enough to blow a little owl-man up and away from the danger in the water.

Above them the sky darkened as the mist rose. Below they could see the river called the Reaching Deep. A gigantic bloated monster with six impossibly long tentacles swam just below the surface. It stared up at them with one bleary eye.

"Now we can see it and it can see us." Moncreed glared at Verdon.

"Let's get Kree up here," Verdon said. "If Iliki's dead, I won't let his life go for nothing." He took a grip on the makeshift rope and, along with Moncreed and Clariel, pulled until they felt the cloth start to tear. Their efforts had taken part of the lightning lizard's weight and Kree had been able to reach the floor of the bridge with one clawed front foot. Using one foot and twisting his body, he could support enough of his own weight for them to pull his right hind leg onto the bridge.

The roar of one cannon and then the other warned them the bridge would start bucking again. Kree added a roar of his own, and whipped up his tail, looping it around the support chain. Verdon, Moncreed, and Rala dashed across the bridge to anchor themselves on the other side. Verdon looked back to see Clariel kneeling by Kree, her arms around the lizard's neck as if her strength alone could keep him from falling.

As the bridge rose and fell with the recoil of the cannons, Verdon stared, willing the lizard to keep his hold. His claws slipped, lost their grip, and found it again as the bridge undulated and stilled. With a heave he threw himself onto the bridge and landed on his back. His tail lost its grip, but he kept his bite on the support cable. Verdon wondered how he kept from twisting his head off.

Clariel hugged Kree's neck as he rolled over and stood up. He worked his jaws, snapping at air and hissing as a tentacle rose over the side of the bridge.

The elf pulled her sword and hacked at it, severing the tip three feet from the end.

"How many arms does the reacher have?" Verdon asked Moncreed as they hurried along the bridge.

"Sometimes I've thought it must have a limitless supply. The dwarfs say they have seen twelve."

"Why doesn't it pull down the bridge?" Rala asked as she trotted along between the two human males.

"It tries, but the tips of its tentacles aren't strong enough—yet. It's still a danger to anyone on the bridge; it can pull you off in one fast swoop."

Clariel hurried forward. Since she and Verdon both carried swords, they decided the group should walk in a tight bunch, with the ex-guardsman and the elf guarding the sides of the bridge. With a surprising move, Verdon grabbed the dwarf and plopped her on Kree's shoulders, facing backward.

"You watch behind us, we can't see everywhere and run too."

"It's not bad enough that I end up riding this monster, now I do it backward," Rala complained. "Next you'll strap me underneath his belly—forget I said that," she added when Verdon raised his eyebrows.

She might have continued her complaints, but suddenly she squealed a warning as a tentacle swung up over the left side of the bridge and veered toward Moncreed. Verdon turned and hacked at the tip. He cut a gash in it and it whipped away.

The disaster she had prevented by riding backward silenced Rala's objections. They continued their run across the bridge, occasionally hacking at the arms of the reacher, until they passed the fourth ballista.

"You can relax now," Moncreed said, and slowed to a walk. "Below us the water is too shallow for the reacher. Even they have their limits."

"They?" Verdon used the word as a query. "How many?"

"We don't know. As few as two, maybe four. There are three bridges crossing the Reaching Deep. We know two bridges have been under attack at the same time." The essencer shrugged. "We don't go into the water and search for them."

"Iliki!" Clariel said, and started to run. Neither the humans nor the dwarf could see the ferran, but they lacked the keen sight of an elf. She had nearly reached the end of the bridge when she knelt, stayed on one knee for several seconds, and then rose. She stood leaning against the support chain of the bridge until they reached her.

The little owl-man sat on her shoulder, one wing drooping, broken when the reacher's tentacle had hit him. The little ferran's face was drawn with pain, but he glared up at Verdon with his spirit unimpaired.

"It wasn't enou—you weren't happy just to get me knocked out of the sky, you had to blow me halfway to Yzeem?"

"Sorry," Verdon said. "I hoped to keep you from feeding the reacher." He was too happy to see the little character safe to worry about the ferran's complaints.

"I was just a few fe-fe—almost to the water when your wind started," Iliki admitted. "I knew it had to be you, since wind doesn't usually blow nearly straight up."

"Did you get a good look at the reacher?" Rala asked. "What do you think it is? Could it be some sort of nocturnal?"

"It isn't a nocturnal," Moncreed said. "It existed a century before Darkfall. Maybe the ferran can tell us what it is. He's been closer to it than anyone else. Anyone that lived to return."

"It looked like a big ba-ba—sack with arms," the ferran said. "The big one. The small ones just looked like multitailed fish."

"It's spawned!" Moncreed stared at the ferran with horror in his eyes. He turned and walked toward the western end of the bridge as if the news was too evil to discuss.

27

When they reached the end of the bridge, Moncreed used a healing spell on Iliki's wing. They ascended a trail that climbed gently, though Verdon could see a much steeper slope ahead. The essencer from Overlook stopped at a fork, where a second path led off into the sparse woods.

"May wisdom guide your footsteps and your tongue," the essencer said to Clariel. She nodded and, with a wave, continued up the main path. Kree followed behind her, and Iliki, sitting on the lizard's back, turned and twisted, looking from the elf to Verdon.

"Where are you go-go—taking me?" the ferran demanded of Clariel.

"It is not necessary that you go," she reminded him. You can stay with the others."

"Where are you going?" Verdon demanded. Her leaving seemed like a betrayal; telling himself he had no claim on her did no good at all. Was she walking into danger? He would trust her with his life, but knowing she felt she had no right to live after leading her companions to their deaths, he doubted she could be trusted to care for her own safety.

"The wise do not count successes before they try," she replied. "If I succeed, I will tell you of it."

Verdon took a step as if to follow Clariel, but Rala caught his sleeve. The dwarf had been listening in silence, glancing from one to the other, looking as confused as Verdon felt. She shrugged away the mystery.

"By now you should know she won't tell you anything more. Her mind is made up, so let her go. You have your own mission."

The dwarf was right, but he hated the thought of the elf traveling with only the lightning lizard and Iliki. He turned away and followed Moncreed.

"I don't know where she's going or what I'm doing," Verdon complained. "I just keep following people from one place to another."

He kept glancing back at the trail until Clariel and Kree were out of sight. She had broken up the group. He realized the fallacy in his emotions and it caused him to wonder. Aktar had been a part of the original group, but he had not been concerned over leaving the desert man at Overlook. The two rapacians knew their territory and could take care of themselves, and he had not given a thought to Obrin, the dwarf who guided them to the castle.

Clariel, Iliki, and Kree seemed closer to him than the others. He glanced back once more and saw the elf climb on the lizard's back. At least she would travel quickly to her destination, he thought.

Moncreed led them up a gentle slope for half a mile. Sickly pale grass bordered the stone path and grew among the boulders. The few trees were tall and spindly, doubtless from the lack of light. Moss and lichen were everywhere, since they grew better in deep shade. The mist that had hung over the Reaching Deep kept the ground damp.

Moncreed led the way through an area strewn with large lichen-covered boulders, and when they stepped out into the open again, they stood in front of a low stone cliff. The essencer frowned.

"I thought we were expected," he said, and just as he spoke, a portion of the stone moved, swinging out.

A small thin dwarf stepped out to meet them. His pants, tunic, shirt, and short jacket matched his gray hair and beard. Only his pale face and hands prevented him from being mistaken for a shadow.

"You will enter without delay," he said, leading the way back through the entrance. They followed quickly and he pulled the stone door closed. Moncreed led the ex-guardsman and the dwarf six paces down the passage. Four bouncing lights waited ten feet inside the passage. These floating illuminators were brighter than the faerkin lights and their glow had a yellow cast, a shadow dwarf substitution for the lack of sunlight, Verdon decided. The glowing orbs bobbed in agitation just over their heads. The three travelers waited while their greeter dropped a stout steel bar across the door and hurried twenty steps down the passage. He pulled a handle set in the wall and a huge stone block slowly descended from the ceiling, an added protection ten feet thick.

Above Verdon's head the bobbing light bounced once and steadied as the dwarf joined them.

"Uthrab Digger at your service," he said with a bow. "Know that I am first advisor to our leader, King Thonlo Purevein. I mention it not to raise myself in your eyes but so you will know we do not take your visit or its outcome lightly. The king would have met you himself, but he is recovering from a wound he received in the lower caverns."

He spoke directly to Verdon, who struggled for an answer. On the journey he had become accustomed to Rala's forthright speech and her spirited complaints. He had no experience with dwarfish formal greetings and knew next to nothing about courtesy to her high-ranked kindred.

"We are humbled by the honor of being greeted by the first advisor, and hope the king will soon be well again," Verdon said, trying not to trip over his tongue.

"Forgive my ignorance, but how can you know the purpose of my visit?" He felt his face grow hot as he saw the glances and the suppressed smiles that passed between Uthrab Digger and Rala. He should have known magicians had their secret ways of passing information.

"Then he does not know the price we put on our help?" Uthrab Digger asked Rala.

"I have not mentioned it," she said. "I felt the bargain should be made by your king—or yourself," she said hastily.

"What are you asking in return?" Verdon told himself he should have known a payment would be required. Dwarfs were canny traders and never gave when they could strike a bargain.

"You seek power. We are willing to assist you, but we have need of your help. The reacher in the deep grows. We are constructing a new bridge, but in time the monsters will grow to reach even it. We want their destruction."

"And there is other help you can give to Skar," Moncreed said. "Until we know the power you will wield, we say nothing more about it. The less you know, the safer you will be."

Verdon gazed at the essencer, the first advisor, and over at Rala.

"I won't be alone in my disappointment if I don't find a cluster," he said. "Everyone has plans for me once I have it. I don't even know how to try for it, I certainly don't know what I can do with it once I get it—if I get it—and everyone seems to forget the reason I want it."

"No one wants to prevent you from using it on the sentinels of the thunder train," Rala hastened to add.

"No, do not turn from the course you've set yourself," Moncreed urged. "You won't be able to assist us until you've learned for yourself what your strength is and what use you can make of the cluster."

"I won't promise anything," Verdon replied, his

frustration draining away. He owed them the truth, since he had nothing else to give. "I have vowed to release my foster father from his bondage. Until I've done that, I accept no other responsibilities. I can't, knowing I might not live to return."

"And if you succeed and retain your life?" Uthrab asked.

"I will return and attempt to repay my debts," Verdon said. "I still make no promises."

"Who could ask more than your best effort?" Rala said briskly. "Now if we're to do this thing, we should get on with it."

The king's first advisor led them down several passages. Verdon guessed they had walked two miles when they stopped before a dark vertical shaft guarded with a gate.

"Another water-vator?" Verdon asked. He wanted to object, but at least this one could not be attacked by the crandow. They might face something worse in the darkness, and if he had to fight, he wanted solid ground beneath his feet.

"It draws only part of its power from water," Uthrab said, puffing out his chest. "Water creates steam, and who was the first to learn the use of steam but the dwarfs? It all began here, you know. This is the first riser to be moved by steam-powered wheels."

"It is said among my people that we at the Top of the World made the first use of steam power," Rala objected.

"Tush." The first advisor brushed away her claim. "This is the first lifter in existence, and I will hear no more about it."

"It may be the first lifter, but at the Top of the World, we have a steam—"

"Every clan of dwarfs has the first of something," Moncreed said, using a placating tone. "Each group developed something different, and they enriched Aden in many different ways. Where would we be without our sturdy kindred?"

While the essencer attempted to calm the ruffled feelings, a clanking came from deep within the shaft, and a cage similar to the one on the cliff dwarfs' water-vator came into sight. It stopped three feet above the floor.

"Down a bit!" Uthrab shouted up the shaft.

His answer was a loud clank, a jerk, and the carrier dropped six feet.

"Up a bit!" the first advisor shouted again.

The cage rose seven feet, now four feet off the floor.

"I'd give up and climb in," Verdon said with a laugh. "I'll give you a boost. He knelt and clasped his hands together, providing a step. The gray-clad dwarf steadied himself by grasping Verdon's shoulder as he climbed into the cage.

"It's an old lift," Uthrab said shortly. "As I said, it's the first ever made."

Moncreed had just given a boost to Rala when the cage dropped two feet. Moncreed jumped aboard and nearly toppled off as the lift dropped another five feet. Verdon found himself alone in the passage, staring down at the top flange and the supporting chain.

As on the bridge over the Reaching Deep, many of the links had been doubled, and some had three links side by side.

Without warning the cage began to rise, and as soon as the space allowed, Verdon slid into the open area. He nearly stepped on the first advisor. Behind him the gate in front of the shaft swung closed.

The solid floor and roof of the car resembled the water-vator carrier, as did the vertical bars on the side. The wood was old, dark, and hard. The three horizontal bars halfway up the sides were a newer addition. Verdon discovered their use as the car rose in jerks and he grabbed a bar to keep his balance. The others also kept a tight grip.

"We will provide you lodging for the night," the first advisor said. "You will not wish to start your search for the crystal right after your journey."

Verdon disagreed, though he kept his objections to himself. The sooner he found the thing, if he could find it, the sooner he could be out of Skar. If he stayed much longer, he would miss the thunder train's return trip. He could spend the rest of his life searching for Marchant. He shook away his resentment. He was asking help from people beleaguered with their own troubles and he could not honestly guarantee anything in return. If he thought they were selfish, what about himself? He had come to ask for one of the most valued and rarest objects on Aden. He wondered if he had the right.

"I still wonder that you haven't made a greater effort to find a cluster for your own people," Verdon said. "That is, if the essencers of Overlook are sure there's one to be had."

"Our people have few mages, since dwarfs mistrust magic," Rala said.

"Only three dwarfs in Skar make use of magical power," Uthrab said. "One dwells on the east slope. One lives in the south near the tip of Skar, and the third is here among our people."

"They don't want a cluster?" Verdon asked.

"No," Rala said. "It would be more of a danger than a help. The clusters draw attention to themselves. Clusters dug from the ground and imbued with magic by magic's rules can be used by anyone who knows how to manipulate that power. If I had one, every mage more powerful than myself would try to take it from me. I might get a little use of it, but once a master magician came after it, I'd lose the cluster, my life, and my usefulness to my people."

"But they can't take it from me?" Verdon asked. He knew the answer, Rala had already explained it to him. Once he drew a cluster from the ground, it would only work for him. The power of world essence had its own rules.

No one answered his question. The lift had begun to jiggle, jerk, and bump. From his ride on the water-vator,

Verdon decided the motion came from the huge links of chain moving over a wheel. He was right.

A brightness that dimmed the floating glows to insignificance seeped around the top of the cage, and in moments they were blinking against the bright light of a passage. They were also blinking against a sudden onslaught of color.

Reds, greens, orange, blue, whites, and browns, every color imaginable, had been used to draw scenes on the walls. Dwarfs were wonderful workers of stone and metal, but their painting was garish and primitive. Still, the unnatural twists of tree limbs, the strange, misshapen beasts, and the tales of their own people were lively and cheerful.

As the lift came to a stop three feet above the floor of the passage, Verdon stared at a painting of two deer on the wall. The deer had been drawn escaping from a hunting dwarf who had fallen over a log during the chase. Verdon at first thought the dwarf had broken his leg at the knee, since it bent in the wrong direction. Then he noticed the deer had been drawn with their hind legs backward.

Rala looked from the painting to Verdon with raised eyebrows. She pursed her lips, but not before he had seen the corners tilt up in a smile. Moncreed gave a slight shrug, and they followed Uthrab as he sat on the floor of the carrier and swung his legs over the side. Apparently the first advisor had decided against an attempt to match the floor of the cage with the passage.

The dwarf glows dashed out of the lift, joined twenty of their peers, and bobbed energetically. The others bobbed back, several dipped as if taking a better look at the visitors, and all but ten streaked off down the passage. They sailed along just ahead of the two dwarfs and the two humans, dashing forward and then coming back.

"I'm going as fast as I can, so don't rush me," Uthrab groused at the impatient lights. "We'll get there in our own time."

There was a gigantic dining hall, made bright by hundreds of the small glows. Fifty tables stood in rows of ten each, and ten places were set at each table. Most were full, but prominently in the middle of the room an empty space had been left for the visitors.

Verdon and Moncreed seated themselves and tucked their long legs under the bench to keep from kicking Rala and Uthrab, who sat across the table. Five female dwarfs bustled up. One brought a cauldron of thick, hot soup. The others carried trays of meat, steaming roots, crusty bread, and an ensemble of jars that held honey and several types of sweets and conserves unfamiliar to Verdon. Another came with a pitcher of dwarf mead.

Dwarfs were a talkative race, but all conversation waited until they sated their hunger. The travelers had covered nearly twenty miles since leaving Overlook Castle and needed food.

Verdon would have enjoyed his meal more if the dwarf lights had not been so curious about the strangers. The dwarfs themselves were courteous enough to throw glances their way or watch them out of the sides of their eyes. The glows dipped down and hung over the table, bouncing close together as if in an animated discussion. A small one came down to hang directly in front of the guardsman's nose.

A larger glow, in deep, frenzied discussion with a group of others, sailed down and tried to drive the little one away. The small one dodged with a deft sideways dash, dipped to avoid its pursuer, and fell in Verdon's soup.

The ex-guardsman looked around for help but the dwarfs had their eyes on their own plates and Moncreed, the only one who noticed, shrugged and grinned. Verdon searched for the dwarf with the soup cauldron, hoping he might get another bowl, but when he located her, the cauldron swung in her hand as if it were empty.

His soup was too good to lose, so he reached in the

bowl, picked up the jiggling light, dunked it in his water cup to wash it off, and set it down on the table. He had been surprised to discover the light was solid and not some magical manifestation. It felt soft and spongy and slightly warm. It was some sort of living creature, he decided; one he had never heard mentioned.

He reached for a piece of bread just as the larger light swooped down again. The little light hopped up on Verdon's hand, rolled up his sleeve, and perched on his shoulder close to his neck. Verdon ate the rest of his meal with a glow under his chin and a bright but irate orb swooping at his shoulder.

28

Dwarfs like to eat without bothering with conversation, but once they were finished they didn't seem to care whether or not the person they talked to had finished his meal.

Uthrab questioned Verdon on what he knew about the world above Skar. Verdon answered the first advisor's questions as well as he could. The ex-guardsman knew about the thunder trains and had word on Yzeem and the High Reaches, though his news from those areas dated back more than six months. Rala took the spotlight from him when she had sated her appetite and pushed her plate away.

Verdon had suspected she had been in Urbana to gather information, but he had no idea at what level she had been working. She had held a position of chambermaid in the household of Anslorn Vinrid, a trusted messenger for Lord Urbane. Vinrid, one of the few who could claim to have seen the Iron Tyrant in the past several years, never lowered himself to visit the admirals, generals, and public officials for whom he had messages.

They came to him, sitting in his opulent office or in his dining room if their rank rated more than common courtesy. Rala's predecessor, another dwarf killed by nocturnals, had found a chink in the heating system. By removing a brick in the laundry under the house, she, and after her, Rala, had been able to hear and pass along information vital to King Corben in Arasteen.

"If we had continued on to Tee and crossed through Burcham's Pass, you could have helped me reach King Corben's generals," Verdon said. Aktar had convinced him he would not have been trusted in the northwestern country. The desert man would be chagrined if he learned Rala could have accomplished as much in Arasteen as Aktar had at the Black Citadel.

If he learned . . . Verdon realized he would not pass that information along to Aktar. The thought bothered him.

Rala grinned. "Don't concern yourself. King Corben knows every word you spoke in the Black Citadel. His Gatherers are a dedicated group."

Verdon had been successfully hiding his yawns for half an hour when Uthrab suggested they retire for the night. Two dwarfs escorted Verdon to a chamber and wished him wealth in his dreams. The door had closed, and Verdon sat on the bed removing his boots when he realized the bed consisted of a box filled with fresh soil.

"They think this will help me?" he asked himself as he stared at it. Well why not? The few times he had slept directly on the ground he had awaked rested and full of energy. Perhaps earth would help his essencing power.

As usual, Verdon slept heavily when he felt it was safe to let down his guard. When he woke his first thoughts were of his disappointment. He had expected to dream of a power cluster, but his night could have been only seconds long and had passed without dreams. He was awakened by the small light that had dried during the night. It bounced in front of his face.

It streaked to the entrance of his sleeping chamber

and returned, repeating the action until he opened the
door. Several others sailed in, clustered over his clothing, and bobbed up and down. They were great little
messengers.

"Someone wants me to hurry," he said. When he finished dressing he followed the lights to the dining hall,
where Rala and Moncreed waited. With them stood an
older dwarf Verdon had not seen the night before. By
Rala's deference when she introduced them, Verdon
decided Ird was a mage. The elder wore the gray clothing that seemed to be the uniform work-wear of the
shadow dwarfs. The night before, Uthrab had
explained that the color blended with the shadows of
the mines and helped to hide them from the occasional
nocturnal.

The rapacians had said they had not been bothered
by nocturnals until recently, but the shadow dwarfs
told Verdon a few had been coming up out of the deep
mines for six years.

"Mind you, not all the dangers of the deep mines
began with Darkfall," Uthrab had said. Verdon had
heard stories passed on from the miners in Urbana. He
had not tried to contribute much to that conversation.
Tales often grew in the telling.

Ird—Verdon had not been given a last name—led
them back to the lift, and, with a series of jerks and
drops that caused Verdon's teeth to ache, they
descended beyond the level of the lower entrance and
continued down another few hundred feet. When the
car stopped, this time within six inches of the stone
floor, Ird led the way along a dark passage. Rala and
Moncreed were each accompanied by two of the pale
yellow glows. Three, two yellow and one blue, danced
over Ird's head. Three glows escorted Verdon. The two
regular-sized lights kept trying to push the little fellow
out of their way.

Before long they reached a set of metal tracks,
placed three feet apart. They passed several carts of
ore, ore that Verdon had seen before. The shadow

dwarfs of Skar had located a vein of manite. Ird gave him a searching look, and the ex-guardsman knew what was required of him.

"It's very dark down here, I can hardly see my way," he said. They wanted to protect their secret vein, which was probably the reason the others had been left behind at Overlook. He remembered seeing Siskiel's manite spearpoint on the desert. The rapacian might know the truth, but then his spearpoint might have been a victory trophy taken from the Worms or some other outlaw. The ex-guardsman wondered at the trust the dwarfs had placed in him. They had allowed him to see the secret that could bring war and destruction into Skar. The knowledge of their trust increased his debt to them. It added to the pressure of responsibility he had begun to feel like a physical weight.

They walked for several hours, strolling along the passages, up and down inclines, and twice they returned to the lift to ride down a level. Rala, Ird, and Moncreed could have been on an outing, walking for pleasure. The essencer from Overlook walked in the center, with Rala and Ird on each side. Verdon brought up the rear. He was left out of the conversation and was beginning to feel irritated about it.

He knew he was supposed to be finding a cluster, but no one had told him how. The dark walls, some earth, some almost totally stone, all looked alike to him.

Then, without warning he halted, feeling as if he had just walked point-blank into a stone wall. He reached forward, but his hand met no resistance. Nothing hampered him in front, back, or on the sides. He thought at first he was caught in a spell, but he could move his arms and legs, he just couldn't go anywhere. He felt a compelling urge to raise his right hand and pressed it against the ceiling. Then he couldn't draw it back.

The two larger dwarf lights danced in excitement. The small one zipped off down the corridor. In moments the dwarfs and Moncreed came into view, running toward him.

"You found it?" Rala demanded. Ird gestured for quiet. They stood waiting while Verdon tried to pull his right hand away from the ceiling.

"This is a great day for Skar," Moncreed said, his face glowing.

"This is *stupid*!" Verdon griped. The other three looked shocked and made signs to avert evil. "I'm standing here, my hand stuck to the ceiling, and I don't feel the least bit magical, I don't feel the world essence, I might as well be stuck in the kred net again!"

Was this the ability to find a cluster? He had expected some tremendous psychic experience. He just felt ridiculous, as if some prankster had laid a trap for him.

Maybe he should be concentrating, he decided. Concentrating on what, the cramp developing in his shoulder?

"Try thinking magic thoughts," Rala suggested.

"How can I think in magic when I don't speak the language?" he retorted, but he knew her advice was wise. Not magic, but world essence. He reached out with his left hand and touched the earth wall. In moments he seemed to drift away. He saw images of strange lands and people dressed in odd clothing. They spoke in words unfamiliar to his ears, but he understood them.

He saw the flames of a burning land and the stones of a tower melting into the ground. A dark, roiling presence reached for him but he jerked away, lost his balance, and fell.

His awareness returned as he crashed into the wall of the mine passage. He slid to the floor. He had no idea how long he sat with his mind shut against the evil presence that had reached toward him. The horror had to be cleansed from his mind, and he worked to drive it away. When he could think logically he realized he held a hard, cold object and inspected it by the light of the glows that whirled around his head.

The cluster, if he could call it so, disappointed him in size as well as appearance. It looked to be no more than a rough piece of shale. The joints of his two thumbs could cover it and it was not much thicker than a fingernail. He brushed the dirt from it and saw the unpolished diamonds that nature had formed into a wafer. The stones laced themselves together in an irregular oval, with gaps between them.

He looked down the passage where Rala, Ird, and Moncreed waited. The essencer and the old dwarf were curled in blankets. Rala sat with her chin on her knees, also asleep. Around them were used dishes and several platters. The remains of a meal had been left on a flat-topped basket.

As he gazed at the food he felt weak with hunger. He hurried to the basket and grabbed a chunk of bread. It was hard from having been left too long uncovered, but he ate it ravenously. A jug of dwarf ale sat on the floor by the hamper. He grabbed it and, with shaking hands, poured some into a cup. His thirst was terrible.

Rala opened her eyes and stared at him. She blinked as if she doubted her vision.

"So you're finally out of it," she said.

"Out of what?" He would have said his hand had only touched the ceiling for a few minutes, but the food and blankets had not been there when last he spoke to them. "How long did I stand there?"

"More than two days," Rala said as she rose stiffly. "Did you get it? Silly question, you must have."

He showed her the cluster. "Not very impressive," he said with a shrug.

She grinned. "Just wait until you've used it a few times. You'll change your mind. But just so you won't be ashamed, wear this." She handed him a slightly larger cluster, one that twinkled in the light of the bouncing glows.

"Two?"

"This one's only glass," she said. "The others will

think as you did, that anything as powerful as a cluster would have to glitter and sparkle."

"Is it necessary?" Verdon had never liked subterfuge. He had been taught to keep his thoughts to himself in Urbana, but he felt he could trust his friends.

"It is," Rala said. "Those you could trust before you found the cluster might turn on you now. Power is a poison. Just the thought of it can taint the mind."

Verdon considered the dwarf's advice and decided the decoy could be used to protect the genuine cluster.

An hour later they had awakened the others and had returned to the upper caverns, where the dwarfs lived. On the way Rala told him Aktar, Siskiel, and Woos had crossed the bridge and waited for them in chambers just inside the upper entrance.

Once he had eaten, Verdon felt as rested and refreshed as if he had slept for the two days he had been in the trance. With the cluster in his possession, he discovered his urge to travel made him anxious over the delay. Uthrab was also concerned.

"You will try to return?" he asked as he escorted them to the upper entrance.

"I plan to stay alive if I can, and I believe in honoring my debts," Verdon replied, surprised to be gripped by a strong desire to repay his debt.

Aktar made no complaint about being left behind. Siskiel, Woos, and the dwarfs who manned the cannons on the bridge had told him only a few at a time could cross safely.

"Next time *you* can travel with Kree," Verdon told him. "I don't mind waiting while you fight your way across."

Verdon's answer seemed to satisfy the desert trader. Aktar's harsh, hawklike appearance softened until he looked around at the colorful murals. He averted his eyes as if he thought them shameful. Rala had noticed the reactions and hurried them toward the entrance.

"We should be on our way," she said, glaring at Aktar. "We've wasted a good part of the morning and we've a long climb ahead of us."

Verdon turned his head away to hide his smile. She had not been too fond of the bright paintings on the wall, but she would not allow a human to criticize her kindred. The rapacians were gazing at the walls as if enraptured.

They made their farewells to the dwarfs that had guided them to the door and stepped out into the brightness of a sunlit fog. The dark green moss and lichen on the ground and the rocks contrasted with the glowing whiteness and faded to ghostly obscurity ten feet away.

Siskiel, walking by Verdon, turned his head to look back in the direction of the entrance to the dwarf caverns. "Do they eat meat?" he asked. When Verdon nodded he gave a gusty sigh. "If we could destroy the reacher, we could trade meat for service. I'd like paintings on the walls of my house."

Rala laughed, glancing at Aktar, who looked away and pretended not to hear. Verdon only heard Siskiel's desire to have the reacher destroyed. He wondered if everyone in Skar would importune him to return and attempt the destruction of the reachers. While he groused to himself, Aktar stepped up to pace him and threw a dissatisfied glance at Siskiel, who walked at Verdon's right.

"Was your visit a success?"

In answer, Verdon pulled out the stout cord that held the decoy cluster. When Verdon had washed the dirt off the silicate cluster, it had glittered with all the brightness he had expected from the diamond wafer. The true cluster remained dull and uninteresting to the eye. A second stout cord, tied to his belt and hidden by the stiff leather of his scabbard, secured the real cluster. He had tucked it beneath the wide leather band. Siskiel and Woos glanced at the decoy, but drew back as he held it out further.

"Leave the power to those who know how to use it," Siskiel said. "I trust in my arms and legs."

"When they're intact," Rala retorted, reminding the

rapacian of his condition when they found him. A foul
mood had honed her usually acerbic tongue. She disliked being wet, and the mist had soaked their clothing
before they had been on the trail an hour. Her bright
curls had tightened until they clung to the top of her
head and around her face. She pushed at the wet hair
impatiently and held her clinging skirt away from her
legs.

The trail was overgrown but still recognizable. They
wound around boulders and small trees as they
climbed the western slope of Skar. They traveled
south, under a gigantic overhang. Verdon kept looking
up as they neared the southern end of the cliff. Below
them, the mist thinned and they could see the dark
water of the Reaching Deep through patches of fog.
Late in the afternoon the ascending trail turned north
again, and they gazed at the tallest trees Verdon had
ever seen.

"I hope the Iron Tyrant never learns of these," Rala
said as they approached the dense wood. The eaves of
the forest were dark beneath the thick branches of
large trees, but in the distance they could see giant
boles rising into the sunlight, their dark brown bark
thrusting several hundred feet into the air before being
hidden by their leafy branches.

"He might learn of them, but they are not his to
destroy," said a voice from the undergrowth.

Verdon gripped the handle of the pistol in his holster as he looked in the direction of the speaker. At
Siskiel's hiss he glanced back at the trail. Twenty feet
away, a drawn bow and the point of an arrow were all
they could see of a guard on the path.

29

"**H**o-hol—don't shoot," cried a small voice from above. "These are our frie—companions." Iliki fluttered down to land on Verdon's shoulder. "Clariel is waiting ahead," he told them, and turned back to glare at the elf. "And you have orders to le—allow these people to travel through your land." He fluffed his feathers.

Before Iliki had finished speaking the bow had disappeared. Verdon had not seen the archer, and as they walked up the trail, he glanced several times at the tree, but no movement gave away the elf's presence, even if it were still there. Verdon knew the guard still hid in the shadows; he felt the watching eyes like a touch on his skin.

"You're not to le-lea—step off the trail," Iliki instructed as he shifted until he found a secure position on the ex-guardsman's shoulder and dug his claws into Verdon's cloak. The trail led through a depression between the main part of the wide cliff and the slope behind it. They walked beside a small bubbling stream that traveled in the same direction. The light that had brightened as they climbed up from the ledge of the shadow dwarfs began to dim. To their right they could see the sunlight shining on the tops of the tall trees, but the shadows had faded from beneath their feet. The air was warm and they walked through another mist. A sound grew on their minds for some time before Verdon realized he was hearing a waterfall. Moss and lichen became more abundant as they progressed. The fungus smothered all the undergrowth but wide-leaved ferns. Here, too, they were aware of being watched, though they could see no one and no movement except for a desert hawk that flew lazily away.

The sickly sweet odor of decay hung in the air. Piles of rotting leaves and tree limbs lay in orderly rows with paths between. Mushrooms grew everywhere, some as small as Verdon's little fingernail, and others stood eight and ten feet tall with caps six feet wide.

"Yum!" Rala said, reaching down to pick one of the smaller caps.

"Leave it alone," Verdon ordered. "We don't want trouble."

Rala gave him a sour look, but she obeyed. He understood her desire, he liked mushrooms, too. Aktar looked around and shuddered. The meat-eating rapacians weren't tempted.

Later, out of the corner of his eye, Verdon saw Aktar rising, as though he had been walking stooped over. He slid something into his pouch. Since the trail offered nothing but mushrooms, he had probably picked a few. Verdon hoped the desert man's greed did not cause them trouble.

If Siskiel and Woos had been alone, they would have raced along the trail and out of the valley of the mushrooms. They seemed to dislike the moisture and kept wiping it off their skins.

"It's one thing to wash away the scent for hunting, but another to spend all day in a bath," Woos complained.

"It's not fa-fa—we're close to the stair," Iliki said as the path turned west, into a narrow valley. The shadows deepened and the air seemed even more moist, but the sound of the waterfall receded. They had walked nearly a mile when they smelled smoke. A few minutes later they rounded a grove of tall mushrooms and saw Kree lying under one. Beneath another, Clariel knelt on the ground, tending a pot of steaming mushrooms.

"One should always store fuel for the body before making a strenuous climb," she said as they walked up. She raised her bright, tilted eyes to Siskiel. "I'm sorry, but the elves of these ledges do not allow their animals to be hunted."

The rapacians snorted at the softness of the elves, but they had brought a supply of food, so they ate from their packs while Verdon, Rala, Aktar, and Iliki took advantage of Clariel's culinary skills.

Clariel carefully extinguished the fire while the others rested. She kept well away from them, busying herself by checking the extra pack the dwarfs had sent for her, by petting Kree and walking through the grove of tall fungi.

Verdon understood her message, that she did not want to speak of the reason for her visit to the ledges of the elves. Aktar surprised him by shouting at her.

"Did you enjoy your visit with your kindred?" he called.

The elf threw him a sharp glance and nodded. She abruptly turned away, but Aktar's curiosity had not been satisfied.

"Did you actually get to see them, or do they hide from their own people as well?"

"Some people value privacy, I guess," Verdon said, wondering at the trader's lack of sensitivity. On the desert he had seemed subtle in most of his remarks. The young warrior had already noticed the change in the man. His complaints had lessened when they began the climb up the western ledges, but his picking the mushrooms and then questioning the elf about what she obviously did not want to discuss bothered the ex-guardsman.

When Rala offered to clean Verdon's plate at a small spring, he leaned to the left to hand it to her. As he

balanced himself with his right hand, he felt a pull
from the damp soil. No thought suggested he take out
the power cluster; his hand moved automatically. He
slipped it from its hiding place and palmed it as he
took the sparkling duplicate from around his neck. To
anyone watching his actions were obvious, but only
Rala knew there were two clusters. He felt the warmth
of the real stone under his palm. He kept it still, trying
to concentrate on drawing power. The movement of
the others distracted him, but the cluster seemed to be
pulsing slightly. It had been warm from his own body
heat, but it grew warmer, then uncomfortably hot.
While he waited, wondering what would happen next,
the pulsing stopped and the stone cooled. When he
slipped it back into his belt, it felt as cold as when he
had first drawn it from the earth.

The damp ground made an uncomfortable resting
place. The rapacians squatted while they ate, but when
they finished they walked around the still-smoking
ashes, as if hoping the diminishing warmth would dry
their skins. Verdon rose and picked up his pack, but
Clariel came over and took it from him.

"Climbs are easier when they are made unencum-
bered," she said with a sly look at Rala. The dwarf had
not missed either the remark or the glance.

"If it's steep, I'll forgo my usual remarks with my
pack." The dwarf handed over her burdens, and Clariel
fastened them to the makeshift harness she had devised
for Kree. She added Aktar's load to what the lizard
would carry, but the rapacians scorned her assistance.

Clariel led the way a hundred paces further down
the narrow valley and turned on a trail that led to the
bottom of a stair. They paused before stepping onto it
and stared up. The steps diminished in the distance
until not even a pinpoint showed the top.

"Are you sure you don't want Kree to carry your
packs?" Verdon asked Siskiel with a grin. The rapacian snorted his denial, but Verdon thought it lacked
the assurance of his first refusal.

The steps were stone at the bottom. Verdon guessed they had been climbing for a mile when the stone lightened and changed in color. Before long they were walking on marble. Another mile and the composition of the steps gave way to a slick, glassy surface. A hundred steps further and the clear glass beneath their feet gave Verdon a queasy feeling, as if the stair had lost substance.

Clariel had begun the climb with Kree. He brought up the rear of the column, and she wanted to be sure he could handle the steps. Verdon had led, but soon the two rapacians had passed him by, taking the human/elf-sized steps two and three at a time. They were nearly out of sight.

Rala and Aktar were a hundred or more steps behind Verdon when Clariel passed them by and suited her pace to Verdon's.

"You can see why they call it the crystal stair," she said. "It could be dangerous in the rain." They both turned weather-wise gazes on the sky, but they could discount that peril for the moment.

"Will the rapacians be in any danger if they reach the top of the steps ahead of us?" he asked. He knew the humanoids had trouble slowing their pace to human speed, but he had thought of warning them about going on ahead. His warning might have had the opposite effect. They were vain about their abilities, and the suggestion that they might run into trouble could have been taken as a challenge. Verdon also remembered what his rescuer from the net of the kred had told him about the reason his people had been driven into Skar. Elves had longer memories than any other race on Aden.

"The elves of these ledges know we have permission to pass," she replied. "They wish you success."

He tensed, waiting for her to tell him they wanted him to bring the power cluster back to assist them, but she looked out over the steep slope as if the conversation had ended. After a moment she glanced back at him.

"You have not said. Were you successful in the shadow dwarf caverns?"

"A trade," Verdon grinned. "Did you achieve your aims with your kindred?"

"If we are to speak only of completion, I did what I was asked to do. Nothing more can I say until we are out of Skar. There are ears that are strangers to the deafness of distance."

"Fair enough," Verdon said. "I possess what I went to get. I don't know if I can use it."

"No weapon is truly yours until you know your skill with it. You will need to try it before you attack the thunder train," she said.

"Missing your battles with the nocturnals?" Verdon grinned.

"The creatures of evil will prove sufficient for my needs. I have but to live to complete my tally. I referred to your need to develop your skill with the cluster. Now that you have what you sought, we need a plan for attacking the train."

"That's what's worrying me at the moment," Verdon said, putting his finger on the restlessness of his mind since leaving the dwarf caverns. "We number eight if the rapacians stay with us, and Iliki is too small to be noticed. We won't even be considered a threat, not to something as large and as well guarded as the *Dominant*. They don't release the sentinels except for a large number of nocturnals or a major battle."

"Where do you plan to get a larger force?"

"I don't know."

They continued to walk in silence. The stair continued until Verdon decided he would age to a graybeard before they reached the top. Midway through the afternoon they saw the end, and everyone except the reptilians and the elf complained about sore muscles when they reached the second elf ledge. Kree gave a sigh and dropped to the ground. Verdon noticed the rapacians seemed stiff, but he doubted their problem came from the length of the climb. They had found the steps too small for their comfort. Even Clariel admitted she suffered from the sustained effort of the stair.

They had reached the upper ledge of the elves and could look down on the thick forest. The outer rim of the lower plain still glowed in the sunlight. Some of the trees had bright, light green leaves, as if they were just getting their spring foliage. The dark green of the giant trees loomed above the others like brooding shadows.

"We have another hard climb ahead of us," Clariel said. "We have been given the use of a safe haven for the night, but we must reach it before dark."

They continued to climb winding paths that took them up two hundred feet at a time and then flattened out on the terraced levels of an orchard. Verdon kept an eye on the dwarf and the human who brought up the rear, afraid they would fall behind. Aktar seemed tired, but he kept up. Rala had slowed to walk by Kree and talked to Iliki, who rode on the lizard's back, perched on the packs. Clariel took the climb in her stride.

Verdon caught the glint of metal in a fruit tree, the only movement he had seen since they had been halted by the bowman on the lower ledge.

The sun had disappeared and darkness was nearly complete when Clariel led them into a five-sided wooden structure at the top of the terraced orchard. Ten feet from the door of the building Verdon's sword flashed, throwing light from its scabbard. Blue lightning danced across Clariel's arrows and the spearpoints of the rapacians. A glow from beneath Aktar's cloak suggested he carried dweomered weapons he had not admitted to having.

"A strong magic protects this haven," Clariel said. "We would be wise to take full advantage of the safety."

The building consisted of one large room with a fireplace in the middle of the floor. A fire burned in the stone surround and the smoke obediently disappeared through a hole in the center of the roof. Ten wide platforms, two to a side, ringed the walls. They were a convenient height for sitting and wide enough for sleeping. On one sat a basket of fruit, more than the travelers could manage that evening and the next morning combined.

"I hate to disappoint you, dear elf," Aktar said with a trace of his old humor. "But if it's not too disheartening, I'd rather not go searching for nocturnals tonight."

"I'm in agreement," Clariel replied. "But if someone else rids the world of them while we sleep, I will hold you accountable."

While Aktar laughed, Verdon noted the banter and marked it as a milestone in the elf's healing attitude.

Clariel told them her kindred watched through the night, a precaution added to the magic protection of the dwelling. Verdon warned himself it would be his last safe sleep and to take advantage of it.

The next morning he woke before the others and was ready to travel before they had finished their morning meal. The fruit of the elves went well with the travel rations. No one objected to starting, but they ran out of trail within half an hour.

The day before they had ascended half the distance to the desert floor, traveling far faster than they had when descending. Verdon decided he had been spoiled by good trails. He chafed at the delay caused by having to hunt for a path. Iliki had flown on ahead and tried to pick the easiest course, but the bird had no experience in climbing. Twice he led them up easy slopes only to find, when they reached the top, that they had to climb up and down gorges across their path.

At sunset they were only one ledge above the orchards of the elves. Verdon showed his disgust in every step. He stomped through the scrubby trees and around impenetrable clumps of bushes.

"If you knock down the ledge, Clariel's people will have to do without fruit," Rala warned him.

"The *Dominant* should be starting its return trip any day," Verdon said. Perhaps it had already passed Skar. He kept trying to number the days since he had deserted the train, but someone always interrupted him. He had tried to start over several times and had just confused himself.

"We can't go much further today," Clariel unnecessarily pointed out. Her gaze flicked to Rala and on to Aktar. Both were showing their fatigue. Even the elf seemed tired, which was unusual for her.

"Siskiel, does anyone live on this ledge?" Verdon asked. He wondered if they might find friends and shelter.

The rapacian nodded slowly. "On clear nights we sometimes see fires. Who is here, how many and what sort, I cannot say."

"I don't see anyone about," Iliki said. "But who can, through this tangle of brush and trees?"

"Let's find a clear space where we can build a fire and keep a watch," Verdon suggested. "We'll want to gather plenty of wood."

Siskiel and Woos trotted ahead, seeking a place to camp. Verdon, Clariel, Aktar, and Rala spread out and began to pick up dry sticks as they followed. Verdon had his arms full of fuel from their fire when a jurak loomed up in his path.

At least it resembled a jurak. The muscular creature stood seven feet tall, had the usual sloping forehead, large ears, heavy, protruding underlip, a face of appetite with little forethought. Its two tusklike teeth were not as long or as pronounced as most of the race, the eyebrows were not as heavy, and the eyes were rounder. Its skin was darker than average, what he could see of it beneath the brown fur. It was altogether an imitation of a jurak, as if some artist had softened the features, removing the harshness of reality.

The jurak wore a breastplate and cuisse and greaves and carried a heavy, two-handed broadsword. It issued a challenge.

"Stand and fight, human. To die a coward is the worst fate of all!"

30

Verdon did not want to fight. He wanted rest, a meal, and a chance to finish making his plans. The jurak's challenge was only the latest irritation in a day full of maddening events, and while he had no desire to harm the stranger, he was suddenly enraged. The creature stood a foot taller than the ex-guardsman and outweighed him by eighty or more pounds, but Verdon's anger kept him from feeling threatened.

"Don't be stupid!" he snapped. "I've no reason to fight you." He had known several juraks and had liked them. Their race possessed all the tact and diplomacy of a thunder train, but each had been honest to a fault.

The creature in front of him lowered his heavy brows in a frown. "You refuse to fight?" he said as if he couldn't believe what he heard. "The glorious battle is the purpose of life. Honor can only be gained in death." The jurak stared at him, obviously expecting him to understand. The creature seemed so disappointed, Verdon almost felt sorry for him. Almost. His main emotion was disgust at the idea of injuring or even killing another being for no purpose.

"I've no argument with you, I've never injured a

jurak, and I see no reason to. You have nothing against me that I know of." He paused. "Unless you begrudge my friends and me a fire through the night and passage through your land."

The jurak took a stronger grip on his blade and spit on the ground. "We are not juraks. We call ourselves halvers. If I said you had to fight for the fire, would you draw your sword?"

"I suppose I would," Verdon reluctantly agreed. Juraks were, as he had coined his term, naturals, people who belonged in the Known Lands. His challenger, who called himself a halver, had to be partly jurak, mixed with some other natural species. Doing battle for a fire seemed a waste, but the travelers needed rest, warmth, and protection from nocturnals.

He had carefully piled his gathered wood in the shelter of an overhanging bush and drawn his sword when two other halvers came out of the dense shrubbery. They had obviously heard at least part of the discussion. They both wore two-handed broadswords in long scabbards that hung down their backs. They wore armor made of leather, but one boasted a metal helm. His beard was thicker than the others' and slightly gray. Neither had pulled his weapon. They stepped between Verdon and his challenger.

"Don't think you can fight him for wood and a fire, Havman," the oldest said. "Have to check the law. Don't know much about it, but think letting him camp falls under the laws of hospitality."

"What's hospitality?" Havman asked, glaring at the older halver.

"Heard something on it once," said the second, younger halver. "Has something to do with strangers coming to visit."

"But nobody ever comes to visit," Havman pursued, still wanting his fight.

"He did," the older one said, pointing a long, bony thumb toward Verdon. "Have to check the law."

Havman threw his sword on the ground in disgust.

His face wrinkled up as if he were going to burst into tears. Verdon half expected him to stamp his feet.

"Waggin, you *know* old Rancine will recite for four days before she gets to something called hospitality, and by then he'll be long gone."

"Still, you can't go against the law," Waggin, the elder said. He gazed wistfully at Verdon, who felt as if he were being considered a succulent meal. "Shame though. Ain't had a good fight in so long I can't remember. But you can't fight him anyway. Wouldn't be an honorable battle."

"Why not?" Havman demanded. "There's more of them, and they've got some invisible critter with them as won't let you hurt any of their party."

"How come you know that and I don't?"

"Met another of them gathering wood. He started yelling for a Mil-something-nog. I'll tell you, it kicked up some dust coming to his defense. Don't want to get stabbed in the back by a thing we can't see. Not an honorable way to die."

Aktar had been gathering wood, so the halver had to be talking about the desert nomad. Aktar had not been told Milstithanog was only a lie told by Iliki. Rala or Clariel had probably been close enough to hear the trader's shout and had sent a dust cloud in response. Verdon shook his head, remembering Moncreed had told them that not even magic could rid them of the nonexistent creature. But even if he didn't exist, Milstithanog still had his uses.

"I really wanted a good fight," Havman said again, picking up his sword and sheathing it. Verdon thought he had never heard such disappointment in the voice of an adult of any species.

"If you don't fight, how do you keep off the nocturnals?" Verdon asked, intrigued.

"What are nocturnals?" Havman asked hopefully. "They visiting too?"

Verdon stared at the halver, unable to believe what he had heard. Hundreds of thousands of people on

Aden had been killed, the rest lived with the constant nightmare of the evil creatures, and these halvers didn't know about them? Ridiculous! They had to know. They probably gave the night creatures a different name. He gave them a brief description of the monsters he had fought from the top of the thunder train, the flying corpses that had attacked the sail carts, and drew a graphic word picture of the moss monsters that had come up out of the Rotting Caverns.

The halvers were fascinated. Their excitement convinced him they knew nothing about the existence of the evil night creatures spawned by Darkfall. All three started babbling questions without even waiting for the answers.

"Hold it. Wouldn't it be better to talk around a fire?" he said, wistfully thinking of the campsite Siskiel and Woos had undoubtedly found and where they might have a warming blaze waiting. The others would be looking for him. His stomach growled its demand for food, and his legs ached from the climb.

"We'll build a fire," Waggin said, making the decision for the rest. "We'll sit and tell tales of glorious battles."

Verdon convinced them to help him find the rest of his party, telling them the others would know tales about fights that even he had never heard. They agreed and were arguing about which way to look when Iliki swooped down out of the darkening sky. The ferran led the ex-guardsman and the three halvers to the campsite the rapacians had found.

Havman eyed the reptilian-humanoids hopefully, but lost interest when Verdon said they, too, were saving themselves for a special battle. Waggin, Havman, and Glist, the third halver, grew so excited Glist danced about the fire, unable to sit, and Havman nearly fell into the flames.

"If you're that interested in battle, why do you stay here alone on this ledge?" Siskiel asked. "Skar is full of trouble."

"But if we climbed the slopes and fell, that would not be an honorable death," Waggin said. "Our laws say we must always prepare for the glorious battle. It doesn't say anything about climbing the sides of the gorge."

"Then stay where you have no enemies," Clariel snapped. "It is always safer to talk the big fight than to take part in it."

Verdon tensed, wondering if she had angered the halvers. If they attacked her, he had to be ready. He loosened his sword in his scabbard and checked to make sure his pistols were not caught up in his belt. He'd use the gunnes first, he decided. He refused to risk himself or the others unnecessarily. Attacking the thunder train was too important to him.

"We have no saying that talking is safer than doing," Waggin said slowly. "Still, it is a truth. It sings on the air." He rose suddenly. "I return to Honor in Death, where I will speak of this." He turned away from the fire and disappeared in the growing darkness.

"How long have your people lived on this ledge?" Verdon asked Havman. He understood their militant spirit. Most of the juraks he had met were hired mercenaries.

"More than three hundred years," Havman answered. "Our clan is not of the true jurak blood. Our ancestors were half-human, the get from human female slaves. When they almost outnumbered the rest of the village, they were driven into the desert." He raised his head, his eyes flashing. "But we could return to destroy the descendants of those who took our homes."

"If the law permitted it," Glist replied. "There is much we could do if the law did not forbid it."

The halvers would have talked all night, but the travelers were tired. Havman and Glist were considerate hosts. They volunteered to keep watch at least part of the night, but by their cheerful tolerance, they did it to humor the travelers, not because of need.

Verdon resolved to stay awake, though he rolled

himself in his blanket. Next to him, Clariel turned over. He saw her eyes glistening in the firelight.

"It can't be true that they've never seen a nocturnal," he whispered.

"It might be," she said slowly. "My kindred have a saying, 'Fear creates its own enemies.' Many believe the nocturnals are born of some evil enemy so this malevolence must have great power, and yet we may be giving it credit for more than it can really do."

"You've lost me," Verdon said. "Unless you mean this evil entity uses the power of our fear to create the nocturnals. If that's true, the halvers might have remained safe because of their lack of fear."

"If they seek death in battle—if they have no fear of dying—what could the evil of Darkfall use against them?"

"Do you think peace could be their nocturnal?" Verdon asked with a grin.

Neither Verdon nor Clariel trusted the halvers' assurance of safety. They remained in their blankets, but they divided the night watch. Nothing attacked during the night. Just before daylight the Havman and Glist disappeared. Verdon had risen early and had built up the fire when they returned with fresh meat and fruit in large hide bags.

The fruit resembled what the elves on the lower ledge had given them, but not as large or as succulent. Clariel asked them if it grew wild on their ledge. The halvers said it had for as long as they could remember. Verdon suspected their ancestors had raided the lower ledges and the seeds dropped when they ate their spoils accounted for the trees.

Verdon cut the meat into strips that would roast quickly, while Rala and Clariel sharpened sticks and set it to cooking. The halvers had brought enough to sate the two rapacians and stave off Kree's hunger for several more days.

"We've been singularly fortunate in the people we've met," Verdon observed to Rala as they breakfasted on the sizzling meat. "I expected more distrust."

"Milstithanog has a lot to do with it," she grinned, her eyes twinkling. She dropped her gaze to contemplate her breakfast. "What is this?" She asked. "It's definitely good, but I don't recognize it."

Verdon called to Glist, who had been sitting by Aktar, pumping him for tales of the great battles on the desert.

"Upper ledge flyers," the halver called back. "We call them murids."

"Crandow?" Siskiel nearly choked. "You eat crandow meat?"

"Not much else around," Havman replied. "We hunt them or do without."

Verdon and Clariel exchanged glances. He could read her thoughts in his own. Neither really believed the halvers were fighters. They talked a good fight, but with no opponents, how could their abilities be judged? Still, if they hunted and killed the gigantic reptilian flyers, they were brave enough.

When they finished their breakfasts, Verdon helped to extinguish the fire. He shouldered his pack, then walked around a minute or two to let the others know he wanted to start the day's march. Aktar turned a hopeful eye on Clariel, but when she did not suggest the lizard could carry their burdens, he reluctantly picked up his pack.

The evening before they had walked a mile out onto the ledge of the halvers, hoping to foil any nocturnals that might creep out of caves in the cliffs. Verdon led the way back, with Havman and Glist walking with him.

He liked the two half-breeds, and hated to say good-bye, but impatience to climb out of Skar made him brusque.

"We don't have time for games, we need to get on with our mission," he told Glist, who suggested they could at least match training swords, which were nothing more than wooden sticks used by the children.

When they reached the steep slope the halvers watched them start to climb. They were still standing at the bottom of the hill when Verdon, scaling the rough, steep hillside, looked back one last time before moving around a rocky spur and out of sight.

"They wanted to come with us," Rala said as Verdon turned and reached back to give her a helping hand.

"Wanting is not doing," Siskiel, who followed her, hissed as he scraped his knee on a rock. Rapacians might be the fastest runners on Aden, but they had difficulty climbing.

When Verdon reached a gentler slope, where they could at least walk upright, he looked back anxiously. He felt responsible for the others traveling with him, but the urgency of his mission had taken on an almost-physical force and tugged at him. Every pause seemed to irritate it and made the force stronger.

Clariel took pity on the dwarf and the humans and suggested they load their packs on Kree's back. She added hers to the lizard's burdens, but when they scaled the next steep slope, the lizard passed them by. Clariel hurried to catch up with her mount. Verdon soon discovered the lizard had a trail sense he lacked.

When they reached a spot where they could look back and gauge the distance they had traveled, Verdon's spirits rose. The sun had yet to reach its zenith, and they had traveled at least two miles above the ledge of the halver. Ahead a gentler slope promised easier walking. They would soon need to stop, rest and eat, but Kree moved away from the others, and the elf trotted by the lizard's side.

"The elf shouldn't get too far ahead," Rala said as she quickened her own pace. "She could find nocturnals even in the daylight."

Verdon tried to remember if either Clariel or Rala had ever used the other's name. It always seemed to be "the elf" or "the dwarf." Still, each seemed to care about the other's safety. Was it because of loyalty to a companion, or just the knowledge that a lessening of the group's numbers would weaken the whole?

Iliki had been riding on Kree's back, but he soared up and flew back to light on Verdon's shoulder.

"Cla-Cla—she's found a spring and some shade, and says it's a goo-goo—safe place to take a rest," the ferran said. "She's found some woo—sticks and has started a fire."

"Tea," Rala said with a sigh. They had been given some innin bark in Faerkin Fields, and had been carefully hoarding it. The night before they had not camped close to a source of water and had decided not to use up the supply they carried in their flasks. The prospect of tea speeded Aktar's pace, and the rapacians could keep up and pass anyone on a slope where they could run.

Clariel had rummaged in the packs, found a pot to boil water, and had the steaming brew ready. The rapacians snorted in disgust at the smell, but the two humans, the dwarf, the elf, and the ferran finished the pot as they chewed on strips of meat cooked that morning.

"We should rest a little," Rala said when Verdon showed his restlessness. "At the rate we're climbing, we should reach the top by tomorrow."

Verdon hoped she was right. He turned to ask Siskiel if he had any idea how far they were from the western rim of Skar, but the rapacian ignored him and stared at the elf. Verdon glanced over at Clariel, who shaded her eyes, looking east. She rose slowly and pulled her bow from her shoulder.

"Crandow," she said. "It's flying in this direction."

Verdon pulled his own bow and Rala rolled up her sleeves. The rapacians each drew a spear from the long heavy quivers on their backs.

The flying reptile rapidly approached and before long they could see it carried an antelope, probably taken from the Lakwar slopes. As they waited they heard a screeching from directly above their heads. The calls were definitely crandow, but lighter, higher in pitch.

"We've stopped beneath a nest," Clariel said.

"Then there's no hope it will ignore us," Verdon replied, knowing the flyer would believe they endangered its young.

31

The crandow was still a mile from its nest when it spotted the travelers. It dropped the antelope and swooped up, screaming its defiance. Verdon wondered why it had not immediately attacked, but he knew when he heard the answering calls. The scream alerted its kindred. As it hovered threateningly half a mile away, five other flyers zoomed into sight and formed with the first crandow.

"Try to drive them off," Clariel said. "They're just natural creatures doing what they think they must."

"I think we've heard that before," Rala said as she rolled up her sleeves. Before the attack on the watervator she had said the flying reptiles were resistant to magic, but she seemed willing to try it. She saw Verdon's appraising glance and shrugged. "I might not do any good, but I'll do less harm with magic than with one of your pistols."

"They raid our herds to feed their nestlings, and they grow up to feed more little ones," Woos said as he stepped forward, gripping his spear. The normally happy rapacian had no sympathy for the crandow.

Verdon knelt, slipped the power cluster from his belt, and put it on the ground, his hand over it. As he

concentrated, he felt the heat and the pulsing. The
cluster reacted more forcefully and more quickly than
it had the first time he had tried the exercise. He found
it harder to concentrate and then wondered if he
needed to. The cluster seemed to have a life of its own.

The crandow hovered for a moment, squawking at
each other like warriors deciding how to outflank their
enemies. They streaked in together, diving toward the
overhang.

Verdon raised his hand, summoning a wind like the
one he had drawn on the desert. He tried several
times. Instead of a wind, a cold chill ran up his backbone. For a moment he felt as if his limbs would be
frozen. Then the feeling passed. His essencing had
failed him. He felt the hollowness of a lost skill and
helplessness. Then he shook away the feeling. Where
magic failed, he would rely on his warrior's skills.

Rala threw a fireball, but the birds were still in the
open air and her target dipped, sailing below her missile.

"Yes, they can avoid magic," she muttered.

Clariel held her shot though the flyers were within
her range. Verdon grabbed his bow and sent an arrow
into the wing of the lead crandow. His shot delivered a
crippling blow, but the reptile flopped to the ground
without further injury. The other five swooped in,
their necks outthrust and their wings flapping as they
lit. The first narrowly missed taking a nip out of
Siskiel's arm as he fended it off with his spear.

Verdon dropped his bow and pulled a pistol, firing
directly into the mouth of the nearest, which had been
reaching toward Rala. Clariel had grabbed a burning
brand from the fire, determined to hold off a crandow
without killing it, but with reptilian speed it grabbed
the torch between the grip and the burning end. Its
clawed foot raked her arm before Verdon could pull a
second pistol and put a ball into its head.

Kree, who still wore the makeshift harness of rope,
had been freed of his packs. He had paid very little
attention to the crandow's attack on the water-vator

on the eastern side of Skar, but now his mistress had been injured by the creatures. He roared and charged, his normally yellow eyes red with rage. With a leap that took him six feet off the ground, he careened into the crandow Siskiel had been holding off and toppled it onto the creature attacking Woos. They both went spinning, but not before Kree had bitten the head off the nearest. He was still chasing the second one when a flight of eight appeared just above the overhang. Verdon grabbed his bow and shot at one of the two who seemed to be leading the charge. Blood spurted from the crandow's neck, but the wound only seemed to enrage it. Kree scuttled back toward the shelter provided by the overhang, but a crandow landed on his back. He roared and twisted, but the reptile had bitten into the lizard's neck and held on with a grip of its strong jaws.

"Kree!" Clariel shouted, and dashed out into the open, her sword in her hand.

Verdon grabbed his last pistol and fired at the reptile that dropped down to grab her. Blood and bone showered the elf and the lightning lizard, who rolled on the ground, trying to dislodge its attacker. Another crandow swooped down, his target the exposed Clariel, who hacked at the neck of the one still holding on to Kree. Verdon had dropped his bow when he reached for the gunne. He glanced at the spot where he had dropped it, but Woos, jabbing at a reptile that had landed, stood on the tip of the weapon. Verdon pulled his sword and raced to the defense of the elf, fearing he would be too late.

He ran directly under the dropping crandow, his sword up to score the beast as it dropped, but a four-foot arrow pierced the creature's breast. He narrowly escaped being knocked down by the lifeless flyer as it fell to the ground.

A second arrow and a third flew past him, the second so close he felt the breeze of its passing on his cheek. Both missiles struck a dropping crandow. Both were glancing blows, but the reptile gave a screech and soared away.

The air filled with the large arrows. Verdon ducked to the ground beside Clariel and looked to the south, where twenty halvers yelled battle cries and charged, shooting as they came. None of their shafts did more than surface damage. Verdon wondered why they didn't slow to take better aim, but as the last crandow took to the air, bleeding from four flesh wounds, none of them in the wings, he realized the halvers had driven the creatures away without killing more than one.

"They seem to feel the same way you do," Verdon told Clariel as they rose and looked around. Five of the flyers lay dead, but the rest had limped away, most superficially hurt, but they would recover.

Waggin came running down the hill, his iron helm gleaming in the sun. For clothing he wore only a thin leather skirt that covered him from his waist to mid thigh. Two large packs bounced on his back, one sloshed and gurgled. Odd pieces of hardened leather armor had been tied to them, and it clattered as he trotted up to clap Verdon on the back with a huge brown hand.

"You do like to fight," he said with a grin that quickly disappeared as he looked around and shook his head. "A waste of good meat."

"It was eat or be eaten," Verdon retorted. "We didn't call them, they came after us."

"Never thought to tell you, they hear good and they remember," Waggin said. "They know from our battle cry, we hunting them. They leave."

"I wish you had told us," Clariel said. "Now the fledglings will starve. It's not the way of elves to unnecessarily kill natural creatures."

"Won't starve," Waggin replied. "One gets hurt, the others feed it, or feed its young. The ones we drove off will heal. Never kill more than we need for food. Halvers shoot too good. Wouldn't have anything left to eat if we killed all we could."

Verdon thought about the precisely placed arrows of the halvers and knew Waggin's arrogance was not an idle boast.

"If you're leading a hunting party, we've already made the kills for you," Verdon said. "Sorry if we overdid it."

"Not hunting," Waggin said. "You go to fight, and we go with you. We did not find a law that says we cannot climb out of Skar. Many will find honor in death."

"Not too many, I hope," Verdon said as they walked back to the overhang. Waggin stared at him with narrowed eyes.

"We go to aid you. Why wish us misfortune?"

"It's good fortune to die?" The jurak liked to fight, but not even they wanted death. The halvers were certainly a different breed.

"To continue life is to die of old age. Where is the honor then?" Waggin glanced around, noting the fire and the packs. "The murids will be back to protect the nest. Better we leave. Once we are away, we can drive the others off. They will go at our call if their young are safe."

Verdon had already felt the tug of his mission and he had no desire to stay and fight more crandow. The *Dominant* had to be on its way back to Urbana, and intercepting it was his prime goal. He hated to disappoint the halvers and Clariel, but if they could escape the nocturnals or any other creature that promised a fight, he would be delighted.

The professed haste of the halvers did not include leaving the flesh of the crandow that could be eaten, carried, or disguised. Siskiel and Woos ate their fill while the halvers dressed the carcasses, packing what they could carry, and spreading the rest around.

"Stupid murids won't know they're eating their own if we take the skins off," Waggin explained as he shouldered his pack.

Kree, whose wound had not been as bad as they

feared, had been healed by Clariel's elf magic. He joined the rapacians and ate with relish. His stomach bulged when Clariel tied the four packs to his back. He led the way again, and his ability to climb took them well above the ledge of the crandow before the sun dipped beyond the rim of Skar.

Iliki had flown ahead to find a spot for them to camp, and guided the lightning lizard to a narrow ledge. The ferran had found the flattest area they had seen since they had left the overhang beneath the crandow nest.

The vegetation had become sparser as they climbed, so they had picked up sticks as they walked, tying them in bundles to use for their nightly fire.

The embers were glowing and they had allowed it to die down after cooking their meal. The halvers were gathered around the two rapacians and Aktar, listening to their stories. Kree had curled into a large ball near the fire, and Iliki perched on his back, his head hidden by his wing. Verdon went to sit by Rala. She gazed into the darkness with an intensity that alerted the ex-guardsman.

"Why are you worried?" He stretched out his legs, thinking he would welcome the heat of the desert if the muscles in his legs would stop aching. He decided the human frame had not been designed for climbing steep slopes.

"I heard your conversation with the elf last night. Do you really think the lack of fear in the halvers will keep away the nocturnals?"

"I hope so."

The dwarf frowned, as if she did not like his answer.

"You want them to attack?"

Clariel, sitting on the other side of the fire, had been watching them. She rose and came over to sit close to the dwarf.

"Wisdom would dictate a trial of the power cluster before you reach the thunder train," she said. She had mentioned the need before.

"I agree," Rala nodded. "How can we make a plan if we don't know what you can do?"

"I wonder if I can do anything," Verdon replied. He told them about his effort when the first crandow attacked. "On the desert I called up a wind that blew us as fast as we could safely travel—"

"Faster, since we went over the edge," the dwarf interjected.

"But that was my fault, I controlled the wind and its force. I just didn't know we were that close to Skar. Today I tried to use the cluster and I got nothing. It didn't increase my power, I had none at all."

Rala groaned and hid her face in her hands. She scrubbed at her cheeks with her palms.

"It could not have been for nothing. If you couldn't use the cluster, why did it come to your calling?"

"Perhaps the cluster didn't work because it wasn't needed," Clariel said softly. "The crandow aren't evil. They're predators, but nature made them so. They only fought to protect their young—mistakenly today, but how did they know we meant them no harm? They are creatures of the world, and so is the cluster."

"But do we dare go on with our plans before we know if the guardsman can make use of the cluster?" Rala asked.

"I would say not." Clariel repeated her observation of the night before, but she used slightly different words. "A weapon is not yours until it fits your hand as though it were part of you."

"Are your platitudes the sayings of your people, or do you make them up as you go along?" Rala demanded.

"Truth has its own origins. Who is to question it?" Clariel rose and rounded the fire to check on Kree. The truce between the two females had ended.

Verdon thought about the cluster as he pulled his pistols from his belt and cleaned them. He had no oil, and they were beginning to develop rust spots. He scrubbed at the oxidation and then untied a half-empty pouch of black powder to measure out the charge. As he pulled the bag open, the little dwarf light popped out and jiggled in front of his face. By the jerks and spins, he decided it expressed its irritation.

"How did you get in there?" he demanded.

The glowing ball spun around in a circle and settled to float just above his forehead. Rala stared at it and shook her head. "I don't know how the shadow dwarfs will like it when they find it's missing," she said. "If they had traded them, I would have known of it."

"Will they think I stole it?"

"I've no idea, and it's too late to worry about it now." She rose and went to her pack, where she found her blanket and stretched out by the fire.

The glow gave Verdon the needed illumination to finish loading his pistols. He looked across the fire at the elf and the dwarf, both curled up close to the lightning lizard. He wanted his own rest, but they would need a watch through the night.

He rose and walked around the fire when the floating glow started to dance. Suddenly it sailed off fifty feet to illuminate a column of gray mist that swirled as it came toward the camp.

"Nocturnal!" he shouted a warning to the others. The word had hardly left his mouth before ten large arrows disappeared into the column. They had no effect.

Rala threw a fireball without stopping to roll up her sleeves. The nocturnal burst into fire, but it continued toward the camp as if it had begun life as a column of flame. Two large arms reached out, ready to intercept anything it could reach, but the travelers were retreating.

"This is a nocturnal?" Waggin shouted at Verdon. "How is it you have an honorable battle with what you cannot wound with an arrow?"

"You point your finger at it and say bang, you're dead," Verdon retorted, suiting his actions to his words, as he backed away. He wondered about the intelligence of the halvers, but he stopped in mid-thought as he watched the fire die and the column disappear.

"Well, now you know what you can do with the cluster," Rala said. She joined the others, walking around the camp, peering into the darkness. After several minutes of searching and finding nothing, they settled down again. Rala returned to her blanket. Clariel called Kree and the lightning lizard curled up by the fire again. The halvers began to question each other about what had happened, but the elf and the dwarf had seen too many nocturnals to get excited once the danger had been destroyed.

Verdon stood staring at the charred ground. A few tendrils of smoke still rose to disappear into the night, and the smell of burning grass met his nostrils. But how had the nocturnal been overcome? he wondered. Had he killed it or had Rala's fireball destroyed it? Perhaps its composition required a minute or so to be consumed by her fireball.

The elf and the dwarf seemed convinced that he had accounted for the nocturnal, but he knew better. He had wished it gone, but his command had been a facetious remark to the halver.

He had not learned to use the cluster. That was his only certainty.

32

The group had spent the rest of the night in peace. Luckily for his purposes, Ag-Aktar had been asked to stand a short stretch of guard duty during the night. While the others had been asleep, he had sent out the call to Akbaran Wiss, and the magician's messenger had arrived within minutes. The magical construct that resembled a small desert hawk had been waiting at the top of the western rim. It had been keeping an eye on the progress of the travelers.

The creature listened as Aktar told it of Verdon's plan to scale the rest of the slope the next day. They would then travel north-northwest until they reached the established trail of the thunder train. The bird stared unblinking as Ag-Aktar finished his message and then glided away into the night.

The rhanate's cousin became more frustrated with each report. The construct gave him no information. Did it pass on what it heard to the magician and relay it to the soldiers who were supposed to be following the party? Would he find reinforcements when he reached the desert floor again? If not, someone would pay—if he reached the Black Citadel again. His chances of crossing the desert alone were slim.

By the middle of the next afternoon, they reached the western rim of Skar. Their climb was over. Ahead lay the deceptively flat expanse of the Sundered Desert. When they paused to rest, Ag-Aktar stared out over the rim of Skar. From the rim the ledges below, at least those close enough to see with any detail, looked like a carefully painted picture. From above, the vast cut in the world lost perspective and reality.

He thought about what he had learned in the deep gorge. Everything he had seen had been carefully committed to memory, ready to be recalled in a full report to his cousin, the rhanate. When he had seen Siskiel's manite spearpoint, he had hoped to discover a manite mine in Skar, but nothing he had seen justified his suspicion. The cliff dwarfs on the eastern slope worked exclusively with iron ore. He had seen little of the caverns of the shadow dwarfs at the bottom of the western slope, but they were pathetic creatures with their garish, primitive paintings.

The herds of antelope on the Lakwar slopes, the Faerkin Fields, and the orchards of the secretive elves would be worth owning, but were they worth conquering? That would be for the rhanate to decide.

The ruler of the Black Citadel might be irritated with Aktar for his failure to lead the Urbanan deserter to the Burning Coast, but the main object of the journey had been achieved. The ex-guardsman had obtained a power cluster. His dramatic use of it against the nocturnal had proved both its existence and its power. Akbaran Wiss had been wrong when he said the essencer would not be able to use a cluster. The magician had been referring to the ones left in Aramyst at the beginning of Darkfall. Did a power cluster from the caverns of the shadow dwarfs have other properties?

Verdon Stramel's success had been a surprise to Aktar. While they were still on the trail between the ledges of the elves, he had called the messenger and sent a hasty message. His plan had been for the following contingent of soldiers to attack the group and Aktar would take the cluster after the deserter, the elf, the dwarf, and the rapacians were dead.

The halvers had forced him to rethink his plan. They were too accurate with their bows, and their fanaticism could destroy his escort. The group of soldiers from the Black Citadel that had followed Aktar had been limited in number to ensure secrecy. He did not want his safety threatened by their diminished numbers. He wanted to return to the comfort of the castle as much as he wanted the cluster. It would be necessary to take the artifact by stealth.

After the short rest, they traveled west, toward the Thunder Trail. Aktar was relieved to discover the surface was smooth and hard, and not many gullies broke up the desert floor. If he could obtain the cluster, he needed to get away quickly and join his escort. Since they should still have their sail carts, they could easily outdistance any pursuers on foot, except the two rapacians.

He hoped the humanoid reptiles would follow, but not until he had reached his own people.

A shadow covered his face, but all around him the desert was still in bright sunlight. The shadow moved and traveled along the ground directly in front of him. The shadow, as perfect in silhouette as if it had been the hawk itself, hovered for a few moments and then turned, angling northwest. It flew away, but in moments it was back again, hovering so that the shadow fell just in front of his feet and angling away again to the northwest. His spirits rose. He understood the message. The bird was with him, and his escort, which had remained well back to prevent discovery by the ferran, would not be far away. Now he knew the direction to travel when he had the cluster.

After the cool dampness at the bottom of the great rift, he reveled in the heat. The dust, stirred by a light wind, carried a clean dryness, just the opposite of the damp and decay of the lower ledges of Skar. He hoped his cousin would not be interested in the fissure and its products. Once Aktar made his report, he never wanted to see or think of the place again.

Up ahead of him, Verdon led the way, walking between Siskiel and Waggin. The dwarf followed close on the deserter's heels. The column had spread out since they reached flat land. The rest of the halvers and the second rapacian were a hundred yards behind them. In the empty space between the deserter and the end of the column the elf walked with the lightning lizard.

Rala fell back to pace Aktar. He smiled as she glanced up.

"At least we're walking on flat ground again," the dwarf said. "I'd think you would feel more at home here than down on the ledges."

"And you'd be more at home in caverns than in the desert?" Aktar countered. "You never said how your people at Top of the World fare against the nocturnals."

"They're having a rough time," Rala admitted. "There have always been creatures living in the depths, but now my kindred spend more time standing guard or fighting than mining."

"The des—" He reminded himself to watch his description of Verdon. "The guardsman's cluster could help them. It could help us all if your people were protected. The more weapons Aden has, the better we can protect ourselves against this evil."

The dwarf's wide forehead wrinkled in thought and Aktar left her to consider the idea he had planted in her mind. After a few minutes he slowed his steps, dropping back until he paced Clariel. The elf had raised her hood and fastened the veil that covered her mouth and nose, a protection from the dust.

"I imagine you enjoy the dryness as much as I do," he said. "I was beginning to think I'd never be rid of the damp." He had to be more cautious with the elf. She nodded, acknowledging his remark, but she was never very talkative.

"At least we can see any danger during the daylight

hours, but at night you may have a better chance to increase your tally," he continued.

"The wise warrior watches for enemies both day and night," she replied with one of her irritating platitudes.

"I'd think the wisest warrior would also be searching for the most effective weapon to vanquish his or her enemies," Aktar replied.

"You know of one that's better than my bow?"

"I am awed by your skill. Are you unique among your people?"

"Perhaps a little better than the average, but all my people are trained with the bow. Sand elves begin their schooling as warriors when they are still children."

"Ah." He let the sound drag as if he were considering, though he'd rehearsed his speech for days. "Just think what an army of sand elves could do if they were led by the guardsman with his power cluster," Aktar said. "You'd be the greatest scourge the Darkfall could face. I wonder what your tally would be then."

Clariel turned her head to stare at him. Her long, tilted eyes were all he could see above her veillike scarf, but their expression gave him warning she had not accepted his suggestion.

"The human has made a vow, and to ask him to break it would be dishonorable."

The lightning lizard had sensed the mood of his mistress, and he hissed at Aktar. The cousin of the rhanate promised himself to kill the creature if he found the chance. He regretted his need to escape with the power cluster would prevent him from taking his revenge.

"The guardsman saved our lives. We *all* honor his vow and support him in his mission," Aktar said smoothly. "But afterward . . ." He let the suggestion hang for a moment while she absorbed the implications. "You are not the only one who has lost friends to the nocturnals."

"You make no mention of asking him to return to the Black Citadel," Clariel observed.

"Pride in my race and my people doesn't blind me to the difference in our fighting abilities," Aktar replied. "Nomads are good fighters, but we don't compare with yours in battle. I shudder to think what would happen if our two races warred against each other."

He walked in silence for a moment, wondering if he had spread the flattery too thick. It needed salting, he decided.

"You and yours are the obvious choice to rally to the cluster, but if you choose not to do so, then I *will* ask him to return with me to the citadel. The warriors of the rhanate are not badly trained, and our leader would fill Verdon Stramel's purse beyond his dreams if he would lead our army. I will ask him; it's my duty to my people. The choice, after all, is his."

Aktar decided he had said enough for the moment. He walked in silence, wanting to get away from the elf and the lizard, but to just walk away would signal a mission accomplished. He knew better than to underestimate the subtlety of elfin understanding. Luckily one of the packs the lizard still carried had slipped and the elf stopped to secure it. He walked on, lost in his own thoughts.

Just before the sun set, Iliki found a deep gully with a smooth sandy bottom, and Verdon led the way down a barely accessible slope. Throughout their climb and during the late afternoon on the desert, they had picked up sticks and dried cactus to use as fuel for their nightly fire. Earlier, reconnoitering, Iliki had spotted a pair of large desert antelope. Kree and the rapacians had cornered and killed the beasts.

They butchered the meat and set it to cooking while they ate the crandow meat they had roasted the night before. In the heat of the upper slopes and the desert it had begun to turn, but had not yet spoiled.

"Eat what must be eaten, save what we can save for tomorrow," Rala advised Aktar when he grimaced at the food.

The halvers stoically ate the meat, and none of the

others complained. When Verdon had finished his meal, his new allies wanted him to describe the *Dominant* and speculate on the enemies they would face as well as the odds of survival. He spent nearly an hour answering questions about the sentinels. Aktar turned away, uninterested in the subject that fascinated the people of Skar. For three days the thunder train and the sentinels had been the main topic of conversation. Most people, even the best warriors, would be terrified at the thought of attacking an eighteen-foot-tall mechamagical construct, but the halvers rubbed their palms together, their eyes bright with anticipation. They would have questioned the deserter far into the night, but Waggin ordered them to roll themselves in their blankets and leave the human to rest.

The rapacians, Kree, and the halvers bedded down for the night, but the five original companions still sat around the fire.

"And what happens after the attack on the train?" Aktar asked Verdon, putting his minor plan into action. Any dissension would aid his cause. "If we live through it, what will you do then?"

Across the fire, he saw the elf's mouth tighten and her almond eyes flash. The dwarf paused, her cup of tea halfway to her lips, the curling tendrils of her hair bobbing as she glanced from Verdon to Aktar and back.

"If I live through it, I'll take the cluster back to Skar," Verdon replied. "It came from Skar, it should first be used to help the people there."

"And when you've cleared the gorge of its nocturnals, what then?" Aktar pressed.

"Who can say?" Verdon shrugged, but his shoulders were tight with tension. He picked up a splinter of dry cactus that had fallen on the ground when the fire was last fed; he used it to draw circles in the sand. "Darkfall doesn't give us a chance to plan far in advance. First we attack the train. I won't promise more."

"We're all agreed on attacking the train," Rala said slowly. "I also admit you owe a debt to the people of Skar, but after that, it might be wise to give some thought to the cluster's use. To clear the nocturnals out of the Known Lands will require many types of resources and strong arms do need weapons."

"And armies need leaders," Clariel said slowly. "Leaders with the power to instill heart in the fighters as well as helping them with magical powers."

Verdon threw the sliver of cactus in the fire and jumped to his feet. He walked off into the darkness. In a moment he had disappeared around a bend in the gorge.

Aktar waited a couple of minutes while the two females glared at each other. When the elf appeared to be ready to go after the human, the desert man stood, staring in the direction the deserter had disappeared.

"He shouldn't be out there alone in the dark. I'll find him and make him understand you only meant for him to think about the future." Aktar gave them a deprecating smile. "This is my fault, you know, the result of our talks today. I'll explain it to him."

The elf relaxed and Aktar walked away from the fire, following Verdon, elated with the result of his day's work. In the half-light of the fire, just before the bend in the gorge, he noticed a rock sticking out of the vertical gully wall. He plucked it out and carried it with him.

He moved quietly on the sandy surface as he followed the depression, and had begun to wonder if he had missed the deserter in the darkness. Then he saw Verdon just ahead. He allowed himself an exultant smile. His plan to create dissension had worked better than he had hoped and had provided an unexpected side effect. He had not expected to get the deserter away from the group, or to upset the ex-guardsman to the point where he did not even hear Aktar approaching.

Afraid Verdon would turn, he kept his right hand at his side. Aktar knew he was no warrior. He could not afford to alert the ex-guardsman, but Verdon stood staring up the gorge, unaware of his approach. When he was two feet away from the unsuspecting deserter, Aktar raised the rock, held it with both hands and brought it down on Verdon's unprotected head.

The ex-guardsman fell without a sound. Aktar waited a moment to make sure Verdon was unconscious and turned him over. He pulled his knife and cut the thong that hung around Verdon's neck and held the cluster. After he tucked the shining jewel into his pouch he raised the blade again, intending to cut the deserter's throat. Then he remembered the life debt. He had no gratitude to spare, but superstition said only bad luck came to those who harmed their benefactors. He was too much a man of the desert to go against custom.

While he warred between his desire and the code of behavior that restricted him, he saw a winged shadow.

Aktar looked around, spotted a shadowed break in the gully wall, and dragged Verdon to it, shoving him into the shadows. Then he continued walking up the gully. If the flyer was Iliki, he would pretend he was still searching for the deserter.

He traveled twenty paces before he identified the dark shadow in the sky as Akbaran's construct.

"Lead me to the sail carts," he told the hawk. "And you can tell your master I have completed my mission."

33

"**I** see him, here he is! I don't know if he's alive."

Verdon heard the voice from a distance, but with each word the speaker zoomed closer. A part of his mind recognized the little owl-man and knew neither of them had moved. His awareness was growing, forcing itself around the throbbing pain in his head.

He tried to sit up, felt as if he were bound, and then slender hands tugged at him. They were joined by clawed fingers and he heard Siskiel speaking.

"How did he get wedged into this crevasse?"

"You mean who wedged him?" Rala said as they pulled Verdon out and he struggled to his feet, holding onto Siskiel for balance. When his head stopped spinning and his eyes could focus, he saw the dwarf staring pointedly at the front of his tunic. He glanced down and realized the false cluster was missing.

"Are you wounded?" Clariel asked, her slanted eyes full of concern.

Verdon's exploring fingers touched the tender spot on the back of his skull. He felt no blood and shook his head—slowly or it might fall off. The dizziness and the throbbing were already easing.

"My pride is the greatest sufferer," he said, and managed to grin at the elf. "I departed from the path of wisdom, allowing myself to be alone and unwary."

"I never trusted that nomad," Rala said. She stood with arms akimbo as she stared up the gully, and to the surprise of the others she chuckled softly.

"The power cluster has been taken," Waggin said. He turned and shouted the news to the rest of the halvers. Until then Verdon had not realized the entire camp had turned out to search for him.

"Get the weapons, be ready to travel," Waggin shouted to his people. "We'll not let the traitor get away!"

"Rapacians are faster," argued Siskiel, but Clariel, her dark eyes flashing as if with a light of their own, interrupted him.

"And a lightning lizard is the fastest of all. Leave him to Kree and me."

"No!" Verdon and Rala both shouted together. The effort caused Verdon's head to spin, and he caught the shoulder of the rapacian again to steady himself.

"Let him go," Verdon ordered. "Don't try to stop him."

Everyone started arguing at once. Verdon felt incapable of overriding them, so he reached beneath his belt and pulled out the real cluster. The narrow upper gully had kept some of the halvers more than ten feet from the injured human, but those close enough to see were surprised into silence. Rala laughed aloud.

"Let him go," she said. "Let him think he has the real cluster. The longer he believes the lie, the further away he will be when he discovers the truth."

"You knew he was a traitor?" Clariel asked, her eyes narrowing.

"I knew and I didn't," Verdon said quietly. "We've been followed by a small black hawk. I suspected it was a messenger, but I didn't know whose, so I had to suspect everyone. When Rala suggested the ruse, I agreed."

Clariel, Siskiel, and Iliki approved the thought, but Waggin took offense. He stepped forward, his hand on his knife.

"Honor requires an explanation or an apology for your doubt," he announced.

"I never suspected *your* people," Verdon replied with a touch of impatience. "I saw a desert hawk in the sky the day after I left the thunder train. After that I seemed to see it nearly every time I looked up."

"Hawks?" Clariel frowned. "Hawks are everywhere. You never said anything to me." She seemed put out that Verdon had shared his suspicions with the dwarf and not with her.

"Rala felt something was wrong at the citadel and warned me to be careful, so I was suspicious. And maybe the bird, or birds, were just coincidence," Verdon agreed. "I just suspected so many sightings. And I could have been wrong. There may have been three or ten hawks, or only one, following in the hope we'd leave food behind. I just saw them—or it—too often for a quiet mind."

Rala nodded, her hands on her hips, her expression saying "I told you so" as loudly as if she had spoken.

"Still, it is not honorable to let a traitor escape without punishment," Waggin insisted. Behind him Havman and Glist agreed. Clearly the halvers wanted Aktar's blood.

"Those who sent him will shed his blood, and that is a more fitting punishment," Clariel smiled with wicked humor. "Our revenge will be all the sweeter when we think of his anticipation turned sour. The rhanate of the Black Citadel is not known for rewarding failures."

"Enough of this talk!" Rala snapped, her hands still on her hips as she tilted her head back, glaring from the elf to the halver. "Even if he denies it, Verdon has been injured and needs his rest. So do the rest of us."

The large human-juraks eyed her warily. The halvers might not fear the glorious death, but they were wary of the two females in the group. Verdon wondered what the halver women were like if their warrior males were afraid of them.

The ex-guardsman did not object to returning to camp. Rala bullied him into his bedroll and ordered Waggin to set his people to watch through the night.

"Because even if you're not worried about nocturnals, just remember, the nomad wouldn't leave us and attempt to cross the desert alone. A troop of the rhanate's soldiers must be around somewhere." She frowned when they seemed to shrug off the danger. "Remember, Verdon was struck on the back of the head; that was not an honorable blow, but then maybe *you* can achieve glory by being murdered in your blankets."

The halver leader stared at her. "They fight without honor? It would be wise to guard the camp." He strode away shouting out names. Verdon grinned, knowing the rhanate's people would be hurrying back to the Black Citadel. Clariel used a healing spell on Verdon and he was asleep before Waggin had finished instructing the night guard.

The guardsman awoke twice during the night; a tiger lizard nearly blundered into camp, but the fire scared it away. It proved to be fleeing a quartet of nocturnals. The two halvers on guard chased the lizard, howling with glee. Two more took over the duty of guarding the camp, but they soon dashed off after the nocturnals. The next morning Verdon asked Waggin if he knew what happened to his four guards. The halver shook his head sadly.

"They fight too well to find honor in death," he said, the corners of his mouth drooping.

"What a shame," Rala snapped. "Now they'll just have to live until we attack the thunder train."

"Aye, there is still the train and the sentinels." Waggin seemed happier when he lumbered off to join his people.

As soon as the sky was light enough to see, Verdon led the way west. As usual, Iliki flew ahead to make sure they were skirting the gorges and gullies, but the smaller breaks in the ground lessened in number as they left the immediate vicinity of Skar. The small amount of vegetation near the rim, fed by the occasional rain cloud that rose out of the giant fissure, had been left behind. The desert colors, orange, yellow, and purple, with the occasional rosy hue, took over from the greenery.

Rala had been bullied into riding on Kree's back again. Verdon led as fast as he could walk, knowing they still had an additional thirty miles to cover before they reached the Thunder Trail.

During the heat of the day they stopped in a small canyon that offered a little shade from the burning sun. Verdon's blood pounded with urgency, but he forced good sense to override it. The constant fast travel in the heat would wear down the strongest halver or the fastest rapacian. Waggin and his people were all for continuing. Verdon let Clariel and Rala deal with the halvers.

He watched, grinning, as the sturdy little dwarf, no more than knee-high to the jurak half-breeds, bullied them into the inadequate shade the canyon's stone towers provided. She was still bossing them about when Clariel wandered by. Verdon called her over and shared his shade with her. Her almond-shaped eyes gazed into his for a moment before she sat and leaned against the stone that supported his back.

"Indecision weakens the arm of the best fighters," she said quietly.

Verdon felt the now-familiar withdrawal of his mind, believing she had read his most private thoughts. He told himself he should be used to it, but somehow he always felt invaded.

"Are you sure you don't read my mind?" he demanded. She had denied the ability before, but he was never sure.

"I cannot see your thoughts, but eyes speak to those who know how to listen with their own. You are troubled because you lack a plan, I think."

Verdon picked up a rock and tossed it from hand to hand, but his frustration drove him to slam it to the ground, sending up a little dust cloud.

"It's all for nothing! We're not even thirty. The guards on the *Dominant* will laugh at us. Adralk will send up a few more men, but we can't stop the thunder train. They won't send out the sentinels for us."

"Can we enter the compartment of the sentinels?"

"That would be certain death. No, we're out here on the desert with a power cluster I don't know how to use, and I've brought"—Verdon made a quick count—"twenty-seven people on a fruitless journey that must fail. Maybe we won't waste their lives if I admit it now and we turn back."

"You would consider breaking your vow?" The elf's voice was soft, without any inflection. Verdon decided she was being careful to hide her contempt, but he refused to let the idea intimidate him.

"What did you say when I offered to help with your tally of nocturnals?" he demanded.

"It is not the same. You owe me no debt, but I do owe you."

"You have more than repaid that. I'm speaking of my need to free Marchant. He was a valiant warrior and a fine man, but he would be the first to say his spiritual peace was not worth twenty-seven lives. To put my life into a vow to free him is my choice, but to allow so many others to die for my need is wrong."

Verdon had not noticed the arrival of Iliki, who had dropped down to perch on a stone to his right.

"And one of those twenty-seven can't even fight," he said morosely. "Why don't you ever find any small enemies that I can handle?"

"I had plans for you," Verdon said. "I wanted you to repeat your glorious victory on the train."

The little owl-man turned an inquiring face toward the ex-guardsman and Verdon explained.

"You've bragged about firing that ballista. Any attack on the train must be at night, we don't stand a chance otherwise. I had planned for you to slip aboard the train and fire as many of the ballistas as possible. The longer it takes the guards to reload the heavy weapons, the better chance we have."

Iliki fluffed his feathers until he resembled a round ball. "If I stayed close to the side of the train and flew just below the roof, they wouldn't see me," he said.

"Did you have plans for me?" Clariel asked.

"Can you create images?"

"Nothing that would fool a magician. I might deceive the guards on the top of the train, but not for long. If there's a strong magic user up there, I'd be no good to you at all."

"I can handle strong images, but I can't make them move," Rala said. She had walked up while the elf was speaking. She stood too close to Iliki, sneezed, and moved away to sit beyond the elf.

"Could you make me look ten feet tall?" Iliki asked. "If you can, I'll never hide feathers in your cape again."

The dwarf's eyes blazed, her cheeks reddened with her anger, and she wove a spell with her hands. Verdon jumped and had his hand on his sword when he realized the rock worm wriggling on the sand was an illusion.

"I won't do it anymore anyway!" the illusion squeaked.

Rala wove another spell and Iliki reappeared in his original shape, this time fifteen feet high. They watched as he strutted about, admiring his new size. Woos came trotting around the side of a column and whipped his bow from his shoulder. Before they could stop him he sent an arrow through the enormous figure, but Iliki remained unharmed.

The illusion faded and the ferran stood where the left foot of his huge image had been. The ferran glared at the rapacian.

"You tried to kill me," he accused.

"A reflex action, I thought you'd be good to eat," the irrepressible rapacian retorted. "Are you making plans?" he asked Verdon.

"Trying to," Verdon replied. "How would you like to be twenty feet tall?"

"I might get scared and shoot myself," Woos replied. He handed them a water flask newly filled at the tiny spring. He took Verdon's and Clariel's water bags and went off to replenish their supply. Rapacians liked the heat of midday, and the sun toughened their skins until their scaly hides were like armor.

"What we really need are nocturnals," Verdon said. "And if we can find some and draw them to the train, don't shoot them." This last was an instruction to Clariel.

Siskiel and Waggin had been strolling up to join the conclave and overheard Verdon's last remark. They stared at the ex-guardsman as if he had lost his mind.

"You want to go searching for nocturnals and not kill them?" The rapacian's yellow eyes flashed.

"We need enough potential danger to draw the sentinels out of the train," Verdon said, realizing he had made a decision. "The creatures of Darkfall will ensure the release of the constructs."

The allies traded looks, and by their expressions they were certain the sun had baked Verdon's brain. Verdon wondered if they were right, but he could think of no other way to reach Marchant Worsten.

"Using evil against evil," Clariel murmured thoughtfully. Her eyes glistened with combined humor and anticipation. "It is fitting."

34

Ag-Aktar—he would no longer think of himself
without his title or allow anyone save his cousin
to use the familiar—had spent a terrible night
on the desert after stealing the power cluster. He had kept
to the canyons and gorges as much as possible, fearing
pursuit and knowing his silhouette could be seen for
miles when he traveled across the flat plain of the desert.

He had been walking for two hours before the hawk
found him and led him to the five carts and twenty warriors that would be his escort back to the Black Citadel.

Knowing the soldiers of the rhanate could be overcome by the halvers that traveled with the deserter, he
reluctantly gave up his plan to kill the elf, dwarf, and
the ex-guardsman. He would reap a better reward if he
took the cluster back to his cousin.

As the sun dropped below the horizon, Ag-Aktar sat
by the small fire and waited impatiently while a spearman poured his tea into a silver cup. The time had
passed when he would help to tend the fire, dress
desert antelope, and clean his own dishes. He looked
down at his hands and grimaced, thinking there was
not water enough in the Sundered Desert to wash
away the mental stain of manual labor.

He hoped his cousin appreciated his efforts. His reward for his adventure should be the governorship of any new land the rhanate conquered. He reached into his pouch and pulled out the power cluster, wondering if he could use it. He had never allowed the infidels to know he possessed any magic of his own, but he didn't consider himself a slouch.

Perhaps he could enhance his own powers with the cluster. If he could, if he could best Akbaran Wiss, he might even take over the throne in the Black Citadel and become the new rhanate.

The thoughts were new and daring. His breath came quickly, and he slipped off the intricate folding chair that had been carried in the lead cart. He dropped to the ground and placed the stone on the hard-packed earth as the deserter had done.

He concentrated but felt nothing. Maybe the ex-guardsman had felt nothing either. After a few minutes he stood and sat on the chair again.

As the evening darkened the soldiers of the rhanate moved closer to the fire. The captain had ordered a watch set. They were worried about nocturnals.

The cousin of the rhanate concentrated on the stone in his hand. He imagined himself the rhanate, subduing the rest of the tribes on the desert, conquering the High Steppes and then Yzeem. His blood pounded harder, a sense of euphoria grew until he could hardly breathe.

Lost in his dreams, he barely heard the alarm as the nocturnals attacked. Then he realized the soldiers around him were fighting grotesque six-limbed crawlers with huge toothless maws.

As one approached him he stood and thrust out an arm. He had intended to shout the words the deserter had used on the slopes of Skar, but the creature was too close. He backed up, tripped over his chair, and fell. His right hand slammed down on a rock. He heard the tinkle of breaking glass and felt the pain of a deep cut.

He was still staring at the broken glass of the false cluster when the monster pounced.

35

Verdon paused and opened his pack, letting out the little light ball that had traveled with him from the caves of the shadow dwarfs. It bounced in front of his face as if telling him off for keeping it shut inside the pack.

"Just do as I tell you," he said, and pointed down toward the ground. "I need to get a look at the trail."

When the sun had dipped to the west and the desert cooled, the twenty-seven members of the party had begun their trek again. They had walked far into the night.

Verdon's neck was stiff from turning his head from side to side, but he had finally ended his search. Stretching out in both directions, a trail of powdered soil marked the repeated passage of the monstrous cargo carriers. He had reached the Thunder Trail, but were they in time to meet the *Dominant* on its return trip? Siskiel and Woos crouched on the ground illuminated by the ball. Woos stretched out one clawed finger and scratched at the loose soil. He crept along, his thick tail in the air as he kept checking. At Verdon's order the little glow traveled in front of the crouching rapacian. Woos settled back on his tail, his razor-sharp teeth glowing in the light as he smiled at Verdon.

"The tracks are here, the trains do pass this place, but the marks are deep and old. No new ones have been made in weeks."

"How can you tell?" Waggin asked. The halvers hunted flyers and fought with hand weapons, spears and bows. Tracking and the reading of ground signs had not been a part of his people's training.

"The wind has been calm, not strong enough to fill in tracks made in the past few days," Woos said. He knelt again and brushed away the sand from the old tracks. "See how deep these gouges are? Only a windstorm or a light breeze blowing for weeks could fill the holes made by the—how do you say it—tread biters?"

"Tread grippers," Verdon said, turning his head again, gazing first north and then south. His hopes rose. Kneeling by a deep gouge in the powdery soil, he put his hands on the ground, but the world essence told him nothing.

"Clariel, Rala, can you feel the passage of magic here? Is it to the north or south?" He doubted the elf's magic would detect rote arts since his abilities gave him no clue to the passage of the train. As he expected, she felt the area and shook her head, but her mouth tightened.

"An elf has lost his life on this path, his spirit is calling for release, to have his death avenged. I feel nothing else."

Rala had walked away from the others; her hands spread before her, she shuddered and stepped away from the crushed ground.

"What do they do to those tortured creatures?" she asked. "If you know, don't tell me. I feel the passing of tortured spirits, the stain of their pain is in the soil, like spilled blood, but the newest is weeks old." She looked up at Verdon, and in the light of the little glow, her cheeks were white, horror darkened her eyes. Verdon read something in her gaze that she had left unsaid. Her expression told him he didn't want to know.

"We are in time. The evil approaches again, but I cannot say how close it is." She hurried away from the crushed ground of the train's path. She clutched her cloak around her as if attempting to enclose herself in a cocoon to keep out the evil she had felt.

Waggin and the half-jurak watched her go and cautiously backed away. They fingered their weapons, tugged at their lanky hair and beards. They were fighters, ready to vanquish foes they could understand, but she spoke of things beyond their experience. Their nervousness bothered Verdon. He wondered if they had any understanding of what he proposed to fight, or if they could stand against the terrifying auras of the sentinels.

Evil stained all it touched, even those who fought against it, and the halvers were like newborns. They were unsullied by Darkfall, as most of Aden had been ten years before, when not even the juraks or the dreaded ilithix could overcome their fear and fight effectively.

"Where pow-pow—magic fails, wings are more effective," Iliki announced, and leapt from his perch on the lightning lizard's head. Kree looked up and hissed, as if calling the bird-man back, but the ferran had disappeared into the night.

"Nocturnals seldom attack the train on open ground," Verdon said thoughtfully. "Let's walk up the trail. If I remember my maps, there should be a wide valley not far from here, and possibly an oasis."

"A spring means animals, a place where travelers camp, and nocturnals," Clariel said softly. "You still intend to make use of the creatures of Darkfall?"

"It's still the only way I know to be sure the sentinels are released," Verdon replied.

They continued to walk through most of the night. Dawn was not far away when they reached the end of the valley. The passing of the thunder trains had crushed the narrow gorges into a gentle incline of gravelly rock.

Verdon had walked along the path of the train to be

sure he did not lose the way in the darkness. Rala paced him, staying fifty feet off the beaten surface, surrounded by most of the halvers. When they reached the slope that led into the valley she stopped.

"We could wait here until the sun is up," she suggested. "There might be nocturnals down below."

"And you could find your way down the slope without setting foot on the trail of the trains?" Verdon asked, referring to her refusal to walk on the Thunder Trail. His teasing was an effort to put her horror into his own personal perspective.

"I can't help it," she snapped. "And you don't want me to if I am to help you in the attack. I feel drained just walking across that path, as if something were pulling at the core of my existence." She glared up at him as if asking him to deny it.

"You understand rote magic better than I do," Verdon said. "I'll accept your word."

They rested on open ground until the sun rose and the sky was light enough for Rala to climb down the steep sides of the gorge. The others walked along the incline and met her at the bottom. They searched for and found the spring. The water welled up in a rocky depression and spread out in a six-foot pool. Some moisture seeped out and damped the surrounding area, allowing some short-cropped grass and a few bushes to flourish.

Clariel suggested they make camp a good distance from it so the animals could drink in peace.

The morning sun was climbing up the sky, and Verdon was beginning to worry about the little ferran, when Iliki flew in to hover over the elf. The human watched while Clariel and Iliki talked and the elf scratched in the dirt with a small stone. Then she rose and came to sit by him with Iliki perched on her shoulder.

"The train will not reach here today. We think it will arrive late in the night, but possibly not before dawn."

"I fou-foun—located it last night," Iliki said. "I rod—rested on it until sunup and left it then."

"When Iliki scouted for me we worked out the time it took him to fly the distance an elf could walk in an hour. My people can walk half again as fast as the train travels. Since I know when he left the train, we can give you an approximate estimate."

"And if it doesn't reach here until dawn, we can't hope for nocturnals." Verdon clenched his hands in frustration. "If we attack after daylight and they see our number, they'll destroy us without even pausing or releasing the sentinels."

"Iliki can go back to the train later in the day and leave it at sundown," Clariel suggested. "It will be closer, and we can make another, more accurate estimate."

"The next question is, how do we stay alive in a valley of nocturnals through the night?" Siskiel asked. "If they're here, we have to hold them off without killing them through the dark hours."

"And there's to be no honor in death while we do this?" Waggin asked. "This adventuring is more difficult than I supposed."

Knowing they faced a fearful night, the others made use of the day to sleep, but Verdon was restless. He wandered around while the others slept, wondering how they could hold off the nocturnals through the night without destroying them.

There would be creatures of the Darkfall; the spring and the sparse vegetation in the valley drew the desert wildlife, and the presence of the animals drew the night creatures. The periodic passing of the thunder train brought them out. The oasis had to be known to the local traders. Their caravans probably used it also. Verdon passed the bones of a tiger lizard; only the creatures of the night could have destroyed it so completely, proof of his theory. For the first time since the beginning of Darkfall, evil and good would be allied, but how did he keep both alive until the arrival of the *Dominant*?

While he paced the perimeter of the camp, a gust of wind whipped through the canyon. The dust stung his

eyes and blew the little ferran off his perch on Kree's
back. Iliki flew up, wobbling slightly with sleepiness,
and landed on Verdon's shoulder. The owl-man
yawned, politely covering his mouth with his hands,
when he noticed the direction of the ex-guardsman's
gaze.

Verdon stared up at the tall, stone columns, where
diggings of desert worms had scoured holes in the rock
for centuries. The wind, finding additional surfaces to
scour, had gnawed at the openings, creating caves and
ledges out of old lairs.

"Don-don—stop thinking about it," he said. "You
can't hide up there in the worm caves."

"Why not, if we destroyed the worms first? We'd be
out of reach of the nocturnals until we were ready to
attack the train."

"Kil-ki—destroy the worms?" Iliki frowned. "How
do you plan to do that?"

"Well, I thought we might use the ropes the halvers
brought with them. You could carry up a loop and
anchor it. I could climb up beside a worm hole and if
you were to—"

"Fl-fl—approach close enough to draw out the
worm, you could cut its head off," Iliki finished for
him. "I knew I would be the bait, that's why I don—
refuse to think about it."

"Then you suggest an alternative."

"It won't work," Iliki said. "I can—I'm not strong
enough to manage that much rope. I might get a length
halfway up that column, to that outcrop." He pointed
at a narrow, wind-worn spire that jutted out of the
nearest stone tower.

"Let's try it," Verdon suggested. "If we clear the bottom of the tower, you can add a length later."

"Why is it always me?" Iliki demanded. He was
being unfair, he had only been the bait once before,
and then at his own suggestion.

"And it won't be necessary for him to carry the
rope." Clariel spoke from just behind him. Verdon

turned to see the elf standing in the shade of a column. Had she just arrived or used some elf magic to blend with the stone?

Clariel, who, when she chose, moved nearly unnoticed, like a gentle breeze, returned to the camp and brought back a length of rope taken from Waggin's pack, her bow and arrows. Verdon showed Iliki how to knot the rope securely. The elf took one end, fastened it around her arrow, and sent it up the column. The force of her shot could have carried the line across the canyon, but when it passed through the narrow opening between the main column and the stone spire, she whistled. The arrow stopped and hung dangling from the end of the line.

After Iliki knotted it, Verdon climbed the rope, and, with Clariel directing him from below, he half stood, his feet anchored against the rough column, his left hand bearing most of his weight on the rope, and his sword in his right hand. He was poised just beside a ledge with a worm hole. Iliki flew close and gave a hoot, imitating an owl. For a ferran who was half-owl, he was surprisingly inept at mimicking his species.

The noise was enough to bring out the worm. The annelid lashed out so quickly Verdon nearly missed it. It was drawing back when he severed the head with one sharp swing. He reached for the still-twisting body of the worm and was just pulling it out when he was startled by shouts from below and nearly lost his balance.

"Honor in death, the glorious battle begins!" Havman shouted. In an instant all the halvers were on their feet, their weapons in their hands. Two stumbled over their fellows as they looked for the foe. Verdon had caught his balance and had thrown down the body of the worm when they realized what he was doing. "He means for us to hide in the holes during the night!" one halver snarled, but Waggin turned on him with a snap.

"It is no dishonor to take the habitation of a crea-

ture you have vanquished, but we must do the killing
ourselves, else we cannot use the shelters."

Verdon sighed and watched as the halvers knotted
their ropes together. Clariel shot the long lengths sky-
ward and Verdon lost his bait as Iliki was put to work
tying off the ends.

The halvers swarmed up the ropes, working in pairs.
The first would lure out the worm while the other
waited to kill it. Four stone columns were free of the
worms before Clariel could get the other ropes
anchored.

"There's a fallacy in your plan," said Rala, who had
been awakened by the commotion and stood watching.

"That is?" Verdon asked, while he tensely watched a
halver struggling with a worm that had wrapped itself
around his arm. The human-juraks quickly tired of the
easy kills and were adding a challenge to the fight by
going after them singly.

"The elf cannot hide in the worm holes while Kree is
on the ground."

Verdon had forgotten about the lightning lizard.
Rala was correct—Clariel would not leave her mount
to fight off the nocturnals, and Verdon could not aban-
don her. If they stayed on the ground, the halvers, not
keen on staying in the worm holes anyway, would
refuse to climb. His bright idea about the worm holes
would amount to nothing but a game for the halvers
unless they could hoist the lizard up a tower.

"Try the cluster," Rala suggested as her thoughts
traveled along the same lines as his. "It might be possible to lift."

Verdon sighed, knelt on the ground, and drew out
the cluster. He placed it on the ground under his hand
and felt the heat and the pulsing. For nearly half an
hour he concentrated on absorbing the power of the
world essence. Then he gave it up. When he had knelt
to draw the essence with his bare hand he had succeeded. With the cluster, nothing.

He had wasted his time and effort getting a talisman

that did him no good at all. The knowledge opened his spring of frustration and anger until everything around him seemed coated in red. Had Rala used him too? Common sense took over. He trusted the dwarf, she had acted in good faith, it wasn't her fault he could not use it. Without it, could he still draw on the world essence?

He put the wafer back in its hiding place and knelt again. He would not use it. He was better off without it. His empty hand on the dry soil of the canyon instantly became a conductor for the power. He felt it grow in him, he felt the euphoria as his fatigue fell away and his strength grew. The power came to him so fast he was full to bursting with strength before he knew what was happening to him. He stood and looked around, needing a use for some of his stored power.

No target presented itself, and he felt as if he would burst. The essence had never before been uncomfortable, but this time his entire body hurt with excess energy. He turned and planted his feet. He pushed against the fifteen-foot-thick stone column behind him in a need to exert some effort. The stone cracked with a rumble like thunder and slowly toppled.

Luckily none of the halvers had been working on the column. As the tower fell, Verdon and Rala had raced away from the base. The halvers clung to their ropes, the worms forgotten as the ground shook with the impact of falling stone. Verdon was still coughing and wiping the dust out of his eyes when Rala glared up at him. He saw fear in her eyes, and it had made her angry.

"The idea was to raise Kree, not lower the landscape."

Verdon ignored her remark. That tremendous power had to come from the cluster. He *could* use it, but how had he done it? As important, could he do it again?

36

Kree had been perched on the high ledge for most of the night, but he still worried about falling. He alternately hissed, whined, and roared, keeping the wandering nocturnals around the base of the column.

Lifting the lightning lizard up the column had been a terrible job, but the halvers had managed it. Clariel adamantly refused to let Verdon attempt levitation. She valued Kree too much to allow him to be risked by an unproved power.

The fact that Verdon had caused the destruction of the stone column had been spectacular, but it was not enough for her to trust him with Kree. They had also discovered Verdon's feat had not been as great as they had supposed. The base of the column had been riddled with old worm holes, and for years the desert wind had whistled through them, eating away the stone core. Everyone had insisted it had taken strong magic to knock down the column, but, looking at the crumbling base, Verdon thought the next good gust of wind could have toppled it. They still had no idea of his limits.

During the evening hours they had pulled dry grass

and had made small torches. When the nocturnals appeared after sundown, all twenty-seven members of the party were ensconced in the larger worm hole caves or on ledges high up on the stone towers. Luckily there were no flying nocturnals in the canyon.

When the nocturnals attempted to climb, the halvers, the dwarf, the elf, the human, and the rapacians dropped their torches. The shadowy forms fled the flames and no one had yet seen their evil allies well enough to know what they were or to judge their number. Before long the night creatures were seeking easier prey, but they stayed within the canyon. They kept wandering onto the crushed path of the Thunder Trail as if they knew the *Dominant* was on its way.

And the train would be stopping, or at least slowing, since the fallen column lay in broken pieces across the trail.

Iliki had flown back to meet the train, with the announced intention of leaving it at the moment the setting sun touched the horizon. When he arrived back at the canyon, he and Clariel had worked out the time and distance. If the elf and the ferran were accurate in their estimation, the *Dominant* would reach the canyon an hour before the sun rose.

During the afternoon and evening they had all managed snatches of sleep. Some of the halvers in the higher worm caves and on the ledges were softly snoring as Verdon anxiously watched the stars.

Iliki had left a short while before, on his way to fire off all the ballistas he could safely reach. Verdon worried about the little ferran, but Iliki had been excited about his part in the attack. It took time to reload the ballistas, time that might make the difference between a successful defense by the Iron Guard and a need to free the sentinels.

Verdon raised his head, recognizing the sound of the train, as a shadow hovered overhead and dipped to land on the ledge where he waited.

"The two ballistas on the fro-fron—by the cannon of

the engine car are still loaded and the two on the rear barge," Iliki panted. "They never saw me or noticed the discharge of the weapons." The ferran paced back and forth, his feathers puffed out as he boasted of his success. "They didn't see them fired in the darkness, and no one can hear anything over the noi—clatter of the treads."

Verdon nodded. Iliki's task had gone according to plan. In the darkness the guards on the ends of the train were not aware he had fired off most of the ballistas, but if he had attempted to shoot off the two at the front and the two at the back, they would have seen him. Even though he could have escaped into the night, they might have called out extra guards to check the rest of the heavy artillery.

"You've done your job," Verdon said. "When the battle starts, you stay up here, out of the way."

"I've ear—deserve a rest and I need it," Iliki agreed. "But I want to see the fight."

"Just stay out of the way," Verdon warned. "We don't want someone to shoot at a shadow and hit you by mistake." He moved his pack to give Iliki more room and accidentally brushed the flap in the darkness. Before he could close it again, the dwarf light sailed out, bounced its irritation at being shut up, and settled to float over his head.

"Get back in the pack or hide behind me," Verdon ordered. "You're not helping. Do you want to get me killed?" The light whisked behind him and stayed until the noise of the train became the roar of the thunder that had given it its name. On the floor of the canyon, shadows began to move toward the established path of the *Dominant*.

On the columns, the halvers, too excited to wait, started down the ropes.

"No, it's too soon!" Verdon heard Clariel echoing his own shout, but the roar of the train covered their warnings. He saw the elf swing out on a rope and start down from her place by Kree. The lightning lizard had been hissing and roaring at the nocturnals below; he crept to the edge of the outcrop that supported him and leaned over, roaring at his mistress. When he overbalanced, Clariel raised her hand in an attempt to stop him.

Verdon placed one hand on the stone and used the other to cast a levitation spell. In the dim light he could see Rala reaching out. The lightning lizard hissed his fear as he walked down the side of the column headfirst, reaching out with a cautious foot, afraid of falling, yet held back by the spells of the three magic users. They would never know whether the lizard safely reached the canyon floor on his own, as a result of all their spells, or only one use of the arts.

When Kree was safely on the ground, Verdon's hands stung with rope burns as he rapidly descended the rope and raced after the halvers. He was too late to keep them from attracting the notice of the nocturnals.

The evil creatures of Darkfall lacked the intelligence of humans, elves, or dwarfs, but they were capable of limited knowledge. They were not known for any loyalty to each other, but they did band together for a combined strength and they understood enough of the principles of warfare to use the tactic of ambush. They realized Verdon's broken column would bring the *Dominant* to a halt.

Lord Urbane's mechamages chose open, flat ground for the trail when they could, but in this particular area of the desert, the deep canyons, gouged out by the ancient ice floes, all ran north to south. Through the years, the runoff from the Pours had dug deep gullies in the ground, most on an east-to-west course as the water sought the canyons.

Even though the canyons, with their stone towers, offered more danger from attack by nocturnals and other enemies, the path was smoother and faster, and the mages who steered the trains had taken advantage of the easier travel.

This particular canyon stretched for four miles, and

the Thunder Trail wound through it in long, easy curves. The mechamages at the controls would be within a quarter of a mile of the broken columns blocking the trail before they knew they faced a problem. Since the giant cargo carrier could not back up, and the fallen rock was too heavy for the blade on the front of the car to push aside, the mechamages would need to call out the sentinels to clear the path.

The nocturnals had worked out where the cars would stop and were positioning themselves behind boulders and stone pillars, waiting for the train to come to a halt.

If the halvers would leave the nocturnals alone, the creatures of Darkfall would keep the guards occupied, but Verdon's allies were too anxious for a fight. The ex-guardsman raced to intercept them, but he was too late.

A monstrous shape, six feet wide and more than twice as long, lunged for Waggin. It appeared to be a cross between a spider and a worm, with half its head given over to a mouth full of gleaming teeth. The leader of the halvers gave a shrill yell and leapt toward it, plunging his spear deep into the creature's right eye. The half-human, half-jurak had put all his weight behind the thrust, and the point had broken through the back of the nocturnal's skull. Waggin tugged at his weapon, trying to free it. He pulled and tugged until the monster flipped over on its back. The half-jurak turned his back on the creature as he threw his shoulder into his attempt to free his weapon.

Still in its dying throes, the nocturnal swiped at its killer with a foreleg. Verdon brought his sword down across the hard shell-like leg and severed it.

"There's more glory in killing the enemy than dying for him," Verdon told the halver, who turned to glare at the human. He had been lecturing the halvers on the subject of staying alive to destroy evil, trying to plant the idea that to allow themselves to die was to allow evil a victory. They had listened in silence, but by their expressions they completely rejected his theories.

Around him the halvers were gleefully destroying the nocturnals. Three halvers had backed a huge creature that looked like a bloated, two-armed cactus against one of the columns and were taking turns poking at it with their spears.

"They're demented!" Rala, who had scuttled down from her perch, shouted to Verdon over the noise of the approaching thunder train. "Will they stay alive long enough to help with the sentinels?"

Verdon shrugged, indicating he could not predict the outcome of their gleeful fight and dodged a creeping creature that seemed more slime than body. He ignored the nocturnals and the halvers as his feet searched out the crushed gravel of the Thunder Trail. He estimated the distance to the obstruction and hurried south, trying to estimate where the last car would be when the *Dominant* came to a halt.

Two vaguely human shapes loomed up out of the darkness, but Verdon dodged them, circling a large boulder that had broken away from the fallen column. Before long they would have quarry enough on the train.

A shadow loomed up beside him and he had jumped away, his sword ready, when he recognized Clariel astride Kree.

"No eyes can see everywhere at once," she shouted over the roar of the train. "We will guard your back."

Verdon had hoped to reach the spot where the last car of the train would stand when it came to a halt, but he had covered only half the distance when, out from behind a column so large it could be called a small mesa, came the glaring eye of the *Dominant*'s trail light. Because of a curve in the trail, the light was directed to his left. Behind it loomed the bulk of the engine car, blocking out the stars. The thunderous sound washed over him, assaulting his ears and mind until he had to fight to think.

Kree had roared, his voice hidden under the thunder of the train, but Verdon had seen his mouth open with his cry. The lightning lizard had bolted to the other side of the trail and behind a column, taking Clariel with him.

As the engine car of the *Dominant* rounded the curve, Verdon was caught in the glare of the huge trail light. He dashed behind a boulder to keep from being too clear a target, but as the stationary illuminator passed, the battle light on the top of the train swung his way.

He kept low, determined not to be a target for the guard. The little dwarf light whizzed by his head and hung directly in front of his face. It bounced and spun slowly, as if asking a question. Verdon ignored it, waiting for the passage of the train to make the battle light ineffective. Suddenly the dwarf light shot up in the air and out of sight.

"*Now* what's it up to?" Verdon muttered, and forgot it as he judged the distance to his next shelter and made a dash across the uneven canyon floor.

The front battle light on the *Dominant* swung wildly. Verdon looked back to see the dwarf light diving over the head of the guard. Verdon could see it sailing away as the silhouette of the armored human stabbed at it with his sword. The light disappeared. The *Dominant* continued its lumbering passage though it was approaching the broken column. Verdon could see the obstruction clearly in the combined glare of the battle and trail lights, but the mechamage driving the train had not attempted to slow the engine car.

The engine car plowed into the fallen column with a crash and the scream of metal. An unearthly wail rose out of the depths of the steam compartment and two of the pipes on the roof split. The little dwarf light came sailing out from the front of the train and dropped out of sight behind a piece of broken column. It had a greenish tinge and wobbled as it flew.

Verdon understood why the mage steering the train had not stopped it. The dwarf light had flown into the front compartment and had probably been harassing the driver. The shadow dwarfs of Skar could be proud of their brave little light creature.

Crashes louder than the thunder of the engine car followed as the momentum of the barges kept them moving. The first slammed into the back of the engine car and angled right. The second struck the first and careened off to the left. The fourth had nearly overturned, and by the time the crash and clang stopped, the *Dominant*'s barges were twisted back and forth as if some giant hand had folded the entire train.

Four guards had been standing watch. Verdon saw the first two fall from the roof. The second hit the ground in the midst of a group of nocturnals. He gave one terrible yell and was silent.

Verdon winced at the damage. He had not intended to destroy the train. He hated the Iron Tyrant of Urbana and most of his works, but the Known Lands needed the trade goods the *Dominant* and her sister trains carried. On the roof of the engine car, the scream of the battle Klaxon gave a belated warning of trouble.

When the cars were still, Verdon sprinted toward the end of the train, knowing the sentinels would be released. He nearly tripped over a guard lying on the ground. Sturwid, and by the angle of his neck, he had died in the fall. Verdon leapt over his still body and continued to run.

He had not reached the last barge when he heard the grind of the heavy doors. The clang of metallic feet on the metal step warned him the first sentinel had stepped out into the night. He paused, looked around wildly, and dashed for the cover of a boulder. He dropped to the ground and laid both hands flat on the ground.

Each time he called the world essence, he felt it come faster and more powerfully than before. Only three sentinels had left the car when he rose, the discomfort of the power pounding in his head, throbbing in his hands, arms, legs, and feet. He felt as if his body was a vessel that had been filled far beyond its capacity.

He gripped his sword and it glowed in his hand. Without knowing how the knowledge came to him, he was sure the blade would slice though the side of the train if he chose to strike at it. He stepped out into the path of the first sentinel and waited, his blade raised, but as the monster approached he was unable to strike.

He knew Marchant Worsten could be the spirit powering the mechamagical monster. He could not strike without knowing.

What was wrong with him? Everything he had done since leaving the thunder train had been in preparation for destroying the sentinel that kept Marchant's spirit prisoner, and now that he had the chance, he could not destroy the creature.

37

Verdon backed away, afraid the spirit within the huge armored body belonged to his foster father. He forgot the power of the cluster, the efforts of his friends and all his planning. What made him think he could destroy the last earthly vestige of the man that had loved him, raised him, and protected him from the dangers of Darkfall and the Iron Tyrant of Urbana?

He heard the whiffle of an arrow passing close to his head and something fall behind him. He glanced back to see Clariel's arrow arcing up away from one of the partially rotted human corpses that had tried to ambush him on his way to intercept the sentinels.

Her slanted eyes questioned his hesitation, but he was unable to answer her. How could he tell her the journey had been for nothing?

On the roof of the train, the guards were racing along the top of the cars. He heard the explosion of a wheel lock gunne and looked around, wondering who or what or had been the target.

Adralk had freed the stabilizing lock and targeted the right ballista on the rear of the engine car before he realized its weapons had been spent. He roared his frustration and ordered up more shafts. The guard, who had been operating the forward battle light, left it as he ran to help his commander. The other guards were boiling out of their quarters, racing down the train, gunnes, bows, and swords in their hands.

Verdon stood in the shadows where the human guards could not see him. His major concern was the huge mechamonster, whose magically enhanced vision was not encumbered by darkness.

The sentinel raised its ax. Verdon dodged its swing with the ease of the world essence that had been enhanced by the power cluster. His fifteen-foot jump had taken him well out of the reach of the metallic creature, so it had found another target. Two halvers rushed up, screaming their battle cries, their spears raised. Like Verdon, they were able to avoid the swing of the double ax with the two four-foot blades, but the giant weapon hacked through their spears as if the shafts had been made of straw.

The halvers stared at the broken shafts in their hands, too startled to notice that the sentinel had taken another step toward them. As the sentinel raised its ax once more, Verdon charged, sure the war machine could not be his foster father. Marchant Worsten would not attack two unarmed foes. His sword sliced completely through the leg armor of the monster and toppled it on its face. Before it could get to its feet, Verdon had jumped onto the huge metallic shoulder and hacked at the neck, the one spot where the head could be completely severed.

As the head rolled away he stared at the huge body. He had destroyed it. The realization came slowly. The feeling of power that still throbbed in him did nothing for that niggling doubt that said one puny human stood no chance against the power of the sentinels.

His doubt was not shared by the halvers. The two who had lost their spears pulled their swords and stood directly in the path of the next mechanical to leave the train. His need to protect them from a power

they had yet to understand drove him into action. He
ran down the huge metallic body, slipped on the leg,
and fell to the ground. His outflung hand came to rest
on the handle of the large ax. As he touched it, the
blade glowed with his newfound power.

He withdrew his hand and the light died out of the
ax. He touched it again, and the power flowed back
into it. Could he use it? The weapon probably outweighed him by fifty pounds, but when he lifted it he
needed less effort than it usually took to heft a wheel
lock pistol.

Near the end of the last barge, the halvers were
shouting as they tore toward the next sentinel. The
mechamonster held its ax low, drawing it back to take
a swipe at the half-juraks. Verdon was too far away to
help them. He drew back the giant ax and threw it in a
desperate attempt to protect his allies.

The huge double blades retained their glow as the ax
sailed through the air. It caught the sentinel in the
front of the huge face shield and split the head and
neck and cracked the chest plate.

Behind the second inert sentinel, a third had
encountered a huge, wormlike nocturnal. It hacked at
the thick coils as the giant creature of Darkfall
writhed. The monster worm tore the body of the sentinel in half with a painful jerk of its coils as the nocturnal lost its head to the sentinel behind its fellow.

On the roof of the train, Adralk was still shouting
for the guards to reload the ballistas. The cannon on
the engine car fired. Someone had remembered the
nocturnals could be burned and flaming chips arced
out over the gorge. Two guards manned the battle
lights. In the illumination from the last barge, Verdon
saw four halvers dashing behind a boulder just as a
blast from a pistol echoed through the canyon. The
crack still echoed when one of the humanoids stood
with an arrow drawn. His shot brought a scream of
pain from the roof of the train. A second arrow arced
toward the base of the battle light. The illuminator

swung wildly and came to a stop, its light shining down the length of the train's roof, spotlighting the guards on the top of the cars.

"Good shot!" Verdon shouted to the halvers.

Waggin's head popped up from behind the boulder. "We will make a new law. It is more honorable to kill enemies than to die."

"Don't kill the roof guards unless you have to," Verdon replied. "They aren't our primary targets." He was wasting his breath; the halvers were ready to fight anything that moved.

"Can we kill the nocturnal creatures now?" Waggin asked, his tone almost begging.

Verdon sighed. The halvers should leave the Iron Guard and the nocturnals to fight each other. While those two groups were busy, the half-juraks and the rest of Verdon's companions might overcome all the sentinels, but he knew better than to ask. The jurak-humans were starved for a fight.

"Just don't kill me," he griped, and turned away, hoping they understood his restriction was also meant for the rest of their companions.

Verdon heard a victorious shout from behind him and looked to see one of the war machines down, the shaft of a spear sticking out from the back of each knee. The sentinel scrambled to raise itself to its hands and knees. It spared one hand to strike out at Woos, who went sailing through the air. Siskiel jumped up on the broad metallic back and rammed his dweomered spear into the waist joint. He twisted the broad point and drove the shaft three feet into the opening between the armored plates. The sentinel crashed to the ground, its huge arms lifeless. Siskiel jumped to the ground and dashed into the shadows in search of his friend Woos.

The damaged illuminator on the train's roof spot-lighted the guards and threw a deep shadow over the ground close to the wheels of the barges. Verdon took advantage of the darkness while he looked around.

The problem with a pitched battle was always confusion as allies dashed after or away from their opponents. They often got separated in the dark, and Verdon found himself alone. He had no idea what had happened to Rala, Clariel, or most of the halvers.

On the roof of the train the guards had succeeded in loading several ballistas. Half a score of huge, bestial nocturnals were approaching the middle barges. Four fell to the heavy shafts of the large, stationary crossbows.

Verdon turned back to look at the rear of the train, but no other sentinels had appeared. They had certainly left their compartment, so they had to be on the other side of the train. He hurried along in the shadow of the sixth barge and ducked under the coupling.

He skidded to a halt only inches from the maw of another of the giant, wormlike nocturnals. The slowly moving creature had coiled its fifty-foot body in preparation for reaching up to the roof of the train, but it lashed out at Verdon, who jumped out of the way just in time. He slashed at it with his sword, but the blade's light had died and he missed with his blow at the nocturnal. The night monster swung its head at him again but jerked back as a light flashed in front of its bleary eyes.

The little dwarf light bounced around the nocturnal's head. The worm drew back within range of the ballista on the rear of the fifth barge. The thick shaft plunged down, pinning the worm's head to the coils of its body.

Verdon looked up as he ran past the dead monster. Adralk Stunthfel glared down at him.

"Thank you for the assistance," Verdon shouted as he slipped back into the shadow of the train. He grinned. The knowledge that he had saved the life of the man he hated and thought dead, was a wound the contingent commander would feel for the rest of his life.

Verdon counted to three and ducked into the shelter of the barge's track, knowing just how long it would take Adralk to pull his gunne, estimate the deserter's course, aim, and fire. The ball hit the ground on a trajectory that would have sent it through Verdon's back if he had continued on his course. Before the echoes had died away Verdon was sprinting forward again. He could see the ground by the glow of his sword, even before the dwarf light caught up with him.

"You're making me a target," he complained to the light as he ran, though his blade was doing the same. He sheathed his sword, wondering why it had lost its glow when he encountered the nocturnal worm. He still had a lot to learn about the power of the cluster, he decided.

Where were the rest of the sentinels? He had not seen any at the rear of the train. With a moment's thought the answer was obvious—the mechamages who ran the *Dominant* had called them to clear the train's path. Normally they would be defending the barges from the nocturnals, but the creatures of Darkfall were climbing up the sides while the guards on the roof used pistols, swords, bows, and magic to hold them off.

Verdon ducked under the barges to escape the fight and ran a zigzag path beneath the long cars. The dwarf light sped along in front of him, as if knowing where he wanted to go.

From beneath the engine car he could see, by the glare thrown by the trail light, the legs of six sentinels. Two were hacking at approaching nocturnals while four were pushing at one of the broken lengths of the fallen column. Four mechamages had descended from the train and were directing the sentinels.

Verdon stood for a moment watching, considering his best course of action. He looked into the shadows, but he could not see any of the halvers, Clariel, or Rala. Had they been killed in the fight or were they staying back in the shadows, like himself, waiting for an opportunity to strike?

While he watched, the tallest of the mechamages

stared into the darkness. After a moment he raised his hand and threw a bolt of fire into the shadows. Verdon choked as he saw Rala engulfed in flames. Before he considered his action he whipped out a pistol and fired, blasting a hole in the back of the magician from the train. The mechamage fell, but Rala still stood. Next to her a sparse desert bush shriveled in the unnatural heat, but she and her clothing were untouched. She glared in the direction of the train, and by the illumination of the flames that danced around her, Verdon saw her put her hands on her hips. Her lips moved and, as the fire died away, she sent a bolt of flame toward the second mage, a goreaux. The small, dwarflike creature had protected himself and was untouched by the fire. As the conflagration died away he returned her volley, but his magic only ignited another scrawny bush by a large boulder. The dwarf had moved on.

Verdon's shot had drawn the attention of the mages and the sentinels. He ducked back behind the heavy treads of the front left wheel as the goreaux sent a lightning bolt under the train. He felt the tingling shock as the sparks touched the metal treads. He jumped away just in time to avoid a fatal shock and pulled a second gunne, firing at the second of the mechamages. He had not taken the time to aim carefully, but the shot tore away the large pointed ear of the goreaux. The effete little creature gave a howl and rose in the air, levitating out of Verdon's sight when a silver arrow sailed out of the darkness and the goreaux fell, the shaft through his throat.

The ex-guardsman's activity had alerted the other two mages and drawn the attention of the sentinels. Another bolt of lightning and a fireball shot under the train, and Verdon skipped across the narrow space between the two huge front left wheels. He had successfully dodged the mechamages, but he nearly fell over the foot of a sentinel.

He staggered aside and his near fall saved him from

the swing of the war machine's ax. He dashed around
a boulder as he heard a shout from the shadows. A
heavy arrow, shot from a halver's bow, struck the sentinel's right elbow joint and caused it to drop its ax.
While it was bending to retrieve the weapon with its
left hand, Verdon dodged the second huge mechanical
and sprinted into the shadows.

"There would be great honor in destroying one of
the giant war machines," a halver said, his voice coming out of the darkness. The half-jurak leaned forward
so Verdon could identify him. Glist.

"The more dangerous the opponent, the greater the victory," Clariel said, also from the shadows. "Guardsman, you have accounted for four of the sentinels?"

"Only two," Verdon answered and told her about
the others, one destroyed by a nocturnal and one by
the rapacian. "Siskiel has proven himself like no other
rapacian in history."

He watched the six sentinels who stood in the light
of the train. The four that had been rolling a section of
the column aside had turned away from their work
and were striding toward the shadows where he hid.
The others ignored the advancing nocturnals as they
followed, commanded by the other two mechamages.

Verdon had no idea whether the power of the cluster could stand against six sentinels and two mechamages, and he decided not to learn its limits by having it
fail him. He looked around, searching for the safest
escape route. Then he saw their danger. He, Clariel,
and Glist were only fifty feet from the cliff that formed
the western wall of the canyon.

38

Clariel backed out of her hiding place as the sentinels approached. Her face looked calm and serene and she was silent, but something had alerted Kree to her danger. The lightning lizard dashed up and brushed against her, roaring and spitting at the giant mechanicals that strode in their direction. Her first fear, that for her mount, showed in her face, and she shoved at him, ordering him away. When the lizard refused to go, she vaulted on his back.

"Dr-r-rin!" she trilled, and shot three arrows in rapid succession as she disappeared into the darkness. Her first arrow caught one of the mechamages in the shoulder. Her second stuck in the eye of the lead sentinel, and the third flew into the darkness on the other side of the engine car.

"How is it we fight these things?" Glist asked.

"You don't; you get back into the shadows and away," Verdon replied. "If you can get off a shot without endangering yourself, aim for the joints. Knee joints are good or the eye, as the elf did." He knelt and touched the ground. He needed all the power he could get. The power came in a bursting need to release the

excess. His sword was nearly blinding when he pulled
it from its scabbard.

"Yi-i-i!" He charged at the first sentinel, the one
Clariel had shot. His cluster-powered blade cut
through the heavy metal foot and he ran on, hacking at
the handle of the next mechanical's huge ax. The shaft
held, but the weapon flew out of the mechamonster's
hand.

He hoped to draw their huge foes away from Glist,
but the half-jurak charged along with him, getting in
one good shot with his bow. He brought a sentinel to
the ground with an arrow in the knee joint just as the
human had advised.

Verdon ran toward the front of the train, hoping to
use the broken rock of the fallen column for shelter
while he caught his breath and decided on his next
method of attack. He knew he would be illuminated by
the glare of the train's trail light, but the shadows
could not help him against the mages or the sentinels.
His change of direction had caught both by surprise,
and he was nearly through their midst when he fell,
unable to move.

He was caught in a holding spell.

He tumbled and rolled onto his back, his hand still
on the glowing sword, but the power cluster had not
protected him from the magic of a tall, spindly human
with a bald head and the most evil eyes Verdon had
ever seen. A second mage, completely hidden by a
hooded cloak, raised his hand and pointed in Verdon's
direction. The deserter from the train saw the flame
shoot from his fingers, but a shimmering wall
appeared just inches from his hand and the fire
splashed back on the hooded mage, setting his cloak
afire. He blazed like resin-soaked bark.

"I did it! I really did . . ." Rala's surprised and
delighted shout was lost under the mage's dying
screams.

"You spawn of slime . . ." the last mage shouted at
Verdon, and the evil of his glare was nothing to the

hatred in his voice. He strode forward, a short stave in his hand. He pointed it toward the helpless ex-guardsman. He took one last step before a sentinel's ax cut him in half.

The upper torso of the mage still twitched when Verdon felt the release of the spell and he sat up. Down the length of the train he could hear the roars and howls of the nocturnals that were still attempting to get to the guards on the roof. Their battle continued without interruption.

In the glare of the trail light at the front of the train, Verdon watched the sentinels. The one with the severed foot and the one with the arrow in his knee joint had fallen over and struggled as if they had no idea how to get up. Three wandered mindlessly, bumping into each other and the broken stone that still blocked the train's path.

The fourth took two steps toward Verdon before Glist stepped in front of the human with a drawn bow. The sentinel reached out with the broad side of his ax and pushed Glist aside without harming the halver.

"Vonny," the mechamonster said, the voice coming from some unimaginable depth. Volumes of meanings sounded in that one word. Verdon heard gratitude, love, sadness, and farewell. The mechamagical armor that held the dead body and the spirit of Marchant Worsten walked away into the darkness.

"It is honorable to let it go?" Glist asked, his half-bestial face drawn into a labored frown.

"He's free," Verdon replied, getting to his feet, his gaze still on the shadows were Marchant had disappeared.

Glist still frowned his confusion, but Verdon understood. He had not freed Marchant Worsten; Marchant's spirit had freed itself. Verdon's part had been to put himself in danger and his adopted father's love for him had overridden the magician's hold.

"He lived his life as a man of honor. Freed of the mages, he will be the same."

A fireball, thrown from the train, landed close to the halver. It disappeared almost at once. The limited life of the magic and the inaccuracy convinced Verdon the caster had been Adralk. The contingent commander had some skill, but he was not an adept.

Verdon and Glist raced for the protection of the fallen column. When they reached cover, Glist looked back.

"I can shoot the rest of the iron men and the human on the roof?" he asked hopefully.

"No, leave them," Verdon replied. "Adralk may know enough magic to direct the three remaining sentinels. He needs them to clear the train's path and get it back on course."

"Then can we fight the rest of the nocturnals and the guards on the train?" the halver asked.

"Leave the guards on the train. You can go after as many nocturnals as you can find," Verdon said. He pointed to the eastern horizon that looked to be aflame with the rising of the sun. "You'd better get to it if you want them. They like sneaking up on you out of the darkness. Facing you in the daylight when you can see them and aim with accuracy is not their favorite way of fighting."

"I will be quick," Glist said, dashing along the length of the train.

The glow of Verdon's sword had died. The exuberance that had come with the power disappeared. Fatigue rolled over him as if he had been carrying a sentinel on his back. In a sense he had.

He walked away from the battle, wondering what the halvers would think of him, but the Iron Guard could handle the rest of the nocturnals. The halvers were only fighting because of their love of battle.

As he trudged away from the *Dominant,* he was joined first by a tired little dwarf light that came to rest on his left shoulder, while Iliki settled on his right. The little ferran held his bloodstained sword in his hand, but he seemed too weary to brag about his feats in the battle.

As the ex-guardsman walked up the canyon, back toward their campsite, he was joined by Rala, Clariel, who was followed by Kree, and, on the lizard's back, Woos, whose left foot was torn and bleeding. Siskiel watched over his companion. Siskiel was concerned for what he thought was Verdon's failure.

"We could find the sentinel," he said.

"It is unwise to top a growing sapling, or to tug at it to make it taller," Clariel said, and glanced down at the dwarf. "That is an ancient saying of the elves."

"Then maybe you know what it means, but I don't," said Woos, who had lost his sense of humor with his wound.

Iliki shifted on Verdon's shoulder. "I don't understand why, after the death of the last mechamagician, the sentinel that was Marchant Worsten walked off while the others wandered around like they were stunned."

"The halvers could tell you," Clariel said. "True honor is harder than stone and can withstand more force than solid steel. The weak-minded can be overcome, but this Marchant Worsten must have had strong beliefs, else he would not have overcome the spell and killed the mage. He must have resisted their magic, and, because of his desire to protect the guardsman, he had broken with the mages before the last one was destroyed."

"Then you're saying he wasn't evil, even if they did use his spirit, so all we did was for nothing?" Iliki glared from the elf to Verdon.

"For nothing?" Verdon was outraged. "Is it nothing that we rescued a spirit in bondage?"

"It was well worth the journey," Rala said. "And I understand the elf's meaning. Marchant Worsten is no longer under the control of the mages, and if he can continue his existence, he must learn who and what he is. We would hamper him." She looked out at the growing dawn. "But it would really be worth a walk to see him rise up in the path of those Worm bandits."

The halvers caught up with the group who surrounded Kree. Verdon glanced at their long faces and dreaded counting the survivors. Waggin was shaking his head mournfully, so Verdon had to ask how many jurak-humans had been lost in the battle.

"We fight too good for any to find honor in death," Waggin said sadly.

"I thought you were making a new law that said it was better to live and kill enemies," Verdon replied.

"It will be needful. If we cannot keep one law, we must make another," Glist said. "Now we wait out the day. Too many nocturnals were killed. The rest will not come again before nightfall, when they can sneak dishonorably out of the shadows."

Verdon hoped he had not given the halvers the impression nocturnals never attacked during the day. While he was framing an explanation, Rala stared up at the large warriors and shook her head. "Don't they ever get enough?"

"They will if they follow the guardsman," Clariel replied. "But between my need to increase my tally and their desire to fight, Skar may soon be shy its share of the evils of Darkfall."

"Are you reading my mind again?" Verdon asked the elf.

"Did I need to? Obligations must be honored, and I cannot think you will leave a debt unpaid."

No, Verdon thought, he would not, but what would he be paying for, and what did he have to offer? He owed a debt for a power cluster he still did not understand. He had no clear idea of what it could do, or how he could use it to help the people of Skar. It had given him added strength in his arms as well as in his weapons, but it had failed him at a crucial point, when he had faced the wormlike nocturnal. Why had it failed him at that point?

He had thought he needed the additional power to destroy the sentinels, but the rapacians, Clariel, and Glist had proved him wrong. The elf and the halver had seriously wounded two mechamonsters without additional power and the rapacians had destroyed one.

Verdon looked around at the others who trudged along with him. They had followed him into battle believing in his power, and they had succeeded, much as they had depended on the nonexistent Milstithanog while working their way out of their dangers.

Perhaps it didn't matter whether or not he ever learned to use the cluster. They had used the nocturnals for their own purposes, they had stopped a thunder train, held off the guards, killed four mechamagicians, freed a soul in bondage, and destroyed or damaged six sentinels.

They had succeeded by strength of arms, good hearts, accident, and total stupidity, but they had succeeded. Could he hope to do more in the service of the king of Arasteen?

Verdon glanced down at the dwarf. "Are you sure King Corben's spies passed on the information I gave to the rhanate's generals?"

"I'm certain," she smiled. "They also took my report." She twinkled up at him. "Just because I couldn't talk doesn't mean I couldn't communicate."

"Then let's move farther away from the train. We don't want to fight the Iron Guard; they'll have enough to do just starting their trip again. Kree, find us something to eat." He grinned at Rala. "It's a long way back to Skar."

And a long walk back, he thought. Somewhere on that waste, Marchant Worsten traveled alone in the desolation. Clariel was right, a new sapling needed time to gather strength, and the freed sentinel was a new and powerful entity, something unknown on Aden.

Verdon made another vow. The sentinel would not be alone for long.

CALIBAN'S HOUR by Tad Williams

Can an eternity of love be contained in an hour? The answer lies in the enchanting tale of magic and mystery from the *New York Times* bestselling author of *To Green Angel Tower* and *Tailchaser's Song.* ($4.99 Paperback)

DEMON SWORD by Ken Hood

An exhilarating heroic fantasy, *Demon Sword* takes place in the Scottish lands of a fanciful Renaissance Europe where our hero, an aspiring prizefighter named Toby, finds himself possessed by a demon spirit. But soon it appears that the king is possessed by the demon spirit and Toby is possessed by the spirit of the king! ($4.99 Paperback)